It was like a flash bulb went off behind her eyes. Then it dawned on her that it actually was a flash, right in her face, as one of her fellow guests snapped a quick candid of noted *Délicieux* columnist Miranda Wake in a public brawl with hotshot chef Adam Temple.

The copy wrote itself.

Adrenaline surged up, chasing away the lingering haze of alcohol, and Miranda blinked.

A man with dark hair came into focus, nearly close enough to kiss—so close she could only see one feature at a time. His hair was too long on top and completely disordered, curls standing up like devil horns. His tan skin stretched taut over a broad forehead and sculpted jaw. His wide mouth was drawn in a sneer that couldn't quite hide the sensual shape of his lips. He had dark, flashing eyes. The light was too dim to really make out the exact color, but the expression in them was clear enough: a sort of stunned fury, hot enough to burn.

Miranda felt heat scorch along her cheeks and neck, and wasn't sure if it was from the vodka, the intensity of Adam Temple's regard, or the gaze of fifty tipsy foodies. Probably a combination of all three.

Can't Stand The Heat

Louisa Edwards

St. Martin's Paperbacks

This is a work of fiction. All of the characters, organizations and events portrayed in this novel are either products of the author's imagination or are used fictitiously.

CAN'T STAND THE HEAT

Copyright © 2009 by Louisa Edwards.
Excerpt from *On the Steamy Side* copyright © 2009 by Louisa Edwards.

For information address St. Martin's Press, 175 Fifth Avenue, New York, NY 10010.

EAN: 978-0-312-35649-1

Printed in the United States of America

St. Martin's Paperbacks edition / September 2009

St. Martin's Paperbacks are published by St. Martin's Press, 175 Fifth Avenue, New York, NY 10010.

10 9 8 7 6 5 4 3 2 1

*To my husband, Nick, who bears the brunt of all my
research and experimentation, in the kitchen
and elsewhere . . .*

ACKNOWLEDGMENTS

Writing is a solitary gig, but I could never do it alone. I want to thank my handsome husband, Nick, for his tireless support and for the fact that his career ripped us away from Manhattan and plunked us down in a tiny town in Ohio—without that move, this book probably would never have been written. The other person directly responsible for this book's existence is my fabulous agent, Deidre Knight, who was wise enough to make me quit trying to write about vampires and start writing what I really loved. Thanks, D! Best advice ever. And a huge thank you to Rose, for loving this book as much as I do, and championing it at St. Martin's. I have the best editor in the world!

Since starting to write full time, I've made some of the coolest friends I've ever had: my brilliant critique partners, Mel and Maria, my partner-in-crime Nic, Naughty Kate, Diva extraordinaire Kristen, gorgeous Gena, Miss Marley, rock star Rocki, kick-ass Kresley—all of you make it so much fun to get behind that desk every day!

This book also belongs to my chef and foodie friends: Chef Jason Smith and Lauren Martin at 18 Seaboard in Raleigh, Dan Dilworth at Lever House in NYC, and all the other chefs who welcomed me into their kitchens and answered my fan-girlish questions. Megan Blocker, one of the best cooks I know, gets credit for helping to test the recipes, along with my wonderful parents, who first taught me to cook, and my sister, Georgia, who happily tested multiple versions of the champagne cocktail.

You should all know that Nick was the one who actually invented the GINger Lemonade. Everything else in the book is mine, mistakes and all.

ONE

It was the sort of party where Miranda Wake knew every guest by face or reputation, but had never spoken to any of them. At least, not in person. Of course, she'd received irate phone calls from several of the chefs present, after one of her less-than-glowing reviews, but that didn't really count as a formal introduction, she didn't think. Well, not enough to form the basis for polite cocktail party conversation. *Im*polite conversation, maybe.

Miranda caught herself smirking, and pulled her mouth back into its customary noncommittal line. It was harder than she expected. She blinked. The room and everyone in it wavered slightly.

"Why won't all of you no-talent hacks stand still?" she said, a little startled at how loud her own voice seemed in her ears. When had she lost volume control?

Several people turned to stare, and Miranda tilted her chin up, daring them to say anything. She felt brittle and dry, like crumpled-up paper—after the day she'd had, it wouldn't take much of a spark to make her go up in flames.

Someone jostled her elbow, and Miranda turned with a frown to find her editor, Claire Durand, staring at her. There was an incredulous look on Claire's normally serene countenance, her perfectly plucked eyebrows arching upward as she took in Miranda's struggle to keep a straight face.

"Miranda," she hissed, her French-accented voice giving the *r* in the name extra emphasis. "How many of these *apéritifs* have you had?"

Miranda leaned in a little and whispered, "In America, we call them 'cocktails.'"

Claire pursed her red-lipsticked mouth, and Miranda tried to remember what that was called in France. "A *moue*?" she said out loud, without meaning to.

The eyebrows snapped down. "*Merde*," she cursed. "But I watched you! I would swear you had no more than I."

Miranda thought about it. "Yes," she agreed. "But you're French. You were probably given wine as an infant." Miranda blinked. "I . . . wasn't."

Looking around wrathfully, Claire said, "Of what are these concoctions made? Is the chef trying to poison us?"

Miranda, who still had her empty glass, took an experimental sniff. "Don't think so," she said. "Smells like roses. Which are edible. Or, in this case, drinkable. No, that's wrong. What's that word?" Why was she having such a hard time with words tonight? They were usually her specialty.

Callously ignoring Miranda's vocabulary difficulties, Claire flagged down one of the circulating waiters. "You. What is in the cocktail, please?"

The young man appeared to shrink under Claire's stern glare, but stammered, "Rose-petal-infused vodka and fresh Hudson Valley raspberries."

Claire let go of his arm, and the boy wasted no time in making his escape. Miranda watched him go with some disappointment; that rose-vodka-berry thing really had been yummy. She thought she might quite like another one. Third time's the charm. Or was that fifth?

But all visions of sweetly perfumed liquor left her head

when Claire turned the eyebrows on her again. This time they were accompanied by a tight pinch at Miranda's elbow, as Claire manacled her arm and attempted to sidle them both closer to the wall.

"Ow," said Miranda, allowing herself to be led.

"Thank God for atmospheric restaurant lighting," Claire breathed, smiling graciously at a curious fellow guest. Miranda peered at his face as she was hustled past.

"Was that the critic for the *Post*?" she asked. Miranda's volume control was evidently still hit-or-miss, because Claire winced and tightened her grip.

"Ow," Miranda reminded her with greater emphasis. "Randall Collins. Was it? I should say hello. His one review, of that tapas place, was inspired." She paused. "Or do I mean 'inspirational'? Because it sure inspired me. Before reading that review, I didn't know you could even print some of the names he called that chef."

"Oui, oui, I'm certain he changed your life, and I, for one, am grateful to him, but you are in no condition to tell him so. If I permit you to speak with him now, tomorrow you would throw yourself from the Brooklyn Bridge, and then what should I do? I would have to find a new restaurant critic with your gift of vitriol. Who else could I find to take on the titans, like Devon Sparks and his new Las Vegas monstrosity? Remember how much fun that was? And think—if you commit career suicide, you'll never have the chance to write your book and become a world-famous best-selling author."

The remark flicked right over the raw, open wound of that afternoon's letter from Empire Publishing. "It doesn't matter," Miranda wailed. "No publisher is ever going to buy my book."

"That's simply not true," Claire stated, as if being decisive about it would make it so. She succeeded in manhandling Miranda to a standstill in a shadowed alcove.

Miranda felt a wall at her back and leaned gratefully. "The room is spinny," she told Claire.

The older woman laughed and said, "I'm sure it is. Whatever has gotten into you tonight?"

"I got another rejection on the book," she confessed.

"Oh! You poor dear." Claire was instantly sympathetic, and Miranda smiled at her. "What was the reason this time?"

The highlights from the letter were emblazoned on her brain. "They thought my publicity platform wasn't strong enough for a nonfiction proposal, and the part about the restaurant culture didn't feel believable. It just wasn't 'authentic.'" She made sarcastic air quotes with her fingers, still burning with frustration over that particular comment. "I mean, I know I haven't worked in a restaurant, but I reviewed them for three years, freelance, before you hired me. And Jess has been waiting tables since high school!"

"How is your adorable brother, by the way?"

Claire was awfully quick to leap onto a new subject, Miranda noticed. It was possible she was getting tired of commiserating over the stack of rejection letters Miranda had piled up as she shopped her idea for a book examining the rise of celebrity chefs and modern restaurant culture.

Unfortunately, the topic of Jess was a minefield all on its own.

"Funny you should ask," Miranda said. "Not funny, ha-ha, though. More like funny, oh, crap."

"What has happened at that godforsaken college of his?"

Claire had sniffed disdainfully when Miranda was proud that her younger brother had been accepted to Brandewine University in Brandewine, Indiana, on a full visual communications scholarship. Claire distrusted pretty much all the states in the middle and had a hard time believing anything good came from them.

The thought of that scholarship was enough to bring some of the room back into unpleasant focus. Where was a waiter bearing rose-vodka-berry things when you needed him?

"Jess is home," she said.

Claire brightened. "But that is marvelous! Now you'll have all summer together."

"It is," Miranda said. "But it's not just for summer break—he quit Brandewine. Showed up at my apartment this afternoon, about ten minutes after I opened that rejection letter from Empire Publishing. Jess brought three duffel bags, his camera, and not a single word of explanation."

"And you took him in without a murmur."

It wasn't a question, but Miranda nodded. "He's my brother. Even if I've got no idea what's going on with him, what would induce him to leave a full-ride scholarship— even if he refuses to tell me what happened? It doesn't matter. I could never turn him away. But he's damn well going back to Brandewine next semester, or I will know the reason why!"

No matter what was going on with Jess, Miranda would take care of him. That was her job. It had been her job since their parents died in a car crash when she was eighteen, leaving a heartbroken ten-year-old son and a daughter who'd had to grow up overnight.

"I guess we're not as close as we used to be," she said, and the words tasted like ash in her mouth. Like failure.

Claire shrugged with Gallic fatalism. "But that is normal, no? How many younger brothers tell their sisters, especially a sister who has been both mother and father to them, what is happening in their lives?"

"Well, it's not normal for us," Miranda insisted. "At least, I don't want it to be. He's all I have."

Claire frowned at her. "Nonsense. You are becoming maudlin. Stay here." Muttering something about Americans being unable to hold their liquor, she left Miranda leaning against the wall.

Miranda rolled her head to the left, scratching her cheek against the chic exposed brick. The rough edges caught at her hair, pulling like a hundred tiny fingers. She rolled her head to the right, then forward, just to feel it again.

Once she'd tilted her head down it was sort of hard to lift it up. She contemplated her sensible, all-purpose black cocktail dress. The fruits of her first week's labors at *Délicieux* magazine. It had turned out to be a good investment; the Ralph Lauren design was a classic, still in style, even a year later. The neckline plunged enough to give her cleavage, but not so much that men spoke to her chest rather than to her face. And the clingy material outlined the waist she worked so hard to keep trim while trying all those innovative desserts for her monthly column.

The shoes, though. Miranda gazed at her crimson pumps, her spirits lifting slightly.

The dress was nice. Serviceable. The shoes were a decadent indulgence. Red satin with black lace overlay, peep toe and wickedly sharp heel. Every time she put them on, she felt just the teeniest bit vampy.

She wouldn't normally wear them to a professional function, but after the soul-crushing news that yet another publishing house wouldn't be helping her break into the prestigious, lucrative world of book publishing, and Jess's dramatic arrival, she'd needed something. The shoes had beckoned her from the back of the closet, whispering about boosting confidence and the lift a woman gets only from a truly stunning pair of heels, and that was it. She'd kicked off the plain black pumps and slipped on the red satin, and left the apartment before she had a chance to reconsider.

God, she so didn't want to be here right now. Half her brain was still at home in her cozy apartment, staring blankly at her brother's tight mouth and exhausted eyes, wondering exactly when she stopped understanding the one person she always thought she knew better than anyone else. But no. The rest of her brain was soaking in vodka at this meaningless party for a restaurant that wasn't even open yet, but would probably close in a year, because way more than half of them did, and what was the point of it all anyway?

"What are you scowling at?" Claire demanded, startling Miranda out of her reverie. "Never mind," Claire continued, before Miranda could open her mouth. "Drink this."

She was holding two delicate glasses full of darkly pink liquid. Miranda licked her lips, reaching for one. "Really? I thought you wouldn't let me have more." She drank eagerly, making a disappointed noise when she reached the bottom of the glass. The alcohol hit her system like a kick to the head, and the room's colors suddenly pulsed a shade brighter, going in and out of focus.

"When one has reached the sentimental stage, the only way out is more alcohol. I need you *up,* not drooping. The show is about to start."

So saying, she shoved the second drink into Miranda's hand and pulled her back into the throng of mingling guests.

But even with the renewed buzz of icy sweet vodka burning in her stomach, all Miranda could really hope was that the party would be over soon. Red shoes or not, she was in a dangerously bad mood.

TWO

"Man, this is nothing. What are you so jacked up about?"

The guy in the mirror had no answer, just a wild-eyed stare and unruly dark hair.

"Hi, I'm Adam Temple. Welcome to Market!"

The guy in the mirror looked, if anything, more dismayed.

"I know. That sucked. Maybe less enthusiasm?"

The guy in the mirror was clearly desperate enough to try anything.

"I'm Adam Temple, and I want to thank you for joining me in my newest venture."

A knock on the staff bathroom door saved mirror guy from commenting on that one. He looked relieved.

Adam cursed and ran his hands through his hair one last time, and watched the waves tumble back into place, as messy as ever. His fingers positively itched to be doing something useful, like piling mounds of microgreens on trays and topping them with fresh peach chutney and creamy chèvre. In fact, he'd been in the kitchen, cooking like a fiend and ignoring the clock, until his restaurant manager had finally forced him downstairs to put on a tie.

All to impress the assembled food snobs of Manhattan. And the critics! Christ, he really hoped they hadn't invited that woman from *Délicieux,* the one who never had a nice thing to say about anyone. He knew he should've kept a closer eye on the guest list, but he'd kept accidentally-on-purpose forgetting about the party.

Like he didn't have enough to do, getting the crew and the restaurant ready for the actual opening next weekend. The damn menu wasn't even finalized yet, and here he was, about to go upstairs and dance for the assembled gourmet elite like a trained monkey. Well, okay, he was giving a speech—there'd be no dancing. But still.

He huffed out a sigh. Why couldn't he just impress them all with the food? Why did they have to put on to-night's ridiculous show?

Because Eleanor fucking Bonning says so, Adam re-minded himself. *And until the restaurant is a giant-ass success and you can buy her out, you've gotta follow her instructions like a suburban housewife watching Julia Child.*

Anything that would get that woman out of his hair faster was, by definition, a good thing.

Eleanor was supposed to be attending the party tonight, checking up on her investment, and Adam grimaced. Yet another reason to hide out in the bathroom. It hadn't al-ways been like that, but lately, whenever they were in the same room, it got kind of ugly.

Eleanor wasn't technically a woman scorned, since she'd dumped him, but she couldn't have been any more furious if she had been.

There was a second, slightly less tentative knock, and an unfamiliar voice called out, "Chef? Are you in there? Grant's looking for you. He says it's 'time and past.'" The kid's voice went into an exaggerated drawl on the last few words, mimicking the restaurant manager's distinctive

Virginia accent. Fucking out-of-work actors masquerading as waiters.

"I'll be right there. Are the canapés going over well?"

There was a pause, just long enough to make Adam's heart freeze in his chest.

Electric rage pulsed through him a moment later, reanimating everything, when the kid quavered, "Uh ... Frankie said not to serve the food yet. So we waited. Was that not what you wanted?"

Adam threw open the door, and the kid winced at whatever he saw on Adam's face. Not that Adam usually had to work at intimidating his underlings, since he was built more like a boxer than a cook, but he imagined his current expression was probably pretty fierce.

God damn Frankie, anyway. Best friend, sous-chef, and indispensable kitchen asset or not, Adam was going to kill him.

"Get back to work," he snapped at the kid, who hurried off like the hounds of hell were after him. Adam turned to the stairway up to the dining room, any concern over the state of his tie forgotten.

He could hear the party in full swing, voices and laughter echoing down the stairwell. It sounded good, like happy customers, and Adam let the fantasy spin out for a second, let his mind and chest fill up with the satisfaction of running a really fine restaurant, full of people enjoying themselves.

Possibly enjoying themselves a little too much. He took the stairs two at a time, visions of magazine critics crashing into TV Cooking Channel executives dancing before his eyes.

A wave of chatter and tinkling glasses broke over Adam like boiling water from a kettle as he reached the top of the stairs. He felt his neck flush hot, but he grinned his signa-

ture grin, the one Frankie said made him look like an escaped lunatic, and started shaking hands.

The third time a woman dressed all in black—seriously,
did women in New York ever wear any other color?—fell
on him, gushing about the raspberry cocktails, Adam knew
he'd been right to panic.

These people were hammered.

Christ, how long had he been in the staff bathroom?
While he'd been angsting out over his speech, these people,
these serious professionals of the food world, had obviously
been up here swilling down rosewater-flavored vodka at an
alarming rate.

He righted another tipsy woman, this one in a black pant-
suit, and she smiled beatifically as she thanked him. Adam
smiled back, and made his slow way toward the horseshoe-
shaped bar in the middle of the restaurant, hoping to find
Grant Holloway, restaurant manager and tightass extraordinaire. Who, if Adam had to guess, was probably pissing
himself right about now.

Several of the newly hired wait staff passed by, trays full
of empty champagne flutes, and Adam swallowed another
bubble of angry panic. Loose and relaxed was one thing—
out-and-out knee-walking plastered was another. One of
the waiters tried to give the single full glass on his tray to
Adam, who shook his head and held up both hands to ward
him off.

Someone in this joint had to keep his wits about him.
Which reminded him, he was searching for Grant. Adam
spied a bright blond cap of hair bobbing behind the bar,
and headed for it.

The crowd around the bar wasn't as deep as Adam had
feared, probably because most of the drinks were being
served by the wandering waiters, but he still had to throw
an elbow to get close enough to catch Grant's attention.

Adam's restaurant manager was slight of frame and disarmingly boyish. Meticulous in all things, including matters of appearance, it was he who had decreed that Adam must wear the striped silk instrument of torture currently choking off his air supply. So it was something of a shock to see Grant ducked down behind the bar, rummaging frantically for, Adam could only assume, the last bottle of house-steeped vodka with rose petals. He bounced up, triumphant, tie askew and collar open, one end of his shirt untucked from his trousers. Adam gaped for a moment at the wild glint in his normally staid employee's eye, then took a deep breath.

Wits, he reminded himself. *Keep them about you.*

"What the hell is going on here?" he yelled over the din. Okay, so he wasn't great at following his own advice.

Grant started violently and nearly bobbled the vodka. He grabbed at it with both hands and a curse before turning to face Adam with a look of manic aggravation on his face.

Which smoothed out instantly once he saw who it was. The expression that replaced it was closer to joy. Mixed with relief, Adam recognized grimly.

Not a great sign. Any crowd that could ruffle Grant was not a crowd Adam wanted to be within cocktail-garnish-lobbing distance of. And Grant was looking pretty seriously ruffled.

"Boss," Grant cried. "You're finally here!"

Adam put his hands on his hips. Yeah, okay, so maybe he'd dawdled. First in the kitchen, and then in the bathroom. But it wasn't like he'd taken a month-long siesta or anything. You couldn't tell it by Grant's rapturous tone, though.

Grant held up a peremptory finger in Adam's direction, and turned to a hovering waiter, who'd been eyeing the vodka bottle covetously since Grant had unearthed it. With a few terse, low words, Grant handed over the bottle, and shooed the young man toward the kitchen, where the cocktail trays were being staged.

"Supplies are running low and the natives are getting restless. Honestly, where have you *been*? We're understaffed. Frankie came out here and said not to serve the *food*! And then he took off for the Lord only knows where," Grant said in a rising rush, his relief turning to exasperation faster than Adam could follow.

"His ass better be working the pass, getting everything plated," Adam seethed. Everything in him ached to storm the kitchen and take care of it himself.

Something of that fervent desire must have shown in his eyes, because Grant interjected a quick, "Stay here! Don't disappear again."

Adam huffed and glared around the corner of the bar to the slice of kitchen visible from the main dining room. There was movement, hustle, and his chef senses tingled. It looked like chaos from here, but it wasn't. Those guys, his crew, they knew what they were doing. More than that, they knew he'd kick some ass come morning if they didn't get it done. Adam caught sight of his sous chef's spiky tangle of black hair as Frankie strode down the line, barking orders, and felt the tension in his shoulders relax a bit. Unpredictable and thoughtless, for sure, but Frankie was a good man to have on the line.

"I'm not going anywhere," he told Grant. "It looks okay. Frankie's got the crew working, and everything's under control."

"Not yet, but it will be," Grant promised, eyes narrowed. "That was the last bottle of rose vodka, we're nearly out of raspberries, and the line cooks are on point with the first round of hors d'oeuvres. We can get the food trays going while you do your welcome speech, let these folks soak up some of the alcohol."

That was Grant. For all his fussing and bossiness, and occasional friction with the authorityphobic Frankie, Grant was a master of organization.

Adam . . . wasn't. He liked to get involved with things, get his hands dirty, explore. Which led to hours of playing in the kitchen with a new recipe, or driving all the way up through the Adirondacks to check out a new possible source for fresh goat cheese. He needed someone like Grant to keep him grounded. On track. Bounding along in the right direction.

Which, in this case, seemed to be behind the bar. Grant had swung open the movable piece at the side while he was giving Adam the rundown, and now he was tugging Adam's sleeve to get him to step behind the bar and up onto the raised platform that helped the bartenders reach the top-shelf liquor.

Suddenly, Adam was head and shoulders above the milling crowd, and before he could blink, Grant had clapped loudly enough to get the attention of those standing closest.

Word spread throughout the room like a line of fire around a pan of cherries jubilee, and pretty soon it was quiet. Mostly. Adam paused long enough to hear several people clear their throats, and one inebriated guest tittered loudly before being shushed.

Grant beamed up at him encouragingly, and rather than wring his scrawny neck for shoving him up here with no warning, Adam settled for narrowing his eyes in a way that he hoped promised future, painful retribution. The answering sparkle in Grant's gaze suggested that the message had been received, and was mainly fodder for amusement. He took off for the kitchen at a fast clip, clearly relieved to finally be allowed to feed the hordes.

Gritting his teeth, Adam carved out a "company" smile. The wide grin reserved for high-profile diners who wanted to see how a professional kitchen worked, and figured their status out in the real world entitled them to an all-access pass to Adam's.

"Ladies and gentlemen, thank you so much for being with us tonight, as we celebrate the launch of Market. A new way to eat."

There was applause, enough to relax him and make him think soaking the audience in liquor hadn't been such a bad idea, after all.

"At Market, we want to bring back an old-fashioned idea: bone-deep knowledge of what you're eating, and where it came from. Everything I serve, every ingredient I cook with, has been sourced from local suppliers. I don't know about all of you," he continued, falling into the comforting rhythm of this discussion he'd had so many times, with Frankie, with Grant, with the loan guy at the bank, with anyone who would listen, "but I'm sick of the grocery-store culture that has kids thinking chickens are born shrink-wrapped in plastic, or that peaches ripen in December. We're so removed from our food! And it turns the experience of eating into a mundane chore."

The house lights were dim, but the bar was lit from underneath and the spillover light reflected off the glassware and bottles, casting dancing white sparks over the upturned faces of the crowd.

"My mission here is to let all of you know—to let everyone who loves food and loves to eat know—it doesn't have to be that way. Food is personal. It should be personal. Dining is an intimate experience, and I want to close the gap between diners and food producers. This is nothing new. Alice Waters has been talking about this since the sixties. What makes Market different is our dedication and our creativity. I refuse to cook boring food.

"No," he continued, putting a hand flat on the bartop, feeling the solid wood under the heel of his hand. "More than that. I refuse to cook empty food, pretty presentations with no substance, all flash and no heart. I don't want to impress you. I want to nourish you."

"Ha!"

Adam frowned. The vehement exclamation came from somewhere in the crowd, and he lifted a hand to shade his eyes, as if that would somehow help him identify the speaker.

"At Market . . ." He tried to find his place, but the momentum, the passion, was gone. He felt sweat spring out cold on his palms. "We . . . I was saying, I want to nourish not just your bodies, but your minds. Your understanding of what food is, and how it comes to you."

That same damn voice spoke up again. "It hasn't come to us at all!"

Movement by the swinging kitchen doors caught his eye momentarily. Adam looked over to see the waiters pouring out of the kitchen, food-laden trays in hand. The perfection of Grant's timing staggered him, and all he could say was, "What?"

"There isn't any food," a woman said, detaching herself from the rest of the fascinated audience. "You've invited us here, apparently, to talk at us about your fabulous food for hours on end, but have yet to serve us any."

Adam raised his eyebrows. He didn't think the "hours on end" comment was totally fair.

The woman, a redhead, Adam noticed, nodded once, decisively, as if pleased with herself. An attractive older woman at her side attempted to pull her back out of the limelight, but Red was having none of it. She tossed her head and marched right up to the bar, wobbly in her heels but purposeful in her movement.

Adam divided his attention between the waiters, finally beginning to offer their trays of pastry puffs and roasted vegetable skewers to the guests, and the approaching heckler. As the guests began to notice and enjoy the food, most of them turned away from the bar and fell on the waiters like lions on a herd of lame gazelles.

The heckler was wearing the requisite black dress, draped over what looked like very nice curves—but the shoes. Bright, shiny with a glossy patina like you get on good *crème anglaise,* the color of pinot noir held up to the light. Heels like ice picks, and above them, her legs stretched on for miles, slender and perfect. Those shoes sparked his interest.

Interest that ratcheted up by a billion as the light from the bar finally illuminated her face. She was gorgeous, like a Botticelli angel, all flaming hair and startling blue eyes, round cheeks and sweet, sweet mouth.

What was coming out of her mouth, though? Not so sweet.

She pursed those pretty pink lips up at him and sneered, "It always makes me wary when a chef feels he has to climb up on his soapbox and philosophize to justify his cooking."

"You're right," he said, baring his teeth in a parody of a smile. "It's crap. My food is a more eloquent expression of the benefits of local, seasonal produce than anything I could come up with to say." He gestured to the other guests. Most of them, he noted with gut-deep satisfaction, were licking their lips and reaching for a second or third canapé. "Seems like they all agree with me."

Now it was her turn to blink. She looked pretty and owlish, confusion softening the hard line of her mouth; too damned intriguing. Anger and attraction coiled in his belly, a pleasantly unsettling mix. Like what happened when he added a splash of lemon juice to a rich cream sauce.

"What's your name?" he asked her.

She tossed her head again, the motion making her sway a little. Adam looked more closely. Her pupils were blown wide and dark, and her cheeks were flushed in a lovely contrast to her fair complexion.

"Miranda Wake, *Délicieux* magazine," she said defiantly, as if expecting him to take issue with it.

Ah-ha, he thought, somehow unsurprised, even though he'd always pictured the New York food scene's most notorious critic as being considerably older and more dried-up looking than this fiery little piece.

Miranda Wake. You are blitzed out of your mind, on cocktails I designed, mixed with liquor I steeped with my own hands.

There was something weirdly erotic about it, and Adam covered the momentary oddness by stepping down and coming around the bar to shake her hand. The speech portion of the evening seemed well and truly over, now that the food was getting out.

"Adam Temple," he said, taking her limp, warm hand. "Pleased to meet you."

"Are you?" she asked, confused again, and Adam smirked. Her fingers were impossibly slender, making him notice the fine bones of her knuckles, the turn of her wrist. He wanted to force-feed her something rich and decadent.

"Absolutely," he assured her.

"Well," she said, frowning. "Well, I'm not pleased to meet you. I didn't even want to come here tonight. Restaurants that espouse a cause are trite and pretentious, and your food is bound to be atrocious." She slurred over the twin *shus* sounds and wrinkled her nose, working her mouth as if stretching the muscles around it would help get it back under her control. "I've reviewed lots of 'local produce' restaurants, and it's never been anything more than a stupid gimmick to cover the fact that the chef has no imagination."

"Is that right?" Adam said, irritated beyond belief. Why did she have to be so gorgeous and snotty? "Damn. If

there's one thing I hate to be accused of, it's lack of imagination."

Incredibly, she blushed at that. Fantastic.

"You know," he said, "I don't think I like the way you
talk about my food without ever having tried it. What
makes you the authority?"

Her cheeks pinked again, this time probably more due
to annoyance than booze. "I'll have you know I'm the top
critic at *Délicieux*. I get more fan mail than any other columnist."

"Yeah, but I bet half of it's hate mail," he said, baiting
her.

"Some," she admitted with the careful dignity of the
drunk. "I have exacting standards which few restaurants
can meet."

"Don't your standards usually require you to at least
taste the food before passing judgment on it, sweetheart?"

"I . . ." She paused, disconcerted. "Yes, of course. But
it's not my fault I haven't had any of yours yet. And don't
call me 'sweetheart.' "

"Sure thing, doll," he retorted. "And you could've been
sampling the wares for the last five minutes if you weren't
so focused on giving me a hard time. But I understand," he
went on. "The hands-on approach isn't really your thing.
You spend most of your time hunched over a computer in a
cramped little office, right? All alone in your ivory tower,
while the rest of the world struggles to meet your 'exacting
standards.' "

"I . . . I . . ." Her eyes were wide and shocked, and her
chest heaved, giving tantalizing glimpses of the shadowy
valley between her breasts as she strained the fabric of her
dress.

He sneered. "You wouldn't last a day in the real world.
You wouldn't last ten minutes in my kitchen."

That soft, round chin shot up, and she took a step closer.

Her eyes flashed with something, but at this point, Adam was too ticked to decipher it.

"Oh, wouldn't I?"

He stepped in, too, until they were toe to toe. "Not a chance," he declared. "In fact, I dare you. Spend one day in the kitchen at Market, work with me and my crew. See what it's like from the other side. After that, review my restaurant, rip my cooking to shreds, I'll take it like a man. Until then, sweetheart?" He leaned down close enough to see just how long and thick her eyelashes were. She smelled like raspberries and sugar, and something deeper, more complex.

"Keep your opinions to yourself."

THREE

It was as if a flashbulb went off behind her eyes. Then it dawned on her that it actually *was* a flash, right in her face, as one of her fellow guests snapped a quick candid of noted *Délicieux* columnist Miranda Wake in a public brawl with hotshot chef Adam Temple.

The copy wrote itself.

Adrenaline surged up, chasing away the lingering haze of alcohol, and Miranda blinked.

A man with dark hair came into focus, nearly close enough to kiss—so close she could only see one feature at a time. His hair was too long on top and completely disordered, curls standing up like devil horns. His tanned skin stretched taut over a broad forehead and sculpted jaw. His wide mouth was drawn in a sneer that couldn't quite hide the sensual shape of his lips. He had dark, flashing eyes. The light was too dim to really make out the exact color, but the expression in them was clear enough: a sort of stunned fury, hot enough to burn.

Miranda felt heat scorch along her cheeks and neck, and wasn't sure if it was from the vodka, the intensity of Adam Temple's regard, or the gaze of fifty tipsy foodies. Probably a combination of all three.

There was an expectant silence, and the longer it went on, the more insufferably smug Temple's expression became. Miranda shook herself slightly, attempting to reorient her brain.

What just happened? Did he seriously challenge me to spend a day in his kitchen?

And just like that, she was back.

She'd have to be a whole lot drunker than this to allow the opportunity of a lifetime to pass her by. This was her chance to move beyond magazine writing, to get that insider look that her book proposal was obviously lacking.

She looked him right in his smug, self-satisfied (*gorgeous, sexy*) face, and said, "I accept."

He took a step back.

"What?"

"I said, I accept your challenge," Miranda repeated. She was already itching for her notebook and pen. From here on out, everything was fodder for The Book. *A Critic in the Kitchen.* Or *What the Chef Doesn't Want You to Know.* This was it, the angle she'd been looking for. A serious exposé of the gritty underbelly of American professional cooking, from the point of view of an embedded journalist.

She frowned. It was going to take more research than a single day, though.

Adam was frowning, too. Like a thundercloud.

"What are you doing?" he hissed.

Miranda blinked, trying to look as guileless as possible. "I'm taking you up on your offer. Unrestricted access to your kitchen, your crew . . . and you."

Adam blanched. "I didn't offer that . . . Wait, what?"

"But yes, I heard you." Claire appeared at Adam's elbow, widening her eyes gravely. "You invited Miranda into your kitchen."

"It was more of a dare, really," Miranda pointed out, enjoying herself.

Claire waved a languid hand. "As you say. The important thing is that I'm sure Chef Temple would not wish to renege on his offer. Not when so many were here to witness it."

Adam opened his mouth, then closed it again in a firm line. Miranda studiously avoided noticing how the angry set of his jaw made his dimples pop out.

He attempted a smile, but it looked more like a grimace. "Maybe we could discuss the details later," he said, belatedly cautious.

"That would be lovely," Miranda cooed, already trying to work out how she could finagle a longer stint in Market's kitchen.

"Certainly," Claire agreed. "I'll need to get input from the *Délicieux* editorial board as to what sort of piece Miranda will do."

Miranda could almost hear Adam's back teeth grinding. She smiled, alcohol and excitement fizzing through her veins.

And to think, she hadn't wanted to come to the Market prelaunch party.

"Last night," Grant moaned, "was a debacle. I'm so not ready to go clean that mess up. Thanks for having the postmortem at your place, Adam. I couldn't face Market yet."

"Not without a pot of strong coffee, no," Adam called from the spacious kitchen, where he was searching for his French press. After an event like the preopening publicity party, he liked to meet with his top guys, in this case Frankie and Grant, to discuss how it went, what could've been better. He expected today's meeting to be short. What was there to say beyond "we totally screwed the pooch"?

His apartment was actually the first floor of a small brick-front townhouse. It was a weird living space, comprised of two largish rooms. One was the kitchen and the other was the dining/living/bedroom. His bed was partially screened from the rest of the room by a wide bookcase, full of an assortment of cookbooks, science fiction novels, mysteries, and historical fiction—not that he had any down time for reading. All in all, the apartment was a tad cramped for company, but it suited Adam fine.

The whole building used to be a single home, when his parents were still living in New York. But they'd retired to Florida a few years ago, leaving Adam the building. Which, as Eleanor had immediately pointed out, was one of Adam's few financial assets. As long as he put it to use. So he mortgaged it to the hilt, and rented the second floor to a dizzy blond grad student who hosted late-night pizza-and-study sessions. Adam looked forward to the day when Market turned a profit and he could afford to have his house to himself again.

Adam cursed under his breath at the dizzying array of kitchen implements cluttering his cupboards. More than half of his kitchen stuff had migrated, slowly but surely, over to the Market kitchen, and what was left at home base had abandoned any semblance of order.

With a bit of luck, he managed to close his fingers around the French press fairly quickly. Some boiling water, a little finely ground espresso, and Adam was carrying mugs of coffee strong enough to hold a spoon up vertically into the other room. Grant snatched one mug out of Adam's hands and Frankie took the other, setting it down on the coffee table to cool.

"Wasn't so bad, last night," Frankie disagreed, lighting up a Dunhill in flagrant disregard for Adam's no-smoking-in-the-apartment policy. Frankie took a deep drag and squinted up from his boneless sprawl on the living room floor. "Until our boy here lost his head over some magazine bint."

Frankie happened to be lounging just below the crown jewel of Adam's poster collection, a pressed-tin sign for the Clash's *16 Tons* tour. Sallow, angry faces of punk rock icons, from Siouxsie and the Banshees to the Sex Pistols, glared out from Adam's walls. It probably wasn't a sign of perfect social adjustment that the sight always relaxed him. Johnny Rotten's snarling visage was never meant to put anyone at ease, and yet Adam found himself already starting to unwind. Which didn't mean he was ready to absolve Frankie of any responsibility for last night's clusterfuck.

Adam looked from the group of skinny British punks on his wall to the one currently taking up space on his floor.

"You started it," Adam accused, pointing a finger and not caring how fourth-grade it made him look. "You got the guests all smashed and kept the food in the kitchen. What the hell were you thinking?"

"Oi," said Frankie, around an aggrieved puff on his cigarette. "Was thinking you'd be nervous, and a half-in-the-bag audience would be better than a bunch of sharp bastards waiting to cut you to ribbons."

Adam deflated slightly. He should've considered the Frankie version of logic. Of course it all came down to, in the end, what it always came down to: Frankie had his back. No messing around, no exceptions. It was hard to keep a good mad going in the face of that.

"But listen, guys," Adam beseeched them, flopping down next to his best friend. He took a sip of coffee and leaned his back against the sagging chenille sofa he'd been dragging around since college. "We have to get better at communicating. Fuckups like this'll kill us once the joint opens for real."

The guests had finally gone home around midnight, partied out and stuffed full of Adam's food. The French lady and the redheaded heckler had left early, presumably to rub their hands and cackle while they plotted Adam's downfall.

He couldn't believe he'd lost his cool like that. One snarky restaurant critic got in his face, and he went all macho and chest-thumpy on her. Daring her to spend a day in his kitchen! If she'd refused, what would his follow-up have been—*I double dog dare you*?

Only she didn't refuse. She fucking well jumped on it. And now he had to come up with a way to back out. No way was he welcoming a critic into his kitchen.

He knocked his head against the hard wooden arm of the sofa, then deliberately did it again. Before he could whack himself a third time, Frankie reached over and cupped the back of his head, cushioning the blow.

"Here, now," he said, cigarette hanging from his lips. "No need for that."

"Yeah," Grant said, squatting in front of them, both hands cupped around his coffee mug. "We'll pull it together. No sweat, boss."

The sound of the front door's deadbolt made them all turn their heads.

"You'd better be discussing how to make Market an enormous success," said Eleanor Bonning, stripping off her sunglasses and folding them carefully into their case. She slipped the case into the pocket of her Burberry and looked down her nose at the trio on the floor. "Because I'm not ruining my perfect investment record over you."

Adam clambered to his feet.

"She's still got a key? Glutton for punishment, you are," Frankie muttered under his breath. Adam aimed a swift kick in his direction before approaching Market's financial backer.

"Eleanor, I didn't know you were coming by." He tried for casual and probably missed it by a mile, but what could he do? Eleanor Bonning held the future of Market in the palm of her hand. Pretty fucking far from ideal, given their complicated history.

"We need to talk, so I juggled my schedule to fit it in," Eleanor said with a tiny frown. Adam resolutely did not look at Frankie; if he had, the grin tugging at the corners of his mouth would bust out. Over the past year, numerous witticisms had been made at the expense of Eleanor's iron-clad schedule.

The dreaded words "We need to talk" pretty well killed any incipient grin, however, and Adam said "Oh?" as evenly as he could manage.

Eleanor was all business today. "I don't know if you're aware of the repercussions of your conversation with Miranda Wake," she said.

Shit. Adam had hoped Eleanor missed that excruciating ten minutes. Or at least that he'd have a chance to set the record straight with Wake and her magazine before he had to face his financial backer.

From the corner of his eye, he saw Frankie and Grant both standing up. They moved to flank him, and the gesture of support fortified his frazzled nerves.

"Yeah, okay. Miranda Wake."

Red curls, creamy skin, raspberry-stained mouth.

"Precisely. Everyone is talking about your little contretemps with the infamous Ms. Wake."

Adam could well believe it. For all of New York City's eight million–strong population, in some ways, it was a very small town. Each neighborhood functioned as a distinct little community; Adam was a born-and-raised West Villager; he had neighbors who'd never been above Fourteenth Street. He knew several dedicated denizens of SoHo who wouldn't be caught dead in Times Square, and Brooklyners who hated Queens with a passion.

Similarly, the culinary community of Manhattan was

tightly knit and incestuous. Everyone knew everyone else, and gossip spread like clarified butter in a hot pan.

"Look, I'll blow her off and this whole thing will be over in a few days, as soon as Mario Batali pulls a crazy stunt or Tony Bourdain blows back into town or something. If we stay cool and let it die down—"

Eleanor was shaking her head. "No, no, no. That's exactly what I don't want."

"Then what—"

"The buzz, Adam." Eleanor's eyes glittered with that intense look she got when discussing the high rate of return on her portfolio. "All those people, those industry professionals, talking and blogging and posting pictures of you and Miranda Wake. You can't buy publicity like this." She paused. "Actually, you can, but it's very expensive. Better to get it for free, if at all possible."

Adam choked on a laugh. "Are you shitting me?"

Eleanor's mouth pursed again, and Grant poked Adam, hard, in the back.

"No," Eleanor replied, familiar disapproval heavy in her tone. "I am not shitting you." The cuss word sounded extremely dirty in Eleanor's modulated, Ivy League accent. "And the very last thing you're going to do to Miranda Wake is 'blow her off.' In fact, I've already spoken to the editor-in-chief of *Délicieux* magazine—they're set to promote it online and in print, maybe even some TV and radio ads."

A feeling of dread was surging up from Adam's gut, tightening his belly like bad shellfish. "What, exactly, are they set to promote?" he asked through numb lips.

"Their newest feature. 'Dish It Out: The Adventures of a Critic in the Kitchen.'"

Grant spoke up. "I don't get it. All that for one day of Miranda Wake sitting around the Market kitchen? Doesn't sound so exciting or buzzworthy to me."

"Of course not. A single day would be pointless. A true publicity happening like this one builds over time."

"How much time?" Adam felt slippery cold sweat break out on his palms.

"We were thinking a month. To start with."

Adam's jaw dropped. But while he may have been struck momentarily dumb, Frankie suffered no such affliction.

"I think I speak for everyone here when I say: bollocks to that."

FOUR

Jess Wake had a dream. It was a pretty simple one, as these things go.

He wanted to be normal. Like everybody else, for once, instead of the weird kid who lived with his sister. The orphan. The shutterbug. The nerd.

He deliberately didn't think about some of the nastier names he'd been called. There was no point tormenting himself over what couldn't be changed—he was never going to be normal. That's why it was a dream, not a goal.

His *goal* was to try and find his way through the confusing mess of lies and half-truths he'd told his sister over the years in hopes that she wouldn't notice how completely not normal he was. To get to some kind of honest place where he could feel okay about himself again. Or, really, for the first time.

So here he was, in New York, the city he'd longed to live in ever since he was a little kid, socked away in the boonies upstate. He'd left Brandewine, shaken the dust of that craphole off his shoes, and he was ready for a new start.

The morning sun illuminated everything so clearly. The quality of the light had changed, from bright spring to hazy summer, and Jess wished he'd brought his camera out with him.

But no, this was a specific errand, he reminded himself. A good-houseguest errand, to make sure his sister knew how much he appreciated being allowed to stay.

More than that, being welcomed. With open arms and no questions asked.

At least, not out loud. Not yet. But he could feel them lurking in the shadows of the apartment, ready to pounce and claw, and he'd had to get out, just for a little while.

Jess shivered in the brisk breeze, hugging his packages close to his chest, and turned his feet toward home.

Miranda blinked her eyes open and immediately squeezed them shut again. Why was it so bright? Her tiny Upper East Side apartment only had a single window facing the street, and that was in the living room. The other window in the glorified closet masquerading as a second bedroom looked directly onto another apartment building's brick exterior. So how could her bedroom suddenly have developed a glare?

After the first abortive motion of the day caused pain and suffering of the don't-turn-that-way-or-your-head-will-fall-off variety, Miranda stayed carefully still and reviewed her options.

One: she could lie on her back in this bed for the rest of her life. That sounded all right, at first. Until the insistent need to visit the bathroom poked its way into her consciousness. Scrap that.

Two: she could get up, but keep her eyes closed and try to make it to the bathroom blind. This had several advantages: minimization of the head-falling-off effect, as well as the satisfaction of the increasingly urgent demands of her bladder. On the other hand, she couldn't remember if she'd followed her usual nightly ritual of putting away every garment and accessory before bed last night. In most bedrooms, that probably wouldn't matter, but in Miranda's, where there was barely space for one person to turn sideways and scuttle between the wall and the bed to get to the bathroom, any debris on the floor could spell potential disaster. Especially for someone with her eyes shut, and her head in danger of defecting from her shoulders at the slightest provocation.

Miranda was fairly certain that tripping and smacking her head into the wall, bedstead, or doorframe would hurt exponentially more than opening her eyes enough to see where she was going.

Simple, really, when you looked at the cost/benefit ratio, she reflected. Of course, most of life was.

Cracking her eyes the merest sliver, Miranda gritted her teeth against a grunt of pain and breathed out through her nose. Moving creakily, like an old, infirm woman, she managed to haul her aching body from the bed and hunch her way to the bathroom, avoiding a tangle of cocktail dress, ripped stockings, and red satin pumps on the floor. Considering how out of her mind she must have been last night to forgo the putting-away ritual, it was a minor miracle that she'd managed to somehow locate and pour herself into her favorite white-and-cream-striped pajamas.

She took care of bathroom business with a sigh of relief. The longest pee of her life, and maybe the most satisfying. It gave her time to squint down at her bare knees and register that, joy of joys, her pupils had evidently recalled how to dilate and contract in response to light, because it actually seemed comfortingly dim in the bathroom.

Dim enough to make it possible to glance at her no-doubt terrifying reflection in the mirror over the sink without passing out. Or throwing up, which was starting to feel like a serious concern.

But moving around had woken her up a bit, and her

head hadn't fallen off, so Miranda supposed she ought to keep going. She brushed her teeth, twisted her hair up into a knot on top of her head without bothering to brush it, and made her cautious way out to the living room.

Confronted with a problem, Miranda preferred to compartmentalize her thinking until the most immediate, pressing issues had been taken care of. Hence the trek to the bathroom had been made in perfect calm, every dehydrated, alcohol-soaked fiber of her being focused on the task at hand.

Now, however, Miranda's busy brain was turning to other things. Like finding out what time it was, and taking a shower. Because, ew.

Not just yet, though. First things first. A direct IV of coffee, loaded straight into the veins, would be nice. But she'd settle for a nice, hot cup of the blackest, strongest stuff she could brew.

Her mouth watered; she could almost smell it. She inhaled again. Wait, she *did* smell it.

Sure enough, the coffeepot on her minuscule countertop was nearly full, steaming merrily. Miranda paused, befuddled, then blew out a long, gusty sigh.

Jess.

The selective memory loss caused by last night's overindulgence had momentarily blotted out one of the reasons she'd succumbed to the lure of that floral berry concoction from hell in the first place.

Jess was home.

Although apparently not, just at the moment. She listened hard, and even though the fresh coffee was evidence he'd been up and about, she couldn't hear anything moving in the apartment now. And with hardwood floors as old as hers, stealth was impossible.

The sound of the front door opening made her jump. Shuffling footsteps and the rustle of paper bags preceded her younger brother down the short hallway and into the main room.

Jess froze for a second when he saw her standing in the kitchen, then smiled brightly. "Good morning!"

"Morning," she answered, turning to search through the cupboard for her favorite blue china teacup. Any intelligent conversation was going to require caffeine.

"You're up! I thought you were going to sleep all day. I just went out to pick up a few things. I hope that's okay." Jess was talking too fast, and it made Miranda's heart hurt.

"Of course," she said. "I had a late night."

Jess laughed, the sound tight with nerves. "I know. I heard you come in around two." He was clutching the shopping bags like a shield. Miranda swallowed hard.

"What did you buy?" she asked.

A light flush stained his cheeks; the curse of their redhead complexion. Jess's hair was a shade or two darker than hers, more auburn than strawberry blond, but they both had fair skin that tended to show every flicker of embarrassment.

"Boring stuff like toothpaste. And I didn't want to raid your kitchen, so I went to the German bakery on the corner for breakfast rolls. No raisins." One corner of his mouth kicked up, and he suddenly looked just like the boy she'd raised, when it had been the two of them against the world. Before he left for Brandewine and her freelance writing gigs landed her a Manhattan magazine job.

Miranda smiled back, even if it felt a bit shaky. "You didn't have to do that, Jess. What's mine is yours; this is your home, too. Until you go back to school."

He looked down at the bags. His fingers clenched hard enough to show white at his knuckles at the reference to Brandewine, but that was the only indication he gave that he'd noticed it. His voice was steady and wry with good humor when he said, "Sheesh, now you tell me. Couldn't have been before I spent five bucks apiece on pastry. I forgot how freaking expensive everything is here."

"It can be hard to get used to," Miranda agreed, letting the scholarship issue go, for the moment. She probably wasn't up to tackling that without at least one more cup of coffee, anyway. "What's in the other bag?"

Jess scrunched up his face. "Flowers. To soften you up, so you'll let me stay." He pulled out a bunch of peonies, their brightly colored faces vibrant with good cheer.

Miranda caught her breath. "God, Jess." She didn't know how to feel; it was sweet enough to make her teeth ache, but the idea that Jess didn't know he was always welcome made her throat close up.

He shrugged awkwardly. "I know I didn't have to. I wanted to." He held them out to her, and Miranda set down her coffee and took them.

The moment felt fragile. Miranda fought back a totally counterproductive spate of tears. How had she let things come to this point?

"They're gorgeous. Thank you." She held Jess's gaze. "Mom's favorite."

"I remember," he murmured. His mouth firmed into a straight line and he straightened his shoulders. "Thank you for taking me in and not hounding me with a lot of questions. It's not easy for you, I know. You want to know what's happening with the scholarship, my future. You're worried about me. I just . . . I couldn't stay there, Miranda."

She took a deep breath. "It's okay. Everyone needs a break sometimes. You deserve to enjoy your vacation, like every other boy your age. You were the one who insisted on working through the summer. Jess, if something happened out there . . ."

He tensed visibly. "Nothing happened," he denied. "And it's not just a break. I'm transferring to NYU. My application's already been accepted."

Miranda's head whirled. There wasn't enough caffeine in the world to prepare her to deal with this right now. "I know you haven't settled in there yet, but I thought you'd at least made some friends. And there was a girl, right? Tara? The one you worked with at the bistro. You seemed to be getting along really well with her." Miranda had been thrilled about that. Jess hadn't been a big dater in high school, but then, their parents had met and fallen in love in college. Even though she knew it was premature, part of her couldn't help envisioning Jess and this Tara, who was surely a wonderful girl, falling deeply in love and settling down together.

"Tara and I . . . it turned out she wasn't who I thought she was." He gave a short, unhappy laugh. "And, I guess, vice versa. Anyway, it's over. She didn't factor into this decision. Come on, I spent two years at Brandewine! I think if it were a matter of settling in, I would've managed it by now." Her little brother's blue eyes darkened to a flinty blue-gray with determination.

"I'm doing this, Miranda. I'm not asking for you to support me; I'm going to take care of everything myself. Get a job, get loans and financial aid to pay for school, an apartment, whatever I need to do. I just wanted you to know what's going on, and to thank you for letting me crash here for a few weeks while I get situated."

"You are not working your way through college."

"Why not? It's what you did."

"I didn't have a choice," Miranda pointed out. "I didn't get a full scholarship to a good school, and I couldn't have gone away to college even if I had."

Jess looked down at the floor. "Because of me," he said.

"I didn't mind," Miranda said. "I never minded taking care of you—it's what Mom and Dad would've wanted. And it's not a habit I can break, so you're just going to have to live with it."

"For how long?" he asked. "I'm nearly twenty."

Forever, Miranda thought, but didn't say it. Looking into Jess's eyes, she knew now wasn't the time to have this fight. Jess could be unswerving once he got his mind set on something. She hadn't given up on getting him back to Brandewine, but failing that, she certainly wasn't allowing him to spend precious time at some job rather than on his studies.

"Okay." She blew out air, got up to pour herself another cup of coffee. "Give me one of those rolls."

Jess handed over a raisinless cinnamon bun, and joined her at the table with his own. Miranda took a bite, but the sweet, doughy mass was hard to choke down. She ended up shredding most of it while she talked.

"Something is going on with you," she said. When Jess opened his mouth, she cut him off with the patented Big Sister Glare. "Shut it. I'm talking now. You think I can't see something's up? You don't want to tell me what it is, and that's fine," she emphasized, summoning up as much conviction as she could, considering every particle of her being shrieked at her to sit on him until he confessed everything. Sadly, he wasn't fourteen years old anymore.

"If you can't stay at Brandewine, then you did the right thing coming home. I want you here, in my apartment, where I can keep an eye on you. And it's not just for a few weeks, kiddo. If you want to transfer to NYU, you live with me. And you let me pay your tuition. I won't have you splitting your focus between some crappy minimum-wage job and your college experience. You have to promise me you'll focus on your future."

Jess clouded over, but Miranda held firm. "That's the price you pay for giving up that scholarship."

"Fine," he agreed. "But I get a summer job and save up my earnings to help pay for books."

"Deal," she said, mouth twitching. "You drive a hard

bargain. But it's probably a good idea for you to find work this summer—I'm going to be busy enough for the next few months that you'd get awfully lonely sitting around this apartment."

"Problems at work?" he asked, looking concerned.

"Challenges," she corrected, excitement trickling back in. "Big changes, new goals. I'm going to write a book. I've always wanted to, and I finally have the perfect platform."

She couldn't contain the thrill she got when she said it out loud. Just the thought gave her a giant happy shiver, and she took another sip of coffee to settle down.

Jess's eyes went wide. "Hey, that's awesome. What kind of book?"

"Nonfiction, about my experiences in the kitchen at Market. It's a new restaurant opening up across town."

A plethora of recent books and articles had appeared, extolling the virtues of eating locally and seasonally—but was there another side to the story? How possible was it, really, for a restaurant to carry out a mission like Market's? Would the menu suffer from or be exalted by the limitations imposed by Adam Temple's strict policy of only serving local, organic food? There was a story here, Miranda was sure of it. Now if she could just convince a publisher of that . . .

"Cool!" Jess took on a calculating air, which made him look like a little boy trying to figure out how to scam an extra cookie at snacktime. "You think this place needs waiters? If they're still getting started, maybe they've got slots to fill."

"Maybe," Miranda said doubtfully. "But the chef . . . well, let's just say he's not too overjoyed at the prospect of having a journalist observing him. I'm not sure being related to me is going to give you any kind of leg up. Possibly quite the reverse."

Jess shrugged. "All I can do is try, right? You going over there today?"

She nodded. Claire had promised to call with a battle plan after she spoke to the editorial board, but whatever the outcome of that conversation, Miranda was determined to strike while the iron was hot.

Jess nodded decisively. "Then I'm coming with you."

Miranda hid a smile behind her coffee cup. It wouldn't do to let Jess see how much she liked the idea. He wasn't a contrarian, by nature, but with this new fiercely independent streak he was sporting, he might react badly to the realization that Miranda loved the idea of having her baby brother under her direct supervision practically twenty-four/seven. Living together, working together—surely with all that togetherness, she'd be able to puzzle out how things had gotten off track and set Jess back on the right path. Then she'd sell her new-and-improved book proposal for tons of money, and be able to pay that tuition!

Nothing soothed Miranda's frazzled nerves like having a clear, step-by-step plan laid out.

She took another bite of cinnamon roll, and this time it went down easily, sugary icing and dark spice bursting over her tongue.

Yes, she thought with deep satisfaction. *Everything is coming together.*

FIVE

Nothing is coming together!" Adam yelled.

The skeleton kitchen crew dashed around him. It was just section leaders today, the main guys from grill, sauté, garde-manger, and pastry, plus Adam and Frankie, all cooking feverishly side by side as they attempted to finalize the menu for opening night.

And nothing was working. The custom-made, heinously expensive wood-burning grill was turning out fillet that tasted like the charred ends of cigarettes, the sauce for the rabbit *rillettes* kept separating, the vinaigrette for the endive salad was boring and flat, while the rosemary and olive oil flatbread wasn't flat *enough*.

Adam gritted his teeth. He had to bear down and get through this day, put everything out of his head but the food. He couldn't be one of those temperamental chefs who fell apart over every little thing.

It was just . . . having a damn critic in his kitchen, scrutinizing his every move, judging his food and his crew and his methods. That was not a little thing. He might even feel justified about this freak-out, if he hadn't invited the woman himself.

Self-recrimination boiled up in his belly, bitter and acid.

Not only had Adam lost his head and beckoned a viper into their midst, now he was screwing up the kitchen dynamic and taking his aggravation out on the crew.

Unacceptable. He had to pull himself together. And he knew just how to do it, too.

Adam was going to make pâté.

Two hours, a deep clean and re-seasoning of the grill, one perfect *sauce moutarde,* vinaigrette, and flatbread dough later, and Adam was up to his elbows in duck fat. It was the best way he'd found to get calm and collected: make something with a lot of steps, in intricate layers that all had to harmonize together.

He was finally starting to breathe normally again, and, not coincidentally, so was his crew. Everyone was back to focusing on specific tasks, refining the details of every dish until it could be achieved perfectly, night after night.

Adam looked down and contemplated the work he was doing. There was a bowl of duck's liver, sautéed, diced and whipped together with foie gras, minced shallots, and port, sitting in an ice bath to his left. Another small bowl sat beside his right hand, filled with prunes steeped in veal stock and more port. There was duck confit in a bin, and the long, narrow cast-iron terrine pan was ready to be lined with duck fat, which would seal in the moisture and flavor of the pâté as it cooked. He was still trying to come up with one last element, something surprising to cut through the richness of the confit and the liver mixture. Lemon zest?

And then Grant hung up the kitchen phone with a long-suffering sigh.

"She's on her way."

Adam's fingers stiffened against the urge to clench. He held still, with effort. He refused to tear this beautiful piece of fat he'd just painstakingly skinned from a whole free-range duckling.

"Couldn't you hold her off?" he said around the tic in his jaw.

"You want me to tell the newest member of our staff that she's not welcome?"

Adam's stomach rolled. "She's not on staff. She's vacationing here. She's a fucking tourist."

"With pen and paper in hand," Frankie grumbled.

Adam shot Frankie a quelling look. He didn't want the rest of the crew knowing just how disastrous this could turn out to be. Not to mention the fact that it was all his fault.

He'd apologized privately for his part in this fiasco to Frankie and Grant. They were his partners in crime, his friends. But even though Adam preferred a collegial atmosphere in his kitchen, he wasn't about to have subordinates second-guessing his judgment. Flawed or not, it was his damn kitchen. He had to be in control.

Restaurant brigades were like nothing so much as a pirate crew; any hint of blood in the water could incite a mutiny. A lot of his employees lived rough lives around the fringes of normal society. That was why most of them worked in restaurants; the insane hours, the intense pressure, the adrenaline rush of service—only a misfit could thrive under those circumstances. Adam ought to know.

Benevolent pirate king that he was, Adam knew everyone's name, from grill cook to dishwasher, and the names of their wives and girlfriends and kids—but if any one of them screwed up during service? They got the full, sharp edge of Adam's temper.

Screwing up outside of service, away from the restaurant—well, Adam liked to know about that, too. In the interests of being prepared. If someone didn't show up for work, the whole kitchen scrambled to make up the difference.

Keeping on top of that was Frankie's department.

Somehow, some way, Frankie knew everything that went down with their crew. He could find out any information on anyone in the restaurant business, through shady, circuitous means best known only to himself. He was Adam's first mate. His strong right arm, the sword arm. Adam would be lost without him.

All of which made Frankie's occasional dickishness easier to swallow.

"Do you want to go get cleaned up, boss?" Grant asked, wrinkling his nose at the duck fat.

Adam caught Frankie's glance and smiled slowly when his friend winked, eyebrows arched devilishly.

"No way, man," Adam said, letting the familiar sounds and smells of the kitchen wash over him. "Let her come talk to me right here, see what it's all about."

See what I'm all about, he thought. Because this was him. Messy hands, busy mind, every sense trained to seek perfection. This was where he lived. And no snotty little magazine scribbler, gorgeous red-gold hair and feisty spirit or not, was going to change that. ·

There was something strange about a restaurant before opening. Like a classroom after school was out, familiar surroundings where every item has its place and purpose, but none of it's meant for you at the moment.

Miranda hadn't noticed much about the décor last night, but by day Market was a welcoming little place. She glanced down the tree-lined Upper West Side block, noting the cozy, bustling feel of the neighborhood even at ten o'clock on a Sunday morning. There was a school across the street, the large, fenced-in paved area in front entirely taken over by the weekly farmer's market she assumed had given the restaurant its name.

Young families mingled with old ladies carrying cloth shopping bags, all of them poring over fresh produce. The air had a beguiling warmth to it, the first harbinger of New York's sultry summer heat.

Claire had called, as promised, and delivered the exciting news that the magazine's editorial board had arranged matters with Market's financial backer, a woman named Eleanor Bonning, and Miranda would be spending an entire month in the kitchen there. A whole month! And that was just to start. Claire had mentioned something about the Cooking Channel being interested. The possibilities were endlessly exciting.

Jess whistled, low and appreciative. "Sweet setup. I like this neighborhood."

"Location isn't everything," Miranda said. "Let's see if the inside lives up to the promise of the exterior."

Bursting with anticipation, Miranda pushed open the front door and led Jess into the dimly lit restaurant. The soft gold-green of the walls and burnished golden wood of the bar glowed in the late afternoon sun. And wow, how far gone was she last night that she hadn't even noticed the lovely, open flow between the main dining room and the smaller, more private room? The U-shaped bar held court between the rooms, the mirrored backsplash reflecting the green-gold walls and making the space feel even more open.

Before she had a chance to berate herself over missing the tasteful copper wall sconces shaped like abstract Art Deco leaves, she was distracted by noise and movement from the main dining room to the right.

Peeking around the bar, she could see that the back wall of the main room had an open pass through to the kitchen, which was teeming with activity.

She glanced back at Jess, who shrugged and motioned her forward. Music was pouring out of the kitchen, a pounding bass beat layered over with screaming guitar. It was the kind of music the bad boys she went to high school with had blasted over the speakers of their souped-up muscle cars.

Moving closer, she saw the mastermind behind this little jewel of a restaurant nodding his head to the beat and mouthing along with the lyrics. Something about being an anarchist.

A young blond man she vaguely remembered from behind the bar the night before stepped up to the pass and caught sight of Miranda and Jess. Eyes widening, the bartender grabbed at Adam Temple's sleeve to get his attention, gesturing toward the dining room.

Adam looked over his shoulder, locking eyes with Miranda, and she had to gulp in a quick, discreet burst of air.

Damn. She'd really been hoping that was a cocktail-induced hallucination. If there was anything worse than the ego of an executive chef, it was the ego of a good-looking executive chef.

Most chefs had women throwing themselves at them like groupies tossing their panties on the stage at a rock concert, especially in these fallen times, with the rise of the popular television Cooking Channel. Chefs were celebrities, even the ones who didn't have their own show. And unbelievably sexy specimens like the one in front of her?

Well. The only sensible option was to stay as far away from him as possible. Which shouldn't be a problem, since he was looking about as pleased to see them as if she and Jess were a party of twenty women with infants in strollers, showing up for a Mother's Morning Out brunch.

Miranda held her head high and marched forward, Jess trailing behind.

Adam met her at the kitchen door, wiping his hands impatiently on the towel tucked into his apron. His mouth was set, his dark eyes flashing caution, but Miranda wasn't about to let him intimidate her.

"Chef Temple," she said breezily, holding out her hand.

"Miranda Wake," he replied, putting his hands on his hips. He glanced down to her outstretched palm, then back up to her face. "We've met," he said. "You may not remember."

Heat scorched her cheeks, but Miranda refused to acknowledge it. "Of course," she said, dropping her hand to her side. "But you haven't met my brother. This is Jess Wake."

Jess stepped up, and Miranda felt a momentary glow of pride in his manners. "It's an honor, sir." He grinned. "My old boss would have kittens if he knew I was standing here with you."

Okay, glow-of-pride moment over. "Jess," she hissed.

But Adam laughed, the hardness melting from his features as if it had never been. "Hey, it's always good to meet a fan," he said easily. "Or someone who once worked for a fan. Your boss, he was a foodie?"

"You could say that," Jess replied. "He owned the self-proclaimed fanciest restaurant in Brandewine, Indiana. I waited tables there for two years. When Miranda told me the news, I couldn't resist the chance to tag along."

"Right. The news," Adam said, his voice noticeably cooler. He slanted a glance at Miranda. "That your sister's got herself a job peeling potatoes in my kitchen for the next month."

"Speaking of jobs," Jess said brightly, "are you still hiring front-of-house staff?"

"Jess recently moved back to the city, and he's looking for work this summer before he goes back to school," Miranda said.

Adam's eyes widened. "Jesus, what is it with your family? Every Wake in the country have a hard-on to work at Market? Should I expect your mother next?"

Jess flinched a little, but stood his ground. "Nope," he said. "Our parents died when I was a kid, so you don't have to worry about them."

Miranda held in a gasp with some effort. What was Jess thinking, offering up such a personal thing to a stranger?

Adam looked taken aback, the annoyance in his eyes morphing into the shocked pity Miranda'd seen and despised in the face of everyone who found out about her family.

Miranda braced herself for semisincere platitutes or stammering sympathies, but Adam said, "I'll have to check with the restaurant manager. Grant's taking care of hiring the wait staff. Hey, Grant, can you come out here for a sec?" That last bit was shouted through the pass.

The blond man Miranda had mistaken for the bartender appeared a moment later, and Adam introduced him as Grant Holloway. Adam filled him in, and Grant offered to take Jess down to the office for an interview. Miranda watched them go, trying to be grateful that Adam had allowed the awkward moment Jess created to pass without comment.

The gratitude evaporated when Adam turned on her, eyes snapping. "I'm not crazy about the idea of hiring your kid brother. Bad enough I've got you for a month—if we hire that kid, you'll have an excuse to be around even longer."

Miranda's temper kicked into high gear. She snatched her reporter's notebook from her purse, unscrewed the cap on her favorite tortoiseshell fountain pen, and flipped to a blank page.

Writing in the shorthand she'd developed over the years, she spoke the note aloud. "Makes hiring decisions based on personal and evidently volatile emotions, rather than fair, open-minded business practices."

"What the hell are you doing?" Adam was practically snarling.

"My job," she told him. She made another note. "Appears to hold a grudge. Unable to see the benefits of increased publicity for a new restaurant?"

"I'm not a moron," he said, barely moving his lips. "Publicity is a good thing. I just don't happen to think having a critic in my kitchen is worth it."

"Journalist," she corrected him. "I'm embedding myself in your kitchen like a war correspondent embedded with the troops. Although I'm hoping this assignment won't be quite that bloody."

Adam arched a brow. "Don't count on it. Things get nasty in the kitchen; it's inevitable. Tensions run hotter than boiling water and sometimes the testosterone overflows. I don't need some pretty little scribbler getting her panties in a twist over bad tempers or rough language. I'm not censoring myself for you."

"Excellent!" Miranda wanted to clap her hands. He was too perfect. She couldn't wait to write about him.

He stared at her. "Shit. That was exactly what you wanted to hear, wasn't it?"

She nodded. "I need to get an accurate impression of what it's like in a professional kitchen."

"So you can crap all over it in your magazine."

And a best-selling book, if I'm lucky. "I've been given to understand that I'll have unrestricted access to you and your staff for the next month. Whether you like it or not, Chef Temple, this is happening." She gripped her pen and notebook a little harder, only noticing when the spiral rings cut into her palm painfully. "Look, this isn't exactly how I imagined it would be, either, getting my big break. I should apologize for the way I behaved last night. It was unprofessional and insulting."

Adam crossed his arms over his broad chest. Miranda tried not to notice how that made the corded muscles in his tanned forearms bulge.

"Yeah," he said, not blinking.

"Yeah?" Miranda repeated. "That's all you have to say?"

"I'm agreeing with you," he said. "Unprofessional. Insulting. You should apologize. I can't wait to hear it."

Miranda clenched her jaw so hard she was afraid her teeth would snap. "You're an ass," she seethed.

Satisfaction glittered in his dark eyes, as though she'd confirmed something for him. "Maybe, sweetheart," he said. "But for the next month, I'm also your god and king."

He leaned down until she felt his hot breath brush her cheek. "When you're in my kitchen, my word is fucking law. Be sure to write that in your little notebook."

Miranda shuddered, his nearness affecting her in unwelcome ways. But she refused to step away. She held her ground, and when Adam straightened, she looked him directly in the eye. She thought she caught a fleeting glimpse of something like respect, but she couldn't be sure, because in the next instant, he was clapping her on the back and saying, "Come on, scribbler. Let's go introduce you to the crew."

SIX

A professional kitchen was almost never completely abandoned; there was always prep to be done. But things were at a low pitch, Miranda could see through the open pass; only three or four cooks worked industriously at their stations. They glanced up at her curiously, but mostly they stayed focused on what their hands were doing.

Adam led her into his large kitchen, saying, "We're still finalizing the menu for the opening next weekend. Tasting and tweaking, getting it all down so it's perfect every time. Restaurant cooking isn't like throwing a dinner party at your apartment—it's not just about how good the recipe is, or how well you execute it that night. It's about consistency. Being able to do it perfectly, over and over, so if a guest comes in and loves a dish, he can come back and order that same thing every time and always get exactly what he expects."

Miranda made a few notes. Her heart pounded with excitement. In spite of Adam's hostile reception, this was already fascinating.

The cooks were mostly men, dressed uniformly in the standard-issue white jackets and loose, black-and-white-checked pants. They wore leather or rubber clogs on their feet, and they moved past each other in the small confines of the kitchen space like football players on the field, instinctively knowing where everyone else was.

The exception to all of that was leaning over the huge range, holding the lid of a red enameled cast-iron pot. He whooped loudly before turning and throwing a long arm around Adam's neck.

"Adam!" The voice was raucous and rough, with a Cockney edge. "It's done, come taste. Hello, hello, what have we here?"

Miranda looked up . . . and up, into a pair of knowing black eyes. Tall, skinny, shock of black hair, muscular bare arms, and a ripped T-shirt sporting a coy, half-naked cowgirl and the words THE NEW YORK DOLLS. She looked back to see Adam close his eyes briefly, as if praying for patience. "Miranda Wake, this is Frankie Boyd. My second in command."

Frankie grinned, a quick flash of teeth and the tip of his tongue, and said, "Know who you are already, luv. But it's ever so nice to meet you, all formal like."

He extended a hand, and Miranda took it cautiously, not sure what to expect. "So . . . you're the sous-chef?" she asked.

"Sous-chef, informer, enforcer, first mate, punk rocker," Frankie said extravagantly, "and worshipper at your divine altar, oh, gorgeous one. May I kiss your hand?"

His eyes laughed down at her. Miranda lifted her chin, completely unwilling to be overawed by this tornado of a man.

"Pucker up, buttercup," she said, and watched Frankie's eyes widen in comical surprise as he dropped his arm from Adam's shoulders. Adam laughed, and Frankie bowed low over Miranda's hand, pressing a soft kiss to her knuckles.

"Oh," he breathed. "I see why you lost your head over this one. I wish you luck, mate; I think you're going to need it."

Miranda flushed, acutely aware that it was half embarrassment, half accomplishment, the thrill of holding her own.

Frankie gave her one last cheerful leer, before turning to his boss. "Hate to interrupt, and for once I really mean that, but that braised pork belly you started isn't getting any nicer sitting in its sauce, going cold."

"Go on and get it plated, you hooligan, I'm coming."

Frankie leaped for the stove, grabbing his pot with the towel tucked in the waistband of his black jeans. Adam shook his head, obviously used to Frankie's ways.

"I've got to taste this," Adam said, gesturing over his shoulder. He cocked his head suddenly and his eyes brightened for the first time since she arrived. "Hey, you wanna taste it, too?"

Miranda raised both brows. "Really?"

"Shit, yeah. You know, maybe this doesn't have to be all bad, having you around. You can be like our ringer; we can get the critic's take on something before it ever hits the menu."

"You don't think that's cheating?"

"All's fair in love and cookery, sweetheart. I'll do whatever it takes to make this place a success." He pointed both index fingers at her like guns and pulled an ironic face. "Case in point."

Rolling her eyes, Miranda said, "Fine. But just so you know, I'm not going to censor myself, either. Whatever I think of your food, I'm not going to mince words. So be prepared to deal with it."

The insufferable man grinned, lazy and devastating, teeth glinting white and even in his handsome face. "Looking forward to it."

Adam led her over to the pass where Frankie was plating a slice of pork belly. Even after last night and everything she'd said about gimmicky greenmarket restaurants,

Miranda wasn't sure what to expect of Adam Temple's food.

She'd left the party without trying any of the hors d'oeuvres, too eager to sit down with Claire for a late-night conference about the incredible opportunity that had just opened up.

He was so damn cocky about his cooking, she almost hoped it was terrible.

Adam tried the pork belly first, lifting the spoon to his mouth with a considering air that for some reason struck Miranda as unreasonably sexy. He savored it for a moment, his mouth moving slowly, then he and Frankie were off to the races, talking at each other a mile a minute about braising times and the relative merits of clover versus wildflower honey. But Miranda couldn't really follow the discussion; she was too busy having an orgasm through her mouth.

Adam had passed her the spoon when he was done, and she'd innocently, unknowingly, dipped it into the seared, tender creation on the plate before her. Nothing in her experience—and she'd reviewed more than a hundred restaurants in her four years as a food critic—prepared her for what she was about to taste.

Pork belly—humble, fatty uncured bacon—was the current darling of the Manhattan restaurant scene. Every customer wanted it, so every restaurant served it. Mostly, it was oily and tasteless, slippery with pork fat and stringy, meager meat. It was paired with a variety of spices and vegetables, from anise to zucchini, but this.

This.

Was something altogether different. Smooth and dark, thick with meat and juice, tangy with the bittersweetness of apple cider and the round nuttiness of ginger-glazed walnuts. The pork belly was crisp on the outside, the browned top a delicious contrast to the unctuous richness of the braised meat. The sharp notes of acid, the brown sugar on the back of her tongue, forced a sound like a moan out of Miranda's throat.

Miranda opened her eyes to find Adam regarding her with a look of deep satisfaction.

"I know I said last night you should keep your opinions to yourself, but I'd love to know what that noise meant."

Miranda swallowed slowly, not allowing herself to be hurried through the moment. When she'd rolled the after-flavors of caramel and cinnamon across the roof of her mouth, she said, "I'm hoping that if I have to eat humble pie, you'll at least serve it with that sauce."

"Is this going to be your first time working in a kitchen?" Adam was trying to play it cool, but inside, man, he was giving himself the big high five because this gorgeous, prickly woman with *exacting standards* liked his food.

It never got old, no matter how many guests he'd sent home with happy smiles on their faces. Nothing was more guaranteed to send Adam into the stratosphere. He'd never get sick of that look, that blissed-out moment of transcendence when someone tasted a dish he'd thought up and prepared with his own hands (or the hands of his crew, because really, those guys were basically an extension of him) and just freaking loved it.

Always a genuine kick, but somehow, the rush this time was even more intense. And he didn't kid himself; he knew why. It was because it was *her*.

Miranda Wake, whom he'd done his best to run off this morning, who had every reason to resist or deny the evidence of her taste buds, who had, in fact, built her living and reputation on finding fault. Who hadn't even blinked before telling him he was a genius.

Okay, not in so many words, but hey. Adam was prepared to mark this one down as a win for him, no question.

Even if she'd immediately regretted her candor, retreating behind a sniffy attitude that said, "You may be able to cook, but you're still an ass." Which was fine, because he knew he'd been an ass to her. Damned if it was easy to keep disliking someone who so clearly enjoyed his food, though.

Miranda slanted him a suspicious glance, as if she knew what he was thinking and didn't entirely approve. Adam took a stab at doing innocent who-me? eyes, but he forgot about that when she said, "Does it matter if I've ever worked in a kitchen before? This isn't a job interview. I'm here for the duration, regardless of your feelings on the matter."

And the dislike was back, bigger and better than ever. He could feel the blood throbbing in the vein above his left eyebrow. It must make him look like a cartoon villain, about to pop.

"Hey. I'm just trying make sure you're not going to lose a finger if I ask you to dice veg for the mirepoix."

She looked away. "I've cooked at home. And I spent time at the Academy of Culinary Arts."

"Seriously?" Adam blinked, surprised. The Academy of Culinary Arts in upstate New York was the most prestigious cooking school in the country. He never would've taken her for an Academy grad. "You trained at the ACA?"

She blushed, all up her cheeks and down her neck. Adam wanted to know if the flush extended past the stiff collar of her navy blue suit.

"I worked there. In the offices," she clarified. "Occasionally, I had the chance to observe the classes, but I was never an official participant in the program."

Interesting. More clues. Adam was filing them all away, every tidbit she let fall about herself. Never knew what might be useful later. He wondered if that job at the ACA was before or after her parents died. How young must she have been?

"It's just as well," he told her. "ACA grads always think they know more than they do. Chances are I would've had to teach you everything from scratch anyway."

"So I'm actually going to be cooking?" she asked.

"What, you thought you'd be sitting around looking pretty and taking notes? No way. Everyone in my kitchen works."

"Especially you, right, Chef?" Frankie fluttered his eyelashes.

Miranda buttoned up her mouth like she was trying not to laugh. Adam narrowed his eyes at Frankie and said, "No sarcasm in the kitchen. Makes the food taste bitter."

He tilted his head at Miranda, letting himself loom over her a little. "You know what happens to cheeky cooks in my kitchen, Wake?"

She lifted her chin coolly. "What?"

"They get assigned to make stock."

There was a chorus of groans around the kitchen. No one liked the daily slog of making the huge pots of veal stock, chicken stock, fish stock, demi-glace and consommé that formed the base for nearly every sauce that made it onto a Market plate. It was repetitive and basic, boring, but they'd all done their time at Adam's insistence.

"Stock isn't fun. It isn't sexy," he told Miranda. "But it's essential. Without it, you have only canned, processed sauces that taste like stale chemicals, or thin, watery concoctions that taste like nothing. We use fresh every day."

"What do you do with the leftovers?"

"Use them for the family meal—the communal dinner the staff eats together before service. Or for testing recipes. Stuff like that."

He assessed her for a long moment, wondering if he could trust her with the stock. "Might be a good station for you to get your feet wet," he mused aloud. "It'd be a way for me to see what you've got, and it's simple enough that I don't really see how you can mess it up. Stocks are Rob's responsibility right now, and I'm sure he'd love some help."

She looked around. "Rob? Is he here today?"

"Nope. You'll like him, though. Academy extern, all up-tight and eager to please." He grinned. "Unlike the rest of my pirates. Come on, let's do the meet and greet."

Man, this was going to be fun.

Miranda flipped to a new page and shook her fountain pen to make sure there was plenty of ink. Nothing about this day was going quite as she'd expected, from Jess telling Adam about their parents to the chef's changeable moods and mouthwateringly sensual food. She had no idea what the kitchen staff would be like, although she suspected Adam planned to use them to frighten her into backing out.

"Okay," Adam said. "You already met Frankie. And once is usually enough for most people."

"Tosser! I heard that," Frankie yelled from the walk-in.

Adam grinned and steered Miranda toward a towering black man with burn marks scoring his forearms all the way to the elbow. He was chopping shallots, his knife flashing faster than the eye could follow.

"Quentin, I need a minute."

"Yo," Quentin replied. "Yeah, boss. What's up." Everything Quentin said was a statement, not a question. He had a deep, slow voice that seemed to resonate up from the pit of his stomach, and his knife never stopped moving as he talked.

"Wanna introduce the newest addition to our kitchen. Miranda Wake, this is Quentin Thomas, master of the sauté, the braise, poaching—basically, anything that involves meat cooked with liquid. Q is the man."

Quentin slid Miranda a considering look and said, "Yeah. You're the writer."

Again, a simple declarative statement, but she found herself nodding anyway. "I'd love to interview you, sometime. Just a few questions—"

Quentin's big shoulders humped over the cutting board, and Miranda stopped talking, disconcerted.

"Whoops," Adam said, as he took her elbow and whirled her around. "Moving on. Later, Q."

"Later," the large man said, his knife still chopping in unbroken rhythm.

Adam pulled Miranda closer and said in a low voice, "Should've warned you. You're not going to be interviewing Quentin. Like, ever. In fact, don't address him with a question at all."

"Why on earth not?" Miranda had never heard anything so preposterous.

Adam shrugged. "He doesn't like it. Won't answer."

"And you haven't bothered to find out why?" Miranda pursued.

"I respect his privacy. And his knife skills."

"All right," Miranda said, refusing to be thrown. "I'll just observe him, then."

Adam shook his head, and Miranda caught a hint of dimple. "That's what you really like, isn't it? Observing."

"It's a necessary prelude to any good writing," she agreed stiffly, "but especially to reviewing. Details are important."

"Sure. And I bet you rock at the detail stuff. But that's not why you *like* it."

Miranda arched a brow. "No?"

"Nope. Hey, Violet's here!" He tugged Miranda toward a wide wooden table along the back wall where a diminutive woman was turning a huge ball of dough out onto the floured surface.

That was it? Miranda wanted to demand just what the hell Adam meant by that remark, but couldn't bring herself to start a squabble in front of an audience. Twice in two days was twice too many for her.

Besides, there was part of her that wasn't sure she'd like Adam's answer.

"Violet Porter is our pastry chef slash bread genius. If there's anyone who can rival Quentin for number of burn marks, it's Vi."

The tiny woman flashed a broad smile and dusted enough flour from her arms to display rows of shiny pink scar tissue. "Ovens are hot," she said cheerfully. "And bread pans are heavy. Not a great combo."

She had a round, cherubic face with apple cheeks and sparkling brown eyes that turned sly when she poked Adam with a floury finger.

"So this is her, right? Your critic."

Remarkably, Adam colored slightly. Clearing his throat, he said, "This is Miranda Wake. She's going to be observing"—there was that word again, and now that she was listening for it, Miranda could hear the odd stress he put on it—"and helping out in the kitchen for a few weeks."

The pastry chef looked Miranda up and down. "Wow. High heels. That's going to be a barrel of monkeys during service. *Délicieux* magazine, right?" Violet grabbed the ball of dough in one hand and slammed it down on the table, making Miranda jump.

"Yes," she confirmed. Violet folded the dough in a practiced motion, then picked it up and threw it down again. Miranda managed not to flinch at the loud smack of dough on table, but it wasn't easy.

"I've read your stuff," Violet said conversationally. "It's good."

WHAM.

"Thank you," Miranda said.

WHAM.

"You know your way around an insult. I respect that."

WHAM.

Miranda got the feeling Violet's sweetness of face might be misleading. She slanted a glance at Adam. The dimples were out in full force, whatever embarrassment he'd momentarily felt clearly gone.

"I'm paid to express my opinion in an entertaining and informative way," Miranda said.

WHAM.

"Hmm. I'm paid to knead, heft, and work with hundreds of pounds of bread dough a day. I've got wicked upper body strength, let me tell you."

WHAM. This time accompanied by a narrow glare.

"That's . . . nice," Miranda said, glancing at Adam for help. He shrugged, spreading his hands in a what-can-I-say gesture, but then he clasped Violet's shoulder and said, "Ease up a little, Vi. You don't want to overwork that dough."

As they walked away, Miranda whispered, "Am I imagining things, or did your pastry chef just threaten me?"

Adam chuckled. He was having far too good a time with this. "She's a kick in the pants. Swear to God, Violet's the toughest cook in this kitchen, and that's putting her up against an ex-con, an ex-gang member, whatever the hell Quentin is, and Milo D'Amico. Although Milo's not really dangerous, himself, are you, buddy?" He swung a companionable arm over the shoulders of a gangly kid standing at the sink rinsing leeks.

"Nah," the kid said, flashing a grin at Miranda. His straight, white teeth made a striking contrast to his dark Mediterranean complexion. "My family is."

Milo winked broadly, and Miranda wondered if that was Family with a capital *F*.

"Milo runs the garde-manger station, responsible for all

the salads and cold apps. He's a whiz with vegetable garnishes."

The young man twirled a paring knife, boasting, "I can carve a radish to look like your grandmother."

"Wonderful," Miranda said, biting the inside of her cheek. "My grandmother would be so pleased. It's nice to meet you."

"Hey, you, too, beautiful," Milo said, winking again.

"Knock it off." Adam wrestled the kid around to face the sink again, laughing. "Back to work, *amico*."

Another bank of sinks skirted the corner of the kitchen and Adam bounced over to ruffle the dark hair of a wiry kid in a stained apron who stood over a towering stack of dirty pots and pans.

"This here," Adam said, "is the most important guy in the kitchen. Without this dude, all is lost."

The boy turned to Adam with a smile, and Miranda saw that he was older than she'd originally thought. His smooth bronze skin and dark chocolate eyes proclaimed his Latino heritage.

"You only say that to make me work harder," the young man said with an air of wisdom.

"No one could possibly work harder than you," Adam retorted. "We can barely keep up." He shook his head in mock despair at Miranda. "Supplying Billy with a constant stream of dirty dishes is a job of work."

The young man turned, obviously surprised. "Sorry, I didn't see you there."

She could practically see the wheels turning as he took in her uncheflike appearance—no white coat, no clogs, no twinkle of cheerful insanity in her eye.

"Billy Perez," he said. "I won't shake your hand 'cause mine're covered in something nasty."

"I appreciate that," she told him.

Adam jumped in and explained who she was and what

she was doing at Market, and Miranda tuned him out. She didn't particularly care to hear him call her an "observer" again. That word was starting to annoy her.

As Adam led her away from the sink he leaned over and said, low, "That kid's gonna be big."

She shot him a questioning look, and he shrugged.

"It's something you know in your gut when you've been doing this as long as I have, the ability to spot talent. I wasn't blowing smoke—the boy's a worker. And he's hungry to learn. It's a consistently winning combination."

"Does he have ambitions to be a chef?" Miranda wanted to know.

Adam eyed her askance. "Sweetheart, nobody works a backbreaking shit job like dishwasher if they don't want to move up in the kitchen. There's other ways to make minimum wage. Ways that are less smelly."

Miranda pondered that while flipping to a new page in her notebook. She jotted a few notes, wanting to be able to capture it later. There was some really good stuff here, not the least of which was the executive chef and owner.

Adam Temple. Captain of this motley crew, fearless leader, and coconspirator all rolled into one. Miranda looked up from her notes to find he'd been drawn into a conversation with Frankie. It looked fairly serious, their two dark heads bent close together, examining something in a copper pot on the range. Adam was adding pinches from Frankie's assembled bowls of ingredients and stirring them in with a long wooden spoon. After every addition, they'd each grab a clean tasting spoon and sample the new mixture.

Next to Frankie, Adam should seem short—the sous-chef had at least four inches on him. And yet, there was something in Adam's stance and presence that was undiminished, no matter who he stood beside. He radiated vitality and an intense interest in all the doings and workings

of the kitchen. Every cook, every ingredient, every tool—
he was proud of it all, and his passion for what he was doing fascinated Miranda.

It was so foreign to the way she approached her work.
Writing restaurant reviews was a job. A good job, one she'd
pushed hard to get, and continued to strive to do well. But
it was still, in the end, work.

Adam didn't work in the kitchen. He lived it, breathed
it, embodied it.

What worried Miranda—the thought that was going to
keep her awake tonight—was the fact that a part of her
yearned toward the warmth of Adam's intensity. To be the
focus of so much passion . . . Miranda shivered, ruthlessly
quashing any speculation on the way Adam's blunt callused hands would feel on her skin.

It was pointless to speculate. Adam Temple, Miranda
was beginning to suspect, was a true believer. A fanatic, in
his way, and that passion of his was all reserved for Market. Any woman hoping to bask in his warmth would have
to be content with the reflected glow off his love for the
restaurant.

Not that Miranda was that woman. Not at all. Besides
the fact that he'd made it clear he resented every moment
he was forced to spend in her company, she was a professional.

She was here to do a job. Nothing more.

Firming her mouth, she snapped the notebook shut and
ignored the slight ache of longing. She'd learned the trick
of it a long time ago, and she'd do well to remember it now.
The key to happiness, or at least, the key to contentment.

Don't want what you can't have.

SEVEN

Market's nonpublic areas were cooler even than the dining rooms. Jess thought so, anyway. He liked to see the things most people didn't have access to, the dim, poky back stairway, the changing room, the unisex bathroom the staff shared.

Grant had given him the abbreviated tour on the way to Adam's office where they'd do the interview. The restaurant manager was younger than Jess would've expected for someone in that position, especially in a hot new Manhattan eatery. Disconcertingly good-looking, in a preppy way, with his sunny blond hair and cornflower-blue eyes. Not that Jess was going to do anything about that.

Here, with people Miranda knew? Not to mention around people he himself would hopefully be working with.

Jess was going for the super straight-arrow vibe in a big way.

"This could all work out real well," Grant was saying. "We've been having kind of a tough time staffing front of house, and Adam mentioned you have some experience with fine dining?"

"Oh, yeah. I mean, yes. I waited tables through high

school, upstate where we grew up, and I worked at the best restaurant in Brandewine for two years."

"Brandewine?"

"Where I went to school. It's in the Midwest." Jess tensed in expectation of the full interrogation, but Grant only nodded and changed the subject.

"Boss's office is back here. It's a hike—I'm real thankful the kitchen's not down here, too. I've worked restaurants in Manhattan that were set up like that, and they were hell on the knees, let me tell you. All that running up and down stairs in the middle of rush dinner service! Awful." He gave an exaggerated shudder, and Jess let himself smile. Not too much; there were all kinds of cues, and Jess knew how to project the ones he wanted.

"But what can you do in Manhattan?" Grant continued. "Space is at a premium, you can only build up or down. We use the basement mostly for storage. Some pantry items are kept down here, and there's a walk-in cooler. And of course, office space," he finished, as they reached the end of the hall.

There was a handwritten sign posted on the metal door that said BOSS IS in large black letters, and beside it, a cockeyed paper tag that read IN THE KITCHEN. Scattered around the door were other possible ends to the sentence. Jess read HAGGLING WITH SUPPLIERS, AT THE UNION SQUARE GREENMARKET, and A WANKER, before Grant pushed open the door and led him inside.

A large metal desk strewn with papers, files, and an antiquated computer on one side dominated the room. But Grant didn't head over to sit behind it. Instead, he gestured toward a narrow sofa along one wall and sat down next to Jess.

"So," he began brightly. "You're transferring from Brandewine to a school in the city?"

"NYU," Jess confirmed. "I was studying visual media, graphics, and stuff like that. But I'm actually more into photography, and NYU has a great program with some really awesome professors."

Grant tilted his head, those light blue eyes uncomfortably piercing. "And that's why you're transferring? To take advantage of the NYU program?"

Danger. Jess fought to keep his expression from broadcasting his sudden, intense desire to be elsewhere.

"That's right," he answered.

Grant pressed his lips together as if he knew Jess was lying. Sweat prickled at the small of Jess's back.

"You don't have to tell me anything," Grant said. "Lord knows, it's not my business. But I don't like secrets that might come back to bite me in the ass. It's my job to make sure the front of the house runs smooth as glass. And I aim to do just that, no matter what it takes."

Jess felt a flash of anger that this total stranger thought he could make Jess say it when he hadn't even told his own sister, but he swallowed it down. His stomach twisted into knots.

"Look, if you don't want me here, tell me so. I'll get out of your way."

"I didn't say that. And if you hold up your end, I won't have to."

Jess ducked his head, almost dizzy with relief. Grant gave him the shrewd eyes again. "Don't be so quick to give up on what you want. I assume you do want this job?"

"It's not only that I want it," Jess assured him. "I need it. Tuition at NYU is way expensive, and even living with Miranda instead of paying room and board . . . it's going to be tight. I don't want to be a burden on her. She says she won't let me have a job once school starts, because she wants me to focus on my future. But I'm hoping I can change her mind, because the kind of future I want to have involves me being independent and not relying on my big sister to take care of me." A hot mixture of shame and determination boiled in his gut, but Jess kept going. "I'm not telling you this to be like, 'Oh, poor Jess,' or anything. It's not a sob story. It's just—you should understand what's at stake for me. I won't let you down, I swear."

Jess met Grant's eyes dead-on, steeling himself for pity or derision or even indifference. What he saw was more like recognition. And Jess, who'd never believed in "gaydar" or any other sort of sixth sense, suddenly found himself wondering about the restaurant manager. Grant arched a brow, as if he were perfectly aware of the new direction of Jess's thoughts, and gave him another of those big, easy smiles.

"Good enough."

Jess blinked, train of thought effectively derailed. "That's it? That's the whole interview?"

Grant shrugged. "To tell the truth, I think interviews are a waste of time when it comes to most restaurant positions. You could answer all my questions and smile like a pro, get through the whole conversation slicker than deer guts on a doorknob, but I won't have a clue if you can really do the job until I see you do the job. Handle the pressure, keep your cool, don't sass the customers when they get demanding, and you'll do fine."

Jess bounced on the sofa cushions, relieved and happy. "I will, I promise. Hey, can I go tell Miranda?"

Grant laughed, but not in a mean way. "Sure thing. They'll be up in the kitchen, I bet. That'll be good, you can get the rest of the tour, meet the rest of the . . . oh. Hell." He studied Jess through suddenly wide eyes.

"What?" The big eyes were freaking Jess out. "Meet who?"

Grant's gaze was moving quickly over Jess's features, his apparent dismay growing by the second

"Hell's *bells,*" he said. "Just what we need."

"What *is* it?" Nerves rushed back in a torrent.

Grant blew out a breath, loud in the quiet hallway. "Nothing. Maybe. Anyway, it can't be helped. Like my mama always says, these things are sent to test us. Come on, let's go find your sister."

Jess wanted to push Grant for a less cryptic answer, but long-standing habit kept him quiet.

Don't push. You might not like what you find out.

Of course, the silence on the way back up the stairs gave Jess plenty of time to get worked up again. A couple of times, Grant started to say something but stopped himself, and Jess felt himself getting wound tighter than a drum.

As they neared the kitchen, he could hear that same throbbing bass beat from before, punctuated by the sounds of metal pots and pans clattering.

"So, kitchen, right?" he prompted Grant, who'd slowed down.

Grant shook himself like a dog coming out of the water, and said, "That's right. It's an open kitchen so the guests can peek in. Part of Adam's food philosophy is about the value of knowing where your food comes from. Listen, Jess . . ."

"Yeah?" Jess pressed his lips together. *Here it comes.*

"Maybe . . ." Grant appeared to settle something with himself and faced Jess openly. "I don't know what the kitchen crews were like in other places you worked."

He paused, obviously waiting for something, so Jess shrugged. "Pretty standard, I guess. What you'd expect from a bunch of guys under pressure in a confined space. Lots of swearing, lots of sweating."

"Right. Well, here . . . I've worked with most of these people a long time. Adam's known all of them for years, worked with all of them in different kitchens. Whenever he'd move and start running a new kitchen, he'd skim off the best cooks and bring them with him. They're like family at this point."

"So. You're saying I shouldn't worry if they treat me like an outsider?"

"No. Well, yes, you shouldn't worry about that, and if anyone tries any hazing, you let me know, especially if there's talk about a goat."

Jess's mouth dropped open, but Grant wasn't done.

"No, what I mean is that I don't think that's going to be your problem. And I just want you to know, if you feel pressured at any time or uncomfortable with how anyone treats you, if anyone's too friendly, you can come to me. It's not your job to provide the kitchen with entertainment— your only job is to wait on company and shuttle the food from kitchen to table. Okay?"

Jess didn't really get how anyone being too friendly could be a problem, but now Grant was the one looking anxious, so he said, "Sure. It's cool."

Grant lifted his eyes to the ceiling like he was praying for patience, but then he smiled at Jess and motioned him into the kitchen.

Jess didn't see what Grant was making such a big deal about. It looked pretty much like every professional kitchen Jess had ever seen, from the chain family place at the mall where he'd worked during high school, to the pretentious bistro in Brandewine that had taught him what a bad idea it was to let anyone really know him. Maybe Market was cleaner and all the tools were more state-of-the-art than Jess was used to, but that was it.

The bustle of the Market kitchen was familiar, comforting. As long as Jess kept his head down, maybe things could be good here.

Jess looked around for Miranda, a tentative curl of hope warming his chest.

Until his gaze snagged and he stopped dead in his tracks, barely noticing when Grant bumped into him with a startled curse, because the Market kitchen was *not* just like every other professional kitchen Jess had ever seen.

No other kitchen had a cook like *him*.

Tall, lanky to the point of being skinny, except his upper body was clearly too well developed for that—long, wiry muscles stood out along his forearms as he hefted a hotel pan laden with several whole silver-scaled fish on ice onto a gleaming work surface.

Black hair stuck up in tufts all over his head like he'd head-banged his way to work, and *damn,* maybe he had, because he wasn't wearing a white chef's jacket like the other cooks. Instead, he had on a skintight black T-shirt with ripped sleeves, showing off a tattoo of a lean, dark-haired figure in a collared shirt and suspenders on his upper bicep. He moved with an economical grace that wasted nothing, every action utterly intent and focused. But his face . . .

Jess gulped and felt his heart race. That face. Lean and angular, pale skin darkened with stubble along a sharp jaw, high cheekbones. His eyes were dark, too, set under a pair of wickedly curved eyebrows that gave him such a devilish look, Jess half expected him to be wielding a pitchfork instead of a cleaver.

The guy standing next to him—shit, it was Adam Temple, Jess hadn't even noticed him—said something Jess couldn't hear, but the tall cook threw his head back and shouted a laugh to the ceiling. Jess caught his breath at the sound. Totally free and uninhibited.

"Oh, mercy."

Grant's mutter broke Jess out of his trance, and he felt heat sear his cheeks and neck. He dropped his eyes to the floor while everything in him ached for another look at the tall chef.

But Grant was watching him, Jess could feel it, and he willed the blush to fade so he wouldn't make a complete dickhead of himself on his first day at work.

Ignore it. If you don't react, it's not happening.

Jess made himself meet Grant's eyes. Grant was staring at him. Jess could practically see him putting two and two together and coming up with the easy answer. Jess felt his pulse go into warp drive.

"Oh, look, there's my sister," he chirped. "Hey, Miranda!"

She was leaning over a stainless steel countertop writing furiously on her notepad, but she looked up when Jess called her name.

Her smile was a little strained, but still a welcome sight as Jess made his way toward her. He studiously avoided looking to the left or right, and breathed out a soundless sigh of relief when he made it to Miranda's side without any mishaps. With his luck, he was amazed he hadn't tripped over his own feet and busted his ass on the floor.

Jess gave his sister the biggest, perkiest smile he had in him and hastily shored up his mental defenses. He couldn't afford to mess up this job the way he'd screwed things up in Brandewine.

Even if temptation incarnate was standing just behind him.

The moment the kitchen door swung open, letting in Grant and Miranda's kid brother, Adam knew he should've fought harder against even letting the kid have an interview.

A soft, low whistle in his ear pierced even the Sex Pistols' raucous beat. Frankie zeroed in on the new kid, who was a younger, masculine version of his pretty redheaded sister, like a starving man at a feast.

"Well, if that isn't a bit of all right."

Frankie actively encouraged his rep as resident Bad

Influence. In the last two restaurants he and Adam had worked together, Frankie had regarded the wait staff of both sexes as his own personal dating pool. Anything as fresh-faced and innocent as Jess Wake was exactly the type he liked to corrupt.

As if Adam didn't have enough problems already.

"Off-limits, dude. I'm serious." Adam attempted to inject a note of steel, but Frankie just turned to him, all incredulous. As if an impure thought never crossed his mind.

"The bit will be perfectly safe with me, mate. Count on it." He grinned, showing his trademark flash of tongue, and Adam scowled so hard his eyes nearly crossed.

"He can't be more than twenty. And his sister's right there," he whispered, trying not to indicate her in a really obvious way.

Miranda leaned over her notebook, oblivious. Adam glanced back at the unfolding drama and barely suppressed a groan at the thunderstruck expression on the kid's face as he gazed at Frankie.

It was like he'd never seen a punk-rock chef before.

"Ah, to relive my misspent youth," Frankie breathed, laughter running through his tone.

Adam shook his head. "Far as I can tell, you never left it."

Frankie snorted, and Grant wrinkled his nose at him as he walked up. Jess bounded over to his sister and started talking a mile a minute.

"I've hired Jess on a trial basis," Grant announced.

Adam could actually feel himself going gray, one hair at a time. "For real? I don't think that's such a smoking hot idea."

"Why not?" Grant had the balls to affect a look of innocent surprise, when Adam was sure the restaurant manager knew damn good and well what had just happened.

"Yeah, Adam, why not?" Frankie added in a wheedling tone.

"The kid's got potential," Grant pointed out.

"Fucking hell, does he ever," Frankie breathed.

Grant shot him a quelling glance. "Bottom line: he has experience, but he's young enough I can train him to do it the way I want it done. And we need him."

"Christ, mate, it's like you're reading my bloody thoughts." Frankie snickered.

Grant raised a quick hand to smack him on the side of the head, but Frankie ducked away, cackling.

Adam threw up his arms. How often did Grant and Frankie agree on anything? He was obviously outvoted.

"Fine!" he said. "Hire whoever you want. It's on your head." Adam's gaze slid to the pair of interlopers in his kitchen, chatting away without a care in world, and he brooded quietly for a moment. He was really in the shit. A plague of Wakes descending on Market, Frankie in deep shit, and in about two seconds, Grant was going to start nagging Adam for the finalized menu.

Grant turned to him as if on cue, determination firming his chin, and Adam felt a grin start to tug inescapably at his mouth. Energy zinged under his skin like electric pulses and he soaked up the pandemonium of his kitchen like a damp dishtowel. It was all good.

If he'd wanted a boring life with fewer risks, he would've been a lion tamer.

EIGHT

Miranda hung up the phone with a shaking hand and stared sightlessly at her desk. Manic excitement coursed through her so strongly, she had to share it with someone. She picked the phone back up and was already dialing the apartment before she remembered that Jess was at Market, being trained by Grant on server procedures or something.

Crap. She drummed her fingers on her desk, and a memo from her editor caught her eye. Brightening immediately, Miranda pushed back her chair and nearly danced down the hall to Claire's office, pushing inside without even knocking.

Claire raised her eyebrows at Miranda's exuberant entrance, but her only verbal response was a mild, "Can I help you?"

"Oh, Claire, don't go all stiff and proper French right now!" Miranda hugged herself. "I've got huge news."

"Which you are clearly bursting to tell me, so why don't you have a seat?" Claire said with an amused look.

Miranda shook her head. "Can't sit, I'm too edgy. Claire, I got the call!"

"What call?"

"The call," Miranda repeated with emphasis. "From the publisher. About my book!"

"Ah, that call. From your expression, I take it this call was more satisfying than your previous interactions with Empire Publishing?"

"Yes." Miranda paused, savoring the moment. "They want to publish my book."

"Darling, that's wonderful," Claire said, genuine delight suffusing her voice. "I'm so proud of you. What made them change their minds?"

"The month I'm spending at Market! All the buzz about that, and the in-depth research I'll be able to do. I made some notes based on my first day there, and the editor just ate them up. She loved the characters."

Claire furrowed her brows. "The characters? I thought it was a serious work of nonfiction."

"Well," Miranda hedged, "the book they want isn't exactly what I was intending to write when I first submitted the proposal to them. But it'll still be nonfiction; I meant 'characters' in the sense of how over-the-top and wacky some of those cooks are."

"What do you mean, the book isn't what you intended?"

In typical editorial fashion, Claire immediately zeroed in on the weakest part of Miranda's story. Miranda tried not to be annoyed at having her happy moment picked apart, thread by thread.

"I've just had to adapt my original idea, that's all. No big deal." It came out a little sharper than she meant it to. Claire tilted her head down and gazed at Miranda over the tops of the wire-rim glasses she wore for reading.

"This new idea," she pressed, "what makes it different?"

Miranda camouflaged the urge to squirm by taking the seat Claire had offered earlier. "It's . . . a bit less serious," she admitted. "Less of an examination of restaurant culture, more of an exposé. Kind of a gossipy tell-all book, about what it's really like behind the scenes at a major restaurant."

"I see," Claire said. It was uninflected and her expression didn't change, but somehow Miranda felt a wave of disapproval wash over her. She slumped a little in her chair.

She felt a pang when she thought of the proposal she'd sweated over for so long, the one that would've studied the way people related to food and chefs, the one she would've written so brilliantly that she would've become an internationally renowned expert on gastronomy.

That was a fantasy. It was time to grow up and face the real world.

"I know," she said, raising her hands. "But this is what they're willing to pay me for! I need the money for Jess's tuition, and I need it fast—I won't let him work his way through college the way I did. He shouldn't have to do that."

"Miranda," Claire started, then stopped as if she weren't certain of what she wanted to say. When she continued, it was in the gentlest voice Miranda had ever heard from her brisk, no-nonsense friend. "*You* shouldn't have to do something you won't be proud of. Jess wouldn't expect it of you, I'm certain, and neither would your parents."

The kindness in Claire's usually stern face nearly broke Miranda. She swallowed hard around the painful lump in her throat.

"Don't worry. Adam Temple is such an arrogant bastard, I'm actually looking forward to writing it. He's not going to know what hit him." She tried to smile, and found that after the first few seconds, it didn't even feel strained.

"If you'll excuse me," she said before Claire could respond. "I know I'm supposed to be clearing my desk in preparation for being out of the office for a whole month, but right now I'm taking my lunch break."

"Where are you going to eat? Perhaps I'll come with you."

"Someplace I've never gone, even though I've lived in the city for a year. The Union Square farmers' market."

"Ah. More in-depth research?"

Miranda stood up. "This may not be the book I've always dreamed of writing, but I intend to make it the best damned gossipy tell-all exposé it can be." She turned on her heel, ignoring Claire's indelicate snort as she left.

While it was an accepted fact that no one in the history of ever had moved to New York City for the weather—winter was long, cold, and full of snow that turned to icy sludge as soon as it hit the sidewalk, and summer was long, sweltering, and tended to make the whole city smell like ripe garbage—there were two or three months that made up for everything.

May was one of them. Adam could never understand why tourists clogged the streets from July to August, or why they flocked to Manhattan at Christmas, when the glories of late May in New York outshone any holiday or vacation he'd ever experienced.

It had rained the night before and the city looked washed clean, sparkling late-spring sunlight glinting off damp concrete. The market was packed, for a Wednesday, although Adam supposed part of it was that he wasn't used to seeing the place at noon. Lunchtime was a nutty time of day to hit the Union Square market—full of office drones on break, hunting up stuff for dinner, and hip, young mothers using their baby carriages like battering rams to block other shoppers from the last of the white asparagus.

Adam wouldn't normally venture downtown at noon; the travel time on the subway could hit half an hour, easy, and he needed to be up at the restaurant. He liked to get to Union Square at the ass-crack of dawn and open up the Greenmarket, help his buddies from Siren Falls Farm set up their stall. He'd made friends with all his favorite purveyors, so now they let him have first pick of all the produce and even occasionally slipped him tips about specialty items coming into the market.

Like today. Paul Corlie, one of the Siren Falls boys, had pulled Adam aside and whispered that he'd heard a rumor that one of their friends, a well-known shroomer, had gone on a very successful expedition for morels. Morels, those big, succulent members of the mushroom family, were not easy to come by. They stubbornly resisted all efforts at cultivation and continued to grow only in the wild. Shroomers guarded the secrets of their hunts jealously; it was impossible to predict when one would show up at the market, mushrooms in hand. This shroomer was only going to be in town for a few hours, and Adam couldn't wait to work up a special using the tender, earthy delicacy. He'd promised Paul he'd meet the guy back at Union Square at noon.

So here he was. He'd been dreaming of dishes to highlight morels the whole trip down on the C train, so lost in thoughts of what he could do to twist up the traditional pairing with asparagus that he almost missed the transfer at Fourteenth Street.

Glancing around to orient himself—it was wild how different the market was all packed with people like anchovies in a tin—Adam waved at Dava Whitehurst, one of his supplier buddies. She waved back distractedly, her salt-and-pepper dreadlocks bound up in an intricate bundle on her head. She barely took her eyes off the scale where she was weighing out the lump of creamy white goat cheese one of her many customers had ordered.

Adam bulled his way through the crowd, trying to move quickly without knocking anyone down. He breathed a sigh of relief when he got to the Siren Falls stall and ducked around behind the table to escape the crush.

"It's a madhouse out there," he whooped, clapping Paul

on the back. Broad and stocky, Paul spent a lot of his time in the sun doing backbreaking manual labor, and it showed. He was about Adam's age, but he looked nearly ten years older, as if he were pushing forty instead of thirty.

"Yeah, man." His friend grinned, teeth flashing white in his lined, weathered face. He gestured at the nearly empty table before him. The last time Adam saw it, the table had been groaning under the weight of slim, elegant asparagus spears, sweet baby peas, and the first small wild strawberries. "That's what we like to see. We're going home empty-handed tonight."

"That rocks, Paulie," Adam told him. "You're the man."

"Yes, I am," Paul agreed, smug as all hell. "You're gonna think so even more in a minute."

"Why's that? The morel guy here already? Tell me he got at least five pounds." Adam's head whipped around, searching the crowd for a man with a dirty sack of mushrooms over his shoulder. Surely he'd be pretty conspicuous.

"Down, boy." Paul laughed. "He ain't here yet. Naw, it's just that I got your back."

"What do you mean?"

Paul clucked his tongue, clearly enjoying dragging out the suspense. "And man, are you ever gonna owe me. You'll never look at another guy's tomatoes again once I tell you this."

"Damn it, Paul, when are you going to let me live that down? It was one time! One time," Adam groused. "And they weren't even worth it. Pretty to look at, but the texture was for shit."

"And let that be a lesson to you," Paul said. "Just because it looks hot on the outside don't mean it's got any flavor or goodness to it at all. Which brings me back to the point."

"Finally," Adam put in.

Ignoring the interruption, Paul held up a finger. "A certain little redheaded tomato came poking around the stall asking questions, not ten minutes ago. Questions about you, what you like to buy, who you shop with, how much you spend."

Adam bristled. He knew at once who the redhead was and his blood started a slow simmer. "You don't say."

"People pointed her over here, and she wanted to know all about how we grow our vegetables, like were we really organic and whatnot. I gave her the farm spiel. She seemed kinda disappointed to hear that we're all about sustainable agriculture, no pesticides or anything. It was like she wanted to catch us spraying poison all over everywhere."

"I'll just bet she did," Adam grumbled. "Mother of God, she's got to be the biggest pain in the ass I've ever encountered."

"The point is," Paul said, with emphasis, "I didn't know who she was, so I didn't tell her anything about you. I mean, for all I knew she was from a rival restaurant, looking to steal your ideas. So I ask her what she's doing playing twenty questions, and she's like, 'It's for research.'"

"Of course." Adam was really starting to loathe that word.

"But it gets better," Paul promised. "'Research for what?' I ask, and she says, 'For a book.'"

Adam rocked back on his heels as if he'd just taken a heavy cutting board to the jaw. "What. The. Fuck."

"Yeah, man." Paul nodded. "A freaking book. So I told her she'd better move on, because I wasn't talking and she was blocking the line. That was the last I saw of her."

Adam felt his slow simmer heating up to a rolling boil. This kept getting worse and worse! First the kitchen invasion, then the brother, and now this? A magazine article would've been bad enough, but magazines were, by their very nature, ephemeral. Whatever she wrote would cause a stink for the month the rag was on the newsstands, but after that, it would all die down and he could forget Miranda Wake ever existed.

A book, though. That was permanent. A book would haunt him for the rest of his career.

"Did she leave Union Square?" he asked, his voice shockingly calm and low.

"Don't know. I kinda doubt it. She had that look, you know? Like she wasn't gonna be put off."

"Yeah, she's a determined little thing." Adam grimaced. "In fact, I'd lay dollars to doughnuts she's canvassing the stalls right this minute, looking for someone who'll tell her I bought a nonorganic zucchini, or a Vidalia onion from Chile. I've got to find her."

"If you leave now, you're gonna miss the morel guy," Paul warned. Adam shook his head, ignoring the sharp twist of regret.

"Can't help it. Thanks for looking out for me, man."

"You betcha," Paul said, and waggled his bushy eyebrows expressively. "Just don't forget what I said about the tomatoes."

The sick anger churning in his gut wouldn't let him laugh, and Adam just shook his head again as he left the stall and reentered the fray.

Wishing he had some of Frankie's ridiculous height to help him peer over the heads of the shoppers, Adam decided the best way to find Miranda would be to follow his usual path around the market. She was smart enough to have figured out his favorite suppliers, and with any luck, he'd catch up to her.

After checking the stand where he got all his jam and jelly products, and the stall with the weird tropical fruits that they grew in a hothouse in the Catskills, he finally fetched up back at Dava Whitehurst's dairy stand near the front entrance to the market.

And there she was. Miranda Wake, all buttoned up in one of her crisp suits, leaning on the table and chatting away with hippie Dava like they were old friends. Spotting Adam over Miranda's shoulder, Dava waved a languid hand, her many bangle bracelets clinking merrily.

"Twice in one day," she called, her throaty voice carrying over the noise of the square. "It must be a sign. You'd better let me do your chart tonight, see what I come up with."

Adam forced a smile. "Thanks, Dava, but you don't need to. I'm pretty sure I know what the stars are trying to tell me."

He caught Miranda's wide eyes, and she straightened away from the table guiltily.

"Can I talk to you for a second?" he requested, nearly choking on the civility.

It worked, though, because Miranda nodded warily and followed him when he moved toward an empty, secluded area to the left of the entrance to the square.

Adam didn't exactly have a plan for how he wanted this encounter to go, and the moment they had even a semblance of privacy, the rolling boil graduated to a full-on explosion, sending the top of his head into the stratosphere.

"What the hell do you think you're playing at?" he demanded. "Every time I turn around, there you are, fucking with me."

Miranda flinched at his tone, but her eyes were steady on his. "I've told you before. I'm doing my job. It's nothing personal, it's work."

Adam sneered. "Yeah, and that's what you don't seem to get. My work is fucking personal. It's who I am, everything I am, and if you mess with it, you mess with me."

Visibly startled, Miranda let out a slow breath and tried again. "Nothing has changed since the last time we talked.

I told you already that I'd be doing as much in-depth research as I could. And since you've staked your restaurant's reputation on the quality and provenance of its ingredients, your suppliers are obviously a key research point."

"Oh, sure, you've been up front about everything," Adam mocked. "What a shining example of honesty and professionalism you are. I suppose it must've slipped your mind that all this so-called research isn't for some little magazine article." He leaned in, got right in her face, and saw the dawning realization in her blue eyes. "That's right," he said in a near-whisper. "I know. You're writing a fucking book."

She swallowed, closing her eyes for a second. "How did you— Right. The man at the vegetable stand. Okay." Miranda opened her eyes and held Adam's angry glare.

"Yes. I'm writing a book," she admitted. "It's a relatively new development, but I should have told you. But the fact is—" She clammed up, and Adam made an impatient sound.

"The fact is," she said, more strongly, "I don't need your permission to write the book. I already have authorization to be in your kitchen, and as for the rest of my research, it's a free country. I can ask anyone, anywhere, any questions I want. You have very little say in this, so I suggest you get over yourself."

Frustration and rage churned in Adam's gut, eating away at his composure.

"I might have to let you into my kitchen, but there are rules," he snarled. "No pads and pencils, no minirecorders— you're there to cook. Whatever writing or exposure or other shit you want to get out of this, that's on your time. Kitchen time is my time. The minute you start slacking off or compromising the quality of my food, you're out."

"Agreed," she said, and put out her hand.

Adam looked down at her delicate fingers, the thin

wrists that made him want to feed her, put some meat on her bones. He shook her hand once, firmly, then let go, unwilling to examine why the simple touch burned across his palm.

As she turned to leave, Adam caught a glimpse of her smirk in profile. She looked a little self-satisfied, as if she thought she'd played him well, and Adam couldn't resist stepping up behind her. She froze, and he bent his head close enough to smell her hair, which was loose and curling softly around her shoulders. He breathed in the scent of her shampoo, something herbal and clean—rosemary and mint? With one hand, he carefully gathered all that heavy auburn silk and smoothed it over one shoulder, leaning down to whisper into the exposed pink shell of her ear.

"I'll be watching you."

Adam let her go, but not before feeling the tremor that shook her slender frame. Walking back into the market, he grinned. He was pretty sure if he looked behind him, any trace of a smirk would be gone from that pretty face.

NINE

Opening night at Market.

If Miranda were prone to dramatic pronouncements, she might've called this the first night of the rest of her life. It felt epic, this step she was taking away from the small, confined world of magazine writing toward the large, open spaces of book publishing.

According to Jess, who'd spent some of the past week taking reservations, Market was booked solid for the first three weeks after its official grand opening. Obviously the same buzz that had gotten Miranda her book deal was also working in Adam's favor. Squeezing shampoo onto her palm, Miranda worked it into a lather. Would the evidence of Market's reservation book be enough to make Adam happy to see her today?

Somehow, she thought not.

She couldn't believe he'd found out about the book deal so quickly. Obviously, it would've come out sooner or later, but there had to have been a better way for him to get wind of it. Who could've predicted that those suppliers would all count themselves among Adam's friends? And while she was on the subject, was there anyone in the entire city who didn't like Adam Temple? The task of digging up dirt on him was looking more daunting by the day, as every person she spoke to either refused to answer her questions, or had nothing but glowing things to say about the man.

Miranda made a face. She'd be willing to bet that none of Adam's many friends had been raked over the coals by him, repeatedly, the way she had. That scene at Union Square! Adam was forcing Miranda to redefine "undignified." She couldn't help wishing she'd had the chance to tell him about the book deal herself. Maybe she could've spun it so it didn't sound so much like she was taking advantage of him. Maybe that confrontation would've ended differently.

Miranda finished soaping her hair and ducked under the shower to rinse. The thick strands were heavy with water, slip-sliding down her back. She shivered despite the warmth of the water, remembering Adam's hard hand gently pushing her hair aside, the heat of his strong body along her back, the murmur of his breath against the side of her face.

Stop it, she ordered herself. *It's not like he was whispering sweet nothings in your ear—pretty far from it, in fact.*

She'd do her hair in a French braid tonight, she decided. To keep it out of the way and ensure she wouldn't be reminded of that strange almost-embrace by the tickling of hair on her shoulders. She wasn't sure exactly what she'd be doing in the kitchen, and she couldn't afford any sort of distraction.

"Come on!"

Jess rapped on the bathroom door, his excited voice muffled but distinct.

Miranda smiled to herself. Even if they hadn't managed to sit down and have that serious talk she knew they'd eventually need to have, it was still lovely to be living with Jess again. Even the daily ritual of fighting over who took longer in the shower hadn't lost its glow.

She turned off the tap and stepped out of the shower cubicle, whisking one towel around her hair, another around her body.

When she opened the bathroom door, Jess was momentarily enveloped in a cloud of steam and he coughed exaggeratedly as he pushed past her.

"You're not the only one who wants to get clean, you know," he said, stripping off the ratty T-shirt he wore to sleep in.

"I know. What happened to you at Brandewine, Jess? You never used to spend so much time every day beautifying. Is there a cute girl you want to impress at Market?" she teased, hopeful.

She happened to catch Jess's slight, momentary wince in the bathroom mirror, and it made Miranda pause and replay what she'd just said, searching for hidden meanings. Oh, dear, maybe he was still smarting from whatever happened with that Tara girl, despite what he'd told Miranda.

"I'm sorry, kiddo," she said sympathetically. "I didn't mean—"

"Nothing to be sorry for. Hey, what do you think of Grant?"

Miranda squinted at the abrupt change of subject. "I don't know. He seems very competent. And he's been good to you, hasn't he?"

"He has. I like him. I mean, he's a good guy. You know, I think he might be gay."

"Oh?" Miranda felt a bit at sea in this conversation. "What makes you think so?"

Jess shrugged, bending over to fiddle with the drain in the tub. "I've heard stuff."

Starting to feel the pressure of time ticking away, Miranda tucked her towel more tightly under her arms and said, "Does that bother you?"

"No. You?"

"Of course not," Miranda said, surprised. "It certainly doesn't change the way I felt about him before. As long as he treats you with respect and consideration, I don't care what he does with his private life."

Jess was making such a business out of turning on the shower and getting the water to the perfect temperature that his face was flushed when he straightened and glanced over at her. "You'd better hurry and get dressed. Adam wants staff there by three. Big day, can't be late."

Miranda studied him for a moment, feeling that she was missing something. But when Jess hooked his fingers in the waistband of his boxers and looked at her expectantly, Miranda held up her hands and scurried out of the bathroom.

Jess was right. She couldn't afford to be late, today of all days.

Whatever sense of calm Miranda had managed to cobble together disappeared the moment she stepped into Market's earth-toned interior. The place was packed with people, all in a frenetic race to get ready for the big night. An army of young men and women, dressed like Jess in matching forest-green organic cotton button-downs and black pants, swarmed around the coat-check station, bar, and two dining rooms in a coordinated frenzy.

Jess peeled off when he spotted Grant Holloway holding a clipboard and directing his troops like a slender, blond Napoleon.

Feeling a tad abandoned and trying not to show it, Miranda made for the swinging door at the back of the main dining room.

Three in the afternoon, Market wouldn't be open for another two hours, and the kitchen was bustling as though every table in the restaurant were occupied by an impatiently waiting customer.

At first glance, it looked like sheer pandemonium. White-jacketed cooks stood in long rows up and down the bright steel countertops, chopping and pounding and stirring and measuring. The narrow walkways behind the counters were crammed with people, too, spinning and whirling past each other in a parody of a dance. Every second, it looked as if someone were going to run into someone else, but no one ever did.

At the center of the whirlwind was Adam. His dark hair stuck out in spikes, as if he'd been running his fingers through it, and his powerful torso strained at the seams of his pristine white jacket as he hefted a large tray of what looked like chicken carcasses onto the counter beside the range.

A skinny younger man with sharp, bladelike features and a prematurely receding hairline stood by, watching every move Adam made with intense concentration.

As Adam picked through the bones and held one up to the light, his gaze landed on Miranda.

Here we go, she thought, mentally hitching up her pants.

Raised eyebrows were her only greeting as Miranda threaded between a prep cook dicing cucumbers and the round-faced pastry chef, Violet Porter, castigating a trembling assistant for letting the bread dough overproof. Adam looked Miranda up and down, taking in everything from her tightly controlled hair to her unadorned brown leather flats.

"Going to need a jacket," was the first thing out of his mouth. He looked down at her feet and smirked. The glance he shot her from beneath his lashes brimmed with cheerful malice. "By the end of the night, you're really going to wish you'd worn sneakers."

Miranda stiffened. "I'm sure I'll be fine. In any case, no one informed me of a dress code."

"Oh, there's not really a code," Adam said. "Just common

sense. But . . ." He held up a hand to stall her sputtering. "You couldn't know. After tonight, you will. Eh, Robbie?"

The thin-faced man hovering at Adam's side shot back, "Yes, Chef!" Miranda almost expected him to salute.

Cocking a head in his direction, Adam's eyes never left Miranda's. "This is Robin Meeks, our extern."

Miranda went through the polite rituals, holding out her hand with a question. "Extern? How does that work?"

The boy, for he couldn't have been much older than Jess, stood at rigid attention, mouth clamped shut like a private awaiting his drill sergeant's orders. Miranda caught the wry twist to Adam's mouth before he said gravely, "Oh, Rob, here, is a degree candidate at the Academy of Culinary Arts, isn't that right?"

"Yes, Chef!"

The shouted reply was less startling this time, but Miranda had to stifle a laugh at the mischief in Adam's eyes. If she didn't know better, she'd swear he was laughing at Meeks's overzealous adherence to Academy rules— and letting Miranda in on the joke. Maybe he was glad to see her, after all.

She gave Adam a tiny smile, testing the waters, and he let one corner of his mouth kick up, exposing that dimple in his cheek. "Rob," he said. "Run down to the office and grab one of the extra white jackets hanging on the back of the door. Quick like a bunny, Rob."

"Yes, Chef!" The boy appeared embarrassingly happy to be given the task; Miranda wouldn't have been surprised if he'd licked Adam's hand like a puppy as he passed by on his way downstairs.

"So here you are," Adam said.

"Couldn't stay away," she returned, and caught herself up short. That sounded a little too flirtatious, under the circumstances.

The circumstances being that Adam hated her guts, and

was probably cursing her presence in his kitchen at this very moment.

Only, he didn't look too murderous right now. More contemplative than anything else.

"I meant what I said," he told her, his face serious. "You're in my kitchen, you're cooking. There's no room in here for anybody to be standing around with their thumb up their ass. You're going to be on stocks and family meal with Rob. Rob'll show you the ropes; just listen to him and don't mess anything up or get in anyone's way, and we'll be okay. I'm going to be working the pass; I won't have time to bail you out. Ditto everyone else. If you fuck up, you're out of here, I don't care what anyone says."

"I understand."

And she did. This was her chance to prove herself. She wouldn't put it past him to defy his financial backer and cancel the whole deal if Miranda gave him the slightest excuse. He was obviously no more resigned to her presence in his kitchen than he had been three days ago at the Union Square Greenmarket.

Failure was simply unacceptable. She wouldn't have it.

Adam must have read something of her determination in her stance or her face, because he gave her a sharp nod and strode back to the front of the kitchen where he'd spend the rest of the night expediting. Miranda had done her research; she knew what the head chef's job was.

During actual service, the executive chef of a restaurant as large and ambitious as this one didn't do much cooking. Instead, he was like the conductor of an orchestra—he called out the orders, kept the cooks at different stations moving and working toward the goal of having plates ready for each customer at a table simultaneously. He would inspect every piece of food before it went out, tasting for seasoning where possible, because it was his name and reputation on the line if something wasn't prepared properly.

At least, that was the role a good head chef took in the kitchen. Miranda eagerly anticipated the opportunity to observe Adam Temple in action, in his element.

And speaking of eager anticipation . . . Rob Meeks, her guide for the evening, came panting up, red-faced and clutching a white jacket.

As soon as he saw that Adam was at the pass, his manner changed. "Fuck," he grumbled. "Guess I shouldn't have bothered to sprint on the stairs. I almost broke my neck. Here."

He thrust the jacket at her. Miranda fumbled her way into it. She had to turn the sleeves back several times, and it engulfed her completely, but she still felt slightly less like a fish out of water with it on. It was like donning a costume for a play; she put it on and instantly felt more like a cook.

Interesting.

Wishing she could take notes, but not wanting to flout Adam's "kitchen time is my time" edict quite this early in the game, Miranda turned to her companion with a smile.

"How long have you been working with Adam? I know most of the cooks here have been with him in one capacity or another for years."

Rob's mouth turned down in a sullen grimace as he bent to grab an enormous stockpot from the shelf below the counter. "Are you messing with me? I'm an extern. My stint here is a year, total. And the place isn't even open yet. When do you think I met Chef Temple?"

Great start, Miranda. "I'm sorry, I didn't intend to insult you. I thought you might've known Adam before you went to the Academy."

He scowled as he started heaping the bones from the tray Adam had carried over earlier into the pot. "I wish. If I had any pull at all in this kitchen, I wouldn't be stuck making stock every night, or putting together the family meal." He shot her a disgusted look, and Miranda easily read the unspoken portion of his gripe: *and I wouldn't have to waste my time babysitting you.*

She gritted her teeth. "I'm happy to help, if you just tell me what to do."

Rob directed Miranda in a bored, irritated tone of superiority that set her nerves on edge. Together, they diced and caramelized carrots, onions, and celery for the mirepoix, the flavor base of the stock. Miranda watched everything Rob did, hoping to be able to replicate it on her own if she were ever called upon to do so.

His movements were quick and efficient as he added the vegetables, adjusting the heat under the pot, but somehow he lacked the precise grace she'd noticed while observing Adam and Frankie working over that pork belly a week before. It was as if Rob merely wanted to get through it all as quickly as possible so he could move on to something that interested him more.

The rest of the kitchen faded to a fast-moving blur of color and sound. There were shouts, calls and responses that were unintelligible to Miranda, as if they were spoken in another language. In fact, some were; many of the line cooks were Hispanic. The Anglo cooks seemed to have picked up enough kitchen Spanish to communicate, resulting in an indecipherable patois of blended dialects and accents.

Adding to the stranger-in-a-strange-land feeling was the fact that half the conversation was in code; metaphorically speaking, as in references to past restaurants and kitchens she didn't recognize, as well as literally. The dishes weren't called by their full names, but rather shortened versions of their menu description. Discussion of something called "lockets" was actually about the clam starter, spicy steamed Montauk clams served over crusty bread studded with bacon and garlic.

Even though she desperately wanted to be taking notes like mad, flitting from station to station to catch every detail she could, Miranda forced herself to focus on Rob and his slapdash stock tutorial.

This is important, she reminded herself. *Show Adam Temple you can hack it in his kitchen, even for one night, and you'll at least have outlasted the original terms of that ridiculous dare. And maybe you'll have won enough respect that he'll let you actually become part of the kitchen, not just a barely tolerated intruder.*

It wasn't easy, however. Miranda could only hope her sulky babysitter would be more interested in the preparation of the so-called family meal, the meal cobbled together, usually from leftovers and usually by the lowest-ranking kitchen helper, for the staff to eat before service.

Rob grudgingly explained all this while indicating the materials Adam had earmarked for them to work with. Ten pounds of chicken thighs that had been ordered for a dish that ended up being cut from the menu, and a couple boxes of baby artichokes that had been delivered by mistake. In the hubbub of opening-night preparations, Adam hadn't called his supplier to complain as he normally would have, so it was Rob and Miranda's job to figure out some way to use the artichokes to feed the servers and cooks.

"We're going to do a quick pan sauté," Rob said. "Along with the artichokes, some lemon and garlic, that'll make an okay sauce for fettuccine. Think you can manage to steam the chokes?"

"No problem," Miranda said, projecting a breezy confidence she certainly didn't feel. "Just point me toward the right equipment . . ."

Rob stared. "Pot. For water. A couple inches will do it." He pointed. "Steamer basket. The chokes go in there. The water boils, steam rises, cooks them. Shit." He stomped over to the sink to fill the pot, ignoring Miranda's outstretched hand. "Do you even know how to trim the artichokes?"

Miranda froze, and a cook behind her cursed loudly and had to dance sideways to avoid bashing her with the tray he was carrying. Miranda ducked her head, avoiding Adam's sudden laser glare, and pinched the bridge of her nose between her thumb and forefinger.

It was going to be a long night.

TEN

Adam was stoked, hyped up to a level usually reserved for just before orgasm after a long, drawn-out, sweaty bout of sex. Only this feeling had been sustained for more than four hours straight.

Market was a full-on, high-def blast.

The customers surged in, more than they had reservations for, until they were standing three deep at the bar, waiting and hoping for a table to open up. Grant had popped his head in to inform him, ecstatically, that Samara, their new bartender, was handling the pressure well. Grant liked to hire people he didn't know, so he could crow about it later when they turned out to be awesome. And maybe he knew something Adam didn't, because Grant's hires almost always panned out.

Even that kid, Jess. Adam had to admit that Jess Wake had more than pulled his weight over the past week. His demeanor when he came to the pass to pick up his tables' orders was intent, but calm. Focused speed. A quick peek into the dining room, though, revealed him laughing and charming the customers with that wide, bright smile, and Adam liked that.

Keep the punters happy and you can't go wrong, as

Frankie was fond of saying. Adam shot the sous-chef a glance, amused as always to see him manning the grill like a gunner on a battleship. Frankie's wild-man act was toned down a bit, in deference to the steady flow of work, but nothing could shake him out of his intensity when he had meat on the grill. And he undoubtedly set the standard for the rest of the kitchen.

The crew looked to Adam for orders; they looked to Frankie for cues. Tonight, they seemed to have gotten the message, big-time. No playing around, this is not a drill, make or break.

Cook like your heartbeat is connected to the movement of your hands, like it's life-or-death every second.

The orders flew in, so fast Adam could barely shout them out quickly enough, and the food, when it came up to the hot plate, was superlative. The pile of tasting spoons next to the sink was a testament to his crew's dedication to seasoning. Warm pride swelled in Adam's chest.

Even his little scribbler hadn't performed too badly. Aside from a near-collision early on, Miranda had kept out from underfoot, and hadn't seemed to slow Rob Meeks down. Family meal had been adequate, if uninspired. Adam planned to do something about that as they went forward. Restaurants that served shit at the family meal usually ended up serving shit to customers, too, as kitchen morale took a nosedive and cooks stopped caring.

It was nearly ten o'clock and they were down to the last few tickets. The rush was over, and the kitchen was slowing, the fever pitch tapering to a low hum of activity.

That's when it happened.

He'd called a fourtop order, three asparagus salads and one soup. The apps came up, all at the same time. The salads looked good: fresh, unbruised lettuce with just the right amount of dressing, raw asparagus stalks sliced on a precise bias. He reached automatically for a spoon to taste the soup.

It was a cold soup in deference to the warming weather, a variation on the classic vichyssoise. It used parsnips and shallots for the purée, instead of the more familiar potato and leek, but the base of the soup was still chicken stock.

Adam inhaled as the spoon reached his face, and frowned. Something was off. He opened his mouth and breathed in again as he tilted the soup onto his tongue, tasting the scent as well as the cool liquid. It was close to what it should've been . . . but not quite. Seasoning was fine, the vegetables tasted normal. It was something about the stock.

He rolled the soup in his mouth, and identified the problem as it coated his tongue and the roof of his mouth unpleasantly. The stock hadn't been skimmed enough, there was too much fat, rendering the finished soup's mouthfeel thick and disgusting.

"Milo!" he bellowed. "Get up here, now."

The garde-manger station was in charge of cold appetizers, including the soup, and if Milo couldn't identify what was wrong with this vichy, they were going to have a serious problem. Connected or not, Adam would kick Milo's scrawny ass back to Trenton.

Milo was at his side in an instant, looking a little pale under his olive complexion. It was never a good thing to be called up to the pass.

"Taste," Adam said, shoving the spoon toward him.

Milo closed his eyes and took the spoon into his mouth, drawing his brows together in concentration. "The seasoning is . . . I think it's fine, Chef," he said helplessly, and Adam could feel a rumbling roar building in his chest.

But then Milo frowned again, smacking his lips together, and said, "Wait. Is that . . . the stock is too . . . something. Oily?"

"Is that an answer, or a question?" Adam responded, hearing the silky warning tones in his own voice.

"Answer. Chef." Milo was uncharacteristically subdued. "I apologize, Chef, I only tasted for the seasoning and I missed the texture. It won't happen again."

Adam relaxed out of full battle mode and said, "Damn right it won't. You're fucking lucky the other apps are all salads and won't be ruined by the delay. Now get back to your station and open up a new container of stock. This is the goddamn reason we make it fresh every day. Use the fresh stuff."

Milo nodded and turned to go, but paused. "That was the fresh stuff. Sorry, I . . . I was using the leftovers earlier, to get them out of the walk-in. That's what we did at my last . . . Okay, not here!" He interrupted himself, holding up his hands in surrender when Adam took a menacing step toward him. "I just mean, that last bowl? It's the stuff that was made today, because we finally went through yesterday's stock."

Adam ground his back teeth. "Find some good stock. Now. Scrape yesterday's containers if you have to. *Go.*"

Milo hopped to it, leaving Adam seething and staring around the kitchen for a good outlet for this sudden frustration.

The rest of the kitchen was quiet for the first time all night, and it was like the calm at the eye of a hurricane. Everyone was turned away, trying to keep out of the line of fire.

Everyone except Miranda Wake.

She was staring straight at him with an expression of open curiosity, as if he were a clock that had stopped and she wanted to take him apart to figure out why.

That look on her angelic face, plus the knowledge that she'd been the one standing by the stockpot with a spoon in her little hand, built up the hot steam in his head until he was sure it would come whistling out his ears like a teakettle on the boil. His vision narrowed to her face, everything in the periphery like visual static, indistinct and unreal.

"You," he said, rage constricting his throat so it came out all raspy and hoarse.

That startled her out of her contemplation of his inner workings, he could tell. Those big blue eyes got even bigger, and round like a doll's. Her pink mouth dropped open, then closed with a snap as he advanced on her slowly, stalking her backward until she was pressed up against the walk-in door, well out of sight of the dining room.

He loomed over her, using his superior height and breadth without remorse.

"Are you deliberately trying to sabotage me?" he snarled. "You think this'll make for a fun chapter in your book?" He panted for a second, before adding in a strangled tone, "And all this, after you made me miss the fucking morels!"

"What?" she gasped. "Have you lost your mind?"

"The stock," he pressed, getting himself under control. "It was fine yesterday, when Rob made it alone. But today, with you here, suddenly it's fucked. Explain that to me."

"I can't," she shot back. "Rob taught me everything I know about making stock just this afternoon. So if it's not right, I'm very sorry, but I can't explain why. And I have no idea what you mean about morels." That pugnacious little chin went up, as if inviting a hit. Damn her, she didn't back down for even a second, in spite of his blatant intimidation. And damn him, too, for finding that admirable in some corner of his mind. Even at a moment like this.

"You will," he promised her. "Tomorrow. Right now, I have to go clean up your mess and put the rest of the tickets to bed. I want you gone when I'm done."

Something, maybe outrage, maybe simple anger, painted rosy flags high on her cheekbones. "I'll leave when everyone else leaves," she said, stubborn.

There was that tickle of admiration again, but Adam ignored it. It wasn't enough to keep him from smiling gently, the smile Frankie could've told you meant *Danger, Will Robinson,* before saying, "Remember our agreement. You'll leave when I say. And you'll by damn be back here first thing tomorrow morning. We'll discuss this further then."

She pressed her lips together mutinously, but didn't argue.

"My office. Nine o'clock," he said over his shoulder as he strode back up to the pass just in time to intercept Milo with a fresh bowl of soup.

If Miranda made any response, he didn't hear it, and he refused to examine the roiling mix of emotions bubbling just under his skin. If the surging anger he felt was underpinned with a twist of disappointment, Adam didn't want to know about it.

Shut it down, he thought. *Finish the night. Deal with it tomorrow.*

Damn it to hell and gone, he'd wanted tonight to be perfect. Was that really so much to fucking ask?

ELEVEN

Miranda's fingers shook as she unbuttoned the hot, oversized chef's jacket. She stripped it off quickly, wishing the vehement motion would strip away the raw humiliation and general pissed-offness.

To be talked to like that, in front of the entire kitchen. Miranda's stomach tightened ominously, reminding her that she should be grateful she hadn't eaten anything since the meal with the staff nearly six hours ago. None of the people she and Rob (who'd conveniently disappeared before Adam blew a fuse) had served that odd dinner of chicken and artichokes to earlier were looking at her now.

It was as if Adam's tirade had turned her invisible, and part of Miranda really wished it were true, because she had no idea how she was supposed to just leave the restaurant before it closed. There was a door by the walk-in that led out to the alley behind the restaurant, but one year wasn't quite enough time in the city to accustom Miranda to the idea of being in a dark Manhattan alley all alone at night.

Besides, she needed to see Jess before she left. She folded the soiled jacket between her hands and looked toward the front of the kitchen, where Adam had returned to cast his eagle eye over the few remaining plates yet to go out. As if he sensed her stare, he turned his head far enough to catch her eye and Miranda had to fight not to drop her gaze. The berserker rage might have left his face, but from the tight line of his mouth and the thunderous look of his brow, he hadn't cooled off much. Okay, so the guard dog wasn't about to let her past him and into the dining room. Fine. She'd have to hope Jess figured it out when he couldn't find her later.

The glower Adam sent her way stiffened her spine enough to get her to move. She'd rather be out back with the crazies and the rats than in here with him!

Miranda threw back her shoulders and marched to the back door. Every second of that walk, she was aware of having to concentrate not to hobble. The vicious ache in her feet and back, a constant throb of painful pressure, ticked her off even more because Adam had predicted it.

She was not going to give him the satisfaction of limping.

With a defiant push, Miranda knocked open the door and stalked out into the alleyway. It would've been a more impressive exit if she'd managed to avoid tripping over the empty vegetable crates stacked beside the door, but the resulting clatter and cursing probably scared away any resident crazies or rats, so that was good.

The noise also seemed to startle the two people who were standing together a few feet away from the door, just outside the pool of light cast by the bare bulb hanging over Miranda's head.

The dark figures stiffened and drew apart. Miranda saw the bright orange glow of a lit cigarette, and logically, she knew it was probably just an employee on a smoking break. But still, she tensed with one hand on the doorknob behind her. No amount of wounded pride was worth getting knifed in a back alley.

The two walked into the light, and Miranda relaxed when she saw Jess. But the other guy made her frown a little. It was the tall, punked-out sous-chef, Frankie. She hoped Jess wasn't getting too friendly with the cooks. From what she'd seen, chefs were moody at best, certifiably insane at worst.

"Hey, Miranda," Jess called. "What are you doing out here?"

"The restaurant's almost ready to close for the night," she hedged, shooting a glance at Frankie. If he'd managed to miss Adam's meltdown, she didn't feel particularly inclined to give him a play-by-play.

"Suppose I'd better get back to it, then." Frankie sighed, looking like a mournful Goth boy in the harsh direct light.

He stubbed out his cigarette and looked at Jess, who said, "Oh. Yeah. Okay, well, thanks for the . . . talk."

Frankie flashed a grin that startled Miranda with its unabashed wickedness. "Anytime, Bit."

And then he was through the door, leaving a blast of heat from the kitchen behind him.

"What was that all about?" Miranda asked.

Jess shrugged, but turned his face a little to the side. "Frankie was just giving me a hard time."

Miranda didn't like the sound of that. "What was it he called you?"

Her brother made a face Miranda couldn't quite interpret, sort of half rueful, half pleased. "Bit. I don't know why, maybe because I'm shorter than he is? But everyone in the universe is shorter than Frankie, so . . ."

An especially evil throb of pain along the arch of Miranda's left foot distracted her. With a gasp, she stood on one leg and clutched at the offending extremity.

"Are you okay?" Jess rushed over to hold her up just as her balance started to go.

"Oh, I'm fine," Miranda grumbled. "I should've worn different shoes, that's all. I'll know better tomorrow."

Because she would definitely be back tomorrow. If Adam Temple thought he could run her off by yelling at her in front of a crowded room—well, he obviously wasn't a man to learn from his mistakes.

"In the meantime," she said, determination giving her a sorely needed shot of adrenaline. "I'm heading out. Are you coming?"

Jess glanced toward the kitchen door for an instant before saying, "Nah. I think I'd better stay and see if Grant needs any help closing down. See you at home later?"

Miranda smiled at his use of the word "home." "Only if you're planning to invade my dreams. I'll be asleep the moment my head hits the pillow. You're on for breakfast tomorrow, though."

With a nod, Jess headed back inside and Miranda tottered out to the curb to hail a cab.

Before she could raise her arm, however, she was arrested by a hissed whisper from the building corner beside the alley entrance.

Clutching a hand to her racing heart, she made out the amazing disappearing Robin Meeks, her erstwhile partner in crime on stock detail, gesturing furtively at her.

"As God is my witness," she swore through gritted teeth, "if one more person jumps out of the shadows at me, I'm going to stroke out. It's been way too long a night for this kind of nonsense."

"Sorry," Rob said, not sounding all that apologetic. "But I wanted to talk to you, outside the restaurant."

"Oh, is that why you skipped out on me? I thought maybe you knew we'd completely messed up the stock and that Chef Temple was going to lose his marbles over it."

He groaned. "Shit, what difference does the stock make, anyway? It's nothing but broth."

"Tell that to the chef. No, really, tell him. Preferably tomorrow morning at nine A.M., so I have time to sleep in while you get your balls handed to you on a chopping block."

"Listen, none of that's important. It's all small stuff." Rob waved his hand. "But I heard you were writing a book. Is that true?"

She stared. "Did I miss the water cooler on the tour? Because I could really stand to know where you all get your information so damn fast."

"There's no such thing as a secret in the kitchen," Rob told her. "Which is kinda what I wanted to talk to you about. So is it true?"

"Yes, I have a book deal." The thrill she got from saying it was probably illegal in twenty states.

Rob stepped closer and a stray passing headlight caught his eyes in a weird way, making them seem sharp and fragmented.

"Then I'm your guy," he said, his voice tight and high.

"What are you talking about?" Miranda asked, genuinely mystified and really wishing he'd finish creeping her out so she could go home already.

"You want to know all the gossip? The shady backgrounds, the bad pasts, the rap sheets? Who in the kitchen does the dirt, how and when, and with who else? I know all of it. And I'm willing to spill. With one condition."

Miranda's heart started pounding again, this time from excitement.

"What condition?"

He smiled, a thin, unpleasant expression that made him look more like a ferret than ever.

"Keep my name out of it. If you out me as your source,

after what I'm going to tell you, I'll never work in a restaurant again."

It was hours before she made it to bed that night, but they were productive hours. Rob spilled, as promised, loads of dirt. It turned out that he felt he'd been passed over by Adam and Frankie in favor of cooks with less formal training, and it rankled.

Not that Rob put it so succinctly, but Miranda pieced it together. The many and varied comments on the various line cooks' immigrant backgrounds and lack of familiarity with classical French terminology were a big clue.

She couldn't wait to transpose her notes from their conversation and order them into something resembling a narrative. There was a lot to work with here: criminal priors, Mafia connections, insanely dangerous pranks played on other kitchens and bragged about . . . none of it attributed directly to Adam Temple, but that sous-chef, Frankie, was on the hook for enough illicit nookie in and around the restaurant premises to keep the Department of Health and Sanitation hopping for a year. Which only made her retroactively even more anxious about the fact that Jess had been talking to the guy last night. She needed to nip that friendship in the bud.

Once she finally hit her bed, she slept so hard she actually missed her alarm going off and had to scramble to get showered and dressed. She put on one of her office outfits, hoping the conservative dark gray wrap dress would boost her confidence with its associations of delivering the verbal smackdown to bad restaurants across the city.

Jess still wasn't up when she left. He'd been in his room with the door shut when she got home, but his light had still been on. She worried he wasn't getting enough sleep, and thought about trying to enforce a curfew or a lights-out policy while she did her makeup.

Luck was on her side, and she caught a cab right away. The cabbie seemed to know the best way to go, and to not be intent on taking her from the Upper East Side to the Upper West Side by way of Rockefeller Center, so Miranda crossed her fingers and hoped her luck continued to hold.

The cab pulled up at the corner of Seventy-eighth and Columbus Avenue, where Miranda paid up and got out. She was going to have to figure out a bus schedule; all this cab fare was killing her.

Market on a Saturday morning was very different from Market on a Friday night. It already felt more welcoming than it had when she'd been there before during off-hours, and Miranda wondered at that. It wasn't like she'd spent any time at all, really, in the front rooms. Still, the morning sunlight filtered in the dark gold–tinted windows, making the main dining room seem warm and intimate.

Too bad she had to beard the lion in his lair. Miranda sighed. The staircase down to the private offices was dim, and Miranda noticed for the first time how sore her legs were. This cooking gig was pretty intense on the body, she was starting to realize. Who would've thought she'd need cross-training at the gym to be able to get through it?

No one had bothered to give Miranda a full tour, but Jess had pointed out the staff locker room, and he'd mentioned that Adam's office was at the end of the same hall. Miranda ended up in front of a heavy metal door that looked as if it had been installed as a bomb shelter or something.

There were word magnets all over the door, including a sentence right at eye level that said THE BOSS . . . IS IN.

Fighting down a wave of trepidation, Miranda rapped her knuckles hard against the door.

"What?" came Adam's voice, muffled by the thick door.

Great. He sounded as if he were still aggravated.

"It's Miranda Wake," she called, feeling like a fool. It was awkward to cool her heels outside a closed office, but it would be even more awkward to burst in and find him doing something embarrassing. She couldn't quite call up a picture of what that might be, but still.

"Oh, right," he said. "Were you planning on coming in?"

Pressing her lips together, Miranda pushed open the door. Adam was behind a big old-fashioned desk, nearly hidden behind a mammoth computer that looked like it might be the first one ever invented. Like it should have its own room and six men to run it.

Trying not to be obviously in shock over the Stone Age monstrosity Adam was laboriously hunting-and-pecking out keys on, Miranda stood for a moment in the doorway. There was no natural light at all in the basement office, and the greenish reflection from his computer screen should've made Adam look sickly and wan. Unfairly, it didn't. He looked every bit as tanned and delicious as he'd looked every other time she'd seen him, although minus the crackling energy he seemed to exude in the kitchen.

Down here, sweating over what Miranda could only presume to be the books, Adam looked like the definition of stress.

He squinted at the screen, his two forefingers hovering indecisively over the keyboard, and finally blew out a gusty sigh that fluttered the lock of mink-brown hair on his forehead.

Looking up, Adam blinked at Miranda as if surprised to see her standing there.

"Hi," he said. "Um, you want to sit down?"

"Thank you," Miranda replied as she moved to the lone chair. Her voice went a little heavy on the irony, but he didn't seem to notice.

"Right. You're here because . . ." He seemed genuinely lost, and Miranda almost had to laugh. Seriously, she'd been torturing herself in anticipation of this?

"Last night," she prompted him, not really sure why she was helping except that he was bound to remember at some point. Better to get it over with and done with. "The soup?"

His face lit up with recognition. "Yes! Sure. That nasty stock you made."

Miranda scowled. "I made it the way I was told. It's not like I was alone on the station."

"I know, I know." He waved her defense away. "I shouldn't have blown up at you like that. I can get kind of . . . intense during service. My crew knows it's nothing personal—not that I don't mean it," he said.

Miranda shook her head, confused. "I'm sorry, but you mean what, exactly?"

"Well, that everything should be perfect," he said, as if that were eminently reasonable. "That we should always strive for perfection, every night, every minute, and anything less is an insult to the food and the customers. If that's not the goal, why are we bothering? Perfection is paramount. And that stock?" He looked stern. "Not perfect."

"I understand," Miranda said, and she thought she really might be starting to. Despite his unorthodox methods, Adam Temple actually had a decent work ethic. "I'll try not to let it happen again."

He winced. "No, no. You don't get it. Don't *try* not to do it again. Don't *do* it."

Frustrated, Miranda said, "All I can say is that I'll do my best! But I'm flying blind here; it's not like I know how to cook."

Adam stared. "You're a restaurant critic. And you don't know how to cook?"

A flush of heat enveloped Miranda's whole head when she realized what he'd just goaded her into admitting.

"I have an excellent palate," she told him. "I can distinguish flavors and ingredients after a single bite. If I can pick the coffee notes out of a mouthful of dark sauce, is it really necessary that I know the perfect way to skim stock?"

Adam shook his head, evidently aghast.

"It may not be necessary to your bosses at *Délicieux,* but it's sure as hell important to me. Until you have some solid grounding in the basics, you'll keep making rookie mistakes and screwing up my kitchen." He stood up and placed his hands flat on the desk, looming slightly.

Miranda tried not to be nervous.

Then he grinned.

"There's only one thing for it," Adam declared. "I'm going to teach you to cook."

TWELVE

Jess blinked awake from a blurry dream, full of indistinct figures as hazy as a Stieglitz photograph. But Jess could produce from memory a vision of the main player in the dream, a Richard Avedon–esque image of a long, sharp face pale against a crop of black hair, the lines and angles as familiar as the face Jess saw every day in the mirror.

Frankie Boyd.

He burrowed down into the covers, not quite ready to let go of the dream. It had left him with a low-level hum of pleasurable happiness. This was getting to be a regular occurrence, waking up with afterimages of the lanky sous-chef burned onto his eyelids. Frankie was just so . . . wild and different and alive. Exactly the way Jess felt when he was anywhere near him.

For the last week, Jess had managed to avoid any actual conversation with the object of his obsession while silently and unobtrusively (he hoped) stalking Frankie around the restaurant. He was well aware that it was dangerous and dumb, but he couldn't seem to help himself.

Jess had discovered lots of random facts. Frankie smoked Dunhill cigarettes, a British brand reputed to use very fine tobacco and fancy silk filters. He listened exclusively to punk music and would argue long and loud with Adam over which was better, New York punk or British punk. He played bass guitar in a band at an after-hours bar. Frankie was a dog—he'd slept with nearly everyone in the kitchen and front of the house, boys and girls. And the rumor was that Frankie had his eye on someone new.

After last night, Jess had a shameful, flickering hope about who that "someone new" might be.

Jess knew Frankie had ducked outside for a cigarette when he let himself out the back door. He also knew he should stay inside, but something compelled him to follow the guy. Heart pounding, he rationalized that surely there'd be a group of cooks out back smoking, and maybe Jess could join in and bum a cigarette from someone (even though he didn't smoke), and maybe Frankie would give him a light and touch his hand. It was ridiculously junior high. If Jess had considered it for longer than two seconds, he (probably) would've changed his mind.

But he didn't give himself time to wimp out. And when he hit the back doorstep and saw that Frankie was alone in the dark—it was like his brain went offline completely. His feet carried him closer with no clear directive from his mind.

"Evening, Bit," came Frankie's laughing voice from out of the night.

"Hi," Jess responded, then snapped his mouth shut. How lame could he be?

"You know," mused Frankie, taking a pull on his cigarette. "I believe this is the first time we've been alone together since we met. Remember?"

Jess shivered. He did remember; sometimes he had trouble thinking about anything else. It hadn't been anything big or momentous, or at least it shouldn't have been. But somehow that instant when Frankie had first looked him in the eye and really seen him before smiling that naughty, hint-of-tongue smile—nothing, for Jess, had ever been bigger.

"Everything's been so busy, getting the restaurant ready to open," Jess said vaguely.

Frankie arched a brow, the one with a curve like a scimitar. "Not too busy now for a nice little chat, is it?"

Jess gulped, hoping it wasn't audible. "No," he agreed. "My tables have all cleared."

There was the smile again, and Jess watched, fascinated, as Frankie flashed the trademark tip of tongue between his front teeth. There was no earthly reason that should be so ridiculously sexy.

And yet.

Jess cast about for a topic of conversation while Frankie leaned hip-shot against the wall, smoking contemplatively and staring into the sliver of night sky visible between the tops of buildings. Shifting his weight from side to side, Jess let his eyes wander from Frankie's kick-ass black boots, up the black denim-clad legs to the greyhound-lean chest encased in yet another T-shirt, a white one with the black outline of a woman's face surrounded by a pouf of eighties hair.

The sleeves had been ripped out, and Jess noticed again the tattoo that had caught his eye that first day. A skinny figure with shoulder-length dark hair lounged against Frankie's bicep, wearing suspenders and a collared shirt. A pair of dark eyes smoldered out of the tat. Jess wondered with a sudden pang if he was looking at someone who'd been important to Frankie.

"Who's the guy on your arm?" Jess blurted, and could've smacked himself for how completely noncasual he sounded.

Frankie clamped his cigarette between his teeth and twisted his arm so he could see his own tattoo. "Guy? Are you cracked? That's Patti Smith, you plonker."

Jess could feel his face coloring. "A chick. Seriously?"

Frankie took the Dunhill between his thumb and fore-finger and pointed it at Jess. "Not just any chick, Bit. Patti Smith is the Godmother of Punk. She's a genius, Rock and Roll Hall of Famer, fucking Commander of the French Order of Arts and Letters." He shook his head despair-ingly. "Sweet suffering saints, what are they teaching you young squirts nowadays?"

Jess scowled. He hated it when people referred to his age. It's not like he could help being nineteen. "I'm not that young," he said, fighting to keep the sullen out of his voice.

Frankie pushed off the wall and sauntered closer. Jess felt trapped by his own magnetic attraction, as if Frankie were the planet he was revolving helplessly around, and yet he didn't exactly want to escape. Frankie leaned in, and Jess was suddenly enveloped in his scent, the rich to-bacco tang from the Dunhill clashing with the savory smoke from the grill. He breathed in as deeply as he could without gasping aloud.

"I bet you'd like Patti's music, Bit," Frankie said, his sexy lick of an accent rasping over Jess's nerves. "There's this one line of hers makes me think of you every time I hear it, about your youth being for the taking. Makes me want to take your hand and run away."

Frankie shook his head again, laughing at himself, but there was something shadowy in his eyes that made Jess wish for broad daylight so he could puzzle it out. "Don't be so quick to cast off your youth, Bit. Once it's gone, you can't ever get it back."

And then Miranda made a racket entering the alley, and Jess came back to reality with a bump.

Jess sank onto his pillow with a sigh. If she hadn't come outside then . . . but she had. And God, she'd almost seen—he didn't even know what, but something. And that would've been awful, he reminded himself, in spite of the ache of unfulfilled anticipation that still throbbed below his breastbone.

His late night had gotten even later because, of course, he'd had to come home and download every single Patti Smith album he could find. Including the one with the cover he recognized immediately as being the basis for Frankie's tattoo. It turned out to be a Mapplethorpe photograph, which gave Jess shivers when he found out. Robert Mapplethorpe was one of his favorite artists.

Jess twisted and reached to grab the iPod off his bedside table. Fitting in the earbuds, he scrolled to the song Frankie had referenced last night, which Jess had finally pinned down after several hours of intensive listening. By the time he went to sleep, Jess understood exactly what Frankie loved about her. Patti Smith was the essence of cool, brazen and unapologetic. He found the live version of "Kimberly" and let the steady bass guitar beat fill his head.

Jess was fully aware that this was getting out of hand. He was stupidly close to losing his head over Frankie.

Okay. Recognize it and get over it, because no good could possibly come of following through with whatever this was. Miranda would be hurt, Jess would lose his job and all his new friends, and what would he have gained? Only the knowledge that he'd learned absolutely nothing from all the shit that went down at Brandewine. And he couldn't bear for that to be true.

Scrubbing a hand over his face, Jess hauled his ass out of bed and into the shower, determined to get a handle on his hormones.

Following Adam out of his office and up the stairs was like trying to keep up with a bike messenger in rush-hour traffic. Miranda cursed herself for wearing heels yet again, and actually considered slipping out of them.

But barefoot in a restaurant? That had to be a health violation. And anyway, how much farther could he be running?

Adam glanced over his shoulder and made an impatient noise when he saw Miranda straggling, and to her surprise, he reached back and grabbed hold of her hand, hauling her up.

It should've hurt, being manhandled like that, but somehow Adam's hand, hard and callused as it was from years of holding a knife, was nothing more than gently implacable. His dark eyes gleamed down at her in the dim hallway, and when he smiled, his even teeth were white against the darkness.

"Come on, sweets," he said, all gruff and excited. "Keep up. You're gonna learn to cook! I'm telling you, it's the best thing in the world."

Infected by the sheer incandescent joy on his face, Miranda couldn't help smiling back. She'd spent all night and morning worrying about getting screamed at and banished from the kitchen, only to be confronted by Adam in full-on boyish charm mode instead. The reversal of fortunes, added to this insanely good-looking and charismatic man's nearness in the enclosed space of the back hallway, was making her a touch giddy to start with. And when he turned that lethal enthusiasm on her?

Her normal cool reserve didn't stand a chance.

So she found herself smiling up at him, at the warm, solid length of him pressed close to her side, and before she knew what was happening, he laughed out loud and dipped his head to brush their mouths together.

She felt the soft, supple pressure of his full bottom lip moving against hers, the seeking tilt of his head, and they both froze. He seemed as startled as she was by the contact.

The air around them crystallized with tension for one

heartbeat, two, then with a muffled groan, he slanted his mouth down over hers. It was hot and deep and wet, zero to sexy in no time flat, and all Miranda could do was cling to Adam's strong hand. It was the only place they were really touching, other than their lips, and the point of contact steadied Miranda against the rush of sensation when he licked into her and rubbed the velvety nap of his tongue across the sensitive roof of her mouth.

The kiss was a jolt of pure electricity down her spine.

When Adam drew back, running that dangerous tongue over his bottom lip as if seeking to catch the last of her flavor, Miranda knew her eyes were as round as saucers. Her heart was jackhammering away and she felt stunned. Like he'd kissed her stupid.

Adam stared down at her for a long beat before saying, "I've been wanting to do that for days. You've got a mouth that was made for kissing. Did you know that?"

"I—I . . ." *Damn it, brain, kick in!* "I can't believe you just did that."

Smooth.

"Why not?" Adam cocked his head. "It was fun. It felt good."

Miranda fluttered like a startled pigeon. Adam still had a firm grip on her right hand, so she was forced to use her left to gesticulate wildly. "You can't just go around kissing people because you feel like it! My God, where do you come from?"

"The West Village," he said, as if that explained everything.

Maybe it did.

Her heartbeat slowed to something resembling a livable rhythm, although the warmth that had pooled in her belly had yet to dissipate. Miranda shook her head, utterly without a response.

"Come on," Adam cajoled. "It was only a kiss. Chalk it

up to my exuberant personality, or my total fucking joy at being offered an excuse to ditch the books for the morning. Whatever you want."

Getting her feet under her again, Miranda twitched her soft jersey-knit wrap dress more perfectly into place and smoothed her free hand over her hair.

Then she fixed him with the sternest look she could muster, grateful that the poorly lit stairwell would hide the glow of pink she could still feel heating her cheeks.

"Fine. Just promise me it won't happen again."

The son of a bitch had the audacity to grin.

"Not on your life, sweetheart."

By the time Jess hit the apartment stairs, it was already after nine. Thanking whatever gods looked out for penniless students that Miranda had brought his bike when she moved to Manhattan, he unlocked the chain and kicked off.

It was another pretty day, one more thing to be thankful for, and Jess pedaled fast for the entrance to Central Park. He liked to cut across the park in the mornings to get to work, weaving around joggers and people walking their dogs. The leaves were a canopy of vibrant green shading the path. Jess's photographer's eye tagged everything as he whizzed past, on the off chance he'd see something worth stopping for.

His beat-up old Nikon was in the messenger bag slung over one shoulder along with his Market server duds. Jess liked to take the camera everywhere he went, just in case. The city was full of amazing moments that were worthy of being captured on film for all time, if you knew how to watch for them.

Fifteen minutes later, he chained his bike in the alley behind the restaurant and let himself in the back door. His traitorous brain immediately zeroed in on Frankie's

presence toward the front of the kitchen, near the pass, and
Jess studiously kept his head turned away. He couldn't afford to get in any deeper. He had enough going on in his
life already without complicating things with this childish
crush.

Ignoring the quiet internal voice that insisted Frankie
was more than a crush, Jess hurried through the kitchen
toward the staff staircase. He didn't notice there was music
playing, the usual Market kitchen soundtrack of frenetic
punk rock, until it switched off abruptly, to be replaced by
the now-familiar opening beats of "Kimberly."

Patti's whiskey-on-the-rocks voice poured out of the
speakers, trippy lyrics like abstract poetry set to music,
and it froze Jess in place with one hand on the door leading
down to the staff changing room.

Blood thrummed in his ears, nearly drowning out the
music, but before he could turn and meet Frankie's sly,
knowing gaze—the gaze Jess could feel trained on the back
of his neck like a hot photo studio spotlight—the staff door
flew open, knocking him back several paces, and Adam
burst in, dragging a shell-shocked Miranda along by the
hand.

"Frankie," Adam bellowed. "I'm out. Got to school
Miss Miranda, here."

"Go on and skive off, then, you bastard, we've prep
covered," Frankie replied, unruffled as always.

Jess watched the exchange still in the shutterbug zone,
unconsciously noting everything from the exuberant gleam
in Adam's eye and Frankie's wry responding twinkle to
Miranda's slightly mussed makeup and wide-blown pupils.

Which made him raise his brows and take a closer look.
Miranda caught his eye and the blush mantling her cheeks
intensified in color as she tried surreptitiously, and unsuc-
cessfully, to disentangle her hand from Adam's.

Interesting. She looked exactly the way Jess had felt when Frankie shook his hand that first day. Confused, overwrought, and disbelieving. She gave Jess a halfhearted wave as she followed Adam from the restaurant, still looking as though she didn't quite know what had hit her.

Jess sympathized. In his experience, that feeling got worse before it got better.

The thought prompted him to finally meet Frankie's eyes, and the smoky invitation he read from across the kitchen made Jess swallow his heart back down into his chest, where it lodged uncomfortably, beating raucous and loud against his ribs. He shifted awkwardly in his jeans, which suddenly felt too tight, and beat a hasty escape down to the staff changing room.

So much for getting control of his hormones.

THIRTEEN

Where should he take her? Adam wondered. He'd paused just outside of Market, brought up short by the lack of any real plan.

"What are we doing now?" Miranda asked in that snotty tone she used when she felt off her game and didn't want the other players to know. It startled Adam momentarily that he'd already started cataloguing this woman's tones, and he took too long to answer.

"Well?" she prompted, finally succeeding in wrenching her hand away from his. Adam had sort of forgotten he'd grabbed her, but when he thought about it, he knew he'd been enjoying holding that hand for a while now.

Miranda Wake seemed to bring out the impulsive in him. That kiss! Everything perked up at the memory of the hot, sweet friction of her mouth on his.

Adam squeezed his eyes shut for an instant, willing his unruly body to settle down. "You are not the boss of me," he told his dick.

"No," Miranda retorted, making Adam's eyes fly open. "As you enjoy repeatedly reminding me, you're the boss here. So where is this alleged cooking lesson going to take place?"

Rattled, Adam made a split-second decision. "My place," he said decisively. "There's plenty of room, and I know how everything works."

"Your place?" She sounded uncertain. Adam guessed he couldn't blame her. After that kiss—*Down, boy*—it sounded a little like an elaborate plan to get into her pants.

"It's not like I'm asking you up to see my etchings or something," he said, attempting to be reassuring. "We're gonna cook. That's it."

"Hmph. Unless you decide to do something else, just for the fun of it," she muttered underneath her breath. But she didn't make any real protest, and the lines of suspicion next to her mouth softened—*Christ, I'm cataloguing her expressions, too?*—so Adam figured they were good to go.

Taking off across the street at a slow lope, he called over his shoulder, "I want to hit the market, get some supplies." When she didn't move, he turned around and walked backward for a few steps, spreading his arms as a cab zoomed between them, inches from his pelvis. Adam took a moment to be grateful that his dick had absorbed its earlier chastisement. "You coming or what?"

Primming her mouth like a schoolteacher, Miranda waited very correctly for another car to go by before stepping off the curb and crossing the street. Adam supposed she would've preferred to go all the way down to the corner to avoid jaywalking. Something about this woman just tickled the hell out of him, and he knew he was grinning by the time she reached him.

The Seventy-seventh Street market wasn't as big or as varied as the Union Square Greenmarket, but it was convenient. Adam knew some of the vendors pretty well from popping over to grab ingredients when he couldn't wait for his regular suppliers, or when he only needed a tiny amount to tide him over.

"There's a good dairy stand," he told Miranda. "On the far

corner. Not as amazing as Dava Whitehurst's, downtown—this one doesn't have goat cheese or crème fraîche."

"I remember Dava," Miranda said. "She was quite a unique person."

Adam slid her a look out of the corner of his eye, trying to see if she meant that in a bad way. But it didn't seem like she did. Her face was open and bright, taking in everything with that look that said she was taking reams of mental notes.

"Dava's a character," Adam agreed. "I think you can taste it in her product. There's something a little different about all her stuff, from the milk and eggs to the chèvre with lavender and honey."

Miranda gave him an intrigued, if skeptical, glance. "You can taste that?"

Adam shrugged. "Maybe it's all in my head. But it's not like the brain has nothing to do with taste. Who's to say my perception of Dava's dairy produce is less valid just because my knowledge of her as a person influences it? But 'influence' isn't the word I want." He closed one eye, shuffling through synonyms for the right term.

"*Enhance*," Miranda said. "Your personal relationship with Dava enhances your experience of her food."

"Exactly," Adam said, thrilled. She totally got it. "That's what I'm trying to do with Market," he said, getting warmed up. "I want people to feel connected to what they eat, to get that level of enjoyment out of it."

They passed a flower stand and Miranda hovered by the peonies before smiling at the vendor and moving on. "But how can you expect people to taste what you taste when most of them will never meet Dava? Are you going to organize tours of the Greenmarket?"

The idea lit up Adam's mind like the power burner on his Viking range.

"I love that." He beamed. "No, really, I think I might do

that. Maybe an early-morning tour of the Union Square Greenmarket, some lessons on picking produce, followed by lunch at the restaurant. You're a serious genius!"

He grabbed Miranda by the waist and twirled her around, laughing. She gasped, her cherubic little mouth a perfect O of surprise, before she smacked at his shoulder with one hand.

"Put me down, you idiot," she said, tart as vinegar, but a smile tugged at the corner of her mouth.

Adam wrinkled his nose at her and let her feet kiss pavement.

He didn't unhand her waist, though, and after only a second Miranda's pretty pink flush kicked in.

"That's what I was waiting for," he said, filled with satisfaction.

"What?" she asked, a tiny bit breathless as she pulled away and cast a glance around as if hoping no one had noticed her in his arms. Adam could've told her that everyone had probably noticed, but no one had cared. This was New York. Weirder shit happened all the time than two happy people in a clinch.

Instead he said, "That blush. I like it when your cheeks match your hair."

She blushed even harder, but stuck her nose in the air and said, "I happen to be very susceptible to changes in altitude. The blood rushed to my head as a purely physical reaction to being lifted."

Adam snorted and went back to looking for the dairy stall. "Right. And I suppose you kissed me earlier as a purely physical reaction to being belowground, in a basement stairwell."

"I— You kissed *me*," she cried. She looked ready to stomp her little foot in frustration.

"Yeah, but you kissed me back." Adam thought it was only reasonable to point that out.

Miranda threw her hands up in despair. Adam noted with interest the way the movement made the crisscrossing fabric of her dress gape a little right at the best possible spot.

Maybe it made him a pervert, but Adam defied any red-blooded straight man not to sneak a peek at lacy underthings whenever he had the opportunity. Especially if said opportunity took place while the aforementioned lacy underthings were being worn by a smoking hottie like Miranda Wake.

The prim-and-proper aspiring authoress wore a see-through bra made of aqua netting, with a teeny pink silk rosebud adorning the fabric between her breasts. All this underneath her plain, gray, suitable-for-the-office dress.

Got to love a woman of contradictions, Adam reflected as they moved through the market. Right next to a stooped, elderly lady selling honey was the dairy stand. A tall black woman wearing a multicolored kerchief studded with gold charms wrapped around her short hair stood serenely behind the folding table.

"Miss Yvonne," Adam greeted her. "How's it going?"

"Oh, you know," she said in her slow, rich voice. "It's going all right. Who's your girl?"

"Miranda Wake," the girl in question said without waiting for Adam to introduce her. She held out a hand and Miss Yvonne took it languidly, casting a sharp eye over at Adam.

"Pretty," Miss Yvonne said. "You sure got an eye, boy. But this one's got a sweetness to her, like fresh milk." Miss Yvonne nodded her head, making her jewelry chime softly.

Adam flashed a grin, hoping Miranda didn't catch that somewhat veiled reference to Eleanor Bonning. Eleanor hadn't been superpopular with the market vendors—she was a little chilly, a little formal, and a lot picky. Miranda, for all her prickly attitude, was looking around the market like a wide-eyed kid in a toy store, drinking in everything.

That kind of openness and interest would endear her to Miss Yvonne faster than anything.

"Pretty," Adam agreed, "sure, but she's a disaster in the kitchen. I'm teaching her to cook, starting with eggs."

"I know how to cook eggs," Miranda protested.

Ignoring her, Adam said, "Can I have a pound of unsalted butter and a dozen of the free-range ones, freshest you've got?"

Miss Yvonne nodded, but didn't move. She pursed her lips. Adam followed her gaze to Miranda, who crossed her arms over her chest.

"You're right," Adam said. "Better make it two dozen."

Miranda was still fuming when Adam let her into his redbrick townhouse. In spite of her annoyance—a master chef, and all he'd teach her to make was eggs? What a waste of time—Miranda observed that Adam's street was quiet and tree-lined, across from a small park with a baseball diamond.

"Ancient building," Adam explained as he juggled the shopping bag while trying to get his enormous key to turn. "Chock full of charm, somewhat low on the modern conveniences."

"Like a working lock?" Miranda took the shopping bag from his arm, and Adam flashed her a grateful smile. Without the hindrance of a sackful of fragile food items, Adam put his back into it and managed to jimmy the stubborn lock open.

Stepping aside to let Miranda through, he said, "Keep in mind I wasn't planning on having any visitors today."

He sounded nervous, and Miranda went inside expecting to see some shameful evidence of bachelor living, like porn magazines on the coffee table or empty takeout boxes stacked to the ceiling.

But there was nothing like that. The place wasn't neat as a pin, but it wasn't overrun by dust bunnies, either.

Honey-colored hardwood floors gleamed under the natural light coming in from a pair of sliding doors at the back of the apartment. She could see that outside there was a postage-stamp patio edging a small backyard, green with foliage and grass.

Drawn to the unusual sight of an urban garden, Miranda walked over to the glass doors before realizing that put her squarely in the man's bedroom area. It was cut off from the rest of the apartment by a floor-to-ceiling bookcase, so she hadn't noticed the low platform bed.

Rumpled navy blue sheets were twined together with a charcoal gray and blue glen plaid coverlet. The bed itself was wide and soft looking, and Miranda became aware of exactly how little sleep she'd gotten the night before. Surely that was the reason for her sudden, overwhelming desire to crawl in and snuggle down.

"Bed's not made, sorry," Adam apologized, still with that edge of discomfort in his voice.

"No, I shouldn't have . . ." Miranda stopped, feeling extremely awkward.

Why had he kissed her earlier? It made everything so much more fraught and difficult. As if it hadn't already been tense enough between them.

Adam cleared his throat and said, "Kitchen's through here."

Miranda followed where he led with relief, barely aware of the living room with its ratty couch and screaming music posters.

As soon as they hit the kitchen, Adam bounced back from whatever attack of nerves he'd been suffering. Miranda could certainly see why—this kitchen would lift anyone's spirits.

"I've never seen a kitchen this big in an apartment this

size," she said, marveling at the expanse of granite countertop laid out before her.

Running a hand over the smooth chocolate-flecked granite, Adam said, "Yeah, it's awesome. Technically, though, the kitchen isn't just for this apartment. It used to be the kitchen for the whole house. It's only in the last year that the building was converted to two apartments."

"What a shame," Miranda said. Catching sight of Adam's raised eyebrows, she amended, "Well, it's nice for you, of course! But what a gorgeous place this must've been when it was all one home."

"It was," Adam agreed. Something in his voice made Miranda leave off checking out the cabinetry and take a closer look at him.

He saw her looking and quirked a half-smile. Shrugging his shoulders as if to rid himself of an unwanted burden, he said, "I grew up here. This is my parents' house. Or it was, before they moved down to Florida."

Miranda wasn't sure how to respond. He obviously wasn't thrilled about the situation, but he must've had his reasons for renting out the top floor.

"It's fine," he said. "And anyway, it's not a permanent situation. Once the restaurant gets going, I'll get my house back. And until then, I'm not here all that much anyway. In fact, I think this may be the longest I've spent here awake in the past five days."

Miranda bit her lip. He was renting out his home to help finance the restaurant. She thought of all the terrible things Robin Meeks had told her the night before, and started to feel a niggle of sympathy for Adam. Starting a new business was extremely expensive. Maybe he'd hired those cooks because he couldn't pay well-trained employees with no arrest records. Maybe ex-cons and thrill junkies were all he could afford.

Which works out great for me, she reminded herself.

Without those colorful characters, my kitchen exposé would be pretty tame.

Adam crouched and started searching through the lower cabinets, rattling pots and pans loudly enough to jar Miranda from her thoughts.

With a triumphant exclamation, he wrestled out a large stockpot and carried it to the sink. He flicked on the water and let it fill the pot about halfway, then heaved the pot over to the stovetop.

"Hard-boiled eggs?" Miranda guessed. "I hate to tell you this, but I was in charge of the Easter egg hunt at my church, growing up. I know how to boil an egg."

"Sure, but can you poach one?" Adam asked. "One of the simplest preparations known to man, but there's a whole boatload of shit that can go wrong with it."

"Okay, you've got me. I've never poached an egg."

"You will today," Adam stated, cranking the heat up all the way on the burner under the pot.

"Should I put the eggs in the refrigerator?" Miranda asked.

"Nah, leave them. They're perfect for cooking at room temp. If they're chilled, it takes them longer to catch up to the rest of the ingredients. And for boiling or poaching or anything involving water? Forget about it."

"Then I guess I've already learned something."

"Let's see how far we still have to go. How would you get a poached egg?"

She frowned over at him to see if he was kidding. "The truth? I'd order it at a restaurant, usually as part of eggs Benedict."

He laughed. "That's what I thought. But you can have poached eggs right in the comfort of your own home, as long as you have heat, water, and a pan."

"And eggs," she couldn't resist saying.

Adam inclined his head gravely. "Correct. Gee, you're a fast learner. Okay, are you watching the water?"

"I thought a watched pot never boiled."

"All right, that's about enough out of you." Adam brandished a wooden spoon he'd retrieved from a drawer, and Miranda found herself actually giggling.

She struggled to pull a straight face, and Adam cocked his head, watching. "You always do that," he said. "Stop yourself from having fun, like it's not allowed or something."

A chill skated over her skin. "I'm allowed," she said, trying not to sound as defensive as she felt. "But I'm on the clock, here. Sort of. I'm only here because of the book, and I have to keep it in mind at all times."

Adam's dark brown eyes watched her, the set of his mouth thoughtful. "Why is this book so important to you?"

An image of Jess, happy and successful at NYU on the money from this book sale, popped into her head, but Miranda only said, "It's my career, Adam. Isn't yours just as important to you?"

He shrugged. "Yeah, but that's cooking. That's food. What's a book? Entertainment? Food can be that, too, but food is also life. It's who we are. People say 'You are what you eat' all the time, but that's not really how the saying goes. It's not so simple as 'If you eat bacon, you're a pig.' The actual quote is 'Tell me what you eat, and I will tell you what you are.' Jean Anthelme Brillat-Savarin, a French guy who wrote about taste and gastronomy in the nineteenth century, said it. And he meant that food is like this big clue—how we eat reveals a lot about how we feel about ourselves and our world." He broke off with a sheepish grin. "And now I'm starting to sound like a public service announcement about nutrition or something."

"No," Miranda told him, feeling strangely moved by his

passion. "Not at all. I think I see what you mean. Although I reject the premise that the importance of what *you* do negates the importance of what *I* do. Brillat-Savarin and his revolutionary ideas are only available to us now because he wrote them down. In a book."

A slow smile spread across Adam's face until his dimples winked into view. "Well played, sweetheart."

Miranda's mouth twitched. She knew she ought to protest the term of endearment, but the liquid warmth spilling over her insides at the look of approval and admiration on Adam's face made it seem petty and childish to quibble over nicknames.

Adam picked up his head, an alert look on his face. "Hear that?"

Miranda drew her brows together, unsure what he meant. She listened hard for a second, and just when she was about to give up, she heard a soft metallic hiss.

Fiddling with the knob that regulated the burner, Adam said, "It's the water. About to come up to the boil, which is exactly where you want it for poaching. An actual rolling boil is too jarring for the egg, fucks it all up. Just a steady simmer, that's what we want. Grab me that spoon, would you?"

Miranda held it out. It had a long handle that flared to a wide, nearly flat bowl at the bottom.

"These eggs are so nice and fresh, it should be a snap," he said, cracking an egg into the spoon Miranda held.

Which startled her so much, she immediately bobbled the spoon and splattered raw egg all over the counter.

They both stared at the goopy mess for a second, Miranda with dismay, Adam with a dawning expression of amusement.

"This is why I got the second dozen," he said.

FOURTEEN

"Eggs are kinda magic," Adam said. "At least, that's how I think of them."

They were standing over the pot, watching to make sure the water didn't get too hot or too hyper. He'd decided maybe the best thing was to demonstrate the technique first.

He cracked a new egg into the bowl of the spoon, admiring the freshness of the bright orange yolk, the way the translucent white held in a tight circle around it. So different from a regular, grocery-store egg that it might as well be from another planet. Then he slid the egg carefully off the spoon and into the water with barely a splash to mark its passage. He set a timer for three minutes.

"That's it," he'd told Miranda, who looked unimpressed. "Just cook it until the white is set, but the yolk isn't."

As was usual when Adam was working something through in his head, it all came out of his mouth, no prompting required.

"They're the great negotiator, eggs are," he continued. "They call truce between oil and water, get them to finally mix it up together. They can make a meringue light as air or a custard as thick as wet cement. They pair beautifully with everything from brioche toast to wild mushroom ragout, the perfect snack at any time of the day or night. They're probably the most versatile ingredient in any kitchen."

"And it all starts here," Miranda said, tongue in cheek.

"That's right." The timer dinged and Adam checked the egg. The white had feathered a bit on contact with the hot water, but hadn't spread out into untidy fingers. After three minutes on the heat, the white had coagulated into a beautiful sphere around the yolk. Adam had no trouble lifting it out of the water in a slotted spoon and easing it into a bath of cold water.

"You have to cool it down fast if you're not going to serve it right away, or else it'll keep cooking with the residual heat inside it. Which gives you rubber eggs."

"Ick."

"Exactly." He lifted the egg gently out of the ice bath and spooned it onto a square of brioche toast he'd prepared while waiting for the water to come up to the simmer.

"And there you have it," he said. "A little salt and pepper, and you have a lovely snack. Go ahead, break it open. See if it's good."

Miranda took her fork to the egg and made a soft noise of appreciation when the pristine globe of slippery white parted to let the golden orange yolk run out and soak into the bread.

"Beautiful," she said with her usual frank appreciation. Adam was never going to get tired of that. "That seems simple enough. Can I give it a try?"

He handed her the wooden spoon with a flourish.

The first attempt yielded an egg hard enough to bounce on the floor.

"The temperature of the water is key," Adam told a disappointed Miranda. "Remember that the longer the pot stays on the burner, even at a constant setting, the hotter it's going to get. You gotta adjust for that. Right? Okay, try again."

Miranda bit her lip in a totally distracting way while attempting to maneuver the egg into the pot, so Adam missed seeing exactly what happened. When he finally managed to tear his eyes away from that plump pink mouth, he saw egg white fanning out over the bottom of the pot in a way that would have been sort of pretty if it hadn't made Miranda scowl so hard.

"I fixed the water temperature," she complained. "What went wrong this time?"

"Too hot and you get rubber. Not hot enough, and the white spreads when it hits the water and won't coagulate into a nice round shape. You went a little too far in the other direction, is all. Remember, it wants to be barely simmering."

She grumbled a little, but fiddled with the burner until Adam thought it was about right.

But when she carefully—oh so carefully; cracking the eggshell was a surgical act on par with setting a bone—finished her preparations for the third attempt and slid the yellow orb into the water, the white feathered up again, waving its wisps in the current of the simmering pot like algae on the sea floor.

Adam struggled not to show a hint of the amusement he felt at the look of dismay on her face.

"It's not an exact science," he soothed her. "Cooking's not like math. It doesn't come out the same every single time. That's part of the fun."

She crossed her arms over her chest. Adam was starting to adore that particular defensive gesture.

"Not my idea of fun. I have to say, I'm not getting a whole lot out of this."

Adam considered. He was well aware this cooking

lesson was his own brainchild, not something Miranda had come begging for. Maybe she needed extra motivation.

"How about . . ." He hesitated, unsure if he could commit to what he was about to propose, then shrugged.

Fuck it.

"Okay," Adam said. "For every egg you get perfect, I'll answer a question. And I'm telling you now, it's probably the only way you'll ever get me to talk on the record for that book of yours. So I'd take me up on it."

And if she never managed to figure out poaching, Adam got moral credit for making the offer, but didn't have to deliver shit.

"Done," Miranda said instantly, with a Cheshire-cat smile that made Adam groan around a laugh.

"Christ. I'm in for it now."

Miranda lost the grin and huffed. "Don't despair. I've yet to come close to getting one of my eggs to look like yours."

There were no words for what the slight pout of Miranda's lower lip did to Adam's brain. Something similar to a short circuit or system overload or something. He didn't really know tech stuff, but what it felt like was the flare of ceiling-high flame that happened when a cook accidentally sloshed oil over the side of a pan and into the grill.

Instant meltdown. It was the only thing that could account for everything he was letting this cunning little journalist get away with.

"Here, try this." He rummaged through a drawer until he came up with a slotted spoon. "There are a lot of old wives' tales about tricks for poaching, like adding vinegar to the poaching liquid, but chemically speaking, that's all bullshit. The only thing that can actually help is a little bit of a cheat—you strain off the runniest part of the white before slipping it into the water. Then, if you want, once it's in there you can use a wooden spoon to sort of coax the white to wrap around the yolk as it pulls together. Go on, take a whack at it."

Miranda followed his instructions to the letter, with that air of total concentration that just slayed Adam, and of course, the result was a perfect poached egg.

Adam shook his head as they watched the yolk ooze out silkily. When would he ever fucking learn to keep his mouth shut?

But when he saw the giddy happiness in Miranda's face as she turned to him with a victorious "I did it!," Adam couldn't help but feel sort of pleased he'd made it happen. It took some of the sting out of the upcoming interrogation.

"Quid pro quo," Miranda said warningly, after they'd both dutifully tasted and made appreciative noises.

"Okay, but I never thought liver would go particularly well with fava beans, personally. Chianti, maybe."

"Ew," she told him. "Also, don't think you're going to distract me with movie references. I've got an answer coming to me."

"Fine." He sighed. "Hit me."

He wasn't sure what he was expecting—some softball question about how he first got interested in cooking, maybe, or something incendiary about his previous bosses at other restaurants.

Instead, what she asked was: "What's your all-time favorite dish, and why?"

Too intrigued by the question to protest that it was technically two, Adam pondered in silence for a minute, running through his own recipes, things he'd tried and been blown away by in high-end restaurants and roadside stands and pastry shops across the country.

"That's hard," he finally said. "Shit, you don't go for the easy stuff, do you?"

"Never," she replied.

"I didn't go to culinary school," he began, aware that he was answering the softball question she hadn't asked, but the answer to her actual question would be in there somewhere. "When I graduated high school, I took an extended road trip. I had friends come along for parts of it, my parents would fly out and meet me in the places that interested them, but for long stretches, it was just me and the road. I didn't have a car, so I took the bus everywhere, sometimes the train. Met lots of interesting people."

"How far did you get?"

"Made it all the way to Seattle," he said, still proud of it. "On the cheap, too. Whenever I ran out of money, I'd get a job washing dishes to save up enough for the next bus ticket. If there was a great restaurant in town, I'd either try to work there or use my earnings to cop a meal before I moved on. It was an awesome education. I saw people doing things with food that I'd never thought of or heard of—and I grew up in Manhattan with parents who liked to eat out."

"What kinds of things?" Miranda asked, clearly willing to push the limit on her quid pro quo, if Adam was.

"Steamed crabs in Baltimore, pulled pork outside of Atlanta, tacos from the most amazing taqueria in Fayetteville, Texas. There was a guy in Cleveland doing things you wouldn't believe to Great Lakes fish like perch and walleye—seriously haute cuisine stuff with what were basically considered trash fish. And in California . . . hot damn. I know what it was."

"What?"

"The best thing," he told her. "My favorite dish. I saved and saved to get to eat at Chez Panisse. I'd picked up Alice Waters's book in my travels and I read that sucker cover to cover and back again, so she was on my list. I hit Berkeley in the summer, and I remember Black Mission figs were all over that menu. It was the season. I'd never really had anything but dried figs, and I didn't like them. But when I tasted those roasted fresh figs, drizzled with wild honey and dotted with minuscule white smears of triple-cream goat cheese, I just about died."

Adam closed his eyes, lost in the memory of that explosion of tastes and textures, all harmonizing together so simply and beautifully. When he met Miranda's gaze again, she was watching him with a soft smile.

"Good, huh?" was all she said.

"Life-changing," Adam told her, and he knew it was true. "That was the moment when it all came together for me. In my head, at least—it was a long hard road between those figs and getting the whole being-a-chef deal worked out on paper and in the real world—but it was like that afternoon, my brain took a quarter turn to the left and I knew. Food was it for me. And not only food, but local food. Food that tells you where you are, and lets you in on the secrets of the person who cooked it. I ate those figs, and I knew Alice Waters without ever meeting her. I knew myself."

Something soft and sweet passed over Miranda's face, and he thought she might be really getting it. "Sounds like a meal to remember."

"It was, although I haven't consciously thought of it in years." He laughed. "Those figs are behind a good bit of my own cooking, though, one way or another. The marriage of salty and sweet is one I'm still particularly fond of, and I try to never forget the role texture plays in a dish."

"Why didn't you go to culinary school? It seems like a logical next step for a boy who decided he wanted to be a chef."

"Not so fast. No more questions until I see another perfect egg out of you."

"Oh, fine," she muttered, and hurried through the preparations without really checking the water first. She added another rubber egg to the pile in Adam's sink before turning out a good one. They both looked at the spreading yolk for a moment, then turned away.

"I'm getting kind of sick of the taste of plain egg," she confessed.

"Right. We'll try something different next."

"But first, the answer to my question."

"Slave driver." Adam shook his head. "Fine. I didn't go to culinary school because I didn't think they could teach me anything I couldn't learn better on the job. I'm not so sure that's true, looking back, but I did learn a shitload on every line I ever worked, in every position from dishwasher to prep and right on up to two years ago."

"When you worked at the original Appetite on the Upper East Side."

She'd done her research.

"Yeah, I ran the kitchen for Devon Sparks while he was off opening a new hotspot in Miami and filming that TV show about being the greatest chef alive, or whatever."

Adam paused, but Miranda didn't take the bait. Most food writers leaped on any mention of Devon, hoping for stories of his famous temper and antics in the kitchen. Adam never minded obliging with a tale or two, and he had some whoppers, but for the most part the guy had been decent to him.

He sort of liked Miranda's interview style, though, all free-flowing and easy. Although it was getting him to talk more than he would have otherwise, which probably ought to make him nervous.

"In hindsight, I could've saved myself some time, if not money, by doing the formal training thing. I bet I spent as much on books I read on my own as any incoming student at the Culinary Art Academy."

"What books do you think influenced you the most?"

Adam was about to answer when he noticed the crafty

gleam in Miranda's eye. Twisting his mouth shut, he shook his head. "You're a tricky one. But no dice. Maybe I should ask you a question or two instead."

Immediately looking wary, Miranda said, "What kind of question?"

"We've talked plenty about how I know so much about kitchen stuff," Adam said, injecting enough over-the-top pompousness into his tone to make her smile. "How about you tell me why you know so little about it? How did you and Jess eat?" *After your parents died* was the part of the question he didn't vocalize.

For a moment he thought she wasn't going to answer. Her face went kind of blank, but there was a shadow of something like grief in her eyes that made him sorry he'd brought it up. Not sorry enough to stop her when she started to answer, though; this had to be a key to her personality, and Adam wanted to know all about her.

"Jess was ten when our parents died; I was eighteen. I took night classes, got two jobs, and tried to keep Family Services from coming down on us. With all that, there wasn't much time for the culinary arts. We ate a lot of frozen pizza." The flat tone of her voice didn't invite sympathy or pity.

Adam felt like a total shit. He'd wanted to get her to open up, sure, but did he have to choose such a painful subject? Obviously noticing his awkward discomfort, Miranda laughed a little and said, "Don't look like that. It was a long time ago and we made it through just fine."

He didn't buy that for a second—the hollow sound of that laugh told him plenty about the residual effects of those years of struggle and worry.

"I admire your persistence. Not a lot of people could've done what you did, so young. And I bet Jess appreciates it, too."

She made a funny little grimace that should've been ugly, but instead was ridiculously adorable.

"I'm not so sure about that. We haven't talked much since he came home."

"He's settling in okay at the restaurant," Adam offered, feeling hopelessly inadequate.

"I know. And I've been meaning to thank you for that, for giving him a chance."

Adam shifted his weight.

"Frankie and Grant were pretty insistent. And they were right, he's smart and quick on his feet, charming to the customers, and gets along with the brigade."

That brought the smile back. Adam matched it, relieved.

"He did turn out pretty wonderful, didn't he?"

"You should be proud."

"I am. But that doesn't stop me from worrying."

"About what?"

Miranda shook her head. "It'd be easier to make a list of what I don't worry about with Jess."

"Give me some examples."

She started ticking things off on her fingers. "I worry that he won't finish school, that he won't get a good job, that he won't meet a nice girl, that he won't settle down and have a family—"

"That he won't have the life your parents wanted for him?" Adam asked in a burst of insight.

Miranda paused, arrested. "I never thought about it like that." She blinked. "And wow, I did not mean to start talking about that. Have you ever considered a career as a journalist? The way you turned that interview around demonstrates a high level of innate ability."

Adam laughed. "Nope. It's the kitchen for me, forever and always."

"Then what are we making next, Chef?" she said with a deep breath, recovering herself. "Because I really think I've had enough with the poaching."

And obviously she'd had enough with the sharing, too. Christ, getting personal info out of her was like trying to peel a tomato without blanching it first. He decided to let her off the hook. For now.

"Before we quit, I just wanted to mention you can poach lots of things other than eggs, in many liquids other than water. Every variable changes the outcome, but the basic technique is the same."

"Very interesting, professor," Miranda quipped. "Are you sure you didn't go to culinary school? You seem to have quite the knack for teaching."

"Half of running a kitchen is teaching," he said, crouching down for another foray into the disorganized mess that inhabited his cabinets. "Showing the line cooks how to do what you want done, how to make it come out perfect every time. I don't expect my cooks to read my mind and know how I want things. It always drove me bat shit, working for guys like that."

Again, no comment from Miranda on Devon Sparks, and Adam quirked a half-grin to himself. It changed to a full grin when his fingers tangled with the spindly rounded end of a whisk.

"Got it," he crowed, standing up to his full height and twisting a little to get the kinks out of his back. Waggling his brows suggestively, Adam asked, "Are you ready to give the good people at Hellmann's a run for their money?"

FIFTEEN

Miranda worked to contain her "ick" face.

"Let me be sure I understand—we're making mayonnaise? Right here in the kitchen?"

"Yup." Adam nodded enthusiastically. "It doesn't spontaneously generate in those jars with the blue lids, you know. In fact, it's one of the oldest classical French sauces. And a very cool illustration of one of the wackier properties of eggs."

She enjoyed the way he talked about eggs. Such a humble, boring food, but it was as if he could look inside and see the potential for greatness in any ingredient.

"Another wacky egg property?" she asked.

"Emulsification," Adam clarified. "Egg yolk allows us to mix oil with usually unmixy things, like water or vinegar or lemon juice. Mayo lets you see the whole process from start to finish, drop by drop." He surveyed her face carefully. "You're one of those people who thinks they don't like mayonnaise, aren't you."

There was nothing questioning in his tone, but Miranda nodded. "It's grossed me out since I was little."

Satisfaction gleamed in Adam's dark brown eyes. "Just wait," was all he'd say.

With a mental shrug—how different could the home-made version be? Not different enough, she'd bet—Miranda went about the preparations Adam laid out.

She separated the yolks and the whites, pouring the more solid yellow yolk back and forth between the two halves of eggshell, letting the white drain off into a lidded container.

Once she'd done three eggs that way, Adam tamped down the lid on the plastic bowl full of whites and stowed it in the fridge.

"Those are always useful for something down the line. Maybe we'll make French meringues later, if we have time. Now take your bowl of yolks and add some mustard, lemon juice, white pepper, and salt."

"How much of each?" Miranda wanted to know. "Is there a recipe I could look at?"

"Shit." Adam laughed. "Only about a million. But it's really just about what you like. Here, I'll help."

With a quick hand, Adam parceled out the ingredients—more mustard than Miranda would've thought. More lemon juice, too. Not that she'd ever thought too much about the components that made up her least favorite condiment, but she wouldn't have expected so much acid.

"I like it tart," Adam explained when she mentioned it. "When you make it on your own, you can cut down the lemon juice, or substitute white vinegar if you prefer that flavor. You're in control. What you aren't in control of," he continued, "is the amount of oil. Yeah, you add it, and you control how quickly, but the yolks can only absorb so much, and it varies from egg to egg. So you have to watch out for the cues. You'll see. Start whisking."

The light metallic clink of the whisk against the bottom of the heavy ceramic bowl was the only sound in the kitchen for several minutes. Adam started excavating through the pantry for something. Miranda sneaked surreptitious glances at his back.

The view was especially nice when he bent to sift through some items on the floor. Denim stretched taut across the firm globes of his rear in a really pleasing way.

Miranda began to feel warm. Probably from the proximity to the stovetop, or the physical exertion of whisking.

She checked the bowl. Everything was blending together in a highly unappetizing goopy orange-brown mess.

"The bulk of mayonnaise is oil, which is why it's so delicious and fattening. You can use pretty much any kind of oil you want, but I personally think olive oil makes for a very strong flavor. I like it better in small doses, for seasoning. Use something with a neutral taste, like canola or grapeseed oil, for the rest."

He tilted the bottle of grapeseed oil carefully, drizzling the stuff in a drop at a time. The oil was immediately absorbed into the egg yolk mixture, thickening and lightening everything by tiny increments. It was startling to see, and Miranda didn't realize she'd slowed in her whisking until Adam chuckled indulgently and said, "Christ, woman, didn't anyone ever teach you how to stir? I knew we were going back to basics here, but, geez."

With no further warning, he stepped up close behind her, surrounding her with his body, and reached his right hand around to grasp hers over the handle of the whisk.

Instead of demonstrating the correct technique, however, they both stilled.

Miranda was intensely aware of the new level of intimacy between them that came from sharing their histories—not to mention the solid strength of him at her back, pressing so close that the hard line of the counter bit into her side. His hand on hers was hard and warm. It was difficult to believe that those blunt fingers were capable of the artistic arranging of food she'd seen him perform with her own eyes as he plated dishes at Market.

She drew in a slow breath that nestled her even deeper into the embrace. She heard a quiet catching of breath in her ear, and those fingers tightened minutely on her own, making her imagine what else they might be capable of.

The air in the kitchen was thick and heavy, as if the steam from the poaching liquid had spread like fog, invading her lungs and making her struggle for every inhalation.

Adam's heart beat out the passing seconds against her shoulder blade, and just when she felt sure he'd snap and do . . . something . . . just when it became inevitable that Adam would touch her and she knew without thinking about it that she'd respond . . . he stiffened and stepped back.

Bracing herself against the counter, Miranda whirled to face him. All the teasing and humor had left his face and she was shocked at the depth of desire that darkened his brown eyes to black. But he held both hands palm up in front of him, attempting to smile.

"My bad. I promised you wouldn't have to look at those etchings and there I go, wanting to drag them out."

Miranda took him in, the rueful expression, the no-harm-no-foul gesture—the intensity still lingering in his gaze. The gaze he'd locked on her as if it were the one thing he couldn't stop. It reminded her of the way he looked at a tricky sauce, totally engrossed and focused. For some reason, that connection propelled Miranda out of her frozen stupor and into Adam's arms.

Or, more accurately, into Adam's broad chest, because as soon as she moved, Adam squawked in surprise and lifted his arms clear.

In the next instant, about when Miranda was starting to feel brutally awkward, Adam dropped his hands to her shoulders and stared down at her with wide, dilated eyes.

Miranda wanted him. Badly. Adrenaline zinged through her veins, lighting her up with the same devil-may-care bravado that had gotten her involved with Adam Temple in the first place. It felt so damned good, risky and out there and delicious. She grinned, giddy with the unfamiliar pleasure of throwing caution to the winds.

"Show me," she whispered. Her voice was so throaty she almost didn't recognize it, but it seemed to work for Adam. He slid one hand immediately around to the nape of her neck and up into the thick fall of her hair.

"Anything," he said, his awestruck tone making Miranda feel like a femme fatale. "What do you want me to show you?"

Miranda smiled, knowing it was coy, feeling like Lauren Bacall and Cleopatra and Eve in the freaking Garden of Eden all rolled into one.

"Your etchings," she said, and stretched up on tiptoe to kiss him.

The moment their lips touched, Adam broke free of his self-imposed distance from the proceedings. He dragged her into his body with a subsonic moan that reverberated down Miranda's spine, heating things down low and making her squirm in his arms.

She was trying to get closer, not to escape, and Adam seemed to know it. He flexed the hand in her hair, his palm hot and encompassing as he cradled the back of her head and dropped the other hand to her hips. One embarrassingly arousing show of brute strength later, Miranda was perched on the edge of the kitchen counter, her head swimming from the vertigo of being unexpectedly lifted.

Tearing her mouth away, she sucked in air, her head dropping back against the cabinet with a thud. Undeterred, Adam took advantage of the suddenly exposed length of her neck, and moved that voracious mouth down to nip playfully at the tender skin beneath her jaw.

Miranda squeaked when he got to that certain place on the side of her neck, the spot that made shivers run up and down her legs and arms in a furious barrage of pleasure. Adam must've taken note, because he took his time exploring the area with lips, teeth, and tongue until Miranda was an incoherent mess.

All she could think to do was to link her wrists behind his neck and squeeze her knees around the trim slabs of muscle at his waist. The tense and release of her thigh muscles made her aware of the damp state of things between her legs, and the totally inadequate job her lacy little thong was doing of covering it up.

Any second now, she thought hysterically, *he's going to touch me and realize how badly I want this.*

It was an insane thought to have when she'd practically attacked the man in his own kitchen, and was currently writhing in his arms, but it stopped her cold.

"Wait," she gasped, shivering at the feel of Adam's wide hand smoothing up and down her rib cage. "Wait, wait . . ."

"Mmm, what are we waiting for?" Adam asked, nuzzling at the hair behind her ear.

She giggled a touch hysterically. "Um, for my brain to catch up with my body?"

"No," Adam protested. "You don't need your brain for this. Let it take a nice rest someplace else. Just for a little while."

Miranda collapsed forward, resting her forehead against Adam's hard shoulder.

"I can't," she mourned. "My brain won't stop thinking."

"Stupid brain," Adam said, his hands stilling on her ribs. The puff of his quickened breath stirred her hair and made her shiver.

"Maybe . . ." Miranda paused, unable to believe she was contemplating saying it. But how long had it been since she'd acted without counting the cost? Well, when not under the influence of evil, sanity-destroying pink cocktails, at any rate.

"Maybe if you touched me. You know."

One dimple popped out with Adam's half-smirk. His thumbs swept slow circles that brushed the undersides of her breasts. "Can you be more specific? There's lots of you I'm willing—make that *dying*—to touch."

She squirmed, embarrassed. They were pressed so closely together that the movement rubbed her tingling mons into the hard, unyielding button fly of his jeans. She shuddered blindly in his arms for a full five seconds, riding out the feeling.

When she looked down at him again through heavy-lidded eyes, Adam's pupils had dilated hard enough to leave only the thinnest band of whiskey-colored iris. His hands slid to her hips and gripped them like a lifeline. Miranda could feel the indentation of each finger separately through the thin material of her dress, like brands searing through fabric to get to her skin.

"Wow," he murmured. "I don't even know which one of us is getting teased."

The look on his face—Miranda sucked in a breath. He was so completely hers in this moment, and so not trying to hide it. The open, honest lust and admiration in his expression was maybe the sexiest thing about this entire situation.

Except for the way he was sliding his thumbs slowly inward, giving her plenty of time to think about the fact that his palms were caressing the tops of her thighs now, the sides of his thumbs barely brushing the top of her mound through her skirt. The jersey knit had ridden up her thighs when he hoisted her onto the counter and now it had settled into the vee of her legs where her thighs parted to wrap around Adam, leaving very little to the imagination.

Fluttery anticipation invaded Miranda's stomach. Adam's

touch was sure, deft. Using just the right amount of pressure, he rubbed circles into her skin with the fabric. It was smooth on her thighs, a bit rough in between where the dress fabric caught against the lace of her thong underneath. It was more a suggestion of friction than actual friction, but it still made Miranda moan.

Adam closed his eyes at the sound and leaned forward until his cheek nuzzled into the valley between her breasts. She clasped his head to her and rocked forward helplessly, encouraging the continuous gentle brushes of his thumbs that sent shivers all through her.

His hair smelled like green apples.

"Tell me," he breathed hotly against her chest, "that this is one of those dresses where you pull one tie and it magically falls to pieces."

Instead of answering, Miranda found the strings at her side that held the wrap dress closed, and pulled.

"Mother of God," Adam said reverently. "That is my favorite thing ever."

She husked out a laugh. "Better than what's underneath?"

He took the edges of her dress between thumb and forefinger and unwrapped her body as carefully as if her flesh might singe his fingertips.

"I take it back," he said, his eyes riveted to the bright blue-green lace thong and matching demicup bra that lifted her smallish breasts and plumped them to a respectable roundness.

"Take what back?" Miranda asked, suddenly feeling self-conscious at being next to nude while Adam stood fully clothed right in front of her.

"I have a new favorite. Feel free to wear this number anytime you want." He nibbled along the lace edging her B cup.

"O-okay," she gasped. "Thanks."

"Christ Almighty, sweetheart." Adam groaned, lifting his fever-bright eyes to her face. "I could make a meal outta you."

Her heart in her throat, Miranda did her best sultry. "So why don't you?"

And with that, she tugged his face up to hers for another kiss as the heat raged through her, flames catapulting back and forth between them both as they fought to get closer.

SIXTEEN

Miranda Wake was burning him alive. The silky pale expanse of her flesh was highlighted by the ludicrously sexy underwear that cupped and covered everything Adam wanted to touch. He'd never been so goddamned jealous of a couple scraps of lace.

And her mouth. Hot damn, the girl had a mouth made for sin. That cupid's bow shape all puffy and kiss-swollen, rubbed redder than usual from his own mouth. The taste of her was like nothing he'd ever encountered. If he could separate out the flavors and figure a way to re-create it, he'd have the hottest dessert the world had ever seen.

Not that he was at all sure he'd care to share that distinctive flavor with his customers, even in sorbet or syrup form. No, this addictive taste was for him alone. He'd take everything she dished out and keep coming back for more, because this was fucking incredible.

Miranda's small, ink-stained fingers were clenched in his hair, tugging insistently at the nape of his neck to keep him stretched up and kissing her. She ate at his mouth like she was starving for it, or maybe just like she was trying to keep up with Adam and keep him from swallowing her whole. Hunger like he'd never felt crashed through his system. He ripped his mouth away and kissed down her neck to her breasts.

Fumbling behind her to get the clasp of the bra undone, and suddenly Adam was in high school, trying his damnedest to get to second base with Monica Pettuci. Did other guys get suave and debonair with this? The one-handed bra-clasp fumble defeated him every time.

Not that he intended to let it slow him down. Adam distracted Miranda with another searing kiss, and before he could fall so far into it that he distracted himself, too, he got both arms around her and worked some hook-and-eye magic.

She let the bra straps slip off her shoulders but put one arm around her own chest, halting the downward slide of the bra. The image she presented made Adam want to howl.

It should've looked prudish, or at least full of sweet maidenly innocence, the way Miranda's arm covered her lovelies. Instead she was the perfect picture of debauchery and decadence. Her hair was mussed, a deep red cloud around her bare, freckled shoulders. The bra clung to her curves like a virgin clinging to virtue, but there was no denying the course of nature. The pressure of her arm against her breasts made them spill over the top of the bra in glorious, pale abundance, and as Adam watched in rapt fascination, Miranda took a deep breath and one rosy nipple peeked above the aqua lace.

"You're killing me," he told her, meeting her gaze. "But I'm going to die happy."

It must've been the right thing to say, because the momentary shyness faded from her eyes and she let her arm, and the bra, drop.

Creamy white perfection crowned with rosy little nipples like raspberries topping sabayon. They were sweet like berries, too, Adam discovered. Sweeter still were the noises Miranda made under his mouth.

Every lick, every sound, every new inch of skin revealed sent a throb of blood to Adam's already rock-hard cock. If he got any harder, he'd be able to lift her down without the use of his hands. Tension coiled at the base of his spine. His balls ached.

Adam's granite countertops were high enough that when he pulled Miranda forward to rest her ass against the edge, the heavy bulge in his jeans notched right into the lace-covered center of her.

He jerked at the first contact, a hot burst of friction and pressure that shot fireworks off behind his closed eyes. Miranda liked it, too, if the soaking heat against his erection was any indication. Adam inhaled the smell of her desire, musky and rich, and had to get his hands on it.

Dividing his attention between the tight knot of her nipple in his mouth and the tactile feast of lace and the crisp, damp curls over her pussy was like trying to expedite five different tables at once, but he managed it.

But when he thumbed aside the panties and got his fingers right on the wet, silky heart of her, Adam could do nothing but gasp against her breast and zero all his focus down to the first three fingers of his right hand. He petted her softly, learning the shape of her folds and the miraculously smooth texture of her skin down there. Miranda bumped her hips up against his hand, once, twice, as if she couldn't help herself.

When he glanced up at her face, her eyes were glazed with passion, her red mouth slack and moist. That gorgeous pink flush he loved so much was all over her face and spreading down her neck to the tops of her pretty breasts.

"Gorgeous," he choked out. "You are so . . . Miranda." He was at a loss, helpless in the face of so much beauty, all laid out like a banquet for Adam in his own kitchen.

She panted something too low for him to hear.

"What?"

Miranda lifted her head, slowly, as if it weighed a hundred pounds.

"Adam. Show me."

He dimly remembered some extended joke about etchings, but he didn't think that's what Miranda meant. There was something flashing in her wide blue eyes, a flicker he'd seen in her before, but never so strongly. Her whole body was tensed, poised on the brink, as if she were about to take flight and soar up into the unknown.

Adam thought maybe she needed a little push to get her there. It made his heart pound a fast drumbeat to think that maybe he could be the guy to do it.

He flexed his fingers, still buried in her heat, and took her mouth at the same time as he took her deeper. Two long fingers slid into her fist-tight sheath, his thumb searching out the supersensitive bundle of nerves at the top of her slit.

Rubbing rhythmically just to the side of her clit, he plumbed the depths of her clenching pussy and sucked her groan of pleasure into his mouth. Her hands fisted on his shoulders, nails clawing him through his shirt.

Miranda writhed on his hand and he pumped her harder, passing his thumb directly over her clit to make her jump. A delicate touch right there, then a harder caress in a circle all around it, then back again until his probing fingers felt the first flutter of Miranda's orgasm in the walls surrounding them.

Her inner walls clamped down on his invading fingers. She stiffened as if paralyzed. A rush of slick warmth and a pained cry, and Miranda unraveled in Adam's hands.

Adam crushed the iron rod of his cock into the edge of the counter and came in his pants for the first time since Monica Pettuci shocked the hell out of him by actually touching his dick.

* * *

Polishing glassware was oddly soothing. The soft cloth, the hot steam from the kettle, the repetitive motion, the instantly sparkling results—Jess never minded being put on glass duty.

Perched on a stool with one foot hooked over the top rung, he could sit comfortably for hours, polishing and stacking the finished glasses carefully atop the bar. As he watched the cloth go around and around, his mind followed the circles in a dreamy pastiche of disconnected images and impressions.

He thought of the bright yellow peonies in the blue ceramic vase on Miranda's table and the bunch of multicolored flowers with the same burst of small petals that always used to sit on the mantel in the living room of the house they grew up in. That led him to the talcum-powder-and-cinnamon smell he associated with his mother and the memory of soft white arms enfolding him, tucking him into bed at night. The darkness of his old room, painted navy blue with glow-in-the-dark star stickers all over the ceiling, courtesy of a short-lived astronaut phase, made him think of the inky blackness of the alley behind Market. Out there, you couldn't see many stars at all when you looked up. Only the very brightest could compete with the lights of the city that never sleeps.

With a shiver, Jess let his mind flow to the image he'd been wanting to picture all morning.

Frankie Boyd, all low-slung black denim and insolence, leaning one slender hip against the rough brick wall and squinting through his own cigarette smoke up into the hazy night sky.

How Jess wished he'd had a camera in his hands. His fingers itched to capture that moment for all eternity, to get it out of his head and onto photographic paper so maybe he could find some peace with it. Instead, the only place that picture existed was inside of Jess, haunting him.

A lean forearm reached past him, fingers outstretched to trace delicately around the rim of the glass he was polishing, breaking Jess's reverie. The arm was pale, dusted with black hair, and corded with tendons that flexed slightly with every rub of the glass. A thin leather strap wound around the bony wrist enough times to form a cuff, the brown hide scored with marks and burns. Jess had discovered days ago, from careful observation, that the strap had belonged to a WWII soldier, a medic who'd fought in the Battle of Britain.

The arm belonged to Frankie.

When that arm pressed in to rest lightly against Jess's elbow, he shivered so hard he nearly dropped the glass, but Frankie tightened his fingers and steadied it.

"Cold, are we then, Bit?" Frankie husked. There was a laugh in his voice, but when Jess canted his head far enough to look at him, his face revealed nothing but grave inquiry.

Some imp prompted Jess to reply, "Nope. Feeling kinda warm, actually."

Frankie narrowed his eyes, fiendish delight suffusing his expression. "Why, Bit," he drawled. "I do believe you just flirted with me."

Jess felt the despised flush heating his cheeks and turning the tips of his ears red, but he looked Frankie dead in the eye, heart pounding like a bass drum, and said, "Maybe a little. There's no law against it."

"Not officially, no, but you had me wondering if there might not be a rule about it written somewhere inside that pretty head of yours. S'why I haven't pushed." Frankie caught the point of his tongue with his teeth and grinned. "Much."

Setting the glass down before he crushed it in his too-tight grasp, Jess swiveled the barstool until he and Frankie were eye to eye. Or close to it, anyway—even with the added height of the stool, Frankie's long legs ensured Jess still had to tilt his head back a bit to get the full effect.

It was worth it. Frankie's hair was the usual mass of spikes and tufts, his pale, night-loving skin glowing in the gold light reflecting off the bar's mirrored back. His eyebrows were slashes of shocking black in that ivory complexion, demonically arched and insinuating. His grin was openly seductive, teasing Jess with that hint of tongue, but there was something unexpected around his eyes— something soft that made Jess soften in return.

He thought about Brandewine, and about Miranda and her expectations of him. Her wishes for him and the way she thought his life should be, and the fact that Frankie was a self-confessed slut who hit on any Market employee who caught his fancy. Then Jess thought about what an entirely sucky job he'd done of ignoring Frankie and the part of himself that Frankie tempted.

"I do have rules," he admitted, keeping his voice deliberately quiet. "Good reasons for them, too." He took a deep, fortifying breath and got a whiff of essence of Frankie: smoke and tobacco and whiskey. It gave him the courage to continue.

"Sometimes, though, you have to break your own rules."

Frankie nodded. "How you know you're alive, innit? I've broken damn near every rule society, the Church, or my own mum could come up with at one point or another— taken every drug, drunk myself into a stupor, danced with the devil himself, and come out grinning. But it's not for everyone, Bit."

That cautionary note in Frankie's tone gave Jess the good shivers, because it meant Frankie was trying, in his own way, to protect Jess. Even if it meant denying himself what he wanted.

And man, didn't that thought send a zing of pleasure straight through Jess.

Frankie wants me. Me. Maybe even likes me a little.

"I wouldn't break my own rules for just anyone," Jess said, choosing his words with care.

Naked lust and something else flared in Frankie's black eyes and he inched closer, his body a burning line of sinew and muscle at Jess's side. Jess was vividly aware of his own rising desire and the almost uncontrollable urge to wriggle on the tall barstool. He itched under his skin, his whole body jumpy and ready for something, anything.

And then Frankie bent his head and slowly, deliberately, thumbed aside the open collar of Jess's green work shirt and pushed his nose into the divot of Jess's collarbone. Jess jumped at the light, searching touch, the rasp of Frankie's stubble on skin he'd never realized was so sensitive.

"This spot," Frankie breathed, rubbing his prickly chin along the line of the bone where the thin skin burned and quivered, suddenly alive with sensation. "This spot here has been taunting me for days."

And he licked Jess's collarbone.

One hot, wet swipe of rough tongue and Jess nearly fell off the barstool.

Frankie's hand clamped on his shoulder, steadying him, just in time to hear the dismayed, "Oh, crap" from across the room.

Jess jerked upright and stared at Adam in absolute horror. Adam's expression wasn't much better, total exasperation mixed with resignation. His hair was even more tousled than usual and his shirt was a wrinkled mess.

"Christ Almighty, Frankie, what did I tell you about that kid? Were you even listening?"

Jess tensed, his mind whirling with the ugly possibilities of what Adam might have told Frankie, but before he could get himself too worked up Frankie replied coolly, "I heard you, mate. And you knew then it was a waste of breath, so don't bother repeating yourself now."

"Shit." Adam sounded unhappy, but although Frankie's eyes never left Adam's, he relaxed against Jess enough to start fingering the collar of his shirt again. He tugged at the point, nudging the fabric over the still-damp patch of skin on Jess's collarbone. Jess shivered and batted at the offending hand, not quite able to look Adam in the eye.

Until a terrible thought popped into his head.

"Chef?" Jess said, hating the quaver in his voice. "Where's my sister?"

Frankie and Adam broke off their staring contest to zero in on Jess.

Even in the midst of his own burgeoning meltdown, Jess noted that Adam's cheeks stained a dull red at the mention of Miranda.

"Uh, she was tired after the cooking lesson so I sent her home to, um, freshen up before service tonight."

"Right," drawled Frankie.

"Shut your damn mouth." Adam rounded on him fiercely.

"Could you . . ." Jess faltered when the chef turned blazing eyes back on him. "I mean. Could you not mention this to her?"

The fire left Adam's face, to be replaced by dawning comprehension.

"She doesn't know you're . . ." Adam gestured toward Frankie's encroaching fingers, now still against Jess's shirt, and Jess wanted to sink into the ground.

"Um, no. She doesn't. And I'd really like to be the one to tell her."

Adam groaned, sounding even less happy than before. He muttered something that sounded like "the death of me" before giving Jess a hard look.

"Soon. Because I don't like secrets. And I won't out and

out lie to Miranda. So make with the true confessions, kid, before she finds out some other way."

"But not from you, right, mate?" Frankie pushed, as serious as Jess had ever heard him.

Adam gave Frankie another look, sort of a quizzical head-cocked one, and whatever he saw made him smile. "Nah, not from me. Just be careful, boys. You're not the only ones with something riding on this."

And with that cryptic comment, he headed into the kitchen, shaking his head the whole way as if he couldn't believe what he'd agreed to.

"There now," Frankie purred in smug satisfaction. "Where were we?"

He lowered his head to Jess's neck, but before he could do more than breathe one scandalously hot sigh over Jess's skin, Jess grabbed hold of his hair and pulled him back. Stoically ignoring the clingy way Frankie's tangled spikes wrapped around his fingers, Jess said, "Will he keep his promise? If he tells Miranda, my life will be seriously fucked."

"Well, it's a good job you're not too dramatic."

Jess made as if to hop down from the barstool, and Frankie hastened to soothe.

"Now, now. Said he'd keep it close, didn't he? He meant it. Adam's as straight as they come, in every sense of the word. Unlike us."

Frankie's devilish grin was infectious. Jess scrunched his fingers in Frankie's hair and grinned back when he bumped his head up into the touch like a cat.

"Unlike us," Jess agreed.

"Yeah, we're quite bent, us," Frankie said.

Jess laughed, the near-miss adrenaline mixing with relief and the thrum of electricity that always ran through him like a current whenever Frankie was around.

"I like that. Bent. Is that a technical term?"

Frankie shrugged. "Better than the alternatives, innit? Now, if that's settled . . ."

The dark, caressing tone in his voice made a quick chill run over Jess's skin. He relaxed his hold on Frankie's hair, allowing it to become more petting than restraining, and Frankie made a hum of enjoyment that melted Jess's bones.

A cacophonous clatter of a large pan dropping and a shout of raucous laughter from the kitchen freaked Jess into a startled jump.

The move knocked Frankie back a step and broke the moment. Frankie half smirked at him while Jess fought to control his galloping heart rate.

"New rule," he said firmly, very aware of what he was starting. "Never inside the restaurant. Agreed?"

Frankie surveyed him for a moment like a man presented with a feast, unable to decide where he'd like to begin. "Agreed. For the moment."

"For the moment?"

"What can I say, Bit." Frankie trailed his long fingers across Jess's shoulder and turned to go. He tossed the last words over his shoulder, the picture of insouciance.

"I've never been much of one for rules."

SEVENTEEN

Miranda slid into the booth at the back of the empty bar down the street from Market, wincing as the cracked vinyl of the seat scratched at her thighs.

"You're late," Robin Meeks accused, his pointed face pinched into an expression of discontent.

"Sorry," she apologized, trying not to show how flustered she felt. It was an uncomfortable sensation. She could still feel the imprint of Adam's hands on her skin as she stared across the table at the man who, for the last week, had eagerly spilled every tidbit of gossip or innuendo he could think of about the Market crew.

Rob shrugged jerkily, his thin shoulders bulked up by the white chef's jacket he wore. They both had to get to Market to start prep for tonight's dinner service, but he'd called Miranda's cell to ask for a quick meeting beforehand.

"Do you have something for me?" she asked.

"Right to business, aren't you?" Rob said, draining his glass. He was drinking something that Miranda at first took to be a soft drink, until she realized there was no ice. Rob gestured to the bartender for another. When the man moved to the tap and began drawing a draft, Miranda raised both eyebrows.

Catching the expression, Rob scowled. "What difference does it make?" he asked, surly. "Not like I have anything complicated to do in that kitchen. A trained monkey could make stock."

Disdaining to remind him of the events of a week ago, when their stock hadn't been up to Adam's standards, Miranda pulled out her notebook and patiently attempted to work back to the main point.

"What's up, Rob? Why did you ask for this meeting?"

Rob drank morosely. "I don't know. I wanted to talk."

Miranda suppressed a sigh. Rob didn't really want to contribute to her book; he wanted a therapist.

"About last night's service? I thought it went pretty well."

Rob snorted. "You would. Chef let you assist on sauté while I was stuck making that freaking stock and running dishes up to the pass all night. It's not fair! I'm supposed to be learning, and Chef pays more attention to the damn dishwasher than he does to me."

Miranda gripped her pen tightly. Rob was annoying, no question. The frequently whiny quality of his voice grated on the nerves. But that didn't mean he was making this stuff up. With her own eyes, Miranda had seen Adam pass Rob over, time and again. And Rob was understandably frustrated.

None of which meant he was an invalid source, Miranda told herself. Information from disgruntled employees was the backbone of many famous news stories. Besides, every night when she got back to her apartment and started to write, she walked a careful line with what could be considered "libel."

Like that makes it okay.

Firmly squashing the strengthening voice of her conscience, Miranda said, "I'm sorry you're unhappy at Market. But Rob, I can't drop everything to come meet you like this

unless you have something for the book. We're both supposed to be at Market right now, getting ready for tonight. I
can't afford to have Adam notice our joint absence and start
connecting the dots. You can't afford that, either."

"Right," Rob said, draining his beer and setting it down
with a loud clink, as if he'd underestimated the distance between bottle and table. How many had he had? "Guess that
means we don't have time for my dirt on Chef Temple."

His sly tone gave Miranda a chill. This was the first
time Rob had intimated that there was anything negative to
say about Adam. Miranda gripped her pen a little tighter.

"What dirt?"

Fingers playing in the condensation rings left by his
beer mug, Rob smirked. The snotty expression didn't quite
cover the unhappiness in his squinty eyes.

"I saved the best for last," Rob said. "Everyone thinks
Chef Temple is so perfect, we all have to quake in our
clogs when we see him coming down the line, but he's no
better than anyone else."

Miranda forced a patience she didn't feel. "Why do you
say that?"

Rob leaned forward, lank hair falling across his forehead. "You know how he got the money to open the restaurant?" he demanded.

"He has investors," Miranda said, taken aback. "That's
perfectly normal, isn't it?" His financial backer was the
one who'd forced Adam to let Miranda into his kitchen,
Miranda remembered now. Eleanor Bonning. Claire had
described her as "brusque."

"Chef Temple has one investor. Uno. And he didn't exactly make an appointment with her and submit a proposal,
if you get what I mean."

Miranda's heartbeat fluttered into hummingbird speed.
She wasn't sure why. "No, I don't."

"Now, I'm not condemning the man. You do what you

gotta do to get ahead in this business. But it's pretty shady, all the same. That investor lady? Eleanor Whatsit? I heard she wasn't going to give him the money, didn't think he had enough experience or some shit. Then next thing you know, the chef's wining and dining her, taking her out, they're all over town together. The chef gets his deal, she signs the papers, and boom! He drops her like a hot skillet."

Miranda felt sick. "What are you saying?"

"I'm saying Chef Temple fucked his way to the top. He did what it took to get his restaurant—not that it was a chore, I bet. That Eleanor chick is decent-looking, in a naughty-librarian kind of way."

Abruptly unable to handle even one more word out of Rob, Miranda slid from the booth and stood. Her stomach was clenched in enough knots to make her fiercely glad she hadn't drunk anything.

"Okay, thanks," she said quickly. "I've got what I need, so I'm heading out."

Rob was already looking past her, searching for the waiter. "I'll be there in a minute."

Miranda nodded and left the bar, head whirling with unwelcome images.

Adam and Eleanor. They'd had a relationship. Worse than that, Adam had used that poor woman and then ruthlessly discarded her. A chill prickled across Miranda's shoulders. Adam had used sex to get what he wanted before, parlaying his charm and sensuality into a hit restaurant.

Could that be the reason for his pursuit of Miranda? To charm her, seduce her into writing only what Adam wanted? With a sinking heart, she acknowledged it was all too likely. Ignoring the corner of her mind that wished she'd never answered her cell, never gone to see Rob at that bar, Miranda resolved to be on her guard.

No more flirting. No more kisses. And definitely no more insanely hot groping up against the kitchen counter.

She had a terrible feeling that might be easier said than done.

It was disgustingly cheesy, but all Adam could think about was that scene from the Jimmy Cagney movie, where Jimmy climbs a tower or something and says, with this maniacal laugh, "Top of the world, Ma!"

Okay, so the movie was *White Heat* and the premise had something to do with Cagney as supercriminal thug, as near as Adam could remember, but still. The near-psychotic euphoria of that moment struck a chord.

Sometimes life was fucking awesome.

A restaurant that was a smash hit after only one week, phone lines burning up with reservations, insanely talented crew—all the things he'd always wanted, the life he'd been working toward since he was eighteen. Plus one stunning extra to top it all off, like the dollop of crème fraîche on a teaspoon of Beluga caviar.

Miranda Wake. A sizzling hot redhead full of contradictions and surprises. They'd squeezed a few more cooking lessons in over the past week, and even though they'd stuck to the culinary stuff, Adam knew it was only a matter of time. Looks passed back and forth, bodies brushed against each other as they moved around the kitchen—at this point, the sparky tension between them was enough to power a six-burner range.

They'd talked endlessly, conversations ranging from politics (they were both liberal—no shocker there, they both lived in Manhattan) to religion (Miranda went to the Methodist church near her apartment; Adam subscribed more to the Church of Sunday Brunch) to pop culture (they agreed that *Aliens* was as close to flawless as a movie could get).

Adam had noticed that when the talk turned personal, Miranda held back. He'd told her all about his crazy family, his Florida retiree parents, his cranky grandmother, and even his loser cousin, Joey, who blew every paycheck on the dogs. Miranda listened to it, soaked it up like a sponge, matter of fact, but she didn't offer much in return. He'd tried to draw her out, ask about her parents and what it was like to lose them so young, but she snapped shut tighter than a fresh oyster.

So okay. She wasn't ready to talk about that stuff yet. But Adam wasn't discouraged. Something was building between them, layer upon layer every time they met, like a flawless terrine, and Adam couldn't wait to finally dig in.

He pictured her tart mouth all pursed in concentration during that first lesson as she cracked egg after egg, and the image made him want to laugh out loud with joy or hug someone or something.

Frankie, innocently stocking the grill station with his *mise en place*, was the victim of Adam's outpouring of emotion. Luckily, he was used to it.

"Oi," he complained when Adam collared him with one arm around the neck and hauled him in for a bear hug.

"Shut up and enjoy it, you deviant," Adam said, releasing him after a pointed squeeze. "You know you love me."

"You're off your nut," Frankie said, attempting an unsuccessful scowl. "What did that scribbler of yours do to you this afternoon?"

"Nothing," Adam said. Nothing except drive him crazy with her sidelong glances and casual touches. And there'd been a moment, when he'd straightened up from removing the parbaked piecrust from the oven, he'd been sure she was about to jump him.

Frankie raised a brow, and Adam smiled. They both knew Adam would spill his guts if there were anything to tell. They didn't do secrets, not with each other.

Which reminded him of the one and only brown spot on the otherwise delectable peach that was currently his life. He was keeping a secret from Miranda. Kind of a doozy, too. Christ, when was that kid brother of hers going to fess up and make an honest man out of Frankie? Not to mention Adam.

"No time for gossip now. Prep, man, prep! We open in three hours."

"If you can keep your mind on business long enough to make it through service," Frankie said.

"Right," Adam agreed. "Let's all hope for that."

"We'll keep our fingers crossed, yeah?"

"Totally," Milo said, skimming past with a huge stainless steel bowl of chopped cucumber. "What are we crossing our fingers for?"

"For my sanity," Adam told him. "And no mistakes today, right, *amico*?"

"Fuckin' A," was the fervent response. "I think my balls are still hiding somewhere behind my pelvic bone, man. You're scary when you get pissed."

Adam gave him a smile full of teeth. "Don't fuck up and I won't have to castrate you."

"Yeah, boss!" Milo saluted sharply with one hand, nearly dropped the bowl, and hurried off to his station looking nervous but on point.

Adam made his rounds of the kitchen, sniffing appreciatively at Violet's fresh-baked poppyseed brioche rolls and exchanging noninterrogatory pleasantries with Quentin as the big man steadily minced garlic.

When he got to the stock prep station, however, he hit a snag.

No Miranda, no Rob Meeks. No perfectly diced mirepoix, carrots, celery, and onions cut to the same size and caramelized to an even, aromatic tenderness.

He knew where Miranda was—he'd sent her home to take a shower after their semisuccessful stab at quiche this afternoon. Crust always seemed like the simplest thing in the world, until you tried to teach someone else how to make it. She'd been caked in flour by the end of the lesson.

But Miranda wasn't the only one who was missing. Adam stood by the stock station and fretted. Robin Meeks wasn't working out as an extern. Little mistakes, piddling small-time stuff, but it added up, and Adam didn't love it.

Like today. It wasn't exactly late yet—there was still plenty of time to get the stock going. But it needed to happen soon, and he didn't have any idea if Rob was just running behind or if he'd totally flaked or what. Not for the first time, he cursed his own soft streak when it came to hosting culinary school externs. They were never as solid as his handpicked crew.

The rest of the guys were all here. Even Billy Perez, stoic at the dishwashing station, spraying down a set of stainless steel mixing bowls. Adam cocked his head and watched the slight frown of concentration on Billy's face. The way the kid took to his menial task like it was his fucking reason for living.

Adam whistled a shrill wake-up call that made everyone in the kitchen glance up from what they were doing. He beckoned Billy over and the crew got back to business. The kid wiped his hands on his apron and walked over, navigating the bustling rows of workspace and darting cooks with ease.

Yeah, this was gonna work.

When Billy reached his side and raised his dark eyebrows inquiringly, Adam planted his forefinger on the empty cutting block between them.

"You see this?" he said. "Know what station this is?"

Billy narrowed his eyes like he wasn't sure what Adam was getting at. Slowly, he said, "It's stock. Veg prep. Right?"

"Yup. And guess who's on it today."

"Looks like no one yet, but usually Rob. And the new girl?" Billy said, shifting his weight. He still wasn't getting it and clearly sort of wished Adam would just let him go back to his dishes already.

Adam clasped his hands behind his back and rocked up onto the balls of his feet. "But Rob ain't here. You are. I want this station going. You up for it?"

Billy's eyes widened and Adam caught the flash of burning ambition flaring up quick and hot.

"I'm up for it," Billy said, his voice fierce and a little lilting with the accent that only seemed to come out of him in moments of stress. And, evidently, moments of joy as well, because Adam could see that the kid was jacked up to the point of jittery nerves at the prospect of dicing a few vegetables.

"I know you've heard me give the spiel about how to make stock. You could probably say it all back to me, in English and Spanish, that's how hard you were listening. Don't think I didn't notice." Adam gave Billy his very best I-know-all-I-see-all look. The guy was duly impressed. Adam remembered again why he loved the young ones, those eager, bright-eyed kids who were drawn to the magic that happened when food met heat.

He'd been one of those kids once. Okay, so in most ways he probably still was. But that was a good thing! He never wanted to lose the sense of shock and awe he got over a perfectly caramelized carrot or a stock so clear you could read the newspaper through it.

Billy didn't have his own knife set so Adam lent him a good eight-inch all-purpose chef's knife and sent him running for the boxes of carrots, onions, and celery that Adam had picked up that morning from the Union Square market.

Adam watched him long enough to see that he'd gotten a good start, but then he got called over to mediate a heated discussion between Frankie and Quentin on the best way to score the meat to ensure maximum penetration of the marinade. He lost track of things for a while, and before he knew it, there were some angry tones emanating from the vicinity of the stock station.

Ah. Rob was here. Miranda, too, looking a little frazzled as the shrimpy, red-faced extern faced off with the calm Hispanic kid.

Adam knew who he'd put his money on.

He sauntered over. "Problem?"

"Yes," Rob said, puffing right up with indignation and smug self-assurance. "The dish boy," he said, sneering, "is off his station. Worse than that, he's pretending to man *my* station."

Adam was amused. "Not to get all Queen of Hearts on your ass, but all the stations around here belong to me. Nobody works anything except on my say-so. And I say you were late, so 'the dish boy' gets a shot."

The told-you-so look Rob Meeks aimed in Miranda's direction was unexpected, and Adam frowned. Wordless communication seemed to point to a level of intimacy that made something ugly coil and tighten in Adam's gut. They'd arrived around the same time. Together? He took another look at the extern: still thin-faced and sallow, with pockmarks and a bad attitude.

Not possible. Not with the way she'd caught her breath this afternoon when Adam pressed close under the pretext of showing her how to roll out the pastry dough.

Just in case, though, he sent Rob over to help Milo with garde-manger prep. The little pisser went, with a barely concealed glower of dissatisfaction.

Adam winked at Miranda and beckoned her over with a slight nod. "How about you stick with me tonight? See how we do things up at the pass."

She stiffened for a beat, then appeared to force herself to relax. "You mean I get a break from dicing? I'm there. The blisters on my blisters are starting to get blisters."

Adam laughed at her mock-aggrieved expression and

made the appropriately impressed noises over her proffered palms. There were indeed several deeply red and abraded spots, right where the handle of the knife pressed against the knobs of bone at the ends of her fingers. Pretending a need to examine them more closely, Adam took her hands in one of his.

"Yeah, the knife work can be brutal when you're first starting out." He stroked one finger lightly down the center of her palm and was highly gratified by her immediate and pronounced shiver.

"The key," he continued, rubbing delicately at the sensitive skin surrounding her cute little protocalluses, "is to keep at it. Build up new, thicker layers of skin that can withstand the constant repetitive motion."

Miranda jerked her hands away. "So. You're saying I should go help Rob with the prep so I can toughen up?"

Adam frowned. "No, I still want you with me tonight. It'll be good for your book." There, that was believable, right?

Or not. Miranda raised one skeptical brow, but she didn't call him on it, and Adam let out a surreptitious relieved breath. Not that it was a total lie. Truth was, he'd mellowed on the whole book thing over the last week. Once he'd had time to think about it, it wasn't such a bad thing. And after a week of getting to know her better, he trusted Miranda. The kind of book she was sure to write could only benefit Market.

So it was with real sincerity that he said, "I'm serious. I wanted you to learn to cook, and you're well on your way."

That made her laugh out loud, the sound tinged with a bitterness that bewildered Adam. What was going on with her?

"Now I know you're lying," she accused.

He thought of some of the culinary crimes perpetrated by the lovely woman in front of him, from the overpoached eggs to the scalded-milk debacle to the mess she'd made of a simple roasted chicken, and squinted one eye shut. "Okay, maybe 'well on your way' is overstating it. But you're trying and that's what counts. You know, since I'm not paying you or being forced to eat your cooking."

A reluctant smile tugged at the corner of her mouth, and Miranda loosened up enough to slug him in the chest. Adam grinned.

"All I meant was, and *ouch,* by the way, was that there's more than one way to work in the kitchen and every job is important. That's what privileged culinary-school brats like Rob Meeks don't get. He thinks he's better than a mere dishwasher because he's got some classroom training. But Billy Perez has been here since day one, working his ass off doing whatever is asked of him and paying attention. I'd lay you better than even odds he could do nearly any job in here. Whereas Rob can barely manage to show up for his shift on time, and when he is here, he's usually too busy kissing my ass to do his job."

"But Rob has had a lot of specialized training," Miranda pointed out. "It seems like he'd be a more valuable asset than someone with no experience."

Adam shrugged. "It does seem that way. I don't know, all I can tell you is that from what I've seen, hard work and potential? They trump experience every single time." He led her up toward the pass where it was quieter, a little out of the way of the cheerful chaos of the kitchen.

"Interesting," Miranda said. "So, do you think Billy has the potential to do your job?"

Her tone was half teasing, half combative, but Adam took it seriously. "I do, actually. Maybe not tonight, but someday. Yeah. He's got it."

"What?" she pushed, frustrated as always with Adam's inability to articulate.

Adam rocked on his heels, trying to put the indefinable

into words. "Billy Perez has 'it,' that fire, passion, drive for perfection, insanity"—he laughed—"whatever you want to call it."

"Ambition?" she asked, trying to pin it down.

"It's more than that. It's more than a love of food or cooking, or a need to succeed. I mean, it's all of those things, but other things, too. Sorry, I suck as an interview subject." He kneaded the back of his neck with one hand. This was the only time Adam ever felt self-conscious in his whole life, practically, when Miranda was staring at him with those laser eyes, trying to yank a coherent response to some question out of him like tugging the wishbone from a goose.

"No," she surprised him by saying. "I've learned a lot from you these past few days."

For a moment it seemed as if there were more she wanted to say. He could almost see the words forming in her mouth, but she pressed her lips together in an almost unhappy line instead. And then she flushed a little in that way he loved and it made Adam smile, his momentary awkwardness and her strange air of sadness forgotten.

"And tonight, you're gonna learn even more," he said grandly, sweeping one arm out to encompass the long horizontal opening onto the dining room.

"*Oui*, chef," she said, saluting smartly, and Adam loved the way her blue eyes sparkled in the harsh kitchen lights. That feeling was back, that top-of-the-world mojo, and he knew down to the soles of his feet that this was going to be a night to remember.

EIGHTEEN

What a difference a week makes, Miranda thought. A few short days ago, she'd confidently believed in the version of Market she'd presented to her publisher, with a cocky, overrated chef, terrible working conditions, and employees who were the very next thing to criminals. Well, she'd at least believed it enough to commit to basing a book on it and to accept the offer of insider information from a disgruntled employee.

And now? Everything was all jumbled up.

The people working here were happy. The customers were happy.

Miranda was happy.

Well, she would've been if she didn't have this book deal hanging over her head. Not to mention the tension over the true source of Adam's interest in her. Despite Rob's story about Eleanor Bonning, despite common sense, part of Miranda desperately wanted to believe that what she had with Adam was different. Special.

Ridiculous.

She sighed and let her mind wander while Adam went over the menu with Grant. The serving staff was beginning to pile into the kitchen to taste the evening's specials so they could recommend things to customers.

Miranda hung back, her stomach too tight and knotted to handle the pickled-cherry clafouti, a tender puff of lightly sweetened pancake dotted with tart cherries, black with juice, and its little fan of perfectly crisped slices of duck breast. From the moans and groans of the servers, she was missing out, but Miranda couldn't think of anything except the crop of rumors and gossip she'd gotten from Rob Meeks.

This cook has four illegitimate kids, that one has been in rehab six times. The servers are all screwing each other in the locker room except the ones who are screwing the cooks in the walk-in cooler.

Miranda's eyes went automatically to Jess, joking around with Grant and the others, fencing with the tasting forks, and generally acting like the kid he was. Just looking at Jess, Miranda knew that not everything Rob had told her was the absolute truth. Even if Jess had been unaccountably busy for days, out late and up early, she was sure he wasn't here at Market messing around with one of the pretty hostesses or that exotic-looking bartender.

But absolute truth wasn't the point, she reminded herself. Having a source willing to go on record was enough for a trashy tell-all book like the one she was writing. The very thought turned her stomach again. God, what was she doing?

The words she'd written every night this week after getting home from her shift at the restaurant burned in her brain in letters two inches high.

Why not picture them flaming, with red devils and pitchforks cavorting around them? she mocked herself silently, but the shame refused to ease up.

She hadn't been lying when she told Adam she'd learned a lot from him. Not all of those lessons centered around the stove. She was beginning to understand and appreciate Adam's hedonistic love of life, as well. That ability to live so fully and truly that every action, every sensation, was magnified a hundredfold. Miranda had taken many short, exhilarating dips in the incandescent river of energy that poured through Adam, and she thought she could learn to navigate it pretty well, if she had the time. But time was running out. She had a due date looming—her editor wanted the rough draft of the book on Monday.

Miranda didn't fool herself that there would be any more lessons in fun and food with Adam once the truth about her book came out. He'd hate her guts, and rightly so. It was why she hadn't let herself go as far as she wanted to with him. As if keeping her hands off him for the last week would make that damn book forgivable.

She looked at Jess again. It was all for him, when it came right down to it. She needed money for his tuition. Period. The move into book publishing was something she'd always wanted, sure, but she'd never imagined it being like this. She'd pictured a serious, almost scholarly work of investigative journalism—not the horrible, tacky scandal sheet she'd come up with. Between Rob's vicious stories and a looming deadline, Miranda had been shocked at how easy it was to slap words onto paper. Or type them into the computer, as the case may be.

If it were any good, if it had required any sort of thoughtful consideration, it would've taken longer to write.

The question now became, was it worth it? She was in pretty deep, yes. But not over her head. There was still time to get out of it, even if it meant she'd have to sacrifice the advance money she'd been paid on spec. The advance money she'd earmarked for Jess's future.

Watching Jess pass his fork to the next server with a sunny smile and an appreciative sidelong look at Frankie, who'd dreamed up this particular dish, Miranda was pretty sure she knew what her brother's answer to that question would be.

Since it was Frankie's show, his special, Adam seemed to have left the gaggle of wait staff to make one of his tours of the kitchen. He did that periodically throughout every service, doling out compliments and critiques in equal measure. She hadn't heard him raise his voice since that first day, when they'd almost served slimy soup to a customer—until now.

"Christ Almighty! What is it with you?"

Every head in the kitchen swiveled to see who was the hapless object of Adam's aggravated snarl, and Miranda's heart gave a stressed squeeze when she saw that it was Rob Meeks.

He'd been giving Miranda see-what-did-I-tell-you looks ever since they hit the kitchen, and she'd passed jumpy about an hour ago. Now, watching her secret source get chewed out, Miranda couldn't help but shrink back a little. Even knowing that a true journalist would have whipped out her notebook at the first sign of conflict.

The struggle had to do with her own totally inappropriate and intensely inconvenient feelings for Adam.

Hard-nosed journalist or not, Miranda defied anyone to withstand days of unfairly adorable banter, sweetly earnest one-on-one cooking lessons, and the onslaught of Adam's powerful, immensely attractive body, without falling a teensy bit under the guy's spell. If it was all a con to get her to puff him up in the book, it was a masterful one—but, thinking rationally, Miranda was nearly positive Adam was completely on the level. He wasn't a terribly complicated man: what you saw was what you got. His overriding characteristic was passion, which could be a lovely, lovely thing to be on the receiving end of. Miranda's skin tingled just thinking about it.

Or, depending on the situation, Adam's passion could

explode in a far less pleasant manner, all over the person un-
lucky enough to have trifled with his search for perfection.

Poor Rob. Even if she didn't like him very much—
a week of clandestine meetings in sleazy bars hadn't im-
proved on Miranda's initial impressions of Rob Meeks as a
slippery little suck-up with a gigantic sense of entitlement—
she had to cringe at the absolute frenzy of disbelieving
fury Adam was whipping himself into at Rob's expense.

Over . . . what was it? Miranda attempted to pick up the
thread of the tongue-lashing.

"What is it with you, kid?" Adam was asking. "I mean,
seriously, I want to know. What the fuck is it with you that
every single day you come here and screw something up?"

He paused as if waiting for an answer, but when the red-
faced Meeks opened his mouth Adam steamrolled right
over him.

"No, I know what it is. I've seen it before. You just don't
care. You don't care if the veg is diced fine and even, you
don't care if the stock simmers long enough, you don't care
if the parsley's wilted, *you don't care if the leftover roast
gets wrapped up and put in the walk-in before it cools
down all the way.*"

Adam's voice rose to thunderous on that last one. For
the first time, Meeks looked scared and belligerent instead
of just belligerent.

"Do you have any idea how dangerously unsanitary that
is?" Adam asked, dropping his voice to a lethal near-
whisper that was no less frightening than the yell. "The
bacteria that breeds, the sickness we could spread to our
customers if we used that meat?" Adam narrowed his eyes.
"Of course you do. You're an Academy of Culinary Arts
student, as you love to remind us all. I know for a fact this
gets covered in Basic Principles of Sanitation. So why the
hell am I looking at a sheet of plastic wrap around a warm
end of veal roast?"

This time Rob didn't even bother. He hung his head in silence, his mouth a sullen line.

Adam shook his head in disgust.

"Get out."

That brought Rob's head up.

"What?"

"You heard me. Get out of my kitchen. And don't come back, you piece of shit excuse for a cook. I won't have you slopping around here day after day, dragging down the whole crew with that chip on your shoulder. You've never been satisfied with the way we've treated you—so fine. Go."

Rob's mouth dropped open, his narrow face blotched with shock. He looked around the kitchen and zeroed in on Miranda as if he wanted her to speak up in his defense.

Which Adam, of course, noticed. Miranda cursed inwardly and tried to look innocent. Her heart beat out a fast tattoo against her ribs.

Rob's imploring of Miranda only seemed to further enrage Adam, who roared, "Get out!" one last time and accompanied it with a quick shake of the hapless extern by the scruff of his neck.

Gasping and flopping like a landed trout, Rob shook himself free of Adam's big paw and hurried for the back alley door.

"Haven't seen him move that fast in days," Frankie drawled, and everyone laughed, more out of relief at the broken tension than anything else.

Adam blew out a breath and shook himself like a dog coming out of the water. "Okay, that's over. Kick ass at tonight's service and drinks are on me at Chapel tonight!"

He's inviting us all to church?

The crew cheered long and loud, sounding like a gaggle of pirates straight out of an old Errol Flynn movie. Miranda caught her breath as her heart started to pound out of control.

Everything was happening so fast! One minute she was agonizing over her use of a cranky employee's insider info and the next minute that crank was out the door. She hardly knew how to feel. But when Adam caught her gaze and lifted his brows slightly, Miranda couldn't stop herself from smiling back at him and making the line of his shoulders relax away from the tense set of the last few minutes.

She supposed that might be her answer, right there.

Adam made his way back over to the pass as activity in the kitchen spun up into controlled chaos once more.

"Feel better?" Miranda asked him.

"Surprisingly, I do, yeah," Adam responded, laughing and running his hands through his hair. It was all messed up, sort of endearingly bedheadish, and it made Miranda long to smooth it down.

"You're not fooling around, are you?" she said, shaking her head. "That poor kid."

Adam scrunched up his face. "That poor kid, nothing! He cocked up everything he touched for weeks."

Ignoring the exaggeration—Rob Meeks wasn't a culinary genius, but he wasn't a total moron, either—Miranda said, "It doesn't look like he'll be much missed." She gestured to the steadily humming kitchen where ex-dishwasher Billy Perez was skimming the top of the stock like he'd been born to it.

"Meeks never fit in here. I thought it would be okay, since it was just an externship from the ACA, a temporary thing, but no. He had to go. Why?" He peered at her suspiciously. "You gonna miss him?"

And then it hit her.

Rob Meeks's departure from Market was the perfect excuse to cancel the book deal. Her heart beat faster, pulling enough blood from her head to make her dizzy with elation at the thought.

She didn't *have* to do the book. She could throw out the

manuscript—so what if it was half done already?—and tell the publisher she was out. She'd lose the advance money, sure, but Jess was happy with his job at Market. He'd mentioned taking a year off school and working full-time to save up. Or Miranda could go back to doing freelance reviews in addition to her job at *Délicieux*. She'd scrape together collateral and get a loan. They'd make it work.

Miranda felt lighter than she had in days, as if fate had just handed her a big bunch of helium balloons. She smiled up at Adam, who was still watching her expectantly.

"I really won't miss him at all."

"Good," he said, a bit more firmly than Miranda thought the situation warranted.

Before she could do more than raise a brow, Grant pushed into the kitchen. He spared Miranda a quick hello before dragging Adam into an intense, low-voiced conference a few feet away.

By this point, Miranda knew better than to be offended. Around four forty-five every evening, as it got closer and closer to the moment when Market's doors opened, Grant got ratcheted tighter and tighter in the flurry to get everything ready for the night's service. And she supposed, as restaurant manager, it was understandable he'd be freaking a little right now about Adam's summary firing of their extern.

In fact, that's exactly what Grant was upset about. Miranda wandered closer to get a better listen—just because she was no longer writing the book, it didn't mean her journalistic instincts were suddenly comatose.

"You couldn't have waited until after tonight's service?" Grant wanted to know. His voice was a tad shrill and Miranda saw Adam's mouth twitch at the corners as if he were hiding a grin.

"Sorry, man, but no. He was bringing down the whole kitchen vibe with his attitude."

Grant huffed.

"Fine, but you know this is going to cause problems. The ACA is going to want to send another extern, since we committed to a full semester, and who knows what barrel bottom they'll be scraping this late in the game."

"Worry about tomorrow when it happens," Adam advised, nodding his head sagely. "We've got enough going on today."

"Right, like who's going to take over Rob's station."

"Already covered." Adam pointed to Billy Perez like a proud papa at Little League. "He's a champ."

Grant did not appear to share Adam's enthusiasm. "Is that our dishwasher?" he asked through gritted teeth.

"Yup," Adam said. "He's working his way up, just like I did."

"That's a beautiful story, boss, and I'm so pleased we could help Billy's career, but who the hell is going to wash the dishes tonight!"

Adam's eyes widened, then went shifty. He clearly hadn't considered that yet.

Miranda stepped in. "May I make a suggestion?"

"Please do," Grant moaned, one hand on his forehead.

Adam appeared highly entertained, but swept a generous hand in front of her as if inviting her to do her worst.

"First of all, stop panicking," she told Grant. "If worse comes to worst, I'll wash the dishes. Second of all, you've got resources at your fingertips. Frankie knows every kitchen worker in town. See if he can think of anyone to replace Billy."

Adam looked impressed and Miranda felt an instantaneous glow of satisfaction. There was really nothing in the world like solving a problem.

"Hey, not bad. Thanks, Miranda. Yo, Frankie!"

"Yeah?" Frankie shouted from his hunched position over the grill as he gathered his nightly *mise en place*, little bowls of garnishes, marinade, and dry rubs with brushes, and different kinds of infused oils, all arranged precisely to be ready to hand when it came time to assemble his orders.

"C'mere a minute, we need your expertise."

Frankie loped over, wiping his hands on a towel tucked into his pants.

"Go through your mental Rolodex," Adam told him. "Who do we know that can pinch-hit some dirties for us tonight?"

Frankie squinted. "Didn't Finnigan's just close on Eighty-third? Should be some blokes looking for work right about now. I'll make a couple calls."

Adam clapped him on the shoulder and gave Grant a look. "See? All taken care of."

"Sure, thanks to Miranda," he replied tartly. "If it were up to you we'd be buried in crusty dishes before the second turn."

"Yes," Adam said, "but the stock would be perfect."

Service was a breeze. Okay, fine, more like a gale-force wind, but smoother. And the energy in the kitchen! Adam couldn't quantify the change, but he felt it. Heard it in the increased communication between cooks as they worked to get their plates up to the pass simultaneously. Tasted it in the silky white-asparagus soup and caramelized fennel jus for the pan-roasted chicken.

Even Miranda seemed less like a stress case than usual. Not that she was ever annoyingly neurotic or anything. Mostly she was a little tightly wound, in an endearing way.

But up at the pass with Adam, instead of working stocks and filling in where needed with Rob Meeks, Miranda nearly bubbled over with good cheer. It was moderately distracting.

Make that maximally distracting, he thought, as she reached across Adam to place a newly sauced and dressed chicken entrée on the waiting tray. Her sweetly rounded upper arm brushed his chest and Adam felt the jolt zing from his nipple straight to his cock. Fucking ridiculous.

Kinda like the way he probably looked, standing motionless at the pass while both Miranda and the waiter— *Christ, it's her kid brother*—waited for him to release the tray.

What table is this?

"Table twenty-eight, go," he pulled out of his ass, and the kid went. So his voice was a little hoarse, who'd notice in all the commotion, right?

"Are you okay?" Miranda asked, all wide-eyed concern. She even put her dainty little hand on his bicep, which, okay. So not helping the situation with Adam Jr.

"Fine," he croaked. "Ahem. Good job on the plates. You've got a real touch for it, they look excellent."

Score! Pretty pink suffused her cheeks. "It's fun," she said, ducking her head a bit. "It feels artistic, like painting or something. That probably sounds lame to you."

"No, no. Not at all. I don't like to think of myself as an artist—in my experience, chefs who talk about food as art are all douches—but presentation on the plate is highly key. You experience food through all your senses, which is what makes it so powerful. How it looks is your very first sensual contact with it, so it's gotta look perfect. Enticing. And there's definitely a kind of artistry to that."

"Do you ever worry . . . ?" She paused and pursed her lips.

"What?" he prompted her, wanting to take advantage of this short, unexpected lull between tables to talk to Miranda as much as possible. Working the pass with her was exhilarating, but not so much with the communication and getting to know each other.

Something Adam found himself unexpectedly but completely interested in.

"Well," she said reluctantly. "You use the word 'perfect' quite a bit—doesn't it ever bother you that perfection is ultimately unattainable? As a goal, it's not very practical."

That's my little pragmatist, he thought fondly. He knew better than to say it out loud—outside his head, it was sure to sound patronizing.

"I guess you're right," he said instead. "But perfection isn't really my goal."

"No?"

"Nah." He grinned at her, aware with his sixth sense, his kitchen sense, that the cooks were about to start running hot vegetables and meat up to the pass for plating.

"Perfection isn't the goal—the pursuit of perfection, though." Adam reached for words, wanting her to understand. "Striving for perfection, to be better all the time, to be flawless; that's the goal."

She looked utterly bewildered for a moment, which was such an adorable look on her that he almost lost the thread of the conversation for a minute before her brow cleared.

"I get it," Miranda said, like she'd just unraveled the Fibonacci sequence or something.

"You do?"

She nodded. "Perfection isn't your goal; ceaseless struggle is your goal. Never losing the drive to be perfect is your goal. And taking it all seriously—like you said that first night, it's always life-or-death to you."

Miranda was maybe the most brilliant person Adam had ever known. "That's it exactly," he crowed. "I think I'm gonna keep you around to write the Market mission statement and stuff. You put it all into words so much better than I do."

"That's my job."

The reminder sobered him and he paused to search her

face. Miranda usually sort of seized up when she talked about her work, like it stressed her out even to think about it. Not that she ever liked to discuss personal things. But tonight she mentioned her job with a funny little half-smile that Adam couldn't read at all.

He puzzled for a moment, unease filling him. He'd made his peace with the idea that she was writing a book about him, mostly by putting the entire issue out of his mind. But there were moments when he couldn't ignore that it made him nervous. He'd bared his soul to Miranda lots of times, but there was still so much he didn't know about her.

This wasn't the moment for angsty soul-searching, though. The cooks were swarming the pass and servers were waiting to take plates to their tables, and he didn't have time to think about anything but getting the food out.

NINETEEN

Music throbbed in the thick, smoky air of the underground bar, loud and nasty and utterly exhilarating. Miranda was shocked at herself for finding it all so exciting—but heck, she was pretty shocked at everything she did lately.

For once, though, for once ever in her life she was going to live in the moment and not second-guess every damn thing. Somehow she suspected this cramped dive bar had seen more than its share of rebellious moment-to-moment-living devotees.

"Earlier, I thought you said something about going to chapel," she shouted in Adam's ear.

He bent closer so they wouldn't have to scream the whole conversation. "Chapel," he clarified. "It's the name of the bar. We came in the back way, so maybe you couldn't tell, but we're actually in the basement of an abandoned church that was turned into an avant-garde theater decades ago."

"A theater, huh? We must be at least thirty blocks from Times Square."

"Yeah." Adam laughed. "It's way Off Off Off Off Broadway. The director's a real nutbar, has the actors do stuff with bats and glassblowing and feathers onstage."

"Really?"

"It's not as kinky as it sounds," he assured her with a grin.

That smile of his, those deep dimpled creases in his cheeks—Miranda had to firm up her knees. It was ludicrous, she wasn't some swoony teenager.

"And I suppose no one here got the memo about New York's new smoking laws?"

The bar smelled like . . . well, like a bar. The way they all used to smell before New York outlawed smoking in public places. Miranda didn't smoke, had never smoked, so it had really surprised her how much she'd missed that tobaccoy taint when out at night. It just didn't feel like a bar without that haze of blue-gray stinging her eyes.

Chapel was a serious bar.

And apparently very well known to the entire kitchen and front-of-house crew, every single one of whom had taken Adam up on his offer of a free round. She'd lost Jess the instant they arrived. She thought he was up near the stage someplace with the other servers and a few of the cooks.

"Does it look like anyone in here is about to call the cops?" Adam asked, gesturing to the eclectic bunch of patrons propping up the bar.

"If I were a cop, I'd be scared to come down here," she shot back.

"Aw, we're not that bad," Adam protested. "This is our place, we don't let shit get too out of hand. But it's a true after-hours joint—no one even shows up to unlock the door until around eleven. Isn't that right, my man?"

He reached over her shoulder to bump fists with the bartender, a compactly muscled man with shoulder-length brown hair and denim-blue eyes.

"Miranda, meet Christian Colby, the owner of this fine establishment. Chris, this is Miranda. My new kitchen slave."

Christian looked her up and down. "Nice work. And Temple's right. This place ain't no tourist attraction; nobody comes here but folks crazy enough to be getting off work right about now. Cooks, actors, reporters, musicians."

"Sounds very . . . artsy," Miranda said.

The bartender smiled, wide and white against his tanned skin. " 'Artsy'? With that racket onstage?"

He shouted that last loudly enough to be heard over the din of a drum solo that seemed to involve a very excited bald, shirtless man banging away at his cymbals with more enthusiasm than musicality. Frankie was up there, too, she noticed. Playing bass and grinning like a maniac.

"Brought your whole brigade tonight, huh?" Christian asked casually, his intense blue eyes on the crowd by the stage.

"Every last one, so be nice," Adam said.

"I won't rile Grant, so long as he doesn't rile me."

Before Miranda could ask what that was all about, the barman changed the subject with a breezy: "So you want a drink, or what?"

"Gimme something with gin," Adam said. "The good stuff. And Miranda likes . . . actually, I don't know. What's your drink, sweetheart?"

"Don't call me sweetheart," she said automatically. "And what sort of drink do you recommend?" She surveyed the back of the bar, haphazardly piled with an astonishing assortment of liquors.

"My boy Christian, here, is a master mixologist," said Adam. "Any cocktail you can think of, he can make. And probably tell you the history of it, too."

"Then I'll let him surprise me."

"How about I give you what Adam's getting, then? My own creation, called a Ginger Lemonade."

"That sounds perfect," Miranda said. "Thanks." She reached for her purse, but Adam stayed her hand.

"Nuh-uh. Tonight's on me, remember?"

"For the crew," Miranda argued, shaking her wallet at him.

"You're part of the crew," Adam said, and the world around Miranda seemed to stop.

That cemented it. There was no way she could publish that book now. She'd gotten too close, lost all objectivity. Maybe it was weak of her, maybe it meant she'd never be a serious journalist, but the relief that flooded her system when she thought of backing out of her publishing contract convinced her it was the right decision.

Adam glanced over and gave her that long, slow smile, the one that lit him from within. Miranda smiled back with no guilty secrets pressing on her heart. It felt so damned good.

While Christian mixed, stirred, shook, and strained, Adam squinted down the bar, checking out the other patrons.

"I think I've worked with at least half the guys in here."

"Cooking is a very incestuous business," Miranda observed.

Adam whistled low and pointed to the far corner of the bar where a man sat hunched and alone.

"Speaking of guys I've worked with," he said. "Yo, Dev!"

Miranda felt a chill tighten the hair at the nape of her neck. Crap, if this was who she thought it was . . .

With a sense of inevitability, Miranda watched as megastar superchef Devon Sparks raised his head.

He looked strained and exhausted as he scanned the bar, but when his eyes lit on Adam, and Miranda next to him, one sardonic eyebrow rose almost to his hairline. He stood up and Miranda clenched her teeth against a reflexive *Oh, shit*.

Devon sauntered over, a vision of movie-star handsomeness with his artfully tousled mink-brown hair, ice-blue eyes, and overly articulated bone structure. The collar of his black sport coat was turned up, as if against a cold gusting wind, giving his already dramatic visage a boost of gothic mystery.

"What have we here?" he asked in that smooth, TV-perfect voice. "Two of my favorite people having a cozy little drink in the best bar in town."

"You ready for another, Dev?" Christian asked, sliding Adam's and Miranda's drinks across the bar.

"I'll have whatever they're drinking," Devon said without taking his eyes off Miranda.

There was nothing objectionable in any of his comments or even his manner, but somehow the entire interaction reeked of Devon Sparks's contempt for Miranda and everything she stood for.

"Chef Sparks," she said, keeping it as cordial as possible. "I'd never have expected you to frequent a place like this."

"Oh, Devon's an old regular at Chapel," Adam said easily. Was he oblivious to the undercurrents of tension throbbing between his ex-boss and Miranda?

"Yes. And I still enjoy slumming occasionally." Devon's lip curled slightly and Miranda revised her opinion of him from *Overrated Asshole Chef* to just plain *Asshole*.

"Fuck you." Adam chuckled. "You can't go a week without this place. We remind you where you came from."

"Yeah, before you got all high and mighty," Christian put in, handing Devon a Ginger Lemonade.

In all the tension, Miranda had neglected to taste her cocktail and the glass was starting to get slippery with condensation. She took a sip and nearly gasped as concentrated spicy ginger burst over her tongue. The sweet, hot ginger and the cool, tart lemon contrasted beautifully with the subtly herbal flavor of the gin, and Miranda knew she was going to have to watch out.

She couldn't afford a repeat of the rose-berry-vodka incident.

"This is a winner, man," Adam was saying to Christian. "Perfect for summer. I could drink these all damn night."

Devon's attention was still riveted on Miranda.

"I so enjoyed your review of Appetite Vegas," he said silkily. "You have quite a way with words."

"Thank you," she replied. It was usually better not to engage. Sometimes the incensed chef got bored if she didn't provide any opposition.

"The part where you called the restaurant . . . what was it? Oh, yes. 'A romper room of highbrow hackery.' That was simply inspired. My publicist particularly enjoyed the passage that described me as a past-his-prime heartthrob with pretensions of culinary mastery, only interested in catering to the rich and tasteless."

Miranda pressed her lips together. "Yes, Simon Woolf called the magazine to express his displeasure. I'm sorry if you didn't like the review, but I gave my honest opinion."

"Honest," Devon scoffed. "Who gives a shit about your honest opinion? Certainly not your readers. All they care about is that you reliably skewer any chef who dares to make a success of himself."

She shrugged. What could she say? It was no more than the truth, something that she'd thought herself many times in moments of discouragement. Still, it wasn't pleasant to hear it out loud, hurled as an accusation by that too-perfect, multimillion-dollar mouth.

"It's not my fault your 'successful' restaurants have lost the integrity they started out with."

"And it's not my fault you make your living by exposing your bitterness to the world. You need to get laid."

Adam tuned back into the conversation just in time to

catch that last salvo. The deep brown gaze flashed dark and angry for a moment, but Adam was the picture of calm and casual as he looped a friendly arm around Miranda's neck.

"Now, kiddies, play nice. Or I'm going to have to separate you."

"Don't bother," Devon sneered, slamming his untouched cocktail down on the bar. "I'm leaving. It's a little too crowded in here tonight for me." Pinpointing Adam with a narrow glare, he tossed out, "And don't come sobbing to me when this one plays you for the idiot you are. I know all about your little bet, and trust me, brother, Miranda Wake will screw you as soon as look at you."

"But not in the fun way. Is that what you're saying?"

Miranda felt Adam's tension in the rigidity of his arm across her shoulders. She wanted to jump in and tell them both off for talking about her as if she weren't in the room, but part of her was too busy reveling in the feeling of leaning into Adam's solid strength and letting him stand up for her. It was a novel experience. Not one she thought she could ever truly grow accustomed to, but it was fun for a change.

Devon snorted and turned on his heel. He strode out of the bar without a backward glance, leaving poor Christian shaking his head and mopping up the Ginger Lemonade that had sloshed from Devon's glass.

"Thanks," Miranda said. "I could've handled him on my own, but it was nice not to have to."

"Anytime, sweetheart," he replied with a lazy sideways smile. "Devon's not a bad guy at heart but he can get kind of intense. And you really did a number on Sparks Las Vegas. Yowza."

"It was appalling," she protested, feeling defensive all over again. "The food was bad, the service was worse, and the whole restaurant was decorated like Ivana Trump's boudoir."

Adam snickered. "I'm not sure why he cares so much,

anyway. It's not like he cooked the food. He hasn't run one of his own kitchens in years." He shuddered theatrically. "I could never live like that."

He still hadn't removed his arm and Miranda found herself trusting more of her weight to him with every second that passed. The ginger cocktail was filling her with a warm, sleepy contentment despite the eardrum-piercing old-school punk music thrashing down from the stage across the room. It was as if Adam and Miranda were in their own world, a protected bubble that shielded them from harsh reality.

Until reality burst that bubble with a final clash of cymbals followed by a shrill note of microphone feedback.

Frankie's rough Cockney accent filled the room.

"I don't know about you lot, but I think it's time for a change of pace. Adam, mate, you up for it?"

The crowd right in front of the stage, which was made up mostly of Adam's crew, sent up a huge cheer.

Miranda blinked up at Adam and started to smile.

"You?"

He cringed playfully. "Yeah. Not real seriously or anything, but yeah." He raised his voice to be heard over the catcalling brigade. "Not tonight, guys."

A chorus of jeers and taunts rang out as Miranda turned under Adam's arm.

"Why on earth not tonight? I'd pay good money to see you up on that stage."

"That sounds like another dare. What, you think I'll suck? I'll have you know, lady, that I played Curly in Stuyvesant High's production of *Oklahoma!*, with full-on guitar during that square-dance scene."

Miranda giggled before she could stop herself. "Oh, I can so picture you in overalls and a cowboy hat, with maybe a piece of straw sticking out of your mouth. You're the citiest city boy who ever lived."

"Don't knock the overalls, lady," Adam mock-growled before becoming marginally more serious. He actually ducked his head a bit and it suddenly made him look so vulnerable that Miranda's smile faded.

"So you want to hear me sing? I promise not to pull an Ozzy and bite the head off a bat or anything," he said.

Something about the way he was so obviously uncertain but trying to brazen his way through it made Miranda melt.

"Come on, Curly," she said, reaching up to run her fingers once through his wavy dark hair. "Play me something nice."

His smile down at her was just-finished-the-Sunday-*Times*-crossword big. She got lost in it for a moment, the nearness of him, the weight of his arm still holding her close, and the room did that thing where it faded away, leaving just the two of them. So when he dipped his head to take her mouth, Miranda wasn't thinking about the other people in the bar, the kitchen crew, her brother, or anyone else who might be watching.

All she could think was, *Yes. Now. More.*

The kiss was hard and fast, slanting pressure of lips and stubble-rough chin against hers. Adam's tongue stroked rough and sweet into her mouth, and Miranda opened herself up to it helplessly.

A series of wolf whistles finally penetrated the cloud of lust around her head, and Miranda felt the heat rise to her cheeks as she pushed Adam away and settled back on her barstool. She couldn't stop smiling, though, and when he threw her one last jubilant grin over his shoulder before vaulting up onto the stage, her heart expanded inside her chest until it seemed to press against the walls of her rib cage.

The band members left the stage to Adam, and Miranda couldn't help noticing that it was Jess who held up a hand to steady Frankie's jump down. There was something there that made her uncomfortable, but she kept dismissing it. After years of being told by Jess that she was a paranoid worrywart, perhaps it was finally starting to sink in. And her new campaign to let Jess grow up and be independent wasn't really helped by obsessive worrying over and analysis of every person who befriended him.

Still, she noticed when Jess immediately engaged Frankie in animated conversation, pulling him away from the brightly lit stage and into the shadows beyond.

Before she could get too involved in wondering about that, she was distracted by Adam's low, husky voice amplified by the microphone.

"I'm going to play a little song for you guys," he said, looping the strap of an acoustic guitar over his head. The strap brushed through his hair, disordering the curls crazily, and Miranda imagined she could hear the increased heart rate from every woman in the bar. He just looked so damn sexy.

Adam's warm brown eyes caught hers across the room. Miranda felt the force of his gaze like a physical caress; it made her back arch slightly against the mahogany edge of the bar, her breath coming slow and deep.

"This is for Miranda," Adam said.

He started to play. And as Miranda recognized the opening chords to a song she'd heard before, she experienced a weird moment of perfect alignment between life and art. Adam's voice roughed over the familiar lyrics to the Buzzcocks' biggest hit and Miranda felt every word resonate right down to her bones.

And she realized that she had, indeed, fallen in love with someone she shouldn't have.

TWENTY

His first live show! Jess could feel the excitement bubbling inside him, just waiting for the chance to spill over in a tidal wave of inane babble that would immediately brand him as a total loser from Moronville.

But damn it, this was a big night for him. He was *with the band*. Well, sort of. No one except Frankie and Adam knew about it, and Jess himself wasn't entirely sure what to even *call* it, but still. There was a big part of him silently squeeing that his boyfriend played the bass in a punk band.

There was a difference, Jess had discovered as he stared up at the band onstage, between knowing that Frankie was a punk rocker and actually seeing it. Sort of like the difference between Patti Smith's studio recordings and her live albums. No contest, the live stuff was way better. Raw and emotional, thrumming with heat and life and the untamed fury that characterized the best of seventies punk.

Jess had done quite a bit of research since that first night at Market. He thought he could now be considered something of an expert on punk music.

So when Dreck finished their set, and Frankie finished

pretending he was going to stage-dive and finally let Jess help him off the platform, Jess felt perfectly qualified to say, "You were fantastic! The show rocked."

Frankie was pouring sweat, his normally moon-pale skin red at the cheekbones.

"Yeah? That's odd, because we're usually crap."

Exhilarated and giddy with the pulse-pounding thrill of live music, the residual beat of the bass in his blood, Jess couldn't stop himself from crowding in close. He nudged Frankie playfully in the chest, staring up at the taller man's eyes glittering in the dim light.

"Stop it. Modesty isn't believable on you. You rocked and you know it! That last song, the fast, funked-out version of 'Blitzkrieg Bop'? That was insane."

"Better than the Ramones?" Frankie asked, eyeing Jess keenly.

Jess laughed and pulled him aside, away from the front of the stage where too many people were still pressed together waiting for the next set. Jess saw Adam setting up out of the corner of his eye and wanted to smile for Miranda. In a second or two, she'd know how Jess was feeling—although if that soul kiss they'd all just witnessed was any indication, she was already flying pretty high.

"Answer the question, Bit," Frankie said with a grin. He'd snagged a towel from one of the other band members and was mopping off his forehead and neck.

"Not better than the Ramones," Jess decided, taking the towel from him and rubbing at a patch of sweaty skin just below Frankie's chin. "But that's a trick question. No one's better than the Ramones."

"You've learned your lessons well, young one," Frankie intoned, his voice harsher than usual from screaming backup vocals. He sounded like he'd just smoked three packs of Dunhills in a row. The rough gravel of it sent a shiver down Jess's spine.

"You guys *were* better than the New York Dolls," Jess said.

"Enough of that," Frankie replied sternly. "Heathen. I'll make a Dolls fan of you yet."

"I dunno," Jess said, affecting a skeptical head tilt. "They just don't do it for me. Even if Johnny Thunders is hot."

"And famously bent," Frankie said. There was a sly twist to his smile that made Jess want to lick it.

"You're joking," he gasped. *Get it under control, Jess.* "I never would've believed it of a guy who teased his hair and wore more makeup than my sister."

"Mmm. Not to mention tighter clothes and higher heels."

Frankie grabbed Jess's hand, the one still holding the towel to his clavicle, and squeezed his fingers. He had that predatory gleam in his dark eye, the one Jess had come to recognize over the past few days as a prelude to pouncing. Like one of Pavlov's dogs, Jess picked up the cue and responded instantly with racing blood and shallow breaths.

Their linked fingers started traveling slowly down Frankie's chest, grazing over bone and sinew covered only by a thin red muscle shirt with a large yellow banana and the words THE VELVET UNDERGROUND & NICO on the front.

Jess wasn't sure if he was moving their hands or if Frankie was pushing them down, but for a long moment he couldn't do anything other than watch them and feel the soft wrinkle and tug of vintage cotton slip-sliding over hot, sweaty skin.

They were standing so close together now that their thighs were brushing, denim against denim. Frankie's eyes flashed and Jess knew with a sudden shock that he was about to get jumped in front of God, Miranda, and everybody.

Scary, sure, but even scarier was his suspicion that he might not be able to make himself care enough to stop it.

"Outside," he said hoarsely. "Please."

Frankie wet his bottom lip, slow and obscene. "Sure, Bit. Could use a touch of fresh air myself."

Summer had gone into full swing in the last few days, but even the greenhouse effect of all Manhattan's glass skyscrapers couldn't trap the heat for long. The sun had gone down hours ago and a light crispness rode the night breeze. Jess shivered as it teased across his overheated skin as they emerged from the bar.

Chapel was an underground joint, the thick wooden door nearly hidden from the street unless you knew where to look. Jess had been surprised that the Market crew would bother with the forty-five-minute subway ride to the Lower East Side just to get to their favorite drinking hole when there were plenty of dives, complete with peanut-shell-strewn floors and crop-top-clad barmaids, along Amsterdam Avenue just a few blocks from the restaurant. He supposed it had to do with tradition—most of them had been coming to Chapel after dinner service at other restaurants for years—and the fact that lots of the cooks and servers lived downtown or in Brooklyn, so Chapel was on the way home.

Frankie's place was close by, a grotty attic apartment he laughingly referred to as "the Garret," like some bohemian painter in twenties Paris. Jess adored it. Stepping into the Garret was like entering a sultan's desert tent, all dark and enclosed with sumptuous, if threadbare, material everywhere. Everything from woven Navajo mats to faded Persian rugs covered the entire open space, layering over one another haphazardly and forming a soft barrier between the hard floor and the bare feet Frankie insisted on. There wasn't any furniture to speak of, but the patterned satin pillows, round overstuffed bolsters, and huge tasseled cushions Frankie had picked up at flea markets cast every Garret activity in the most leisurely, decadent version of itself.

Frankie didn't sit down at a table to eat, he lolled against a pile of velvet. He didn't lie down on a bed to sleep, he reclined at his ease in a nest of chenille blankets, beckoning Jess to join him. He'd spent many stolen hours holed up in Frankie's otherworldly den of iniquity, lost in softness, silence, and the newness of everything that happened between them.

They talked. A lot. Well, Jess talked and Frankie looked amused. But even with the cascade of details that had spilled out over the Garret, Jess still hadn't talked about Brandewine University, or why he'd run home to Miranda like a wussy little baby. Part of him wanted to tell, and was sure Frankie wouldn't laugh or judge (he wasn't a very judgy sort of person), but shame always choked Jess before he could even try.

There were few lamps in the Garret, and none with bright, fluorescent bulbs. Crazy antique oil lanterns and a table lamp with a Tiffany glass shade were about it. The slanted ceiling sported a grimy skylight, but it let in more ambient city light than moonlight.

Jess imagined even the sunshine through that cloudy window would be weak and muddy. It was just a guess, though. He'd never actually seen the Garret in daylight. Frankie wouldn't let him stay the night. Not that Jess had really pushed, since he'd yet to come up with a plausible reason to give Miranda for staying out till morning, but still. There was something about the firm but gentle way that Frankie ushered him out the door every night at the crack of three that made Jess suspect Frankie was less than enamored of the idea of spending a whole night in each other's arms. Jess worried about it sometimes, after he got home and tucked into his cold, lonely bed with the boring white sheets and extra-firm mattress. But what could he do? He was still reeling over the fact that Frankie was interested in him at all, on any level.

Jess might not have a whole lot of experience in these matters, but even he knew better than to push for more. That'd be a good way to make Frankie rethink the whole thing.

So even though it cracked his heart a little every time he got that subtle push out the Garret door, he didn't say a word. He wanted to hold on to everything Frankie would give him, for as long as he could. Jess resolutely did not think words like "love," "forever," or "partner." Even "boyfriend" felt like a stretch, so he mostly steered clear of that one, too.

It was like an ephemeral Uelsmann dreamscape—too strange and beautiful to exist in the harsh light of the morning.

Now, as Frankie pushed him against the wall beside Chapel's door, Jess began to suspect another advantage to the bar's downtown location. On the Lower East Side, no one batted an eye. At anything. Other parts of the city, he and Frankie would have to be circumspect. Hide what they were.

Things might have gotten cleaned up a tad during the last mayor's reign of terror, but this close to Alphabet City, that infamous rabbit warren of dilapidated buildings housing hookers, pushers, users, and other disaffected youth, the citywide revitalization project wasn't as obvious. Jess felt fairly certain that in Chapel's 'hood, a little innocent smooching wouldn't ruffle any feathers. Even if said smooching occurred between two guys.

Besides, everyone he really cared about hiding from was inside.

So he didn't protest when Frankie closed the distance between them, sliding one sharp knee between Jess's legs. The contrast between Frankie's heat and the cool air was dizzying. Jess's head spun when Frankie immediately targeted his favorite slice of Jess's anatomy, the sloping, slender rise of collarbone peeking out from his shirt. By now, days after that first hot lick by the bar at Market, Frankie's soft kiss to Jess's sternum was like "hello," a warm, exciting taste of things to come.

Frankie set his teeth lightly, testing the resilient flesh, the hard bone. Jess's knees wobbled.

"I saw you from the stage," Frankie whispered, his voice a hot puff of air against sensitized skin.

"Oh, yeah?" Jess gasped. "What was I doing?"

Frankie chuckled. "Watching me like a right groupie, all starry-eyed."

Jess's mouth dropped open and his whole body went rigid with sudden embarrassment. Frankie snickered again, and Jess relaxed enough to put his arms around his shoulders.

"Shut it, you," Jess grumbled.

"No, I liked it," Frankie protested. "Liked seeing your big blue eyes all wide, staring up at me. Your whole sweet body responding to me, just like you always do, but this time from ten feet away. Nearly drove me round the twist, not being able to touch you right then and there."

Jess shuddered and one hand moved to cup the back of Frankie's head as it nudged gently up his neck and across his jawline.

There was no one in the world like Frankie Boyd. At moments like this, Jess had a hard time remembering his personal moratorium on the L-word.

"The things you say to me," Jess muttered, feeling soft lips mouthing his chin, the scrape of teeth against his jawbone.

"The way you look at me," Frankie countered. "Ought to be criminal, the way you tempt a poor, law-abiding citizen like meself."

"If I were really so tempting, we'd have done more than kiss and grope by now." The words were out before Jess could censor them. He cringed inwardly, wishing he could call them back. Sound like a slut, much? Which wasn't actually what he meant by it at all.

Frankie arched his devil's brow, looking like a mischievous minion of Satan in the shadows of their alcove.

"Eager for more, is it? And not very appreciative of the Herculean restraint being practiced by yours truly."

Jess ducked his head to hide his flaming cheeks against Frankie's shoulder. "No," he said in a muffled voice, "I do appreciate it. How slow we've gone. It's just . . ." He breathed in the heady smell of tobacco and clean sweat from Frankie's T-shirt. For courage.

"I know it must be annoying for you," Jess continued, "waiting around for a fraidy-cat little virgin to be ready."

Frankie clucked his tongue and raised Jess's chin on his fingers to look him straight in the eye.

"None of that," he said firmly. "I won't have you shaming yourself into doing more than feels right and good. Ah, sweet Bit. Don't you see? It's only about what feels right and good to you in the moment. That's all that matters. But you have to listen to yourself, to the beat of your heart and the throb of your blood, to know how you truly feel."

Jess did a little wriggle, wanting simultaneously to get even closer and to back up and hide from this conversation that was making him feel so naked and exposed.

"But how do *you* feel?" he pressed, desperate for the answer. "I mean, I know you've been with lots of people. Not just guys, either." Jess felt the corners of his mouth pull down unhappily. "I can't believe you're not bored to tears with me."

Frankie's eyes burned into his as he pressed deliberately forward into the cradle of Jess's hips. The taut bulge of denim between Frankie's thighs shoved into Jess's lower abdomen, igniting a fire there that took him completely by surprise.

"Does that feel like boredom to you, Bit?" Frankie whispered silkily in Jess's ear.

"No," Jess agreed, sucking in air. Frankie's sinful hips swiveled once in a slow, sure rub. Jess was so hard he thought he might die.

"One look at you does it to me," Frankie muttered against Jess's cheek. "One brush of your shoulder or flash of a smile, and I'm done in. You think this kind of reaction is ordinary everyday humdrummery for me? Not likely. It's been an age since I felt anything like this, and I plan to savor it for as long as it's on offer. Take your sweet time, Bit. I'm in no hurry at all."

Jess panted. Maybe Frankie wasn't in a hurry, but Jess was starting to be. He tipped his head back against the building and stared blindly up at the sky while Frankie made a leisurely exploration of the area behind Jess's left ear.

Time seemed to slow down and speed up at odd intervals. It was like a slideshow—flash of Frankie's long, tapered fingers dropping to Jess's waist and burrowing under his shirt to stroke the ticklish skin there—flash of thighs moving together in a deep rhythm, like dancing in place—flash of Frankie's blue-black hair waving in the breeze, and the sudden soaring realization that Jess could touch it if he wanted, which he did—flash of kiss.

The kiss stopped the show. Everything racked focus down to the meeting of mouths, cropping the rest of the sidewalk, the noise from the bar behind them, the cars honking from the street, right out of the picture.

The kiss wasn't fierce, it wasn't harsh, it wasn't demanding. It was . . . searching. Tender. It said things to Jess, things maybe Frankie didn't even mean him to know, or maybe had been trying to tell him for days without saying the words.

That kiss, that sweet slide of tongue and breath and lip,

convinced Jess right down to his soul that he was wanted. And not only wanted, but cherished.

Jess's heart beat with such wild happiness that he almost missed the last frame of the night's slideshow.

Flash: an ugly snickering laugh from the sidewalk where a couple of college-aged guys stood watching, shoving each other and pointing at Jess and Frankie.

The tension in Frankie's shoulders said he'd heard them, too, but he didn't make it obvious. He withdrew his mouth from Jess's with one last luxurious swipe of tongue across his bottom lip, refusing to be hurried.

Frankie pulled back far enough to catch Jess's gaze. Framing Jess's chin in one hand, Frankie said, "All right, then?"

Doing his best to ignore the hooting, name-calling pair of hoodlums not six feet away, Jess nodded. He could feel it creeping in again, that sick humiliation in his gut that had driven him for months, ever since Brandewine. Usually being with Frankie overwhelmed every other feeling, including shame, but with an audience of obviously drunk frat boys looking for targets, the shame was definitely back. With a vengeance.

"Hey," shouted one of the hecklers. Jess looked over Frankie's shoulder. It was the taller one, a rangy kid a few years older than Jess, with preppy crew-cut blond hair and small, mean eyes.

Frankie turned to face them, heedless of Jess's clutching hands at his sides.

"There a problem, mate?" he drawled.

Shit, what is he doing?

"Come on, let's just go inside," Jess said urgently.

"Now, Bit, s'not nice to interrupt. This gentleman and I were havin' ourselves a chat. Isn't that right?"

"Yeah," the kid shot back, all belligerent. "We were just chatting about what a couple of queers are doing out in public where normal people have to look at them."

His buddy snorted and slugged him in the arm, egging him on.

Frankie actually laughed. It chilled Jess's blood; he was terrified that he knew what would happen next. He resumed tugging on the back of Frankie's T-shirt, trying to edge him closer to the bar door. To Jess's dismay, Frankie shrugged off his hands and sauntered closer to the frat boys, hands in pockets, the picture of insouciance.

"Well, my little hooligan friend, if you couldn't tell what we were doing just now, you must be quite the late bloomer. You're not half bad looking, though. Be happy to give you a pointer or two, if you're feeling confused. I'm sure your boyfriend, there, would thank me."

"You piece-of-shit faggot," the tall one snarled, spit flying from his mouth.

That word. Jess shuddered, his mind throwing him back into the past for a disorienting second.

Crew Cut took a menacing step forward, but Frankie didn't back down. Jess was frozen in horror. He couldn't remember how to get his feet to move.

Until Crew Cut drew back his arm and took a swing at Frankie. Maybe Frankie'd been expecting more taunting and verbal sparring, maybe he'd thought the frat boy was too drunk to hit what he aimed at. Either way, Frankie wasn't prepared for the blow, which took him hard on the chin and knocked him off balance. He staggered a few steps to the left into a pile of metal trash cans.

The cans clattered to the ground, making a huge racket, but Frankie kept his feet.

"You like that, you pansy ass?" Crew Cut taunted.

With that, Jess was up and moving.

Adrenaline surged through him like a searing tidal wave, pushing energy and tension into every limb. The guy who'd been standing there cheering on his homophobic friend made a grab for Frankie as he lunged for Crew Cut, and Frankie turned on his new opponent like a rabid dog. Crew Cut reached for Frankie, clearly intending to pin his arms to his sides, but he didn't get the chance.

Jess let the anger and fear fuel him, putting his head down and barreling into the guy who had first hit Frankie. Jess's forehead and shoulder hit him directly in the midsection with the full force of his body. Something sharp—belt buckle?—caught Jess right above the eyebrow, sending a flare of bright pain through his head.

Crew Cut went down. Jess stood over him, hands fisted tight, breath fast and shallow, and waited to see what he'd do.

The guy wheezed a little, the breath knocked out of him. He made one abortive gesture toward getting up, but collapsed back again with a grunt when Frankie slung the shorter frat boy around by one arm to land on Crew Cut's chest.

"Didn't expect a couple of fags to fight back, did you, boys?" Frankie snarled, bouncing on the balls of his feet as if he couldn't wait to get back to brawling.

"Shit, Kyle, are you okay?" the shorter frat boy asked. He was stocky, the kind of bandy-legged, broad guy who often stood on the sidelines of college ball games just generally making Jess wish football uniforms were less tight.

Pudge got to his knees and helped Crew Cut, or Kyle, Jess supposed, to a sitting position.

"Come on, man, let's go," Pudge said, but Kyle spat on the sidewalk and shook his head.

"No way. Fucking fairies, I'm gonna—"

"You're gonna what?"

Jess whirled, eyes wide. He hadn't even heard Chapel's heavy door swing open. Adam filled the doorway, arms crossed and stance belligerent. Behind him, Jess could just barely make out another guy with shoulder-length hair who was resting what looked like a baseball bat on his shoulder. He didn't see Miranda anywhere, but anxiety strung him tight as a bow. These frat boys had to leave. Like, ten minutes ago.

"I'd listen to your mate, there, Kyle," Frankie put in coolly. "You won't get me with a sucker punch twice. And as you can see, the fairies have friends."

Pudge dragged Kyle to his feet, casting fearful glances at the bar door. Kyle didn't want to back down, but when the bat-wielding man stepped farther out into the alcove, he shook his head in apparent disgust and let Pudge turn them around and pull him down the street.

It was over. Jess gulped in air and blinked rapidly, clearing something thick and smeary from his right eye. Shit, was he bleeding?

"I didn't run away," he realized aloud. "I was scared, but I stuck."

"You did," Frankie said, turning to him and cradling his face in both long-fingered hands. There was a trickle of blood at the corner of Frankie's mouth. It made him look even more dangerous and bad-ass than usual. Frankie's long fingers brushed gingerly at the sore place above Jess's eyebrow, drawing a hiss.

"Think we'll have matching scars?" Jess asked with a grin.

Frankie's lips tightened when he looked at Jess's cut, but his voice was light with laughter when he said, "You were my hero, slaid the nasty dragon for me and all."

"And to the victor go the spoils, right?"

Everything Jess had felt before the interruption by the frat boys came roaring back, heightened and intensified by the lingering rush of danger in his veins. High on adrenaline, he forgot their audience and reached out to clasp Frankie's lean hips, pulling him flush against his body.

"That's what they say," Frankie replied. He ducked in for a kiss.

"Adam, did you find Jess? Is everything okay?" Miranda's concerned voice brought Frankie's head jerking up.

Jess's heart jumped, then sank down into his stomach where panic pumped raw acid in a sudden, queasy gush. He dropped his hands and stepped back in a hurry, ignoring the way Frankie's eyes darkened for a moment.

Miranda pushed between Adam and the other guy to get a good view of Jess and Frankie, standing in the center of a circle of light from the streetlamp overhead.

"We . . . heard a noise, and I didn't see you," she said, sounding uncertain. "Jess. What's going on here?"

TWENTY-ONE

N othing. Everything's fine." Jess sounded normal but distant, as if he were in shock.

Miranda stared at her brother. A million excuses were running through her head for why he was standing there, too close to Frankie, watching her with heartbreaking terror in his eyes.

And then she noticed the blood on Jess's face. Anger swarmed up and over her in a welcome rush, pushing her nebulous fears aside.

"You son of a bitch," she said, stalking forward. Adam put out a hand to stop her, but she shook him off. Christian moved aside easily, and, as if feeling that the threat of danger had passed, he turned and went back into the bar, shutting the door behind him.

Little did he know, thought Miranda. Fury made her feel ten feet tall, and whatever was in her eyes was making Frankie scowl in confusion and dawning worry.

Good. He should be worried.

"Miranda, don't," Adam tried, but she ignored him.

"What the hell did you do to Jess?"

Frankie reared back as she got closer, his gaze cutting to Jess as if looking for a clue about how to answer.

"Eyes on me, scumbag," Miranda hissed. "I asked you a question. What the hell did you do to make Jess bleed? Did you hit him?"

"Whoa, wait a minute there, sweets," Adam said, bounding to her side. "I'm sure Frankie didn't do anything to Jess. Right, guys?"

Jess's eyes were wide and almost blank, the blue as opaque and dark as she'd ever seen it. He didn't even seem to be breathing.

"Had us a bit of a scuffle, that's all," Frankie said, who still hadn't taken his eyes off Jess, despite Miranda's very clear warning. He rummaged in the front pocket of his too-tight, ripped jeans and came up with a squashed pack of cigarettes. The casual, unconcerned way he lit up and took a puff made Miranda ache to slap him. There was blood on Frankie's mouth, too, and Miranda's blood pressure shot skyward.

"A scuffle?" she asked through gritted teeth. "Jess, talk to me. Tell me what's going on here, because it looks a lot like Frankie made some sort of . . ." God, she didn't even know how to say it. She ended up spitting it out. "Some sort of *pass* at you or something, and you had to fight him off. Is that true? Because so help me God, if it is, there will be hell to pay."

That shook Jess out of his shock. "No! Miranda. Shit. Calm down, would you, please? I really think I've had enough violence for one night."

"What violence?" Miranda nearly shrieked. "We heard some kind of racket out here, and I looked and looked and couldn't find you, and then Adam said he thought he knew where you were. And now you're saying there was violence?"

"A couple of drunk frat guys hassled us," Jess said. "But it was no big deal. Some trash cans got pushed around, and one of the losers hit Frankie." His voice got hard and angry for a second before he visibly calmed himself. "But it was fine. I'm fine, so can we just go back inside and forget about it?"

Adam closed a hand over her shoulder, but Miranda barely felt it. She was watching Jess, and keeping an eye on Frankie for good measure.

Frankie wasn't looking at Jess anymore. He didn't look at any of them, even Adam. Wandering a few steps away from the group, Frankie examined the end of his cigarette, then stuck the filter back in his mouth. Talking around the butt, he said, "Yeah, good idea. You lot go on inside, I'll be along in a mo'."

All that while squinting off into the distance away from them, as if they weren't worth his time or attention.

Even if Frankie really had gotten that split lip sort of defending her brother—and Miranda was no fool, she knew there was some pertinent information missing from Jess's story—she couldn't help it. Frankie Boyd got her back up in the worst possible way.

Jess was aware of his distant coolness, too, and it seemed to make him unhappy.

"Frankie," he said. "Come on."

Miranda noticed Adam watching this exchange carefully, his brows drawn together as though he were deciphering some secret code.

Frankie hollowed his gaunt cheeks around the cigarette, plucked it from his mouth, and blew the gray smoke in a billowing cloud over their heads. Then he angled his head far enough to slide Jess a quick smile that didn't reach his eyes.

"Go on with your sister, now, Bit. You were spot-on, everything's fine here. I'll see you tomorrow."

Jess sucked in a breath. His face looked the way it had when he was twelve years old and trying out in-line skates for the first time and realized, too late, that he had no idea how to stop.

Adam's worried gaze swung to her, and the concern she saw in his brown eyes made Miranda feel as if she'd hit the same fence post Jess had on those damn skates, a solid thunk of wood straight to the gut.

Her nebulous fears came swirling back. Sweat sprang to the palms of Miranda's hands and her heart tripped all over itself trying to catch up to the lightning pace of her brain.

Time slowed down and white noise filled her ears. Into the silence, Miranda dropped a single, slow question.

"What were they hassling you about?"

Jess looked from Frankie to Miranda and his brow cleared. Out of the corner of her eye, she saw that Frankie himself appeared carved from stone, frozen with the cigarette inches from his mouth. She could feel Adam's solid warmth behind her, and the immediate sense of safety he provided made her want to lean into him.

Jess's quiet response took all choice away from her.

"The frat assholes took exception to the sight of two guys kissing." He swallowed visibly, but firmed his chin and went on. "Specifically, me. And Frankie."

Miranda's knees went watery, enough to make her grateful when Adam stepped up a little closer and lent her his silent support. She blinked. What was she supposed to say to that?

"You and Frankie?" She hated the sound of her own voice, high and thin with something like fear.

A fear she saw echoed in Jess's blue eyes—God, their mother's eyes—but his jaw was set and determined. Miranda watched him nod and saw their father in Jess's stubborn chin and solemn expression.

"Miranda. I'm gay."

There was a momentary flash of recognition—*Yes, I know, I've always known*—before Miranda throttled it.

"But you . . . you like girls," she said stupidly. "I mean, what about that girl at Brandewine? Tara?"

But Jess was shaking his head. "No. Tara was my friend. Or at least, I thought she was. She was the first person I came out to—and she couldn't wait to tell the whole rest of the school and all the people we worked with at the restaurant. Pretty much nobody wanted to have anything to do with me after that."

"This is why you came home," Miranda realized, dazed. "Oh, my God, you must have felt so alone. And confused!" Her heart ached with the knowledge of what Jess had gone through, and guilt at not having dug deeper to find out what had prompted his transfer from Brandewine.

Actually, the guilt ran far deeper than that, but even looking at it sideways made panic start to bloom in her chest, so she shoved it down.

"I wish I'd told you before," Jess said. His face was lightening, as if he felt relieved at finally coming clean. "I should've known you wouldn't hold it against me."

"Oh, honey," she choked out. "No, of course not."

Pulling away from Adam, she rushed to wrap her arms around her little brother. He was only an inch or two taller than she was, and still so skinny and coltish. Not even done growing yet, and he'd had all this bewildering chaos of emotion happening inside him. And he'd had no one to turn to.

It had always, always been Miranda's job to be there for him. She'd failed in the worst possible way—but no more.

"None of this is your fault," she said fiercely, not ready to let him go. "You're only a baby, Jess, how could I blame you?"

He stiffened in her arms.

"Miranda—"

She let him pull away, but kept one hand circling his wrist. She couldn't bear to lose the connection entirely.

"It's okay," she said soothingly. "We're just going to go home and talk this out."

Jess gazed at her uncertainly for a moment, then his

eyes cut to someone behind her. Miranda realized with a start that Adam and Frankie were both still standing there, bearing witness to this incredibly private family moment.

Moreover, it was Frankie Jess had looked to, as if for permission. And suddenly Miranda knew *exactly* who was to blame in all of this.

"How could you?" she hissed at Frankie. "I wasn't so wrong, after all, was I? Maybe you didn't hit him yourself, but what you've been doing to him is a hell of a lot more damaging than a scratch."

"Whoa, Miranda, what?" Jess was shaking his head, but Miranda ignored it. He was a child, he didn't know what he wanted. But this . . . this *man,* with his too-tight jeans and too-cool attitude—he'd tricked Jess into believing something that just wasn't true.

"He took advantage of you," Miranda told Jess. "He picked up on your normal, natural teenage confusion and he took advantage."

Her voice shook dangerously and she had to press a hand to her eyes for a moment before she could go on. Frankie the Scumbag did not get to see her cry.

When she looked at him again, however, Frankie the Scumbag was staring at Jess.

"Bit," he said hoarsely. "Bit, I—"

Frankie reached out a hand, and Miranda lost it.

"Just stop," she cried. "Don't talk to him, don't look at him. And for the sake of all that's holy, don't ever, *ever* touch him again. Oh, my God, I can't stand to think of your hands on him, I can't stand to think—"

"No, you stop it," Jess said, startling her. His eyes were blazing as he shook free of her restraining grasp. "I'm not listening to this for another second. It's a lie, everything you're saying, you couldn't have it more wrong."

He backed away from her and Miranda followed like a puppet on a string.

"You don't understand," she said, making her voice slow and clear so she could explain it to Jess. "This man is older than you, honey. By quite a few years, and they're important years when you'll do a lot of growing up. And he had no right"—she shifted her attention to Frankie and emphasized that point again—"*no right* to make you think he cared about you, or to try to talk you into doing anything you weren't comfortable with."

"No right, is it?" Frankie finally broke in. His spiky hair and weirdly arched eyebrows made him look like a drawing out of a children's story illustrating the damn Prince of Darkness or something. "Maybe you're the one who hasn't the right, to treat your brother like he's mentally deficient, or a bloody child."

Miranda bristled. "I don't believe I have to answer to *you* for how my brother and I conduct our private, personal family affairs. And he *is* a child, you disgusting pervert!"

Frankie tilted his head and smirked that horrible smirk at her. "You wouldn't think he was such an infant if you'd come out here about ten minutes earlier, pet."

Jess smacked him on the shoulder, looking mortified, and Adam hopped into the conversation.

"Whoo kay, Frankie, really not helping. And can I say, we all might need to take a breather here? Seriously, Miranda, deep breath."

"I won't be able to breathe freely again until my brother and I are safely at home, nowhere in the vicinity of this, this, this . . ." She sputtered, unable to come up with anything scathing enough.

"Vile seducer?" Frankie supplied, sneering. "Shameless debaucher of innocents?"

"Okay, enough," Jess said loudly.

Miranda opened her mouth, only to shut it with a snap when Jess continued, "And that goes for you, too. God. This is so not how I wanted this conversation to go."

Forcing a calm she didn't feel, Miranda held up her hands in surrender.

"You're right. We shouldn't be talking about this here. Let's go home, and I promise we can sort it all out."

She'd have to find out what the age of consent was in New York State. Probably eighteen, which was patently ridiculous, but with any luck it would be twenty-one and she could press full charges against Frankie Boyd.

Lost in fantasies of court dates and Frankie in an orange jumpsuit, Miranda didn't immediately notice that Jess wasn't agreeing. In fact, he'd moved closer to Frankie's side, shrinking away from Miranda as if *she* were the one who'd victimized him.

The sight brought that panic that had been roiling beneath the surface bubbling up into her chest and throat. Her throat closed up, making her voice sound tight and terrified when she said, "Jess?"

"I don't want to go home and sort anything out," he said with a tremor that stabbed at Miranda's heart. "Because there isn't anything to sort out. I'm gay. You aren't going to change that with a conversation. And I'm sorry"—his voice broke a little—"that this is so hard for you. But it's been hard for me, too."

Miranda's eyes welled with tears, but she blinked them back furiously. "Jess, it's okay. But please. You have to come home with me."

"He doesn't," Frankie said. Try as she might, Miranda couldn't detect an ounce of smugness in him now, and he seemed to be carefully avoiding touching Jess in any way. Jess looked up at him questioningly. Miranda didn't want to be aware of the way his entire heart was in his eyes. Her stomach clenched.

Frankie cleared his throat. "He can stay with me for the night."

Jess's smile was beatific, and for a moment Miranda

could only stare. But when her baby brother moved to twine his fingers with Frankie's, a loud "No" exploded out of her.

Jess looked at her, his smile turning bittersweet. "This is what I want, Miranda. I know it's not what you had planned for me, but it's who I am. Come on, Frankie, let's go."

With that, he turned to leave, tugging Frankie along behind him.

Miranda couldn't believe this was happening. "Jess," she called, but he didn't turn around.

"Oh my God," she gasped.

Adam stopped her from running after them with a hand on her arm.

"Do something," she shouted, rounding on him. "You're supposed to be his boss—make him leave my brother alone."

"I've never been able to control Frankie," Adam said with a grim twist to his mouth. "Not for a second. I wish I could help."

Miranda felt her breath coming faster and shorter, the tears she'd held at bay for so long spilling over and searing tracks down her cheeks. Her head throbbed painfully and a harsh, racking sob worked its way up through her chest.

Adam's arms came around her, familiar and comforting, and Miranda lost herself in his embrace and in the stormy release of crying.

"I'm losing my brother," she sobbed against his chest.

"Hey, now, no," Adam said, rubbing his hand up and down her back. "You're not. It's only for a night, so everyone can cool off and take a step back."

"Ha," Miranda huffed wetly. "I'm sure it'll all look so much better after a sleepless night of pacing around my empty apartment." The thought of Jess's vacant bedroom made Miranda want to curl over herself in pain.

"Yeah, I can see how that might make you broody," Adam said. "Why don't you come home with me? I promise to come up with something mindlessly entertaining to distract you long enough to fall asleep."

Miranda sniffled and pressed her cheek to the somewhat soggy front of Adam's thin T-shirt. She listened to the steady thump of his heart under her ear and realized how exhausted she was. Nothing like an emotional rollercoaster ride followed by a crying jag. Someone should write a book about it; it could be the new fitness/exercise craze.

It was blissfully tempting, the idea of curling up in Adam's brick townhouse and letting him take her away from herself, from her problems, from the world.

"Okay," she whispered, raising her head. Adam immediately kissed her and it felt good even through the stuffy nose, swollen eyes, and spiking headache.

Someone should write a book about that, too, she mused hazily as Adam ran back into the bar to settle the tab and get their things.

Adam Temple: Miracle Cure for What Ails You.

TWENTY-TWO

What a night.

Adam settled Miranda on his lumpy chenille sofa and moved automatically to turn on the stereo. He hesitated briefly over the music selection; something told him Siouxsie and the Banshees might not be particularly welcome at the moment.

Rummaging through his CDs, he came up with a Nina Simone album Grant had given him years ago. Seconds later, the low, smoky tones of Nina's bluesy voice rasped through the air.

Adam looked over his shoulder at Miranda huddled on the couch. She seemed small and fragile against the over-stuffed cushions. Her eyes and nose were red, swollen and tender with the aftermath of tears. She'd appeared shocked by the torrential downpour, as if she weren't used to letting it all out. Even as he watched, she pressed a furtive hand to her cheeks, the corners of her eyes, and frowned as if dismayed at the evidence of her recent binge.

"It's all right, you know," Adam said. "You can cry some more if you want. I might even have real tissues in the bathroom, so you won't have to use my shirt."

She smiled, as he meant her to, but it was fleeting. Moments later, the pensive look was back.

Adam didn't want to crowd her, but he didn't think she should be alone, either. After some deliberation, he perched on the arm of the sofa, facing her. At first, Miranda wouldn't look at him, and his gut clenched at the volumes her stubborn solitude spoke about the kind of support system she was used to.

There had been a moment when she'd leaned on him, though, when she'd turned to him and let him hold her, and he was hanging on to that memory with everything he had. This was a woman coming apart like an overcooked sauce, separating into an ungodly mess right before his eyes.

"I'm sick of crying," she said. "It's an impractical response to a problem."

"Maybe, but don't you feel better after?"

She blinked up at him. Adam wanted to hate himself for noticing that the tears trembling in her lower lashes made her eyes glitter like sapphires. It was sick to find her flushed, tear-blotched face so attractive. But Adam felt like he was seeing her for the first time, the stripped-down, unadorned woman beneath the put-together image she presented to the world.

"I don't know what could make me feel better right now," Miranda said. "God. Not too dramatic, am I?"

The rueful curve of her pink mouth made Adam ache to snatch her up and kiss her.

"No, it's my fault," Adam said, swinging off the sofa before his shaky impulse control gave out completely. "I promised you distraction and I haven't delivered yet."

"What did you have in mind?" Miranda asked. Her eyes were wide and guileless. Adam must have imagined the sultry note in her tone.

"Um. We could watch a movie or something. Except.

Damn. My TV broke a few weeks ago and I haven't had it fixed because I'm not really here enough to watch anything anyway, plus it's summer so Devon's show is in reruns, and it's the one thing I really watch, and only so I can mock him for it mercilessly."

Miranda laughed, which shut him up. She looked surprised at herself for it.

"Who needs TV?" she said, shaking her head and smiling. "You're the perfect distraction all on your own."

She unfolded herself from the couch and approached, her gaze never wavering from his face.

"Am I?" Adam forced out between suddenly dry lips.

"Well." Miranda considered it. "You could be doing an even better job of it."

She stepped directly in front of him. Her hands fluttered, then settled lightly on his hips.

"I don't want to push you, if you're not feeling . . ." Adam coughed, then started again. "I mean, this isn't why I asked you back here."

"I know," she said, pushing her thumbs in circles against his hipbones. The touch rucked up his T-shirt a little, and then her hands were resting on the bare skin of his sides.

"Is it why you came?" Adam asked, feeling like the wrong answer was a bucket of ice water suspended over his head, just waiting to fall.

"Not that I'm turning you down, no matter what," he hastened to add. "If all you're looking for with me is oblivion, one night to feel instead of to think, I can give you that. But I'd like to know ahead of time if that's all it is."

Her hands stilled on his skin, making Adam wish he'd bitten his tongue and gone with it.

But as he watched, the lines of tension in Miranda's face softened, melting like sugar into caramel.

"That's not all it is," she told him. A new wash of pink

stained her cheeks as she confessed, "I've actually been picturing this moment ever since you hopped up on that stage and started singing, back at Chapel."

Adam's heart started to pound, but he managed a cocky grin. "Liked that, did you?"

"Far more than I expected. I especially appreciated your song choice."

He ran his hands up her arms to her shoulders, enjoying the shivery arch of her body into his palms. It was subtle but addictive.

"One of my all-time favorites," he whispered. "It's been stuck in my head a lot recently. For some reason."

Now they were both breathing too fast.

"Want to give me a tour of the rest of your place?" Miranda asked.

With all their cooking lessons and makeout sessions, they'd never made it past the kitchen to the more private areas of the townhouse.

Adam sucked in air, instantly imagining Miranda's dark red hair flowing over the plain green sheets on his low, wide bed.

"Yeah," he groaned. "Let's do the tour."

She squeaked when he picked her up, but obligingly wrapped her slim legs around his waist for balance.

"The kitchen, you already know."

"Intimately," she said directly into his ear, causing a full-body shudder that almost caused him to drop her.

Adam cursed and firmed his hold on her delectable round ass. Not exactly a hardship.

"This is the living room," he recounted doggedly, rounding the corner of the bookcase that screened his bed from the rest of the apartment. "And oh, look, the bedroom."

"Fascinating." Again with the ear, but this time Adam was ready for it.

He turned her carefully to avoid bashing her head against the bookshelves. Concussion would undoubtedly put a damper on the evening.

His skin was too tight for his body, all of a sudden, as he laid her down and stepped back to take in the vision made real, Miranda sprawled, boneless and sensual, across his bed. She moved a little on the sheets, a sinuous squirm that should've made her look embarrassed or ill at ease, but instead made Adam want to rip her clothes off so he could watch her do it again, only naked this time.

"Come on," she breathed, holding out one hand. "Make me forget. Wrap me up until there's nothing but you."

A hard tremor racked Adam from head to foot. Christ, this woman got to him. He reached for her hand and intertwined their fingers, following the slow tug down to the bed.

She needed this, he thought as he covered her with his body. And it was something he could give her. Okay, let's be honest here, it was something he was dying to give her. But it wasn't all there was.

And as he settled into the curves of her body, his hips sinking into the cradle of hers, that sense of *more* throbbed between them like an extra heartbeat in the room. He'd felt it earlier, onstage at Chapel, while he was fiddling with guitar strings and drawing breath to sing. The whole bar faded away until there was nothing but Miranda's expectant face, her eyes shining and full of something hard to name.

Every beat of that damn song, which he'd meant to be funny and maybe ironic, had turned into a private message for her, tattooed into the air like smoke signals.

It was too much to hope that Miranda, his observant, detail-oriented Miranda, hadn't gotten the message.

And as she pushed up to meet his kiss, Adam wasn't at all sure he was sorry.

* * *

The emotional highs and lows of this insane evening combined in Miranda's system like a double shot of tequila with a vodka chaser. She felt drunk with the aftereffects of adrenaline, the subsequent crash, and the longest crying jag of her life. There was madness coursing through her blood, her thoughts whirling fast enough that she felt she might fly up toward the ceiling at any moment, pulled apart and flung to the four corners of the room, if Adam stopped touching her.

This. Just this, Adam's hardness and heat pressing her into the soft mattress below, surrounding and enfolding her. This was what Miranda needed.

It had been so long—maybe her whole adult life—since she felt safe enough to let go.

Adam slanted his wonderful mouth over hers again, banishing all thoughts of brothers and secrets and guilt. Miranda arched her spine painfully, pressing as hard as she could to get as much coverage as she could. It felt like it would be impossible to get close enough to Adam. They were touching from forehead to ankles, his weight solid and reassuring atop her, but it wasn't enough. She wished he would swallow her in a single bite.

He opened his mouth, taking control of the kiss with a hoarse curse, and made a valiant attempt.

His broad chest ground into the yielding globes of her breasts. The thin fabric barrier of their clothes was insignificant in the face of the heat their friction generated. Adam's hips rocked down in a slow, deliberate circle, teasing Miranda with the growing emptiness inside her. She could feel the hard bulge of his erection trapped in his jeans; it notched in the vee between her legs with short bursts of motion, making her throb with emptiness. And all the time his hungry mouth moved voraciously, sucking at her tongue and tormenting her lips with tiny nips and bites until she could feel the tender flesh puffing and swelling to hypersensitivity.

Miranda whimpered into him, surrendering utterly. It was like the first time she'd tasted his food: a swift shock to the senses, immersing her entire being in a wash of bodily pleasure. Where there was so much pure sensation, there was no room for thinking.

"Whoa," Adam gasped, pulling back. Miranda frowned in protest, prompting him to pet her soothingly.

"Not going anywhere," he said, out of breath and husky. "Just. Damn. We need to slow down a little. We've got all night, don't we?"

A hint of vulnerability shone in the darkness of his eyes as he gazed down at her. It was like he half expected her to toss him out of his own apartment once she was through with him.

Making a sincere effort to curb her own pounding heart and runaway libido, Miranda tilted her chin back and ran a hand up Adam's strong neck and into the soft curls at his nape.

"I'm not going anywhere," she told him. Relief, and something stronger, glimmered through his expression before he smiled.

"Damn right you're not." With a triumphant growl and a lightning-quick maneuver, he trapped both her hands in one of his big fists and pinned them to the bed above her head.

"At least, not until I finally get to see you naked," Miranda said.

Her own boldness turned her on, and from the dazed look on Adam's face, it had a similar effect on him.

That's right, she mused. *He likes the way I talk.*

Improvising, Miranda put on her best sultry voice, drinking in every flicker of expression that crossed Adam's face as she began to speak.

"I want to take off your clothes and taste every last inch of you. You can tell a lot about a person by taste. I can, anyway. It's that overdeveloped, exceedingly discerning palate of mine, I expect." She inhaled deeply, the sharp aroma of masculine sweat and heated flesh rising to her nose.

"Even the way you smell," she went on, forgetting to monitor Adam's reaction and losing herself in the delirium of the moment. "You smell like sex, all musky and warm."

"God, Miranda," Adam groaned, dropping his head in supplicating defeat against her shoulder. "You're killing me with this stuff. The way you use words . . ."

He trailed off helplessly, but Miranda could feel the truth of what he wanted to say in the quick, hitching breaths being panted against her abdomen. In the frustrated thrusting of his hips.

Miranda was making him lose control, driving him out of his mind with desire. The knowledge sent a sharp spasm of excitement straight to her center, and she swallowed against the liquid rush of it.

"So do something about it," she demanded, spreading her legs wider and locking them around his narrow waist.

Adam sank deeper into the cradle of her pelvis. Groaning convulsively at the increased pressure of his sex against hers, he let go of her hands and raised himself up on trembling forearms to stare down at her.

The move bowed his body into hers slightly, jostling them together. The way his denim-clad erection rubbed across Miranda's tight, swollen folds made her shiver with longing.

"Miranda."

She met his eyes. Her head cleared enough to register the seriousness of his expression.

"What?"

"You know I love it when you use those ten-dollar words and make sense out of everything in my head."

Miranda smiled. "I do."

"Wonderful. But unless you want this night to be over before it begins, could you do me a favor?"

"Anything."

"Shut up."

Miranda felt his lips curve against the shell of her ear at the same moment as she felt his hands drift to the hem of her shirt. She moved to help him, and they divested themselves of their clothes in a breathless rush.

In some corner of her brain, Miranda acknowledged that as much as she'd imagined this moment over the last few days, she'd pictured a slow, anticipatory revealing, every inch of newly bared skin kissed and worshipped in a graceful dance toward completion.

It was nothing like that.

This was exuberant and fun, a mad dash toward nakedness. It was like they were in a race, falling against each other, gasping with laughter, hands hot and frenzied on each other's bodies. It had never been easier to be naked in front of someone else.

Miranda wasn't a prude; she'd had her share of boyfriends. Six, to be exact, none lasting more than a few months, but all of them serious enough at the time to warrant sexual intimacy. Not a single one of them had prepared her for this.

Adam tumbled back down on the bed, pulling her atop him. The coarse hair on his arms and legs abraded her skin gently, heightening every movement, however tiny. Surprisingly soft black hairs swirled around his flat, brown nipples, meeting in the middle and narrowing suggestively down his ridged abdomen. Miranda tangled her fingers and smoothed them down his front, compulsively following the trail to the patch of coarser hair nesting Adam's erect cock.

His belly quivered under her questing fingers, but that

was nothing compared to the way his cock jumped when she circled it loosely with her thumb and forefinger.

Adam huffed out a laugh and Miranda gave him a swift, secret smile.

"Got a mind of its own, hasn't it?"

"You have no idea," Adam responded fervently.

She laughed and ducked her head to watch her own fingers dance up and down the taut, straining sides of his erection. Adam was thick and solid, heavy with arousal and already flushing red at the tip. He felt marvelous in her hand; it was like stroking the embodiment of his passion for her, all hot, silky skin over steely hardness. His hips jerked helplessly up into her grasp, making Miranda tighten her fingers.

The look on his face was exquisite, agonized bliss drawing his handsome features tight. Adam's unabashed enjoyment of what she was doing was more exciting than Miranda could have dreamed. It made her want to do even more.

She sighted down his body again. She'd never been a huge fan of oral sex, either giving or receiving. It always felt a little beside the point, to her—strictly relegated to the foreplay period. Adam, though, made her want to savor everything on the way to completion.

Without giving herself more time to think about it, Miranda scooted down the bed and lowered her mouth over Adam's warm, musky flesh. He strained upward with a choked, disbelieving cry, forcing Miranda to draw back a bit and lap contemplatively at the head.

She should've known. Like everything involving Adam, this act was made over new and delightful, merely because it was *him*. Miranda inhaled deeply, imprinting the rich, earthy scent of him on her senses. And the taste!

Sticking her tongue out, she licked again, a long stripe from base to tip. Flavor exploded over her tongue like a surprising *amuse-bouche* sent out by a master chef. Adam was salty and delicious, with an underlying hint of citrus that made Miranda's mouth water.

And when she fastened her lips around the wide, flared head of his prick, and started to suck, the groan that rumbled up from the depths of Adam's chest made blood flush hotly through Miranda's body.

Sexual power surged through her, quickening her breath and making her startlingly conscious of the slick dampness between her thighs. She curled around his hip and bobbed her head in a short, staccato rhythm designed to drive Adam out of his mind.

"Ah, God, no more," Adam rasped, grabbing her shoulders and lifting her away from him.

Miranda allowed herself to pout, quite aware that the swollen, bee-stung state of her mouth made it devastating.

Adam stared.

"Christ Almighty, woman." His eyes were wide and shocked, the aftereffects of her sensual assault still pulsing through him like ripples from a stone tossed into a lake. He reached for her and she went into his arms gladly, straddling his lap with a shiver.

Her most sensitive bits rubbed companionably against his, sending little spirals of delight out from her center to the tips of her fingers and toes. Adam's big hands cupped her waist, keeping her snug against him as he kissed her.

Miranda heard a half-strangled whimper, high-pitched and desperate. With a start, she realized it came from her own raw throat as Adam traced her bottom lip with the point of his tongue before dipping hungrily into her mouth.

She writhed against him, feeling wanton and hot. Splayed open against the hard, defined muscles of Adam's stomach, Miranda's sex burned and throbbed. It was too much.

"In me," she gasped, pushing the words into Adam's open mouth. "Please."

His arms tightened around her like a net, capturing her frantic struggles and taming them down to slight undulations.

"You don't have to beg," he said. "Ever. I mean it. I'm way easier than that. At least when it comes to you." As he spoke, he fumbled with the drawer of his nightstand, rummaging around until he came up with a crinkly packet. He made quick work of the condom, the inadvertent brushing of his fingers along her ass when he rolled it down making Miranda shudder.

"Now who's talking too much?" Miranda asked, hitching herself higher against him and reveling in the feel of Adam's callused palm sliding around to cup her bottom.

"You're right," Adam admitted, flexing his hands and curling his fingers inward. Miranda shifted, knowing he was testing her readiness to take him, and knowing as well that he'd find her body wet and open.

He groaned when the pads of his fingers met her damp inner folds. Miranda threw her head back at his delicate caress. She could feel the throbbing length of his erection brushing the backs of her thighs, the crease of her buttocks, and she wanted it with a sudden ferocity that took her by surprise.

They moved together without words, Adam's hands supporting Miranda's shift onto her knees, her thighs trembling against his flanks as she straddled him. Then the head of his cock was right where she wanted it, so close, tip kissing the wet, aching entrance to her body. Miranda braced her hands on Adam's wide shoulders. Their faces were mere inches apart. Every breath Miranda took was laden with Adam's essence.

Their eyes locked. And she opened herself up and slid

down his length in a lush, controlled glide that forced hoarse cries of pleasure from both of them.

So full, was all Miranda could think as she sank down and sealed herself to Adam.

The wicked pressure of Adam's thick cock made lights flash before her eyes, like soft explosions in her peripheral vision. She clenched her inner muscles without meaning to and they both groaned at the intensification of sensation.

Miranda stared at Adam's lust-blown pupils, his heavy lids and absurdly long eyelashes, and in the midst of the most shattering physical experience in Miranda's memory, Adam bumped his nose questioningly against hers.

Such a silly, sweet thing, but it unraveled her.

With a cry that sounded broken and defeated to her own ears, Miranda wrapped her arms as tightly as she could around Adam. Somehow, Adam took that as his cue to move, and in seconds they were sitting face-to-face. He started a slow rocking that drove his cock up into her in short, powerful pulses. Miranda buried her face in his shoulder and held on.

Sitting up like this, arms pressing each other close—it was terribly intimate. Adam was so deep inside her that every upward thrust touched a place that had never been touched before, forging pathways into her body and making them his own. Adam swept his hands down her heaving sides and along her cramping legs. Lifting her with one sinewy forearm below her buttocks, he used his other hand to straighten her bent legs and encourage them to clamp around him.

Relief sang through Miranda's body as she bounced down, now seated fully on Adam's lap. The new position pressed him even deeper inside her, till she was sure she could almost feel him in her throat. There was something ridiculously hot about allowing Adam to manhandle her pliant body into whatever shape suited his whims.

Twining her trembling limbs around him like an especially clingy vine, Miranda turned her mouth to Adam's neck, taking his salty skin between her teeth. He grunted and moved into her even more forcefully. She smiled around her mouthful and sucked harder. She had a wild desire to mark him in some visible way, just as he was marking her deep inside.

Every thrust ground her into the hardness of his pubic bone, setting off sharp bursts of pleasure that radiated up her spine, threatening to blow off the top of her head. She shook in his grasp, straining toward something so big it scared her.

"Come on, sweets," Adam rasped against her cheek. "Let it go."

He grabbed her waist and pulled her down while thrusting up, circling her hips in a tight spiral that stretched her around him and rubbed her clit against the grain of the crisp, damp curls at his groin. Miranda's head fell back, too heavy for her neck to support as waves of ecstasy washed over and through her. Adam shouted and shook beneath her, losing the beat entirely. He pumped his hips erratically, emptying himself and extending Miranda's orgasm until the pleasure became sharp enough to resemble pain.

She clung and shuddered through the aftermath, pleased to discover, as she came back to herself, that Adam was clinging just as much. They were pretzeled around each other inextricably, and Miranda's heart felt fluttery and warm. She never wanted to move.

If she moved, she'd have to think about things. And really, she'd prefer never to think about things again. Thinking was bad. Very bad.

Miranda frowned and burrowed tighter into Adam's embrace.

"Stop that," Adam said, his warm voice husky and laced with amusement.

"What?" Her reply was muffled against the damp, delicious skin of his shoulder.

"The wheels in your brain are starting to turn again, aren't they? Like a hamster in one of those plastic balls."

Miranda snorted, but allowed her lips to curve into a sleepy smile. "Nice pillow talk."

"Ooh, speaking of pillows . . ."

TWENTY-THREE

The disentangling process was slow and satisfying for Adam. He liked the way Miranda moved as if she were swimming through melted chocolate, sort of boneless and effortful. Her eyelids drooped nearly shut, getting lower with every breath.

Adam settled her on her back, loving her unselfconscious snuggle into the pillows, and drew the thin cotton sheet over her while he went to the bathroom to clean up.

He narrowed his eyes against the harsh glare of the bulbs over his bathroom mirror. One glimpse was enough to tell him he looked thoroughly "shagged out," as Frankie would say. Adam grinned at his messy hair and remembered Miranda's fingers tunneling through it, snarling it up into its current condition.

Glancing back through the open doorway, he was arrested by the sight of her sprawled across his bed the way he'd imagined her, spotlit by the shaft of light from the bathroom. It was a gorgeous picture she presented, and Adam took a moment to enjoy it. The deep evenness of her breaths told him he'd most likely be basking in the afterglow alone, but he didn't mind.

There was plenty of good stuff to think about. He

switched off the bathroom light and stumbled his way back to the bed. Sliding in beside Miranda, he spooned up against her, relishing the silkiness of her skin and the murmuring noises she made. He propped his head on one hand and studied her beautiful face.

Was it stupid and soppy to be happy just watching her sleep?

Whatever. Adam would've shrugged, but he didn't have the energy. Either way, he was definitely justified in the surge of gladness he felt when Miranda turned toward him in her sleep, nuzzling closer and throwing a possessive leg over his.

Thus happily pinned in place, Adam prepared to relive the last hour in his head, from the instant she requested a tour of his townhouse, to now. He wanted to cement it all in his memory, every touch and every look. The tight satin grasp of her body, the breathy, almost shocked sound of her cries, the raw red of the flush that suffused her cheeks and all the way down to her breasts in the moment of climax.

Adam's heart thrummed with deep satisfaction and contentment. The most basic part of him, what he thought of as his hind brain, was cavemannishly pleased to have his woman locked into his embrace, sleeping peacefully under his protection with the livid evidence of his possession fading into light bruises on her hips.

Miranda was his now.

And he was hers.

Morning hit Miranda like a sledgehammer. One minute, she was lost in a dream where Jess was a toddler again, strapped into his car seat in the front of the van their mother used to drive, while Miranda was stranded in the last row of seats, unable to reach him as the van started to move down the road on its own. The next minute, she was gasping awake in an unfamiliar room, a moss-green sheet knotted around her legs.

"Hey there," came a gruff voice from her left.

Miranda whipped her head around, scissoring her legs until she could clutch the sheet to her chest. Adam blinked up at her from the pillow beside hers, his mouth stretched in a drowsy smile. Dark stubble shadowed his jaw, but his eyes were clear and alert.

"Hi," she said, immediately cringing at her own inanity.

"Everything okay?" he asked. "You jerked awake like something bit you."

"Fine," she replied automatically. Her head was pounding, tension tightening her nerves to the screaming point. She furrowed her brow in pain, and Adam frowned.

"You don't look so fine to me, sweets. Head hurt?"

Miranda nodded against the pillow and Adam's hand came up to rub soothingly at her temples. The headache subsided to a manageable level, allowing her to chuckle.

"This reminds me of the morning after I first met you," she confided. "I had the worst hangover of my life."

"I can believe it." Adam grinned, but it faded fast. "I didn't think you drank all that much last night."

"No," she agreed. "I'm afraid this is more along the lines of an emotional hangover. You know, too many ups and downs in a single evening."

Adam's fingers stilled, then combed through her riotous morning curls once before dropping back to the bed between them.

"I'm sorry you're not feeling well after last night," he said carefully, but Miranda could hear the underlying disappointment in his voice.

"It wasn't you," she hastened to say. "You were wonderful, perfect. Exactly what I needed."

He actually blushed a little and turned his face farther into the pillow, mashing his nose and giving her only a glimpse of his crooked smile. Her heart swelled dangerously.

"I mean it," she insisted.

"God, Miranda . . ." Adam faltered into silence, and for a few seconds, she was afraid he wasn't going to go on. When he spoke again, it was painfully halting. "I wish I could fix this for you. I want it to be easy, like math: one down plus one up equals even keel. But I know it's not."

"Not exactly. But, honestly, I don't know how I would've gotten through last night without you. Outside the bar, with Jess, and then after, here. You took me out of myself, made me . . . well, happier than I've been in a really long time."

Fear dragged at her chest with that confession, but even as she pressed her lips together and watched closely for his reaction, some part of Miranda knew that she was safe with Adam.

Her hand fluttered out, unsure where to settle, and he caught it in his, squeezing her fingers reassuringly. His eyes had cleared, and he was watching her with a gentle understanding that wrung the breath from her lungs.

"I'm glad I could help," he said quietly.

"You did," Miranda assured him, her throat aching. "You still are."

Adam's mouth twisted into a lopsided smile. The pall that was trying to settle over Miranda's mood lightened from black to a misty gray.

"How about breakfast? All part of the full-service Adam Temple Experience. Our motto is: sleep with a chef, expect to get stuffed. In more ways than one."

He waggled his eyebrows outrageously and bounded out of bed, entirely unconscious of his own nudity. Miranda rolled over on her stomach to better admire the view.

"I'm not a big breakfast person," Miranda confessed. "I usually grab a bialy from the coffee cart on my way to work."

"Get out." Adam rounded on her, hands on lean, bare hips and a scandalized expression on his face.

Miranda laughed, blushing a little at her own struggle to get her eyes to focus above Adam's waist. "I know, I know, it's the most important meal of the day."

"Fuck that. It's the most lip-smacking meal of the day. Whatever you want, from sweet to savory, pancakes to corned-beef hash. Name it, and it's yours."

Adam flung his arms out grandly. Something about the gesture seemed to clue him in that he wasn't wearing any pants. He looked down at himself as if surprised, but evinced no embarrassment whatsoever as he turned to rummage through his bureau, eventually finding and putting on a pair of plaid pajama bottoms.

"Nice jammies," Miranda teased.

"My mom gives me a new pair every Christmas," Adam said with a grin. "I give all the tops to Goodwill. There's this funny German lady who runs an old-fashioned candy store down the block, and she makes the best iced coffee in the world. Every now and then, I see her sporting a very familiar patterned shirt."

Miranda shook her head. "Have you ever told her she's wearing pajamas as clothing?"

"Why should I? They look great on her. Also, I'm a little afraid to. She's perpetually cranky."

"Oh, please," Miranda scoffed. "Like there's a woman alive you couldn't charm."

Adam raised his eyebrows. "Damn, Miranda. Keep that stuff up, and I'll start thinking you like me."

Miranda threw a pillow at him, which he dodged, laughing.

"Come on," he cajoled. "Get up and cook with me. It'll be fun."

"Fine." Miranda threw back the covers, determined to be as nonchalant and suave about this whole nudity thing as Adam was.

From the corner of her eye, she saw his throat work in a convulsive swallow.

"Okay, maybe I lied," he said. "Jesus. You're even more gorgeous the morning after. How the hell is that possible?"

Miranda pressed her lips together to hide a smile. His appreciatively roving gaze sent sparks of warmth goose-bumping over her skin. It also enabled her to stand up and strike a casual pose.

"Are you sure you've given away *all* the pajama tops?" she asked. "I don't particularly want to face my clothes from last night. A sweaty dinner service followed by a stint in a smoky bar isn't liable to have left them fresh as a daisy."

"Yeah. What?" Adam blinked and dragged his gaze away from her chest. Miranda arched a brow at him and was pleased when he flushed.

"Sorry. I think I have something you can wear. Hold on." He groped ineffectually at the open bureau drawer, never taking his eyes off her. Miranda decided it was time to take control.

"I'm going to borrow your toothbrush while you look," she announced. Head held high, she marched into the bathroom and shut the door.

She took care of her usual morning routine as best she could. At first she avoided the mirror, afraid she'd see the same sort of wreckage that had taken hold after that party at Market. Eventually, of course, she couldn't resist the urge to assess the damage wrought by the previous night's emotional bonanza.

Huh.

In spite of the headache still coiled around her temples,

Miranda didn't see any outward evidence of her inner turmoil. Her hair was an almost attractive mess, rioting all over her head in masses of tumbled curls. Her eyes were wide and limpid, not bloodshot in the least. She'd expected to be pale, but instead she had good color in her cheeks, undoubtedly from the constant blushing she seemed to do around Adam. Curse of the redhead, Jess called it.

She watched her red, still kiss-swollen lips turn down at the thought of Jess. Some of the sparkle in her eyes dimmed.

God, what was she going to do?

Once Miranda was out of his direct line of sight, Adam managed to snap out of the semicoma her pretty, naked body had thrown him into. Hurriedly rifling through his drawers, he unearthed a T-shirt for himself—to cook bare-chested was to risk singed chest hair, which smelled unbelievably awful—and a Yankees sleep shirt Frankie'd given him as a joke. It had escaped the last nightshirt purge, and he thought it should be long enough to cover Miranda's distracting bits. At least long enough to get something nourishing into her.

So one night of sex hadn't made all her problems go away. Fine. Even if it was astonishingly, wildly, life-changingly awesome sex, he could understand that.

Probably they just needed to keep at it, perfect their technique. He grinned to himself.

But in the meantime, he'd fall back on his other great love: food. He was a firm believer in the curative properties of comfort food.

He left the Yankees shirt on the bed and went to see what he could rustle up.

The waffle iron was heating and he was halfway through mixing up the batter for cornmeal bacon waffles when Miranda appeared. She looked sleepy and tousled, swimming in the shirt, which hung to her knees. It was a true triumph of willpower that he didn't toss aside the mixing bowl and bend her back over the counter to plunder that sweet, swollen mouth.

But the waffles were really going to be delicious, and Miranda's mouth was set in an unhappy line that didn't invite kisses. Adam restricted himself to a smile.

"Find everything okay?"

She nodded and dropped into one of the chairs he kept near the movable butcher-block cart for when he wanted to sit while performing prep tasks like shucking corn or snapping peas from their pods.

Fingering the shirt with mock disdain, Miranda said, "I'm afraid this relationship is already on the rocks, though. Are you a Yankees fan?"

Her tone suggested that she could have substituted "serial killer" for "Yankees fan."

Adam gave her a cheeky grin, but inside he was doing a victory dance. She called it a relationship! Score.

Maybe it was weird that he liked that word. At least when it came to Miranda. Adam didn't know and didn't care. Something about the matter-of-fact way it came tripping off her tongue nearly made him giddy enough to forget to level the cake flour.

"I'm a born-and-bred New Yorker," he told her, emptying the hopefully correct amount of flour into the cornmeal mixture. "Of course I'm a Yankees fan."

"You could be a Mets fan," she grumbled. "You know, if you had a soul."

"I enjoy watching a team that wins." Adam shrugged. "Sue me."

Miranda sniffed, obviously unconvinced. Adam imagined taking her to a game, buying hot dogs and popcorn and cotton candy and beer, getting all rowdy with the diehards in the nosebleed section, where he liked to sit.

He pictured her perched ramrod straight on the bleachers. Probably wearing a Red Sox jersey, just to make a point. He'd sit back and let the nosebleeders hassle her until she finally got pissed enough to scrap with them. All of which would be better entertainment than any ball game Adam had ever been to. Something about the way Miranda held her own in a fight, never backing down from what she wanted, turned him right the hell on.

Smiling to himself at the thought, Adam whisked in the eggs and the melted butter, taking care to pull the heavy stoneground cornmeal up from the bottom of the bowl and mix it in well.

"What are you making?" Miranda asked. "And what are you *wearing*?"

Adam looked down at himself, wondering what shirt he'd grabbed.

Ah-ha. He'd thought it was white in the dim light of the bedroom, but out in the kitchen it was clearly pink. The front bore large block letters stating: MEAT IS MURDER. TASTY, TASTY MURDER.

"What?" he said. "You don't like it? I already know you're not a vegetarian. That would've killed this relationship before it ever got started."

He took smug pleasure in stressing the R-word.

"No." Miranda laughed. "Not a vegetarian. There aren't a lot of successful restaurant critics with hard-and-fast dietary restrictions. Anyway, even if I'd been toying with the idea, one bite of that pork belly you made a couple of weeks ago would've converted me."

"Ah, bacon," Adam said blissfully. "Fresh or cured, it's the gateway meat. Speaking of which, can you grab it out of the icebox?"

Miranda unfolded herself from the chair, flashing an enticing length of creamy thigh in the process.

"It's in the white paper wrapper, a big hunk," Adam told

her. "I got it at the market yesterday. The guy said it was slow cured, then smoked over applewood. We'll need, like, four thin slices."

"Okay."

Miranda pulled the scarred maple cutting board from its hook on the wall, and retrieved an eight-inch blade from the magnetic strip under the cabinets. Adam admitted to himself that it gave him a high like the strongest jolt of espresso to see her moving so confidently around his kitchen.

"To answer your other question," he said, "we're making cornmeal waffles. Here, now cut those bacon slices in half. We're gonna lay them in the waffle iron with the batter, so they fry right in. It's awesome, the rendered fat from the bacon makes the waffles all crisp and golden, not oily at all."

Blowing a stray curl out of her face, Miranda gathered up the bacon pieces and stood ready to place them as soon as Adam ladled out the batter.

His little rectangular waffle iron was so ancient, it didn't beep to signal it had reached the correct temperature. You had to watch for the tiny light on the front to glow orange. As soon as it did, Adam opened the iron and spooned out enough batter to fill all the shallow holes. A happy hissing noise filled the air as cool batter hit hot cast iron.

"It's not a Belgian-waffle maker," Miranda noticed.

"Yeah, I like the old-fashioned kind more. Better ratio of syrup to waffle, if you ask me. Also, because less surface area is exposed to the hot iron, the waffle turns out more tender than crunchy. Okay, lay on the bacon. Doesn't have to be pretty."

Miranda obeyed, and watched with great interest as Adam closed the iron. Batter visibly oozed out to the edges but didn't overflow.

"Want coffee?" he asked, picking up the pot.

"Sure." Miranda settled back down in her chair. "How long until the waffles are ready?"

"A couple minutes. Long enough to warm up some maple syrup. Keep an eye on the orange light for me, will you? Once it goes out, the waffles are done."

Miranda accepted the mug of coffee he handed her with quiet thanks. Adam banged through his cabinets looking for a gravy boat or something to serve the syrup in. If he'd been alone, he probably would've poured it straight from the jug, but that didn't seem nice enough for Miranda.

She still looked a little fragile to him. Her slender fingers were white with strain where they wrapped around the coffee mug.

He kept a weather eye on her, so he knew the moment she started thinking about her brother. Her brows lowered and her lips trembled before she firmed them and took a sip of coffee.

Adam considered jumping in with a conversational ploy to distract her, but decided that she needed to think this through. Better now, with him, than later on with Jess looking to her for support and understanding. Adam kept quiet and let her thoughts play out, hoping that eventually she'd open up.

"How could I let him go like that?" Miranda finally said. She set the mug on the table, drew her knees up under the sleep shirt and rested her chin on them, hugging herself as if needing to stay warm.

"You didn't." Adam kept his voice gentle. "It was just for the night, to give you both time to think. You haven't lost him."

You will, though, if you're not careful.

Adam shook his head. He wouldn't say it, couldn't add to her obvious misery. But Christ Almighty, he couldn't fathom what was stopping her from being the loving, caring older sister he'd seen her be to Jess before last night.

Something deep was happening here, something under the surface. Something more than a knee-jerk antipathy to Frankie's brash personality or disapproval of the age difference. And he didn't believe it was as simple as bigotry.

Adam's desperate hope was that she'd stop and think long enough to figure it out for herself; God knew what would happen if it were up to him to ferret out the answer.

He could freely admit that action was his forte. Contemplation, discussion, emotional delving—not so much.

But he truly wanted to help Miranda, so he manned up and said, "Look, I know you hate him but Frankie's really not such a bad guy."

She shot him an incredulous glare and he spread his hands in an earnest, what-can-I-say gesture.

"Hey, it's not what you want to hear. I get that. But I've known him a long time, and I've never seen him act like he does around Jess. I'm pretty sure this isn't a game to Frankie. He may not know *what* it is, himself, but it's serious. And Miranda—" Adam steeled himself for another dose of Miranda's evil eye.

"He's what Jess wants."

Miranda did scowl at that, but didn't issue the instantaneous denial Adam had prepared for. Instead, she paused as if struck by a sudden realization.

Adam did a mental victory lap. Hey, if she was thinking, she was one step closer to reacting like the logical, rational woman she was at heart, instead of like a scared, emotional wreck.

"So. You've seen them together?" Miranda asked slowly, her eyes narrow and intent on his face. "Before last night?"

Oooh, shit. Back up that triumphal float—there will be no parade in my honor today, fellas.

"Ah. Well." Adam cleared his throat. "Um, yes. I mean, at the restaurant. You know."

Very slick. Master of Misdirection, you are.

Adam winced.

Miranda clearly wasn't buying it.

"You knew," she said, all accusing. Her chest started to heave a little bit, which did interesting things to her braless breasts.

Adam always liked to look on the bright side. Which was good, because this was about to get ugly. Christ, he hated secrets.

"Okay, yeah, I knew. I saw them together—you know, *together* together—about a week ago. Right after the egg lesson."

"Days ago," she seethed, jumping up from the chair and starting to pace. "You knew all this time, *you slept with me,* and you never told me. You just allowed it to continue, allowed that deviant scumbag to prey on my innocent brother—"

"Whoa, hold on," Adam broke in before she could build up a good head of steam. "First off, whatever you think of him, Frankie is my best friend and I can't let you talk about him like that. Secondly, Jess is the one who swore me to secrecy. I kept it quiet for his sake, because he asked to be the one who got to tell you."

Miranda balled her fists. She looked ready to take his head off. "That's completely irrelevant. I *trusted* you."

Now Adam was starting to get pissed. "Yeah, well, so did Jess. And give me a break. I made that promise before anything had really happened between you and me."

"Oh, so making out in your kitchen was *nothing*?" He could practically see her blood pressure skyrocketing.

"That's not the point, and you know it."

Jesus, what a cock-up.

Miranda felt as if Adam had taken that thick slab of slimy bacon and thwapped her in the head with it.

"Basically, you're telling me that a promise to my brother,

a boy you barely know—didn't even want to hire until I forced your hand—means more to you than . . ."

Means more to you than I do.

She couldn't say it. The words, the foolishness of the sentiment, stuck in her throat.

God, what was she doing here?

Adam ground his back teeth audibly. "Frankie and Jess both swore me to secrecy. And since it really wasn't any of my business, I kept my mouth shut and my nose the hell out of it."

"You know what?" Miranda stood, aware that her legs were wobbly but willing to ignore it. "Thanks for last night. You really did help me through a rough patch, and I appreciate it."

His jaw dropped. "You're leaving. Just like that."

"You lied to me, Adam. For days, while we stood in this very kitchen and talked for hours—"

"About me!" Adam's shout seemed to surprise him as much as it surprised Miranda. He pulled in a deep breath in a visible effort to calm down. "We always talked about my past, my family. You didn't offer dick about your own history. Shit, all I mean is, Jess never really came up."

Miranda stiffened, renewed anger strengthening her knees. "Never came up? Are you serious? That's your justification? No. That's it. I have to go."

Adam stared at her for a long moment.

"Fine. I guess I can't stop you."

Miranda could have sworn the air between them crackled with angry heat. She could almost smell it burning.

"Crap," Adam yelped, spinning on his heel and grabbing for the waffle iron. "I forgot about breakfast."

The iron smoked when he opened it, released an acrid, burned smell into the air.

"I had high hopes for these waffles," Adam said, poking at the crusty remains sadly.

Miranda left him in the kitchen and went to gather her things. The last view she had as she let herself out of the townhouse was of Adam flaking blackened crumbs into the trash.

TWENTY-FOUR

Frankie snapped the cell phone shut with a grimace. He had no landline for the Garret, always used his cell for everything.

"That was Adam. Evidently your sister's on the warpath and he thought we should know."

Jess snorted and leaned back against a corduroy cushion covered in loud purple paisley. He pondered the inspiring sight of a half-naked Frankie, the lines and hollows of his surprisingly muscular chest gleaming pale in the half-light.

One full night at Frankie's, the best night of Jess's life, in so many ways, and he couldn't completely immerse himself in enjoying it. Not with the memory of Miranda's horrified expression superimposed on the backs of his eyelids.

"I already knew that. One night wasn't going to be enough to cool her out."

"Big Sis has quite the hate on for me, it's true," Frankie bragged, throwing himself down to lie beside Jess.

"I still can't believe how she acted. I was scared to tell her, but deep down, I really thought it was going to be okay." Jess could hear the throbbing pain in his own voice, and he tilted his head up to the brightening skylight to hide his eyes from Frankie's watchful black gaze.

He felt, more than saw, Frankie's shrug. "That's family, innit? They love you too much to let things go."

"How can you be so . . . cool about it?" Jess asked.

"Can't be anything else, Bit. I was born this cool."

Jess looked over in time to catch Frankie's ludicrous eyebrow-waggle.

Laughing like a hyena, Frankie easily ducked Jess's halfhearted swipe with the paisley pillow.

"Watch the goodies! That one bruises."

Jess tossed the pillow aside and wiggled across the few inches separating him from Frankie. With the ease born of a long night of new experiences and expanding horizons, he draped himself comfortably across Frankie's wiry, hairless chest. His skin was cool and smooth under Jess's hot cheek.

"I think it's the corduroy," Jess told him. "Makes the pillow feel all hard and overstuffed. Not that your bony shoulder is much better."

He fought to contain a thrilled shiver when Frankie's only response was a pair of long arms winding around Jess, holding him in a secure embrace.

"I guess I can make do," Jess muttered, pressing his face into the warm, spicy bend of Frankie's neck.

They were quiet together for a moment, Jess greedily absorbing as much sensation as he could, storing it in his memory for later. He didn't know when he'd get another night like last night, all of Frankie's focused attention for hours and hours, followed by this amazingly sweet and wonderful cuddling. If Jess were dumb enough to even *call* it cuddling, he was sure it would be withdrawn. He breathed deeply of Frankie's smoky clove scent and forced Miranda from his mind. He would live this to the hilt, he promised himself fiercely, for however long it lasted.

When Frankie's voice cut the stillness, Jess poured all
of himself into listening to the rough cadence of it, adding
another layer of sensation to the memory.

"I'm cool about it because she's your big sister, Bit. Took
care of you, loved you, protected you. For years, and that
makes it a hard habit to get out of. If I were her, I wouldn't
want me sniffing round, tempting my innocent brother out to
play."

Jess unraveled that with a moment's thought, and when
he did, it just ticked him off all over again.

"I'm not some doe-eyed angel boy getting corrupted by
the big bad punk rocker," he said. "I wish people would stop
acting like they're thinking about calling Child Services
or the Special Victims Unit or whatever." He squirmed in
annoyance, buffeting Frankie in the side with his elbow
accidentally.

"Settle down. I know. But that's just m'point. Eventually, most people will stop looking at you and seeing a
fresh-faced boy who can't take care of himself. You'll get
older, for one thing, and life leaves its mark in other ways,
too. Miranda, though? She never, ever, will look at you and
think, 'Oh, Jess is all grown-up. Well done me, guess I'll
go take a kip.' She'll always want to protect you. That's her
job. Your job is to let her."

That brought Jess up onto his elbows. "You can't mean you
think I ought to let her stop me from seeing you. Or worse,
let her think she can somehow talk me out of being gay!"

"'Course not." Frankie's eyes were deep and black in
the soft, filmy morning light. "But don't throw her care and
concern back in her face, either. You'll regret it as much as
she ever does, I promise you."

Jess, who had never lost the habit of noticing every minute detail about Frankie, saw the way his brows tightened
as if warding off some remembered pain. In the midst of
his own agitation and gut-deep disappointment in his sis-

ter, Jess stared at Frankie and realized that he wasn't giving advice based on some self-help book or movie of the week.

"You lived this, didn't you?" Jess breathed.

Frankie's immediate flinch was all the confirmation he needed. He got more when Frankie curled up from their nest on the floor, hitching his black jeans over his narrow hips and padding barefoot to the jacket he'd discarded by the door. Jess watched the search for cigarettes with impatience.

He waited until Frankie'd lit up and taken one good drag to bounce up on his knees. "Come on! Tell me."

Frankie puffed a couple more times in intense silence. A thought struck Jess like a dart letting the air out of a balloon.

"You don't have to talk to me about it," he offered, unable to completely keep the tremor out of his voice. "Not if you don't want to."

Blue smoke streamed out of Frankie's mouth on a frustrated breath. "It's not that, Bit. I don't mind you knowing. It's the telling part I don't fancy." He cocked his head at Jess. "You see the difference."

Jess got off his knees and walked over to where Frankie was standing. After last night, it didn't feel so daring to put his arms around Frankie's waist and hold on, or to bury his face in the taut silk of the skin stretched between Frankie's jutting shoulder blades.

Not so daring, but oh so right.

"No pressure, no guilt," Jess said. "I swear. But I'm here. Anytime you want to tell me, I'm here."

The noncigarette-holding hand stole up to lie across Jess's tight-hugging arms. Frankie's velvet-soft answer was better than a kiss.

"Not right now, then. But sometime."

"Sometime," Jess echoed happily. He squeezed Frankie's

ribs and reveled in the sense of continuity, of future, that word implied. Nothing concrete, oh, no. Frankie didn't work like that, and Jess knew better than to try and pin him down.

But it was a promise, all the same, a pact between the two of them.

And in that moment, Jess knew he'd do anything, defy anyone, to keep his part of the promise.

Her first emotion when she caught sight of Jess was annoyance that he didn't have the courtesy to look as miserable as she felt.

Part of her had hoped that a night sleeping under whatever rock Frankie Boyd habitually occupied would've cured Jess of his infatuation with the bohemian lifestyle. However, it didn't look like things were going to be that easy.

Jess sauntered up the path toward her looking terribly young and carefree. He was wearing his same clothes from yesterday, but if the lack of freshness bothered him, his loose-limbed stride and neutral expression didn't show it. His short hair glowed dark red in the buttery summer sunlight. When she'd gotten home, she'd been grimly unsurprised to find the apartment empty. Jess had answered his phone promptly, however, even though it was clear he was still with Frankie. She'd asked Jess to come home; he'd countered by inviting her to meet him in Central Park.

Miranda understood, and could even respect, the desire for neutral ground. She also suspected that Jess was hoping a public meeting would curtail her desire to rant and rave and make a scene.

She agreed to meet Jess at the Turtle Pond. She got there early and then had nothing to do but stand and try not to stare at the many partially clothed sunbathers littering the grass beside the pond, scant inches from the path. The banks of the Turtle Pond weren't as packed as the Great

Lawn, she was sure, but the glaring heat of midday had called the sun worshippers out in full force. Every summer, as soon as the mercury topped seventy, the city dwellers left their glass-and-concrete caves and gathered in Central Park to bare their pasty, winter-white skin. Bathing suits were almost never employed; instead it was deemed preferable to wear skimpy tank tops and minuscule shorts that were then rolled up as far as possible, or to strip down to skivvies.

Miranda shaded her eyes from one painfully thin hipster sprawled on a batik blanket wearing nothing but tightie whities and a pair of three-hundred-dollar sunglasses. She experienced a brief, violent surge of hatred—how dare this boho boy lie around in his underwear, looking happy, when Miranda's life was circling the drain? It was a disgustingly familiar bitterness, her lifelong companion, although it seemed all the stronger and more vicious for having abated somewhat in the last few weeks. It was tough to be bitter around someone as unrelentingly generous and lively as Adam Temple.

Quit mooning, she lectured herself. *You had your moment in the sun, soaking up Adam's energy and passion. Now it's time to head back to reality.*

She turned back to watching the path, and that was when she saw Jess loping steadily toward her, pink-cheeked and bright-eyed and none the worse for wear.

Miranda felt a wave of relief that he was okay. She wanted him to come to his senses, sure, but she didn't want him to suffer while doing it. Unreasonable, maybe, but as he got closer, she could see a faint red line at the corner of his eyebrow where he'd been bleeding last night.

He'd already been hurt because of Frankie. No matter what Adam said in defense of Frankie's character, nothing was worth endangering Jess's life. She'd sell her soul to keep him safe.

"Are you all right?" were the first words out of her mouth.

Jess didn't roll his eyes, but with instincts honed by years of parenting a teenager, Miranda could tell he wanted to.

"I'm fine. I told you I would be."

"Good, that's good."

They looked at each other, each waiting for the other to make a move.

Miranda broke first. "Why don't we walk up to Belvedere Castle? It should be quiet up there, and maybe not so hot."

"Sure," Jess said, turning to lead the way.

Was she imagining it, or had some of Frankie's smug, cooler-than-thou attitude rubbed off on her brother?

They followed the winding stone steps up to the top level of Belvedere Castle. The castle was more of an observation point, cunningly worked to look like someone's idea of a medieval fairy tale, complete with arched windows and a turret. There were usually people grouped around the stone platform enjoying the view, gaggles of children running around playing knight of the realm, but today there was no one.

Miranda would've wondered if her luck were changing, except she recognized the stubborn tilt to Jess's chin.

He moved to lean against the granite balustrade, hitching one hip up to get comfortable. Miranda thought it probably wasn't a coincidence that the position accentuated the couple inches of height difference between them. Jess had always been good at strategy games; he'd been beating her regularly at Risk since he was eleven.

Her shoulders tightened. The fact that he viewed this as some sort of power struggle didn't bode well for her chances of getting him to respond rationally. She and Jess shared a tendency to chuck logic out the window while clinging blindly to a fixed idea. Miranda had worked hard to overcome it, but Jess was still so young.

Young, but not without confidence, she saw, as he firmed his mouth and squared his shoulders.

"I'll start," Jess declared. "It'll save time, since I already know what you're going to say. You want me to promise not to see Frankie anymore, and better yet, you want me to find a nice girl and settle down, maybe spawn a litter of kids, and live happily ever after. Am I close?"

Miranda drew in a breath, feeling sucker-punched by Jess's casual scorn for the dreams she'd harbored for him.

"Would that be so atrocious?" she heard herself say. "It's the life our parents had. They thought it was pretty great."

Jess's eyes widened as he acknowledged the hit, then narrowed dangerously. Silence expanded between them like the shock waves of an exploding bomb.

"Oh, nice. Bring Mom and Dad into it," Jess finally ground out.

Miranda flushed with guilt, although underneath it she couldn't help but feel that Mom and Dad were in it already. She could practically feel their spirits swarming behind her, poking and prodding her.

"You're right," she conceded. "We're getting off track. The main issue here is Frankie."

Jess immediately got his back up. "This isn't about Frankie, either, and I hate it that you're trying to make it be about him. This is about me," he continued, more quietly. "And the fact that you can't accept me for who I am. But I'm not ashamed of being gay. And the infuriating thing is, I know you're not a bigot. You didn't have any problem with Grant being gay. But when it's me, your own brother . . ."

"Jess, no." Miranda was very firm. "Listen to yourself. I love you. You know that. I have always accepted you, encouraged you, supported you. But you have to see that I can't support this crazy crush Frankie has somehow suckered you into."

"It's not a crush," Jess cried. "And Frankie isn't the bad guy here."

Miranda's eyes burned. "And I suppose I am? I'm not the one who nearly got you beaten up."

She reached a trembling hand to the cut on his forehead and Jess shook her off as if he were swatting at an annoying insect.

"It was nothing, I told you that last night."

"See, that terrifies me, Jess. This lifestyle you're so eager to join, it could get you hurt, make you sick. You could die. The dangers—"

Jess cut her off with a sharp chop of his hand through the air between them.

"Stop right there. Being gay isn't a 'lifestyle' choice. It's not a choice at all. It's just me."

That statement stole Miranda's breath. "Okay. Okay."

They stood looking at each other while the noises of the park drifted around them.

Miranda gazed at Jess, and for the first time, she saw a young man rather than the small boy who'd slipped his hand into hers at their parents' funeral. Her heart cracked a little at the self-knowledge and determination in his blue eyes—a determination that couldn't quite mask the vulnerability underneath. Miranda breathed, and thought hard about what she was going to say next. She knew instinctively that it would set the tenor for her entire adult relationship with her brother.

"When you first told me you were gay, I did everything wrong. I cried. I yelled. I blamed everyone in sight, including myself. I acted like being gay was this horrible thing, when I don't even think that—but Jess, it *is* different, because you're my brother." She swallowed hard, but the light starting to fill Jess's eyes dissolved the lump in her throat.

"We grew up in such a hurry after Mom and Dad died," Miranda faltered. "The two of us against the world. That car accident robbed you of so much—your childhood, your innocence, countless memories of our parents and the beautiful life they made together. I swore to myself you'd have those things one day. I imagined every detail. Countless dreams of a perfect, normal life—a wife, a nice house in a safe neighborhood, kids. I wanted that for you even more than for myself, and hearing that you were gay . . ."

Miranda lost her voice without warning. She realized she was crying, tears rolling wet and messy down her cheeks.

"God," Jess choked. "Miranda."

"Let me finish," she begged. "I don't think less of you, and nothing you could ever do or say could make me stop loving you. But I'm afraid. I'm afraid of the way the world treats people who are different. And there's a part of me that's afraid it's my fault. That it's something I did, or didn't do, and that if Mom and Dad were alive they'd have done better, protected you or . . ."

Jess took her by the shoulders, his hands sure and steady, his face serious. "But you know that's wrong."

"I do," she swore, pushing every ounce of sincerity she could muster into her voice. "I know that's not how it works. Your sexuality has nothing to do with me, and I had nothing to do with it. I let my own fears and insecurities govern my reactions when you came out to me, and I will regret that till my dying day."

"Stop it." Jess's voice made her ache with love. He shook his head. "I don't care how the world treats people like me. I care about you, and what you think. It doesn't matter that you weren't immediately perfect the instant I told you. You're saying all the right stuff now. That's what counts."

Miranda let him hug her, only slightly surprised to register that he was tall enough for her to rest her chin on his shoulder. She wanted to savor this moment, when she finally felt connected to Jess, the way it used to be when he was little—only better, because he was all grown-up. But she knew the next thing she had to say wouldn't be quite as welcome.

Steeling herself, she pulled away and said, as gently as she knew how, "I understand that being gay isn't something you chose. But honey, Frankie Boyd *is* a choice, and a very dangerous one. He's older than you, more experienced, and look at the way he lives! No sane person would get involved with someone so unstable."

"What's so unstable? He's got his own apartment, he pays his rent, he's got a good job."

Miranda must have made a face without meaning to, because Jess jumped all over it.

"What? Suddenly being a chef isn't good enough for you?" he asked. "Wonder what Adam would say if he knew that."

"Don't talk to me about Adam Temple right now—I'm so angry at him for not telling me what was going on with you, I could scream." She couldn't help but think that if she hadn't been blindsided by Jess's revelation, she might have reacted better.

"But look," she continued. "This is what I'm getting at. The restaurant kitchen culture, especially now, in the age of the celebrity chef, is insane. These cooks have women throwing themselves at them all the time. It's like being a rock star; crook a finger, and anyone you want will be thrilled to bend over your kitchen counter."

Adam had sure cashed in on the chef hoopla, Miranda remembered. He'd slept with that investor, Eleanor Bonning, to get capital for his restaurant. How could she have forgotten that?

Easy. She simply hadn't wanted to think about it. In the glaring light of Adam's personality, his easy charm and warm, flirtatious manner, it had been easy to rationalize what Rob had told her. But she shouldn't have forgotten. Adam was someone who believed the end justified the means—and that included lying to Miranda about her brother.

Nausea threatened to overtake her, but Miranda forced herself to keep going. Jess watched her with big eyes, his face open and searching. He was finally listening to her.

"Sex doesn't mean to them what it does to you and me," she told him. "I don't know how far you and Frankie have gone." Jess flushed and ducked his head, and Miranda hurried to say, "Nor do I want to. But honey, his reputation, even in the kitchen, among his friends and colleagues who presumably like him—he's known for short-term flings."

No one in the kitchen had ever used such decorous language for Frankie's exploits, but she couldn't bring herself to repeat what she'd heard verbatim while staring into Jess's wide blue eyes.

It would be cruel and unnecessary. She could see in his face that he knew exactly what she meant.

Please, oh, please let him believe me. I want him to be happy, and Frankie is going to make him miserable.

Jess stared down at the rough-hewn rocks beneath their feet. When he met her gaze, his eyes were older, somehow. It shocked Miranda out of her brief moment of hope.

"I heard those same rumors when I first started working at Market," Jess told her. "And there's nothing concrete I can show you to prove that what Frankie and I have is different. He could be playing me. Except that he's never broken a promise to me yet."

Jess met her stricken stare head-on. "He could be seeing someone on the side. Except we've spent part of every night together for the past week, so I don't see when he'd have the time. It doesn't matter. I want him. More than I've ever wanted anything."

Miranda's mouth opened and closed soundlessly. All those nights he'd gotten home late, told her he'd been out with the other servers. God. She'd known, of course, that this thing with Jess and Frankie had to have been going on for a while, but she hadn't wanted to believe it was serious.

Getting right to the heart of the matter, she said, "I want you to quit your job. Meet some people your own age. If you stay away from Frankie, these feelings will fade. You'll see. In a few weeks, it'll be like 'Frankie who?'"

"And now we're back to this again." Jess pushed away from the wall and stalked past Miranda. She caught at his shirtsleeve but he shrugged her off, only turning to glare at her.

"Once you're not seeing him every single day, you'll—"

"I like working at Market. I like the people there. Grant's been really good to me, and Adam gave me a shot when no one else would've." Jess sighed. "And honestly, I love seeing Frankie every day. I don't want to give that up. I'm not giving him up, Miranda."

She drew breath to argue, but Jess cut her off with a sharp hand gesture. "The issue of Frankie aside, I can't afford to quit." He squared his shoulders. "You don't want me working my way through college, but I need to help pay for my own education. It's important to me. And I know you don't really have the money for NYU."

"You could get another job, somewhere else," she tried, knowing already that it was unlikely. Waiting tables at an upscale place like Market was a lucrative proposition for a student. Most restaurants at that level wouldn't hire someone with Jess's scant experience, and two weeks at Market followed by a precipitate departure would hardly be inspiring résumé material.

"Will you at least come home and stay with me?" Miranda asked around the hard, scratchy lump in her throat.

Jess smiled tremulously, and there he was, the sweet boy Miranda'd raised, not so far under the surface after all. "If you'll still have me."

"Of course I will," Miranda said, fighting not to sob out loud. He looked almost surprised, but very glad, and Miranda braved another shrug-off to get her arms around him. This time he allowed the contact, and even hugged back, clinging a little.

"I would never turn you away." Miranda spoke fiercely into his shirt. "Not for any reason. Promise me you'll always remember that."

"I promise," Jess said, his voice thick with tears.

Miranda stroked her baby brother's back soothingly and closed her eyes.

She'd always said she'd do anything to keep Jess safe; this was the true test. Would she sell her integrity down the river? Would she betray the people she'd worked with, laughed and talked with, for the last two weeks?

Would she give up her chance at making up with Adam and getting him to fall in love with her?

With a sharp shudder of agony, Miranda acknowledged the answer.

Yes.

Jess was right. She didn't have the money to pay for his tuition—unless she delivered that manuscript and cashed the check from the publisher. It all came down to money, in the end. If she had that check, she could afford to send Jess to school. If she had that check, she could talk him into quitting his job at Market, she knew she could.

If she had that check, she could get Frankie Boyd out of Jess's life and give Jess a chance to fall in love with someone his own age. To have the freedom to meet new people at school and stretch his wings, to be himself, without being tied to a man who couldn't truly care for him the way he deserved.

When she looked at it like that, the decision was really very simple. Heart-wrenching, gut-twisting, but simple.

Later that afternoon, as her finger hovered over the send button, hesitating to make that one final movement that would deliver her manuscript to Empire Publishing, Miranda berated herself.

This is no time to get squeamish. Think about what Mom and Dad would've wanted. Think about Jess.

Whatever you do, don't think about Adam Temple.

Don't think about his hands, his quick smile, his happy laugh, oh, God, that dimple . . . Don't think about the way he makes your whole body buzz with energy or the way he loves to hear you talk. Don't think about how much you lov—

She blanked her mind, and pushed the button.

TWENTY-FIVE

Adam cursed loudly and inventively. A Sunday-night service should not be this fucking busy, it was unheard of, it was ungodly, it was unbelievable.

It was just his damn luck.

The restaurant was fully booked, standing room only at the bar, and Grant had signaled him ecstatically earlier to let him know that the three tables they reserved for walk-ins each had an hour-and-a-half-long wait.

Bountiful Table, another foodie magazine, had come out with yet another article about Miranda and the damn dare. Diners were lined up, presumably hoping to catch a glimpse of a pint-sized redhead screaming invective at Market's chef. Adam hoped they'd go away disappointed on that score, but thrilled with the service and food at Market.

Actually, part of him hoped they'd *go away,* period. Not that he'd ever admit that to Grant, who looked happier than Adam had ever seen him. But then, the tension in the dining room wasn't thick enough to carve like an ice sculpture.

The atmosphere in the kitchen, meanwhile, was such that Adam's frantic cussing went practically unnoticed.

Miranda hadn't called him after she left his place that morning, but he knew from Frankie that Jess was back with her and apparently there to stay, so everything should've been hunky-dory.

Except it so obviously wasn't. When Miranda arrived for prep, she quietly asked to be put on garde-manger with Milo rather than up at the pass. Adam realized that expediting wasn't for everyone, but he'd thought she enjoyed working with him before. He'd been hoping that the stellar sex and hard-core closeness they'd shared might outweigh the small spat, but it didn't take Dr. Phil to figure out that she was avoiding him. Which sucked donkey nuts.

And then there was Frankie, who seemed to be going out of his way to be, well, *Frankie*, talking loudly and throwing himself around the kitchen like he was hyped up on crack. He didn't directly confront Miranda, oh no, but the performance was definitely for her benefit. Frankie's oh-so-subtle *fuck you* in the face of her disapproval. Luckily Jess hadn't come sniffing around the kitchen yet; Grant and the crowds of customers out front were keeping him hopping. Adam was determined not to borrow trouble, so he wasn't imagining what might happen if all three of the key players in last night's drama convened in one room.

One packed, bustling room where Adam was currently striving to pull his crew out of the weeds through sheer force of will.

"Milo! You and Miranda need to hustle up with those mixed greens, the table's waiting on you."

"Yes, Chef!"

Miranda just looked at him. Or, more accurately, looked through him. Christ.

He turned to Quentin, who'd been pressed into service on the sauté station. "Q, man, I've gotta have those shrimp skewers. It looks like you're getting low on rosemary branches—Billy, check the basement pantry, see if we've got more."

"You got it, Chef!" "Yes, Chef!"

"Whoo, you've got these lads trained a treat," Frankie cackled by the grill, his hands a red-hot blur as he flipped and cross-hatched steaks in a complicated pattern.

Adam wanted to rip his hair out. "Frankie! Quit bullshitting and buckle down. I mean it, we're in the weeds."

He didn't add, "And it's all on you," but he was sure thinking it. From the way Frankie steadied his stance and hunched a bit over the grill, he knew it, too. The crew took their cues from Frankie, always had. His personality tended to overwhelm the kitchen, which could be a great thing, when he was on. When he was being a shit? The whole kitchen went to shit.

"What should I do, Chef?"

The unfamiliar voice had him spinning around in a near-panic. He felt like he was balancing a full tray of dirty plates and glasses on the top of his head. One single saucer perched up there with the rest would be enough to bring the whole thing crashing down.

His spin brought him face-to-face with that metaphorical saucer.

Oh, yeah. As if tonight weren't stressful enough, the Market kitchen crew had a brand-new boy to contend with.

Wes Murphy had taken the train down from the Academy of Culinary Arts that morning. He'd arrived at Market wearing fresh, crisp kitchen whites and a cocky grin.

Adam had a new extern. God help them both.

Adam had set him to work dicing vegetables and mixing up salad dressing, the kitchen equivalent of swabbing the decks. Wes handled a knife like a pro, real grace and economy of movement turning the simple chore into a showpiece.

Noticing Adam watching, Wes had shot him that same smug smile. Adam had sighed and sent him off to help Violet roll out pastry dough for tonight's special dessert, rustic peach tartlets.

Wes had done that perfectly, too, his touch with the rolling pin deft and light, ensuring maximum flakiness of the crust.

Adam had left him to it. He'd tried to keep an eye on the kid, but service lurched out of control so damn quick, he'd lost track of Wes.

Now here he was, obviously bored and more than a little judgmental of the frenzied state of the kitchen, if the look in his eyes was anything to go by. Adam stared at him for a moment, trying to pinpoint what it was about the new guy that made Adam want to banish him down to the basement to take inventory of the supplies in the employee john.

Wes was taller than Adam, but years of friendship with Frankie the Giraffe had inured Adam to the sensation of looking up to catch another man's expression. And anyway, Wes wasn't quite as tall as Frankie, but he was broader. Not as wide through the shoulders as Adam, but clearly strong enough to lift heavy pots, which was all Adam cared about.

He had the tanned, hard look of a guy who spent a lot of time at high temperatures, standing over a hot stove. He had a lot of light brown hair falling over his forehead and a pair of thick, straight eyebrows that gave him a broody look. His sideburns were longish, kinda retro. He had those funny eyes that turned different colors in different lights, green to gold to brown and back again.

Adam thought Wes probably had the kind of looks that women swooned over; it reminded him of Devon's polished handsomeness, although not so exaggerated. Devon Sparks was cover-model good-looking. With Wes, it was more his expression, the way he carried himself. Women tended to go for that cocky-as-hell, soulful look; Adam had worked that angle himself often enough when he was younger.

None of this endeared Wes Murphy to Adam. The new guy had sneered at Milo, condescended to Violet, and now he stood in front of Adam, hands on hips and an impatient curl to his mouth. From the vibe of him, Adam could tell Wes was hoping to be ordered up to the pass to work the hot plate with Adam. Get some expediting experience.

This was supposed to be an educational stint for Wes, Adam knew. The guy was in his final year of culinary school, and the externship program was meant to provide practical, hands-on experience before the graduates were shunted out into the real world and expected to earn a living by their knives.

So let him learn, Adam thought viciously. *This is my goddamned kitchen. No one gets to do exactly what they want here except me.*

"Take over helping on garde-manger. Milo, switch-hitter coming in! Miranda?"

He looked away from the surprised disappointment in Wes's eyes to find Miranda starting at him, mouth pinched and gaze narrow. Adam ground his back teeth.

"Miranda, with me," was all he trusted himself to say.

"Yes, Chef." Wes echoed the crew's earlier snappy salutes, but somehow, on him, it sounded snotty. Adam shrugged. He could handle attitude, so long as the guy kept bringing his A-game. Wes would settle in eventually; the kitchen was an amazing leveler. Had a way of bringing everyone down to their true nature.

Adam's gaze fixed on Miranda. The corners of her mouth were turned down unhappily. Something about the look of her made Adam's shoulders relax. Maybe it was that he couldn't see himself having trouble making her happy again.

Making her not mad was another story, but happiness, Adam could do.

"Sooner rather than later," Adam said mildly, scanning the next ticket.

With evident reluctance, Miranda moved up to his side. He watched her gaze immediately search out her brother through the open pass to the dining room. The worry line between her brows made Adam's heart turn over in his chest.

He wanted to tell her Jess was fine, that everything would be fine, but they were in the weeds and there wasn't time.

Just as he opened his mouth to start barking orders, there was a commotion at the back of the kitchen. A scuffle, a short scream that sounded like Violet at her pastry board by the back door, and Adam thought, *Christ Almighty, what now?*

From the moment he glanced over his shoulder, irritated at the new disruption, everything moved into slow motion. His vision sharpened, colors brightened, sounds magnified by a thousand.

There was a guy waving a gun around Adam's kitchen. *Oh, hell no.*

TWENTY-SIX

Somebody screamed and Miranda's blood turned to ice water.

Robin Meeks had returned to Market. And he had a gun.

His sharp, thin face was damp with sweat or tears, his eyes were wide and rolling. He looked deranged, his grip on the gun none too steady.

"Hey, I'm here to talk," Rob said loudly.

"Fucking hell," Frankie swore.

Adam immediately thrust out an arm and pulled Miranda behind him, but she still had a good view of Frankie making a dash for the swinging door that led to the front of house.

Coward, she thought, genuinely shocked but at the same time darkly pleased to have her bad opinion of him confirmed.

It didn't work anyway, because Rob swung toward Frankie and managed to bring his gun to bear. Wavering only slightly, he slurred out, "Not so fast, Frankie boy. This concerns you, too."

Frankie froze a few strides from the pass, putting his hands in the air. But even with a gun trained on him, held by a shaky hand, he couldn't seem to focus on Rob. Miranda saw the glances he kept casting out to the dining room. She couldn't decipher the look on his face; it was more than simple fear.

It was hard to tell if the diners even knew what was happening; the kitchen was open, but there was music out there, the noise of plates and silverware, servers circling. She closed her eyes and prayed that someone had noticed, had used a cell phone to call the police. She sent up a further, fervent prayer that Jess *hadn't* noticed, that he'd stay out there where it was relatively safe.

She didn't have long to contemplate it, however, because in the next moment Adam said, "Come on, man. Be cool. You don't need that gun to get us to talk to you. Why don't you put it on the ground, and you and I'll go down to the office and have a long chat? Whatever you want to talk about."

Miranda reached out and clutched the back of Adam's chef jacket in her fist. She did *not* want him going off alone with Rob, gun or no gun. The guy was obviously on something.

"Shut up!" Rob lurched in their direction, bumping Milo, who cursed and stepped out of the way quickly. Rob turned on him clumsily, and stood blinking in confusion at the man standing next to Milo.

"Who are you?" Rob asked.

"Murphy," the new cook said, eyes never leaving Rob's limp gun hand. "Wes Murphy. Just started tonight."

Rob started to laugh, sending a visible shock through the room. "Oh, shit, that's funny. You're the new me."

"Say what?" Wes Murphy said, his tone icy enough to make Miranda nervous.

"The new extern, right? From the Academy?"

"That's right." The guy's eyes snapped.

Rob's harsh laugh sounded like a sob, and she wasn't

surprised when he brought up a hand to swipe at his cheeks with his sleeve. It was the hand holding the gun. Everyone in the kitchen jumped and gasped as the barrel flailed wildly in Rob's loose grip. Every muscle in Miranda's body tightened at once.

"You can go, if you want," Rob said. He seemed distracted, tired of talking to Wes, or maybe as if he were coming down a little from whatever he'd taken. "You weren't part of this. Didn't do nothing to me. You are me. We're the same. So you can leave."

"No, thanks," Wes said, disdain in every syllable. Miranda caught her breath, wondering what the hell he was playing at.

She wasn't the only one. Rob stared, arrested. "No? Ooooh, I get it. You think if you stay, it'll make them like you. Think they'll respect you for it or something, let you into the club. Well, I got news for you, man, no one gets in this club. They've all been cooking together since dinosaurs roamed the earth, man, they're tight, tighter than a nun's ass. They're never going to let you in."

Miranda could see the muscles in Wes's chiseled jaw working. "All the same, I think I'll hang around."

Adam spoke up cautiously. "Maybe, Rob, if you're okay with Wes going, he could head out into the dining room, round up the guests, get them out of here. They don't have anything to do with this, either, right?"

Rob squeezed his eyes tight and pressed the butt of the gun to his forehead, missing the look Adam telegraphed across the kitchen. Miranda saw it, though, and so did Wes, who nodded slightly in acknowledgment.

"Fine, fine, whatever," Rob said peevishly. "Shit, my head."

Wasting no time, but not running, Wes hurried out the swinging door. Miranda could sense him moving through the dining room behind her, heard movement and low voices. Chills coursed down her spine. *Please,* she prayed, *get Jess out of here. Please, please, please.*

"You ready to talk now, Rob?" Adam asked. "Why don't you give me the gun, and we can get you some aspirin or something?" He took a step closer, hand outstretched. Miranda held her breath.

"I don't want *you* to talk to *me*," Rob spat, opening his eyes and bringing the gun to bear on Adam. "You had your chance. Now I want you to fucking listen. Can you do that, boss?"

Adam held up his hands placatingly. "Sure, sure I can do that. Whatever you say. Just put the gun down."

"No. If I don't have the gun, no one will listen to me."

"I'll listen, I swear it."

"No! No one listens. Except Miranda. Hey, where is she? That you, Miranda? You hiding from me?"

Adam shifted in front of her, shielding her more closely with his body, but Miranda could hear the increasing desperation in Rob's voice. They had to keep him calm.

"I'm right here," she said, controlling the tremor in her voice and stepping out from behind Adam. She kept her grip on his jacket, though. Maybe it was weak, but she needed the anchor of that connection. Suddenly, exactly when Adam knew what and whether or not he chose to tell Miranda seemed monstrously unimportant. Even the all-encompassing guilt about the book faded into the background of this horrific situation.

Adam made a muffled sound of protest as she exposed herself to Rob's view. She couldn't look up and meet Adam's eyes; that would break her calm façade for sure.

"Hi, Miranda," Rob said. He didn't seem all that happy to see her, but he let the barrel of the gun droop toward the floor.

"How are you?" she asked, falling back on manners.

Really, what did one say to an armed gunman? Did Emily Post have a ruling on that?

Miranda's vision swam, making her painfully aware that she was skirting the edge of hysteria. Her ribs heaved, expanding and contracting too fast, until she felt Adam's big, warm hand settle at the small of her back. The weight and heat grounded her. She inhaled and actually got a breath into her lungs.

"Not so good," Rob said morosely. "Since I got fired from here, no one else will hire me. I can't go back to culinary school, they'll fail me for sure. It's all fucked up." He raised his head, the gun in his hand coming up, too.

"It's your fault, everything is." Rob glowered at Adam, blinking furiously. "You never gave me a chance to show you what I could do. You spent all your time paying attention to the others, like that stuck-up bitch, Violet, and that little Mafia piece of shit, Milo. Even the fucking Mexican dishwasher! But the worst was Miranda. She showed up, and it was like you couldn't even see anyone else."

Adam's hand tensed against her back. He shifted a few inches to the side, angling himself in front of her again. Miranda forced air in and out of her lungs in a rigidly slow tempo.

"I'm sorry if you feel I ignored you," Adam said. He was using a deep, soft voice, as though he were coaxing a spitting cat down from a tree. "But it wasn't Miranda's fault."

"She's not even a cook," Rob ranted, like he hadn't even heard Adam. "She's a writer, she doesn't give two shits about cooking, she's only here for one fucking month. It's not like she was even looking for a job! But you acted like you wanted to hire her on full-time or some shit."

"I would," Adam said.

What?

Rob's face darkened, but Adam wasn't even looking

at him, he was staring at Miranda and she was staring back.

"I'd hire her in a heartbeat if it meant she'd stay right next to me for a good long time."

Miranda gaped, searching Adam's eyes for the meaning behind his words. His dark chocolate eyes were almost black, snapping with tension. He raised his brows a fraction of an inch, and Miranda tried desperately to interpret the message he was sending. She refused to believe it was as simple as Adam trying to tell her how he felt about her. That would imply that he thought he'd better get it in under the wire while there was still time, and she couldn't handle that level of pessimism from Adam. Wes was outside by now, the police were probably on their way already. This was no deathbed confession.

No, Adam must mean he wanted her to stay at his side or behind him, not present a target for Rob's ever-shifting gun.

"Shit, a woman like Miranda?" Rob laughed, high and grating. "No way she's sticking around. She's just digging for dirt for that book. Have you let him read it yet, Miranda? There's some good shit in there."

Miranda closed her eyes, blood draining from her head and making her see stars against the black of her eyelids.

"Doesn't matter. Book or no book, she'll always have a place at Market, if she wants it," Adam said, clasping Miranda's shoulder. He shook it lightly, as if waking Miranda from a deep sleep, and she opened her eyes to find him gazing down at her with unmistakable affection.

She gulped. He smiled, dimple winking, and Miranda's heart did a slow spin before leaping up into her throat.

That wasn't mere affection shining in Adam's eyes, written in every line of his face.

Adam wasn't offering her a job, he was offering himself.

Joy rose in her like a storm surge, bright and unstoppable, only to tangle horribly with a crushing coil of guilt.

Adam loved her.

She'd betrayed him.

Those awful things Rob told her, that she'd put in the book. Secrets, rumors, innuendo, about Violet and Milo and Quentin and all the rest. About Adam and the way he'd gotten the money for Market. Any single revelation would hurt Adam, but a whole bookful, splashed out into public for the whole world to pick over and denigrate?

Miranda shuddered. Adam curled his hand around the back of her neck, palm warm and reassuring at her nape. His stare went from tentative happiness to concern in a blink. Miranda had never felt so out of control. She had no idea what he was reading in her expression, but from the tingling in her fingertips and the chill of sweat at her hairline, she must be white as salt.

She opened her mouth, but her vocal cords seemed to be paralyzed. Nothing came out, not even a whisper.

Before she had a chance to clear her throat and try again, Rob made an aggrieved noise that jerked her attention back to him.

"You fucking loser," Rob said. There were tears on his cheeks again, but he didn't pause to sob. His gun hand was steadier now and pointed directly at Adam. "I've got a damn gun on you, aimed right at your stupid heart, and you're still mooning around playing suck-face with her." Rage purpled his face. His whole body shook.

The very real possibility that she could lose Adam before she managed to squeak out one word about how she felt struck Miranda between the eyes. Everything was happening so horribly quickly.

Shoving Miranda behind him again, Adam faced Rob. Miranda gripped the scratchy fabric of Adam's chef jacket, longing to pull him to the ground and cover him with her own body. Anything to get that gun off its target.

"I'm sorry, Rob, calm down. Keep talking. What else is on your mind?"

"What's the fucking point?" Rob screamed. "Oh, shit, what's the point of any of this? I can't do it anymore, I can't, I can't—"

Adam stilled, and time slowed to a crawl. As scared as she'd been before, Rob's sudden breakdown ratcheted up her terror by about a thousand degrees.

The whole kitchen froze into a hideous tableau with Rob at the center, crying silently and hunching over his midsection as if he were slowly crumbling.

Sudden movement in the dining room. A flash of auburn hair stopped Miranda's heart.

Jess.

He peered around the corner of the pass-through and locked eyes on her at once. She made an involuntary movement, a quick jerk of one shoulder, before she bullied her body back to stillness. But in the unnatural silence of the kitchen, it was enough to bring Rob's head up.

Flailing wildly, Rob swayed on his feet, eyes narrowing on the pass.

Time sped up.

Miranda couldn't follow it.

Adam gripped her shoulder and pushed, propelling her away from him.

Miranda careened into the salad station, stainless steel countertop thudding into her solar plexus and stealing her air.

Adam exploded into motion, diving for Rob.

Frankie dashed toward the pass, terror in his eyes and a name on his lips.

"Jess!"

A gunshot. Stench of ozone and fear.

Adam tackled Rob to the ground, knocking the gun from his hand.

Time snapped back into place and Miranda started to breathe again. She clutched the stainless steel table and panted.

Sirens screamed outside the restaurant. Quentin and Milo ran to help with Rob, who collapsed bonelessly. All the fight went out of him as soon as the gun was out of his hand.

Adam wrestled Rob into Quentin's big, capable hands, got off the floor and whirled, looking around frantically until he spotted Miranda.

"You okay?" he asked, circling the salad station and coming up behind her. His arms closed around her tight enough to force the air from her lungs again, but Miranda didn't care.

"I know, it's okay, I'm okay. But Adam, that gunshot—"

"No!"

Jess's agonized voice tore through the kitchen. Miranda pulled out of Adam's arms.

"Oh, my God," said Adam faintly.

Frankie was on the ground, stretched in front of the pass like a rag doll tossed aside by a careless child.

Blood seeped reddish-black, puddling under his left shoulder and spreading over the pristine white tile.

Jess banged through the swinging door and skidded to a stop at Frankie's side, crouching and whimpering, "Please no, oh no, Frankie, please, hold on, hold on."

Adam's knees gave out under him, just for a second, but his arm was still around Miranda's shoulders and she caught the brunt of his weight.

"Adam, honey, come on, we've got to go make sure he's okay," she said urgently. "Stay with me, you can do this."

Nodding, Adam set his jaw in a grim line and straightened up. Miranda kept a cautious arm around his waist, but they stumbled over to Frankie and Jess with no problems.

Frankie lay facedown, his right arm curled beneath his body. Jess hovered over him, tears streaming unnoticed down his face.

"I don't want to move him," he said. "I'm sure we're not supposed to move him."

Miranda helped Adam ease down beside Frankie, careful to avoid the small pool of blood. It didn't seem to be getting any bigger, but she still said, "Maybe I'll get some towels? We ought to put pressure on that wound."

"Hey, Frankie," Adam said, voice gruff and choked. "Come on, man, wake up."

Frankie didn't stir.

Jess met Miranda's eyes, his own swimming with pain and remorse.

"It's because of me," Jess said through white lips. "Rob saw me through the pass. He was aiming for me. Frankie saved my life."

Miranda's heart split down the middle, jagged shards cutting into her chest. God, how could one person be so wrong about so many things?

She'd thought Frankie was a danger to Jess. The man had literally thrown himself between Jess and a bullet.

A thready, heartfelt groan sounded from the vicinity of the floor.

"Ah, fucking hell." Only the accent was so thick, it came out sounding like *fockin' 'ell.*

Miranda wasn't sure she'd ever heard anything more beautiful.

Judging by the dawning elation on Jess's face, he agreed completely. Adam made a sound between a grunt and a cough. A quick glance at his face confirmed that he was caught on the brink of relieved tears, and was struggling manfully against it.

Miranda squeezed his arm. "I'll get the towels," she said gently. She kissed Adam's cheek on her way back to her feet, and he shot her a grateful look, the love she'd seen earlier shining bright and honest in his wet eyes. Miranda paused for a second to take it all in. She hadn't imagined it; Adam loved her.

"What happened?" she heard Frankie ask groggily. And a half second later, in a much sharper voice: "Where's Jess, is he all right?"

Self-recrimination was bitter on the back of Miranda's tongue, but she swallowed it down.

She deserved every bit of it.

TWENTY-SEVEN

"Whoops!" Frankie listed sideways as they led him out of the emergency room, where he'd been bandaged and deemed okay enough to go home. Grant ducked under his arm and supported him from the other side.

"Thanks, mate. Still getting my sea legs under me. That paramedic bint had great drugs. Help me reel over to Adam?"

Everyone in their ragtag little group faded but Frankie and Grant. A lump the size of a ham hock expanded in Adam's throat.

"I'm so fucking sorry," Adam choked out.

"What on earth for?" Grant asked, eyebrows high and perplexed. Grant had organized the efficient evacuation of more than a hundred guests, servers, and other front-of-house staff. Then he'd come back inside with the police, unwilling to leave his friends in danger any longer than he had to.

Adam was half surprised the man hadn't told the guests to get out on their own and come back to the kitchen when Jess did. But of course Grant was too responsible for that. And, unlike Jess, Grant wasn't in love.

Frankie was giving Adam that narrow look he reserved

for idiots and madmen. The knowledge that only sheer, dumb luck was responsible for keeping that sneer in place made Adam shudder.

"Adam's torturing himself over what happened because he thinks he's God," Frankie said. "Right? Shoulda seen it coming, shoulda stopped it before it started. That kind of bollocks."

"It's my place, my restaurant," Adam said miserably. "I knew Rob was a fuckup from the minute I met him. I should've bounced him out of here then and there. It never should've come to this."

"See? Woulda, shoulda, coulda," Frankie said, all singsong and annoying. When it didn't even make Adam want to slug him, he knew things were fucked up.

"Frankie's right. Ineloquent and immature, as always," Grant specified, returning to his usual full-on snark with visible relief. Even a couple hours of being nice to Frankie while he was injured must've been a strain. "But for once, absolutely right. You've got to let the crazy man with the gun take responsibility for this one, Adam."

The lump in Adam's throat started to dissolve. He had the best friends in the whole fucking world. If his arms weren't made of overcooked pasta, he'd totally subject them both to bear hugs.

Frankie shrugged his unbloodied shoulder, barely hiding a wince. "And anyhow, it all turned out fine. No one the worse for wear."

Jess shot Frankie an incredulous look. Adam was with him on that one; the ER doctor had removed Frankie's shirt to get at his left shoulder, and that entire side of his pale, Englishman's body was smeared with a rusty stain of drying blood.

"I'm staying with Frankie tonight," Jess announced, glancing at his sister. "I told the nurse I'd keep an eye on him."

Adam watched Miranda, but he couldn't read her expression.

"I understand," was all she said.

Jess gave her an uncertain look. "So it's okay?"

"Christ, Bit, how much of a blessing d'you want?" Whatever the ER doc had given Frankie was making his eyes slide shut.

Jess hesitated for a moment, and Miranda touched his arm lightly.

"I'm glad you're okay," she told him, a world of feeling in her voice. "And . . . Frankie's going to be fine. I know you'll take good care of him."

"I will," Jess said, all serious eyes and firm mouth. "And he'll take care of me, too."

Miranda pressed her lips together and nodded. Jess helped Frankie over to the curb where Grant had already managed to hail a cab, leaving Miranda staring after them.

"Hey," Adam said. "That was . . . wow, a huge step for you. It was awesome. Are you okay?"

She turned back to Adam, looking a little lost for a second. "I'm fine." Her face cleared almost at once. "Where do we go now?"

"Home," Adam said, stepping off the curb to flag down a taxi.

"Home," she echoed with a soft smile. "I like that."

Once they'd clambered into a cab and were speeding down Tenth Avenue toward the Village, Adam leaned his head back against the cracked vinyl seat and groped along the cushion for Miranda's hand.

"Miranda," he said. His voice sounded strange, tinny, and far away. "There was a guy with a gun. In my kitchen."

Even in the dim light of the cab's backseat, he could see those gorgeous blue eyes fill up. "I know, honey."

"You keep calling me 'honey,'" Adam said. "And I can't even enjoy it. Because of the guy. With the gun. Oh, Jesus."

A sob ripped out of his gut before he knew it was coming. His chest heaved and he brought a shaky hand up to his face.

Miranda's arms were around him in a flash. Nothing in the world ever felt so divine.

The rest of the cab ride passed in deep, cushioning silence. Adam felt like he'd been packed in cotton balls; the world rushing by the taxi window seemed very far away.

When they got to his corner, he let Miranda pay the cab driver and maneuver him into his townhouse. He watched her deadbolting the door and was shaken by a wave of delayed fear and adrenaline.

"I almost lost my best friend today," he said, startling himself. Saying it made it real. He pulled Miranda close.

"But you didn't," she reminded him, coming willingly to his arms. "It's over and Frankie's got lots of people looking out for him. He's going to be better than okay."

Adam nodded, his face in Miranda's hair. No wonder Frankie nuzzled Jess all the time. The Wake hair was addictive, warm and soft. Comforting.

"I could've lost you, too," he said, the words slow but inexorable. He couldn't stop dwelling on the terrible what-ifs.

What if Rob's shot hadn't gone wild? What if Adam had shoved Miranda in the wrong direction, and she'd been hit instead? What if . . .

"But you didn't. You won't." Miranda's voice was fierce. She sounded like she was trying to convince herself, too. "I'm right here and I'm not going anywhere unless you make me."

The only possible response to something so wonderful and longed for was a kiss.

Adam framed her face between his palms and looked his fill. Luminous blue eyes, pink, cupid's-bow lips, soft red hair waving over the milky skin of her forehead. He could feel the butterfly pulse of her heart in her neck, where the heels of his hands met to cup her chin.

He took her mouth, hunger beating in his chest like a wild bird was trapped behind his ribs.

She gasped into it, opening for him, yielding everything. Adam wanted to touch every inch of her, reassure himself that she was real and safe and there and all for him.

Pulling back, he told her, "I meant what I said to Rob. I want you to stay. After the month is up, for as long as you want."

He had to be sure she understood. Should he say he wanted her to stay because he loved her? Would that scare her off?

Miranda gave him a tremulous smile. "I can't tell you how much that means to me."

She punctuated the words with a slip of her hand down his body, to where his dick was trying to leap out of his jeans. Adam didn't know when he'd gotten hard, but it was suddenly all he could think about. Her hand moved delicately, every shifting bit of pressure sending sparks up his spine and shivers through his belly.

"God, yes," he panted. "Need this, need you." *Love you.*

"Shhh," she crooned, looping her arms around his neck. "You've got me. Whatever you want."

Adam kissed her again, desperate for the dark, sugary rush of her taste, the slick press of her tongue against his.

It wasn't easy to make it from the front door to the bed without letting go of the kiss, but Adam put his back into it. He didn't want to let Miranda go, even for the five seconds it took to walk through the living room.

They didn't bother with turning any lights on; the spill of moonlight from the curtainless window was enough for Adam to navigate around the bookcase, to see the hectic flush on Miranda's cheeks, the burnished copper of her hair. When the edge of the bed pressed into the backs of his knees, Adam realized that Miranda was urging him backward, pushing her sweet body tight to his. Intuiting her plan, Adam broke the kiss long enough to turn and strip all the blankets and sheets from the bed. He was too hot already.

The smile Miranda gave him was scorching, but it was the gentle warmth in her eyes that stole Adam's breath.

"Lie back, honey," she told him, and Adam finally thrilled to the endearment the way he'd wanted to. "It's my turn to make you forget everything."

Selective focus was a beautiful thing, Miranda found. Her life had never been in such turmoil, her emotions never so unruly and uncontrollable, but the moment Adam scrambled back and spread himself out on the wide bed before her, the rest of the world fell away.

There was nothing for Miranda, nothing but this.

Adam, his broad shoulders strong against the softness of the pillows, his strong legs stretched toward her like an invitation. Everything about him called to her, tugging at her heart.

Tugging at her conscience.

Miranda pressed her lips together as tightly as she could. She'd messed up everything, so badly. She'd been unbelievably wrong about Jess and Frankie, and when she thought of her brilliant plan to separate them, she felt ill.

That damned book. One hundred and fifty pages of sleazy, tabloidy trash masquerading as pseudojournalism, and Miranda had written it. Not only written it, but sent it to her editor, to be published.

Wrong, wrong, wrong.

Adam made a soft sound, bringing her mind back to the present. This beautiful moment, which felt like a reprieve sent from heaven.

Rob Meeks could so easily have told them what she'd

done. She wouldn't have been able to deny it, would've had to watch the light fade from Adam's eyes when he looked at her and saw someone who would do something so bad. Protestations of "book or no book" aside, Miranda was fairly certain what Adam's reaction would be if he ever read what she'd actually written.

But Rob hadn't told. And Jess wasn't in danger. So there was still time.

Miranda could fix this.

She knelt at the foot of the bed and bent low over Adam's prone form, rubbing her cheek along the heat of his side, bumping up his ribs to his chest and over to his shoulder. He moaned and she smiled.

One phone call on Monday morning would fix everything. Miranda would let the publisher know that she withdrew her consent to publish the manuscript and make them shred their copy. She'd get them to stop payment on the check they'd sent. It would all be over.

No one would ever have to find out how close she had come to selling her soul.

Filled with renewed purpose, and the relief that came from making a decision about what to do, Miranda set about ridding them both of their clothes. Adam was more of a hindrance than a help with the fiddly bits like buttons and zippers, but he was a big help when it came to tossing the clothes to the floor with reckless abandon. She palmed a little foil packet from Adam's jeans pocket, silently blessing him for being a typical optimistic man who always carried a condom.

Adam needed to be taken care of. The shattered look on his face had to be banished. The guilt scraping at Miranda's insides only made her more determined to fill Adam's mind and body with pleasure to replace the tension and panic of the last few hours.

She'd make it all up to him, everything Rob did, everything she'd done.

When they were both naked, Miranda climbed up his body, straddling his hard thighs.

Her eyes had adjusted to the meager light from the window above Adam's bed. She could see every nuance of Adam's expression, every tense and release of his muscular shoulders and arms.

"You feel amazing," he said, eyes dark and wide, watching her.

"It's the two of us, together," Miranda replied, rubbing herself sinuously against him. She felt like a big cat. All the sensation in her body seemed concentrated in her skin, making her need to push hard against Adam and get as much contact as possible.

She stretched out full-length on top of him. A pair of groans split the air.

"So good, sweetheart," Adam huffed.

"I know." She shivered. "We fit."

The thick, solid length of his erection was like super-heated steel against her stomach. Demanding attention.

Miranda gave Adam a deep, lazy kiss, holding herself up on her hands above him. The curve of her spine pushed her lower body into his and she writhed slowly, enjoying the pressure, the hot, slick caress of the swollen cock on her stomach. The way Adam's eyes squeezed shut and he gasped into her mouth, hands clenching on her upper arms.

Licking at his lips, Miranda backed off before nipping at his chin and nudging her tongue along his jaw and down his neck.

She slid down, down, down his body, leaving a trail of kisses in her wake. Adam propped himself up on his elbows to watch her, hot, dark eyes never leaving her face.

"Never want to see anything but this again. Christ, Miranda, you look better than anything."

"Better than a perfectly clear pot of stock?" she teased, lapping at his belly button. The shallow cup of flesh quivered under her tongue. "Better than Violet's buttercream or Quentin's béarnaise, or Milo's carved radishes?"

Adam cracked a smile—his first real smile since Rob had stormed the kitchen. A sense of accomplishment glowed through her.

"Definitely better than Milo's radishes." He chuckled. "Those ones he carves to look like people are freaky."

"Mmm. I won't tell him you said that; it'd break his heart." Miranda licked a wet stripe up Adam's cock, base to tip.

"Thanks," Adam gasped, head thunking back down on the bed hard enough to bounce as his arms slid out from under him.

"You're welcome," Miranda said, intoxicated by the immediate rush of heat that filled her body when she did this to Adam. To be the one to make him moan and flush, smile and pant—how could she ever have thought she'd be able to do without this?

Fierce exultation rocketed through her veins at the thought that she didn't have to. She could have it all—Jess safe and happy, Adam hot and alive and throbbing beneath her.

As she applied herself to the task of turning Adam inside out with pleasure, she reflected that life could be very sweet, indeed.

Adam was lost in a haze of shivery, zinging sensation. Everything inside him felt too big to contain, like he was bursting out of his skin. But in a good way.

Miranda was like magic moving over him, her mouth hotter than the inside of the big bread oven. Wetter, though,

God, so wet and scalding and awesome. The changing pressures of her mouth kept him off guard, nerves awake and begging.

She ducked her head and took him deep, the silky smoothness of her cheeks hollowing against the sides of his dick. Twisting up in a corkscrew motion, her tongue working delicately, a velvet rub against his most sensitive skin. And all of it was amazing. But it was the sharp, light edge of teeth she gave him that made him want to howl.

He should've known she'd be a technique queen, his detail-oriented Miranda. One night together had taught her Adam's hot spots, the ways of moving and touching that short-circuited his brain. The furrow between her brows gave her a look of such dedication to her appointed task— that expression got him right in the balls, made him hotter almost than the way she was touching him.

They had to slow this down or he wasn't going to last.

"Did you get even better at this since last night?" he managed to grunt out.

"Glad you like it," Miranda hummed, the vibration setting off another round of the shakes all through Adam's body.

"That's really not a strong enough word for how I feel about this. And if you don't want it to be all over before it gets started, you should stop touching me. Like, now."

Gripping him in one soft hand, Miranda sat up. "Tell me what you want. All I want is to make you feel good."

"Lucky me," Adam said, drinking in the sight of her, bare and beautiful in his bed. "I'm feeling pretty damn good right now."

Reaching out a hand, he beckoned her up to lie on his chest, then turned them both so that they were side by side, facing each other.

Miranda pillowed her head on Adam's bicep and watched him watching her. It was quiet in his apartment,

the usual discordant jangle of traffic and street noise somehow soft and distant. The peace was like a reset button,
bringing everything back to neutral.

Miranda's slim arm crept across his waist, reminding
him that they were pretty fucking far from neutral. She
seemed to be feeling around for something on the bed behind him, and he almost twisted around to get a peek, but he
didn't really care what it was enough to stop looking at her.

She made a pleased sound and held up a condom packet
between two fingers, waving it triumphantly.

Adam melted. She'd planned ahead. It was so her. "Well,
I declare, Miss Wake. You been carrying that around all
night, just in case?"

Miranda giggled. Actually fucking giggled, and Adam
wanted to eat her up with a spoon, he loved the sound of it
so much.

"Nope. Snuck it out of your jeans when you were busy
getting me naked."

"You're a genius," he said adoringly. "Gimme that. And
gimme a kiss, too, while you're at it."

Tilting her lips up to Adam's, Miranda parted for him
easily, tongue dancing and playing. She distracted him with
her soft, sweet mouth, dragging him in for another kiss, and
another, and before he knew it, the packet was open and the
condom was poised at the damp tip of his prick.

"Whoa there," he said as she started to roll it down.
"You think you're the only one who gets to play?"

"Want it," she breathed against his mouth. "Want you."

God, she was going to be the end of him. "You've got
me," he promised, letting her agile fingers get the condom
on his now-twice-as-hard cock.

For once, Adam and his dick were in agreement. Miranda
saying she wanted it, in that raspy voice, was the sexiest
thing ever to happen in the entire history of people having sex.

Pulling her top leg to rest on his hip opened Miranda up for his fingers. A single touch and he knew she was telling the truth. She was sleek and slippery with desire for him. He parted the slick folds with two fingers and groaned at the way her heat clung to his skin, sucking him in. The bundle of nerves at the top of her cleft beat like a tiny heart against the heel of his hand. When he pressed it, she cried out.

Now. Right now. He had to have her. Later they could take their time, love on each other for hours. But he had to be inside her now.

"Yes," she said, eyes glazed with passion. Adam realized he'd said all that out loud.

He took her mouth again, at the same time as he canted his hips and pushed into the tight, grasping heat of her. Miranda's body closed around him like a fist, forcing a ragged moan up from his chest.

Miranda drew breath for more of those short little bird cries, sharp and high and utterly arousing. She was so lost in it, abandoned to passion. Adam slid deeper, working his hips, reveling in the molten grip of her core. Her nipples dragged across his chest, twin points of searing heat amid the overall hotness of what they were doing. They were joined, connected, in the most basic way possible. Adam's heart leaped like a fucking ballerina. When did she become so necessary to him?

Adam cupped his free hand around her heaving breast and thumbed the pink bud at the tip while twisting his hips against hers. She stuttered out another cry, eyes flying wide and shocked to his face. Another quick bump and grind had her mouth opening soundlessly, body locking down on his in waves of undulating pressure that milked the orgasm right out of his cock.

They lay panting quietly, arms and legs tangled together in a spent, happy mess. Adam became aware of the air brushing against his skin, cool where the sweat was drying.

Miranda stretched luxuriously against him, rolling her shoulders and smiling into a yawn.

Adam yawned, too. "I could sleep for a year."

"Hmm. Not with all the covers on the floor."

"You cold, sweets? Here." Adam swung over the side of the bed and grabbed a handful of cotton, dragging it over them both as he cuddled Miranda to his side. "Lemme warm you up."

She snuggled against him happily. The pure joy of it made Adam's arms contract around her shoulders involuntarily. Propping her pointed chin on his chest, Miranda gave him a searching look.

"How are you holding up?"

Adam exhaled noisily. "Better. Worlds better, here with you in my bed, all naked and pretty. If we could just stay like this for the rest of my life, I'd be extremely happy."

"Yes. But eventually you'll have to go back to the restaurant."

Adam felt a pang. His restaurant, his sanctuary, had been violated. By that loser, Rob, who never deserved even to set foot in Market's kitchen.

The sympathetic tilt to Miranda's head said she knew what he was thinking.

"It'll be easier than you think," she said softly. "Once you're back there, in your groove, everything will fall into place. You were born for that life, Adam. And Market is yours, every inch. No idiot with a grudge can take that away from you."

Adam swallowed convulsively to get his heart back down in his chest where it belonged. "You're so good to me," he said. "Jesus. When I think how I almost messed this up . . . Miranda, I know I made you mad before, about Jess and Frankie and not telling you. But I swear, no more secrets. I hate 'em, anyway. Only the truth between you and me, from here on out."

An emotion flitted across her face, powerful and dark. Something like shame or pain mixed with the fiery light of determination. It was gone before Adam could pinpoint it or describe it to himself, replaced with dancing eyes and a saucy grin that made him wonder if he'd imagined it.

"If you still feel weird when you get back in the kitchen, I bet we can come up with something to exorcise those demons. A little after-hours private party, just you and me and the butcher block . . ."

Adam laughed, his spirits lifting at the thought of his prim little scribbler consenting to semipublic sex, for any reason.

Tilting her chin up with one finger, Adam curled down and kissed those swollen lips.

Yeah. Everything was going to be okay.

TWENTY-EIGHT

Sunlight poured into the room, hitting the bed at a strange, unfamiliar angle. Miranda blinked and squinted into the brightness. It took her a minute to remember where she was.

Adam's townhouse.

Curious to know what time it was, she twisted around in the bed to see if she could locate an alarm clock.

Adam snuffled into the bedding next to her, brows lowered in stubborn refusal to wake up. Miranda grinned.

She finally gave up on a clock and dug her watch out from the pile of clothes beside the low, wide bed.

Eleven o'clock! She couldn't remember the last time she'd slept past eight. Miranda let out an involuntary noise, part squeak, part gasp, and Adam cracked an eye.

"Time's it?" he muttered into the pillow.

"It's after eleven," she told him, wondering if she ought to get up and get home. Her first thought on waking had been that damn manuscript and how badly she wanted to call up the publisher and square everything away so the ugly thing would never see the light of day.

"Not all that surprising," Adam said, ending her internal debate with one sharp tug at her shoulder, pulling her back down beside him. Miranda didn't put up too much of a fuss; his big body generated a cozy, furnacelike heat that tempted her to cuddle at least a few minutes more.

"The trauma of dealing with Rob Meeks's pseudohomicidal tendencies, a stopover at the ER, then a bout of incredibly diligent and impressive lovemaking—that kind of evening takes it right out of you."

"Well, sleep is very healing," she attempted to say primly, but Adam crooked his fingers in her side and tickled her mercilessly until she collapsed in a giggling heap against him.

"I'll tell you what was healing," he mock-growled. He rolled her under him and stared down. Miranda tried to catch her breath, but she couldn't do anything about the smile stretching her lips and cheeks. Happiness bubbled through her veins, popping and fizzing like sparkling wine.

She felt as if she'd been wandering, lost in the subway tunnels for days, and now she was finally climbing back up into the light. She wasn't there yet, still had some things to take care of before she could truly enjoy basking in the sun—make things right with Jess, bury the Market book under a ton of sand—but if she stretched, she could feel the warmth on her face, and it made all the difference in the world.

Adam made all the difference in the world.

He gazed down at her, his heart in his eyes. Miranda's heart fluttered up to meet it, rising in her chest to her throat and expanding there so she could hardly breathe.

"I love you."

For a second, Miranda wasn't sure if she'd heard it or said it. Then Adam's eyes widened, as if he were surprised, too.

"Damn. I didn't mean to blurt it out like that," he said, pinking.

Miranda thought the muscles in her cheeks were in danger of getting sprained from smiling so much.

"I love you, too," she managed to choke out around the obstruction in her throat. "I love the way you blurt things out, and your sexy brown eyes, and your bed head, and every little thing about you."

Those eyes flared with heat and a kind of fierce exultation. Adam swooped in for a kiss that turned into three or four. Miranda pushed into the kisses, fingers dancing across his shoulders and back, up into his tousled dark curls.

"You always get me like that," Adam gasped. "The way you use words. Makes me nuts."

Miranda laughed, all the happy bubbles inside her fizzing up and overflowing into pure joy. "So glad you enjoy that about me, because I don't think I'd make a very good mute."

He traced her mouth with the tip of one finger. The surprisingly delicate touch made her shiver. "I wish I could say something smart and pretty to tell you how much, how big this is to me."

Miranda read his frustration in the downward curve of his full bottom lip, the snap of his brows. Hooking one arm behind his neck, she pulled him down close enough to nuzzle the exact spot where his dimple would pop out if she could make him smile again.

"Don't tell me," she urged, breath starting to come in fast, excited pants. "Show me."

Adam smiled against her mouth and Miranda grinned in triumph before gladly tumbling back down into pleasure with him.

Two hours, about a thousand kisses, and one very long shower later, they were jumping off the L train at Union Square, ravenously hungry and exclaiming over the gorgeous June day. Adam threaded his fingers through Miranda's and dragged her through the bustling midday market.

After the shower, Adam had declared that man could

not live by kisses alone, and besides, there were still the evening's specials to buy for, so they had to check in at the Greenmarket. Truth be told, he was so flipping happy, he was greedy for more. He wanted to have as many of his favorite things together at once as he could.

Farmer's market, perfect produce, Miranda.

Sometimes, life so did not suck.

Miranda laughed and went along with it, in that way she'd recently acquired of indulging Adam's every whim. He wasn't a fool, he realized this new tendency was an early-stage-of-the-relationship thing, and therefore unlikely to last. He intended to take advantage of it while he could.

Hence the market at two o'clock in the afternoon.

"I don't usually like to shop this late," he told her, weaving them through herds of office girls on their lunch breaks and tourists sauntering down the wide stone pathways, goggle-eyed. "Most of the good stuff gets snatched up early. But I bet Paul over at Siren Falls will have saved something for me."

"And if he didn't?"

Adam dodged a pair of SoHo moms with double strollers festooned with scarves, and shrugged. "I'll find something wonderful. I always do. This place is the best inspiration in the world! I get all my ideas for new menu items here."

"You really come here every morning?"

"If we're starting a new special, then yeah. And that's almost every day. I like to cook what's fresh, you know? The stuff that's growing now is the best to eat now."

Miranda gave him a keen look. "So can I take this to mean you plan to open the restaurant tonight?"

"Hell, yes. That moron, Rob, isn't screwing me out of two nights' service. No way. Besides, best way for everyone to get past what happened is to get back in there and start cooking."

They fetched up at the Siren Falls Farm stand, where Paul Corlie was selling a couple of pints of tiny, jewel-like raspberries to an older lady in a garish purple cardigan. Paul's eyes lit up when he caught sight of Adam, then widened in surprise when they slid over Miranda.

"Hey there," he said, handing Purple Cardigan her change. "If it isn't Adam and his little tomato. Everybody's talking about what happened at Market last night. You look okay to me."

"We're good. Better than good. Paulie," Adam said repressively, hoping to God the man would mind his manners. "This is Miranda Wake. She's my . . ." Fuck, what was he supposed to call her? "Girlfriend" sounded way junior high, but "lover" sounded like something out of a soap opera. And "former-nemesis-turned-sweetheart" was a mouthful.

Miranda saved the awkward moment by arching one expressive brow at him before stepping up and offering her hand to Paul.

"Hi, I think we've met before. You probably don't remember me, but I definitely remember the beautiful ramps you were selling."

"There's my smart girl." Adam laughed. "Buttering up the produce supplier for me. Awesome."

Paul's eyes twinkled. "I remember you, missy, sure enough." He clapped his bear paws together and said, "Here, try some of these cherries while you look around."

"Thanks, we're starving," Miranda said, accepting the bag gratefully.

"First of the Rainiers?" Adam asked, eyeing the creamy, yellow flesh tinged with the slightest pink blush.

"Yeah, it was a warm spring. So what can I sell the two lovebirds today? Something for a romantic picnic in the park?"

"Oh, God," Miranda moaned, her mouth full. "How about a couple more pounds of these cherries?"

"Good?" Adam grinned, reaching for the bag.

Miranda tilted it toward him reluctantly. "This is how you know I love you," she said, "the fact that I'm sharing these cherries."

Adam didn't even try to hide the thrill it gave him to hear her say it like that, out loud, in public. In front of one of his oldest friends, no less. Even his first luscious bite of the fruit, sugar-tart juice exploding on his tongue, couldn't overshadow the glow he got from Miranda.

"I've never experienced cherries like these," Miranda said. "They are the pinnacle of cherrydom. The zenith. The apex. The epitome. The *mmph*."

Adam covered her mouth with his hand, winking at Paul. "She turns into a thesaurus when she gets excited. Cute, huh?"

Miranda shoved him away, laughing. "I'll show you cute if you ever do that again."

They wandered back out into the fray. A few stalls down from Dava's perennially jam-packed dairy stand, Miranda stopped dead in front of a tray of croissants.

"Oh. Pretty," she said.

They were, all uniformly crescent-shaped and shiny with butter. "You want to get a couple?" he asked, shifting his weight from one foot to the other.

"I do, but you don't have to wait for me," Miranda said. "Go on, I'll meet you at Dava's. I know where it is from last time."

Shooing him away with a laugh, Miranda turned to order their pastries. Adam snuck in a quick kiss to the side of her neck before he went, laughing and dancing away from her automatic swat.

Not into displaying herself in public, his Miranda.

Lost in thoughts of how he might persuade Miranda to display herself in private, Adam nearly flattened a man he never expected to see at the farmer's market. After all, it was Adam's responsibility to buy that day's produce for the restaurant.

"Grant!"

"Adam! Where on earth have you been? No, don't tell me, you turned off your phone and your cell phone was flushed down the toilet or something."

Adam guiltily pictured the sleek little flip-top nestled in the pile of clothes he and Miranda had shed before tumbling into bed last night.

"Sorry, man, I forgot it."

"What is the point of owning one if you never carry it, much less turn it on?" Grant growled. Adam reeled back, taking in the wide, panicked eyes, blotchy cheeks, and untidy hair.

"What's up with you?" he asked, concerned. "What are you doing here?"

Grant laughed. It wasn't a happy sound. "Oh, nothing. I've just been all over hell's half-acre today, looking for your sorry self. Frankie's out of commission for at least a few days and you're nowhere to be found. Meanwhile, the world is caving in."

"Wow, drama much? And you talked to Frankie. How's he doing?" Guilt bit at Adam, sharp and mean.

Grant shook his head, frustration in every line of his face. "Frankie's okay. Pissed as hell, but feeling fine. You haven't seen the papers yet, have you?"

"No, we woke up and came here. That's it. Grant, what the hell is it?"

"Or checked your e-mail." Grant didn't seem to have heard him.

"No." Adam struggled for patience. "I'm completely in

the dark. And you're scaring the shit out of me. What the fuck is going on?"

"Miranda. That book she was writing. It got leaked this morning on a blog, some editorial assistant or something."

Adam went cold, like all the blood had drained right out of his body onto the ground. Through stiff lips, he said, "How is it?"

Grant looked like he didn't know if he wanted to fucking cry or spit nails. "It's bad, Adam. Real bad. The things she said about the crew—I don't know how she even found out about half of it, but it's vicious, catty stuff. Personal. About Milo's family connections and Quentin's priors. Frankie's parents. Violet's divorce." He glanced away, eyes narrowed. "And . . . your affair with Eleanor Bonning, man. She makes it sound like you basically whored your way into getting the financing for Market."

The bottom dropped out of Adam's stomach, pitching him into a frozen, black wasteland of nausea and disbelief.

At that moment, Miranda walked up, carrying a brown paper bag already showing darker spots where the butter from the croissants had soaked through. She was juggling that with the plastic sack of cherries from Paul's place and a pair of coffees in paper cups, stacked one on top of the other.

"Whew! Thank goodness. I need a couple more hands." She smiled up at Adam, who reached for a coffee and the bag of pastries on autopilot, mind still totally consumed with Grant's bombshell.

"Hey, Grant," Miranda prattled on, wiggling her fingers at the restaurant manager. "You want a croissant? I'd offer you cherries, but I'm afraid I'm too selfish to share." Her smile faded at their silence.

Grant was looking at her as if he'd seen a ghost. And

not one of those wispy lady-in-white type ghosts, either, but a nasty one. Adam could only assume he looked the same. Or maybe Adam looked as gut-kicked as he felt, like he was about to heave in the middle of the fucking Greenmarket.

"Is it true?" Adam couldn't think of anything else to say. It was all that mattered.

"Is what true?" she faltered, but the instant paling of her complexion told its own story. "Adam, is everything okay?"

She put her hand on his arm and he shook it off, dropping the bakery bag onto the dirty sidewalk.

"Is it true?" he said, barely able to grind the words out of his parchment-dry throat.

She shook her head, pretty tears welling up in her dark blue eyes. She looked so confused, bewildered. Adam almost softened, almost reached out to her.

"The book," Grant said, his voice harder than Adam had ever heard it. "Did you write a piece-of-filth book full of lies and gossip about the staff at Market?"

"I'm writing a book, yes, or I was, but it's not happening anymore. I decided not to do it. I swear." Her eyes darted around as if she were searching for an escape before resting on Adam in a plea for understanding.

He couldn't speak.

Grant was not similarly afflicted. Nearly hissing in rage now, he said, "Does your publisher know it isn't happening? Because choice selections from the manuscript appeared this morning on a blog. It's already been picked up by half the media outlets in the city, and the online celebrity-chef-watcher sites are going nuts. It made Page Six, Miranda. Explain to me how it isn't happening."

Miranda wilted before their eyes, like greens under hot bacon dressing. Tears slid down her white cheeks. He hated that she looked beautiful even when she cried.

Even when she'd betrayed him.

"I—I—I . . . Oh, my God." She shook like a brisk wind had her.

"Not good enough," Grant snarled. "Come on, Adam, let's go. We've got work to do to get the restaurant in shape to open tonight. And I will be goddamned if we let all this shit keep us closed."

"In a second." Adam hardly recognized his own voice.

Shaking his head, Grant moved off, muttering under his breath about crazies with guns and scandalmongers with no morals.

"I don't know what to say." Miranda clutched herself around the middle. "It's all a huge mistake, those things should never have been published. I'd decided, I was going to break the contract. You have to believe me."

"You wrote those things. And you sent them to the publisher."

She didn't deny it. The mute suffering on her lovely face was answer enough.

Adam forced himself to continue. "You lied to me. You cozied up to me, for what, for material? Jesus. Was I research?" Adam stopped, sickened, and Miranda rushed to fill the gap.

"No, no. Don't believe that, I couldn't stand it if you—I swear, please. Everything I said last night, about how I feel for you, that's all true. I meant every word, every touch."

She was sobbing openly now, attracting attention from passersby. Adam started to feel suffocated.

"But I don't know how to tell the difference," he said, feeling stupid, slow. How was he supposed to get this? "How do I know what was a lie and what wasn't?"

"You just . . ." Her mouth worked for a second. "You just trust me. I guess."

Defeat weighted the words so they dropped into the space between them like overworked dumplings, doughy and thick.

"I think you can see where the logic falls down, there," he said.

"I should've told you—"

"But you didn't. I don't know why I'm surprised, though. You've got to be the most secretive, closed-off woman alive. You never told me anything. About your parents, about your life. Every important thing I know about you, I learned from someone else. Maybe we all only think we know you; all we really know are the stories we tell each other about you. Maybe it's all lies."

Miranda shuddered. "I'm sorry," she whispered. "This isn't what I wanted, what I meant. I love you."

His heart fluttered, tried valiantly to make Adam feel something, but he throttled it ruthlessly. Numb was good. Numb was his friend.

"I've got to go," he said, backing away. If anything was going to break through the ice encasing his emotions, it would be that sentence on Miranda's sweet, treacherous lips.

"Did you hear me?" she said, desperation roughening her voice. "I said I love you."

"Don't. Don't say that."

She recoiled as if he'd slapped her, but nodded in acceptance. "Sorry. I don't know what else to say. It's a switch, right? Me, not having the words."

"You don't have the words because there isn't anything left to say."

Adam walked away.

He only looked back once before the crowds of market-goers closed between them, blocking his view. She was standing where he'd left her. Her hair shone like a dying fire in the summer sun, casting her face in shadow. The fingers of one hand were white-knuckled on the sack of cherries.

Adam didn't think he'd be able to eat another Rainier cherry as long as he lived.

TWENTY-NINE

The apartment had that echoy, vacant feeling that told Miranda that Jess wasn't home.

She dropped her purse by the door and dragged into the living room, wanting nothing more than a glass of wine and a long soak in a hot tub. Beyond that, she just wanted to forget.

Forget the mess she'd made of her life. Forget the condemnation in Grant's face, the hurt in Adam's eyes.

He didn't scream at her, didn't raise his voice once. After the way he blew up over kitchen mistakes, she'd have thought something like this would make him go nuclear. But now, having lived through both, Miranda was able to categorically state a preference for the yelling and screaming. With Adam, that kind of explosion was fleeting, big and loud and over in an instant. The pain she'd caused today—that wasn't something he'd let go of overnight.

As she was about to lower her aching body onto the sofa, she noticed the blinking light on her answering machine.

Knowing damn well that listening to those messages wouldn't help with the forgetting plan, Miranda found herself gravitating toward the machine, helplessly snared.

Be-e-e-e-p.

"Miranda? This is Claire. You unutterably foolish woman, whatever have you done? The office is abuzz. The editorial board is thrilled with the publicity, of course, but I'm worried about you. Call me."

That was nice. Less yelling than she was expecting. Miranda let the messages play and went to get some wine from the kitchen.

"It's me."

Jess. She poured a big glass with shaky fingers and hurried back to the machine.

"I can't believe this. You're . . . Who are you? My sister wouldn't do— Frankie, quit it, I'm fine . . ."

Be-e-e-e-p.

Miranda knocked back half the wine in one swallow.

Be-e-e-e-p.

"Me again. I had to . . . Fuck. It's still hard. Why is this so hard? Miranda, I moved out. I can't stay with you, I don't even know you, howcouldyoudothis? Those people are my friends. I thought they were your friends, or at least Adam was. And Frankie, God, the things you wrote about him. Look, I'm staying with him. You have my cell number. I don't really want to talk to you right now, but . . . Shit, the machine's gonna cut me off. Bye."

She was going to need a lot more wine.

Miranda abandoned her wine glass and retired to the sofa, cradling the half-empty bottle of cabernet to her chest.

Claire hadn't sounded mad or disgusted, so she was first on the list. Miranda was in desperate need of clearheaded advice, since she was currently drinking away her own clear head and had no intention of stopping.

The minute Claire picked up, Miranda was seized by a hiccupping fit. Claire seemed to know who it was, regardless. Unless she routinely answered her office phone with the words, "My God, but you've made a mess of your life."

"I know," Miranda managed to gasp out. "Claire, it's so terrifically awful, I don't even know where to begin."

"We shall see. Put down whatever it is you are drinking that is giving you such horrible fits." Claire downshifted into practical French mode, every word brisk and devoid of nonsense. The knot in Miranda's stomach loosened slightly; Claire's take-charge attitude was oddly comforting. She set her bottle of wine on the coffee table.

The French accent clipped on, relentless. "You have no mother to go to for advice; I make allowances for that. And my own advice, when I offered it before, you would not take. But that is finished. The book exists and cannot be undone. *Alors,* we must decide how to proceed."

"If your advice involves something more than hiding in my apartment and never speaking to anyone again so I can't do any more damage, I'm afraid I won't be taking it this time, either."

Claire clicked her tongue in outrage. "That is quite enough!"

"It *is* enough!" Miranda banged a fist into the couch cushions. "I'm like a poison, a virus, infecting everyone I touch. I've done enough damage for any one person for a lifetime. Hurt so many people, and all for nothing."

"Yes," Claire agreed. "It was moronic and entirely avoidable."

Miranda sucked in a breath that turned into a laugh. "Oh, thanks. Why did I call you again? Right, it was because of the two messages on my machine, yours was the one that exhibited more of the milk of human kindness."

"I'm not sure what you mean by this milk." Claire's voice held the frigid disapproval she always evinced toward unfamiliar English colloquialisms. "But it is no matter. You've made a mistake. The important question is this: are you going to give up and hide away from the world in cowardice?" Dramatic pause. "Or are you going to use that brilliant mind of yours to discover a way to fight for what you desire?"

Miranda sat up on the couch, wine forgotten, heart starting to pump battle endorphins into her blood.

She'd never been very good at giving up.

"Well, when you put it like that . . ."

The next few days were spent in a flurry of phone calls and planning. Miranda did her level best not to watch the clock and think about what she'd be doing if she were at Market. It was strange not to be there. After only a few weeks, the routine of prep and service, cooking and expediting, was like a physical presence in her body. Her palm ached for the comforting heft of a well-balanced knife, her fingers itched to be arranging garnishes. It was a weird sensation that served to bring home to her exactly how much she stood to lose.

It was harder to avoid thoughts of Market once normal business hours were done, and she had no more cajoling, pleading, bargaining phone calls to occupy her mind. Only visions of Adam in his chef whites, a dark whirl of motion as he bounced from station to station, checking that everything met his standards of perfection.

Miranda distracted herself by dressing carefully for her final and most important meeting. It was tricky. What did one wear to debase oneself before an enemy in hopes of being granted a favor?

Miranda tried to see the upside. Tonight couldn't be worse than apologizing to Eleanor Bonning, the woman she'd essentially labeled a duped sugar momma. And then hearing, in no uncertain terms, that Eleanor broke off the relationship herself, because, while she appreciated Adam's dedication from an investor's standpoint, she didn't enjoy competing with Market for his attention.

That one had stung.

Staring into her closet, Miranda decided she wanted to look competent and serious, but not in an uptight way. Unfortunately, her wardrobe didn't really lend itself to that. She regarded her conservative gray dresses, sweater sets, and suits with dissatisfaction. None of those things worked for the place she was going.

Finally, she grabbed a pair of jeans, so dark blue they were almost black. She topped them with a white button-down with the sleeves rolled to her elbows. Leaving it untucked, she decided, made her look a little less Brooks Brothers. For luck, she slipped on the same red satin pumps she wore that first night she met Adam. As always, they made her feel sexy and a bit dangerous, and now, they had the added benefit of reminding her of the hot look in Adam's brown eyes when he took them in.

Aware that she was fussing over her appearance purely as a stalling tactic, Miranda rushed through her makeup and left her hair down to curl around her shoulders.

She checked the clock one last time. Edging past ten; the Market crew would be winding down, sending out more desserts than mains. The kitchen would be starting to clean up, set things for the next day. She knew the process by now, knew she'd have time to make it downtown before Market officially closed for the night.

But not if she dawdled around much longer. With a last, nervous glance in the mirror, Miranda was on her way.

Twenty minutes later, she was walking into Chapel. The place wasn't marked at all; if she hadn't known it was there, she never would've found it. As it was, it took several turns around the old, abandoned church on the corner of Grand and Orchard before she noticed a heavy wooden door that looked familiar.

The inside of the bar wasn't as loud or as smoky as she remembered, probably because the place had just opened. There weren't any roving bands of cooks or punk rockers yet. But Miranda had hope that the man she wanted to see would be there, propping up the bar. He'd been an early bird the first time she went to Chapel. With any luck, that was his pattern.

Blinking in the dimness, Miranda made her way toward the bar. She could barely make out the silhouette of Christian Colby, the long-haired bartender. He was slicing limes, quick and efficient, but he looked up when she got closer and let out a low whistle.

"Well, look who's here. Damn, darlin', used to be I considered everyone who made it through my door a friend, but you make me want to revise my policy on refusing service."

Miranda stiffened at the open hostility in his voice. "I suppose you've heard about the Market book."

"Darlin', everyone's heard. You're famous. Or is that infamous? Smart little writer lady like yourself ought to be able to tell me which."

"You really do all stick together, don't you?" It was very appealing, that loyalty. When it wasn't aimed at keeping her out.

"Adam's a good man. I've worked with him, and I know all about how he runs his kitchen. No way is Market like you said. No way did Adam Temple sleep with that woman like some kind of gigolo. And no way did any of his crew deserve to have their private lives dragged through the muck."

Miranda wasn't about to explain everything to this guy, but the obstinate twist to his mouth made her think he wasn't upset in the abstract—there was someone special at Market whose secret she'd revealed. She sighed, remembering how ready he'd been to jump in with that baseball bat when she'd thought Jess was being attacked.

"I promise, you don't have to tell me what a bitch I am, I already know," she said. "I'm trying to do something about that. Is Devon Sparks here tonight? I need to talk to him."

Christian's hands stilled their furious slicing as he stared at her. "For the record," he said slowly, "I'd never use such ugly language to refer to a lady. And Devon's not here."

Shoulders slumping, Miranda turned to go, already trying to devise some other way to get in touch with him. It wasn't very likely he'd take her call, and she didn't have his home address—

"Yet," Christian called, stopping her at the door. "Shit, I can't believe I'm doing this."

"Yet." Miranda pounced. "You mean he'll be here later?"

"Almost definitely," he said, as if the words were being pulled from him. "Probably soon. He's here most every night when the show's filming a new season."

Miranda felt a strange mixture of relief and dismay. "Do you mind if I wait here for him?"

The bartender sighed. "Always was a sucker for big blue eyes. Sure, come on and sit down, I'll fix you something."

"Do I need to look at a cocktail menu or anything?"

Shaking his head, Christian started mixing and pouring. The drink, when he set it down in front of her, was clear and fizzy, with a lovely garnish of fresh mint.

"Club soda with mint-lime syrup," he told her as she took a sip.

"It's good," she said. "Very refreshing."

Christian winked. "No alcohol. I figure you're gonna need to keep your mind as sharp as possible for the conversation with Dev."

"You taking my name in vain, Chris?" The smooth, sexy voice slid down Miranda's back like an ice cube.

Devon was here.

"Hey, man," Christian was saying, reaching across the bar to slap Devon's palm. "How was shooting today?"

"It was— Wait, you wouldn't be trying to trap me, would

you? Anything I say in front of Miranda Wake is liable to show up online later tonight."

Pulling her best poised, calm demeanor around herself like a cloak, Miranda gave Devon a serene smile. "Devon Sparks. Nice to see you. Won't you have a seat? I'll buy you a drink."

Devon snorted, but he was obviously intrigued enough to slide onto the barstool next to hers. "It's cute that you think I pay for drinks. Ever. Dirty martini, tonight, Chris, none of your little experiments."

"One day I'm going to send your bar tab to your accountant and give the guy a heart attack," Christian threatened over his shoulder as he picked through the gin.

"Don't skimp on the olives," Devon demanded before settling back and looking Miranda up and down. "To what do we owe the pleasure of your return to this shithole? Looking for fresh material? Or were you hoping to replace Temple in another way"? His sneer was blatantly sexual, but his eyes were cold and flat, like a shark's.

She'd taken a lot of abuse in the last few days, most of it deserved, but this was too much. Her temper flared. "Don't be more disgusting than you have to be, Sparks. I'm not here for that, and if I were, you're the last man I'd choose."

The moment the words were out of her mouth, she cringed, wishing she could call them back.

What a clever negotiating tactic. Insulting and alienating the potential benefactor. Go me. Perhaps next I'll spit in his drink, then see where the evening takes us from there.

To her very great surprise, however, nothing more extreme than curiosity flashed in Devon's extraordinary eyes.

"Then is it the other? You're looking for more dirt on Temple and his pals? I suppose I'd be a natural source, having employed most of them at one time or another."

"That's not what I'm after," Miranda hastened to assure him.

"Good, because I wasn't planning on telling you anything," Devon said, pulling his martini closer, "except that Adam Temple was an exemplary employee and one of the best cooks I've ever had working for me. He chose his people well; poached most of them from my staff, in fact. Which, by the way, is the quote I've given six different newspapers, four magazines, and twenty-five Web sites today."

Miranda smiled for the first time since staring into Grant's accusing face. "That lovely loyalty again," she breathed. "I wasn't sure it would extend to you, too." This made her request so much more viable, she wanted to climb up and dance on the bar.

"I don't know what you're talking about," Devon said crossly. "It's nothing but the truth. I realize you've got only a passing acquaintance with the concept."

Miranda swallowed that down without a flinch, flying on the idea that this might actually work.

"I'm talking about Adam," she said. "And a favor. Not for me, but for him. To sweeten the deal, let me add that this favor will not only help the Market crew, but it will also cause me considerable personal trouble and humiliation."

Devon cocked a brow at her and took a maddeningly long sip of his martini.

"Fine," he said at length. "You've got my attention. Tell me what you have in mind."

THIRTY

How was it that one person being missing from the line for a week threw the whole kitchen into chaos? Adam wondered tiredly as he schlepped up the stairs from his tiny, cluttered office.

He'd slept at the restaurant again, on the narrow couch in his office, after last night's difficult service. They'd missed Frankie and his irrepressible energy on the grill station.

Adam refused to consider who else he'd missed.

Today will be better, he promised himself. Frankie was due back in the kitchen tonight, healed enough from his brush with death to sling some hash under Adam's watchful eye. It was a little sooner than the doctor had recommended, and before Frankie received permission to cook, Adam had endured a very uncomfortable conversation with Jess. While both of them danced carefully around the slim, pretty redheaded elephant in the room, he'd sworn to Jess that he'd keep a close eye on Frankie and make sure he wasn't overdoing it. For a while there, he wondered if he'd have to take out some kind of affidavit signed in blood and notarized by a priest or something. Jess did cave, eventually, to the relief of the whole Market crew.

It had been a weird week.

The first day back was the hardest; Frankie's conspicuous absence, plus the horror of finding out shit he never wanted to know about his employees. The awkward, embarrassed way people moved around each other, each cook in his own orbit, never touching anyone else. No one made eye contact. Adam became hyperconscious of everyone's left ears, the shape of their foreheads.

Some of those so-called secrets Miranda had written about were things Adam had known forever, and the rest weren't exactly a surprise. The fact that Quentin had done time shocked no one; the confirmation that Milo's family was Family, likewise. Adam had known when Violet got her divorce that it was beyond acrimonious, because one day in the middle of all of it, she'd forgotten to add yeast to a whole batch of bread. When the sad, flat goop refused to rise, she'd broken down and told him all about what a bastard her soon-to-be-ex was.

Frankie's parents had mailed the papers that officially declared him no longer their son to his work address, back when they'd both been at Appetite; Adam had actually been standing beside him when he opened the letter, close enough to steady him when his knees buckled.

It wasn't that he was shocked by the skeletons in his crew's closets. He knew who they were, and liked and respected them all. It was the ugliness of having those private sorrows and failures and foibles thrust into the spotlight to be salivated over by the grasping public.

What lifted his spirits was the avalanche of business all the extra publicity had generated.

Adam hadn't known what to expect, that first day. He and Grant had spent the hours before service calling the line cooks and telling them to come in, cleaning up the traces from the stampede of police and ambulance people. Then they'd split up, Adam to comb through the walk-in cooler for ideas for specials, and Grant to stand by the full reservation book, wringing his hands and waiting to see if any of the people who'd booked tables would show up.

They did. And so did about three hundred more would-be customers. As busy as they'd been since opening, it was nothing compared to how slammed the restaurant was now. And they weren't all novelty diners, either—more than half of them went home and called Grant the next day to make return reservations. Every so often, Adam would check in with front of house and hear Grant gleefully informing some hopeful that they were currently booked solid for the next three months.

As messed up as things had been in the kitchen, the cooks hadn't let it affect the quality of the food they were sending out. The customers never knew the difference; it was only Adam and his crew who pined for the way things used to be.

After the past week, they'd lost the fun.

Adam bumped the kitchen door open with his shoulder, hands full of pen and memo pad, trying to compose something appealing and elegant to describe the riff on succotash he was doing for that night's special. Sort of a summer pot pie, with sweet corn and buttery lima beans in a flaky, golden crust.

What exact words would make it sound good to customers? Adam sighed. He sucked at writing menus, always had.

Miranda had been great at it. Not surprisingly, she'd made quite a study of menu wording, the ways the choice of adjectives and which ingredients were included in the description colored the reader's understanding of what was on offer. By switching a couple of words and adding a vivid adjective or two, she'd turned a boring-sounding dish into something everyone wanted to try. Adam swore she could make a vegan order the rib eye, the imagery she evoked was so tantalizing.

Once Adam had discovered this miraculous ability, he'd put her to work on the special addition to the menu every night.

Not thinking about her, he reminded himself. *I wrote a thousand menus before Miranda Wake, and I'll write a thousand more without her.*

Not a particularly cheerful thought.

He tossed the empty pad on the counter and looked up in time to see Frankie clattering into the kitchen, laughing uproariously, one arm slung around Jess's neck.

Adam narrowed his eyes against the almost overwhelming rush of relief.

"Is he high on painkillers?" he demanded, pointing at Frankie with the pen he was still holding.

"High on life, mate," Frankie crowed. "Fucking hell, but it's good to be back in the kitchen."

"I haven't let him touch a knife in six days," Jess explained, watching fondly as Frankie jitterbugged his way to the magnetic strips running along the walls above the counters. Each strip held at least five knives, all-purpose chef's knives of different lengths and weights, carving knives with their long blades and rounded tips, and short, broad cleavers for hacking through bone.

Frankie went straight for his favorite nine-inch stainless steel, lightweight and agile, sharp enough to tackle almost any cutting job. Not sharp enough for Frankie, evidently, since he rummaged through a utility drawer until he came up with a whetstone and began sharpening the knife with reverent attention.

Without taking his eyes off Frankie, Jess said, "I'm going to hold you to that promise you made. If he looks like he's wearing out, send him home."

"I will," Adam said, making a sincere attempt to keep the impatient growl out of his voice. "I don't want him chopping off anything vital or catching himself on fire any more than you do."

Jess finally tore his gaze from Frankie to look Adam in the eye. The kid had that bruised look around the eyes from not getting enough sleep. His eyes, those so-familiar blue eyes, looked old and tired.

"I know," Jess said. "I worry because I'm not sure I can stand to lose anyone else right now."

It was Adam's turn to look away. "Have you talked to her?"

"No. I told her not to call."

"I'm surprised she listened."

"Me, too, actually." Jess sounded concerned rather than pleased. "I still don't understand why she wrote those things, or why she allowed them to go public."

"Don't look at me, kid." The harshness of his own words grated in Adam's throat. "I'm the last person she would've opened up to."

Jess looked startled. "But I was sure the two of you were—"

"We were. Sort of. But she never told me much of anything personal, really. I guess she figured, why expend the energy on a fake relationship?"

The kid's eyes darkened with something that looked an awful lot like pity. Adam abruptly needed this conversation to be over.

He coughed. "I think Grant's out front, if you want to find something to do before everyone else gets in."

"Yeah, I'll do that," Jess said. "Leave you guys to get on with it. Frankie? See you later."

"Later, Bit," Frankie said. "Oi, wait a tick."

He dropped the knife and whetstone with a clatter and bounded over to Jess, pressing a quick, hard kiss to the young man's mouth.

Jess did a fair impression of a lobster on the boil, but his eyes were shining when Frankie straightened up.

"I guess I'd better . . . Grant's probably . . . um, okay, seeyoubye!"

Frankie surveyed Jess's flustered escape from the kitchen with smug satisfaction. "He needed distracting."

"Nice work," Adam commented.

"What can I say? I'm a master distracter. Matter collapser. Masturbator. Ah, it's so damn good to be back!"

"It's damn good to have you." Even Adam was surprised by the wealth of feeling in his voice. Frankie didn't miss it, either, curse him, but turned a speculative eye on Adam.

"Rough week?" was all he asked.

"You could say that. We've had more business than we can reasonably handle while short staffed—no, no jokes about the shortness of my staff, thanks—even with Wes to help pick up the slack, and everyone's walking on eggshells around each other. I mean, bad enough to deal with the fallout from goddamn Rob and his pop gun, but that book . . . "

"Yeah," Frankie said musingly. "That was a weird night. What I remember of it, anyway. Don't actually remember getting shot, although I'm sure I was very brave and heroic about it."

"You whimpered like a kicked puppy," Adam said crushingly. He'd missed Frankie a lot.

"A kicked *boy* puppy, though," Frankie said. "One of those manly breeds, like a mastiff or a bulldog."

Adam broke, snickering. "Shit, at least you didn't cry. I think all matter in the universe might actually have collapsed if you'd shed real tears. Or at least all the matter in my head."

"Violet cried. I remember that."

Adam lost his smile. His chest squeezed tight. "Bitch-on-wheels, tougher-than-nails Violet."

"Yeah. I could see her at her station from where I was standing. She didn't sob or anything, but it was still strange. Like watching that bit in *Terminator 2* when Arnold cries."

"All kinds of wrong," Adam agreed, knowing exactly what he meant. "Well, we haven't had any more tears in the last week, thank Christ, but we haven't had a lot of laughs, either."

"'Course not, you were all too busy missing me," Frankie crowed with a smirk and a twinkle in his black eyes.

"Frankie's back!" The shout came from the door to the back staircase where Milo and Quentin were just emerging, still buttoning their white jackets.

"And better than ever," Frankie shouted back.

"Hells yeah," Milo said, bouncing over like a short, Italian Tigger. "You're working the bad-boy action now, man, you've got a scar to back it up."

Quentin followed more sedately, his teeth shockingly white in his dark, handsome face. "Chicks dig scars," he said in his slow, deep voice.

"He ought to know." Milo laughed. "He scores more than any of us. Apparently, chicks dig the strong, silent type, too."

"That lets you out then, Milo," Violet said, joining the throng. Happiness like Adam hadn't seen for days was clear on her round face.

"All right, all right," he jumped in, forestalling Milo's heated defense. Billy Perez and Wes Murphy came up the stairs, their conversation halted by the sight of the knot of jubilant cooks surrounding Frankie.

"Gang's all here," Adam said. "We're stoked to have Frankie back, but we still have a restaurant to open in, hmmm, less than two hours. So get to work. Wes, come talk to me a minute."

Looking wary, the new guy approached while everyone else scattered slowly to their corners of the kitchen. The vibe was better than it had been in days, not completely back, but they'd get there.

Adam was painfully aware that the rest of it was his own fault. The kitchen would stay noticeably out of whack until he could figure some way to get over Miranda.

Shaking himself out of it, he said, "Wes, now that Frankie's back—"

"I know, I know," Wes interrupted. "I'm off the grill. Where do you want me?"

Adam paused. There wasn't nearly as much of the long-suffering martyr about the guy as he'd expected.

"I want to be clear," Adam said, "you saved my ass last week. Seriously, man, I don't know how we woulda gotten along without you. I'd have had to run a station and the hot plate, both, which might have killed me. You did good on meats, really good."

"But Frankie's better," Wes said simply, his hazel eyes steady on Adam's face. "For the moment."

There it was, that arrogance Adam had come to associate with their extern. But it was arrogance that Wes backed up with a shitload of talent and an unswerving dedication to being the best.

"Best way to improve is to watch Frankie work the grill."

Wes lit up like a power burner. "You mean it? That would rock. I know I could be faster, more precise with the meat temperatures."

"Frankie's a good teacher, when he's not goofing off." Adam yelled that last part, catching Frankie out of the corner of his eye involved in what looked like a pitched battle with Milo, using wooden spoons as weapons.

Lowering his voice amid the giggles as Frankie and Milo got back to work, Adam added, "And it would really help me out if you could keep an eye on Frankie tonight."

"Is he still in pain?"

Adam shrugged. "Probably, but you'll never get a straight answer out of him about it. Which is why I need a pair of eyes on him. Let me know if he starts to flag, if you can tell his shoulder is bothering him, whatever."

"I can do that," Wes said. He glanced up at Adam, then down at his own black kitchen clogs. "Look. I know I come across kind of strong sometimes. But I wanted this externship. Nobody will work harder for you, because nobody wants to learn as badly as I do."

Adam saw the stubborn flame of ambition in the kid's eyes, but he also saw the hidden, flickering hope he'd seen in so many others who'd passed through the kitchens he'd worked in. Hope for friends, an extended family of sorts, people to accept him for who he was.

The combination of desires was invaluable, would bind this kid to Adam for life if he could provide both the opportunity for greatness and a family to cheer him on.

"You don't have to justify yourself to me," Adam told Wes. "I've watched you work; we both know you're good. But I also watched you stand with us a week ago, and I watched you pitch in and do what needed to be done by helping Grant get the customers out. Point is, Wes, I see you. And there's a place here for you beyond the externship, if you want it."

Wes simply nodded. But Adam read the sheer relief in him as easily as reading a recipe. He sent Wes over to Frankie, who welcomed him like a long-lost brother.

Adam watched his crew, humming along better than they had in a while. All the necessary ingredients were mingling and merging in the good way, coming together to make something better than the individual parts, the way eggs and flour and sugar came together to make a cake.

He should've been happy. He should've been ecstatic.

So why did he feel like a key ingredient was still missing?

Ignoring the scoured-out hole in his chest, Adam rolled up the sleeves of his jacket and immersed himself in work.

THIRTY-ONE

Nerves skittered through Miranda's stomach like drunken butterflies. It all came down to tonight.

She'd had days to work herself into a frenzy of anticipation and dread. Devon needed the time to make all the arrangements, and she wanted to wait until Frankie was back in the kitchen.

It was a good thing she'd established a new inside source for information on the Market kitchen and its crew. Miranda hadn't heard a word from Jess or Adam since the book was leaked. Not that she'd expected to.

That's what this is about, she reminded herself, trying to convince her stomach it didn't need to empty itself forcefully all over her red satin pumps. They'd worked on Devon, so they were now a talisman, of sorts. She'd plucked them out of the closet tonight without even considering any other options. They went nicely with the black knee-length pencil skirt and lipstick-red short-sleeved silk sweater. The sweater, which had started life as part of a twin set, was that rare shade of red that didn't clash with her hair.

After tonight, Adam and Jess will have to talk to you. And one way or another, they'll know how you feel.

"Are you ready for this?" Devon asked.

He looked ludicrously gorgeous under the harsh, unforgiving lights of the camera crew. His short sable hair was artfully tousled, his devastating cheekbones and sensual lips enhanced with subtle makeup.

Lifting his chin away from the dabbing sponge, Devon gestured the makeup artist over to Miranda, who submitted.

This was Devon's show, after all. She was just the guest star.

"Am I ready to expose myself in front of a roomful of people with good reason to hate my guts? Sure, bring it on," Miranda replied.

Devon's steely blue eyes mocked her. "You make it sound like you plan to do a striptease. Oh, please, please tell me you're going to strip!" He clapped his hands like a delighted child. Miranda had to laugh, even though she wondered if the sharp movement of her diaphragm might dislodge her dinner.

"Only if it looks like I'm not getting anywhere with the true confessions from the soul," she told him.

"Mmm. Nice. I'm banking on Adam's stubborn streak."

The camera crew rushed around, setting up the shot. Devon was going to film an introductory segment on the street outside Market, then they'd head around back and go in through the kitchen door.

They'd timed their arrival to the end of dinner service. Miranda wanted to cause as little disruption as possible, and if they'd interrupted prep, the whole night would've been thrown off. This way, the customers had all left and so had many of the servers. The cooks would be finishing their cleanup and prep for the next day. She was certain Jess would stay late to help Grant and to wait for Frankie.

Devon beckoned Miranda with an imperious flick of the wrist. She came over to stand next to him and squint into the lights and fiddle with the wireless mic attached to her collar.

"Let your eyes adjust." Devon frowned. "You can't crinkle up your face like that once the cameras get going."

The camera crew settled into place and started a countdown.

"Understood." She breathed hard through her nose, concentrating on smoothing her features back to normal.

"It's going to be all right, you know," Devon said unexpectedly.

"You think so?" Miranda asked, surprised into betraying her desperate need to believe him.

"Trust me. If anyone understands the effects of high drama on human emotions, it's me. And this is one very dramatic stunt we're about to pull."

Miranda had no time to respond before the camera operator reached the end of his countdown and pointed at Devon, who turned and beamed that flawless smile into the lens without pause.

"Hello there, I'm Devon Sparks. If you've seen my show on the Cooking Channel, *One Night Stand,* you know I'm an expert on the way sparks fly and tempers flare in the kitchen."

Miranda struggled not to roll her eyes. She should've known there was no way of getting out of this without several plugs for Devon's show.

"As chefs," Devon continued, "we try to confine our shouting matches to the privacy of the kitchen—but sometimes emotions overflow into the dining room and out into public, for the whole world to see. With me tonight is Miranda Wake, restaurant critic for *Délicieux* magazine and author of a scandalous tell-all revealing the secret lives behind the kitchen door."

Miranda smiled into the camera. She could tell it was wooden and unconvincing by the way her mouth pulled taut, but she couldn't do better.

"Cut."

"The next segment will be a voice-over of me explaining the backstory—the dare, your source inside the kitchen, the book, and how it got leaked after the hostage situation. We'll play it over some spliced-together footage of the inside of the kitchen, which we'll take in a minute, some outdoor shots, stills of Adam and the crew."

"Fine," Miranda said faintly, feeling out of her depth. This was all a lot more real than she'd bargained for. The presence of the cameras was largely symbolic, in her mind; since the nature of her offense had been so glaringly public, so should the apology be. But now that it was actually happening, she had to fight down panic at the knowledge that this segment would be aired on the Cooking Channel for the delectation of millions of people.

Swept along in the tide of the cameras and technicians and Devon's various handlers and assistants, Miranda was shocked to find herself in the alley behind Market, poised on the back doorstep.

You can do this, she lectured herself fiercely. *This is important. Maybe the most important thing you've ever done. Your future happiness depends entirely on the next ten minutes.*

No pressure or anything.

Straightening her shoulders, she glanced at Devon, who nodded at her to go ahead. So she sent up a little prayer and pushed open the door.

She could tell at a glance that they'd timed their entrance perfectly. The stereo above the dishwashing station was pounding out some punk rock anthem, telling her that the front of the house was closed for the night. Cooks in dirtied jackets pushed sweaty hair off their foreheads and hustled through their last-minute tasks of wrapping up leftovers and wiping down countertops.

Miranda had only a split second to take it all in before the camera guys pushed her farther into the kitchen, entering behind her. The noise of a dozen people lugging heavy equipment through the narrow doorway brought every head in the kitchen swiveling to face them.

And it sent Adam, whose back was to the door, into orbit. He lunged for the magnetic strips mounted on the wall and came up brandishing a short, wicked-looking meat cleaver. His cry of "Oh hell, no, not again" died in his throat when he whirled and came face-to-face with Miranda.

She threw her hands up in surrender, the instantaneous jolt of fear making her wonder for a panicky second if Adam were really angry enough to take her head off with that knife.

Everyone paused except Devon. He cracked up, cackling like a hyena, before turning to the cameraman and saying, "Tell me you got that."

"What the fuck is going on here?" Adam snarled. He lowered the arm holding the cleaver, but Miranda noticed he didn't set the knife aside.

Miranda was struck speechless. All she could do was stare at Adam.

He looked good. Well, he looked like he hadn't been sleeping nearly enough, but even with shadows under his eyes and lines of exhaustion etching his olive skin, he looked good enough to eat.

God, she'd missed him.

The feeling didn't appear to be mutual. Adam was looking back at her with a curiously blank expression, as if he didn't even recognize her. She was reminded forcibly of those early days when she'd been an unwelcome interloper in his kitchen.

Devon strolled into the tense moment with easy, liquid grace. "We're here to do a segment for the Cooking Channel, Adam. Miranda, here, has promised to go on record and clear up some of the ugly rumors that have been flying around. My hosting the piece pretty much guarantees a viewership," he said smugly.

Adam shook his head as though he were trying to clear water from his ears. "No. No, you'd have to have permission for something like this. And I most definitely do not agree, so you can all get the hell out of my kitchen."

The cooks chimed in, Frankie vocal and loud about it, arguing with an equally loud Devon, while the camera crew, evidently used to working in war-zone-like conditions, went about setting up their lights and booms. In seconds, the entire kitchen was in an uproar.

Miranda was aware of the exact moment that the decibel level brought Grant and Jess running from the dining room, but she never took her eyes off Adam, his snarling mouth and flashing eyes and the lingering pain he couldn't hide when his gaze hit hers.

"We have permission," Miranda said. She didn't try to compete with the shouting match, but somehow her voice carried enough to shut everyone up.

Adam gaped for a second before realization dawned. "You went to Eleanor," he ground out.

Miranda nodded. The woman who controlled the purse strings and who had a controlling interest in the restaurant, Eleanor Bonning. Since she'd been the one to get Miranda into Market in the first place, she'd been the obvious choice. Once Miranda had groveled suitably, of course.

"She was very helpful," Miranda said.

"I'll bet. She'd cheerfully murder a homeless guy if she thought it would get publicity. Helping out the woman who dragged her name, and mine, through the mud, would be nothing to her." Adam looked thoroughly disgusted.

"Can we start rolling now, or what?" one of the camera guys asked.

Adam practically vibrated with the clear desire to tell

them all to fuck off, but he reined it in. "Bonning signs all of our paychecks," he finally said with ill grace. "We're stuck. Go ahead with your little dog-and-pony show. But I want to say one thing," he burst out, pinning Miranda with an accusing eye.

"Yes?" She was determined to take whatever he dished out, knowing she deserved it.

"You knew," Adam said, lowering his voice to a near whisper. "After what Rob did, you saw what it did to me. He forced his way into my kitchen. He fucking violated this place. What you're doing now—it's the same."

Miranda flinched, eyes going wide as her body absorbed his words like a blow. The stubborn wish she'd been harboring, that this might actually do something to turn her stupid, messed-up life around, withered and died.

"I'm sorry," she said numbly, fighting through the utter desolation of all her hopes. "I know it's inadequate, but it's also true."

Adam scowled. "But you're going ahead with this no matter how sorry you are, huh?"

Miranda was vaguely proud of the fact that she was still standing when disappointment was crushing down on her so heavily. "Yes. I understand that nothing I can say will change how you feel about me, but I think I can do some good here. Please, for the sake of your crew, please let us do this. I only want to help, I swear it."

The impassioned plea seemed to reach Adam. He glared down at her, brows lowered and lips tight, but he didn't sneer or scoff or shrug her off. Miranda held her breath.

She didn't legally need his permission to proceed, but she desperately wanted it.

Adam acquiesced with a short nod that sent the camera guys and Devon's people into a flurry of motion. Miranda barely registered them chivvying the cooks into a group and getting ready to shoot. She closed her eyes, digging down deep for any reserves of strength that would help get her through the next few minutes.

When she opened them again, the room was quiet. Her eyes fell on her brother, who'd come to stand by Frankie. Jess looked worried, pinched and pale, and she sent him a smile that only seemed to increase his distress. He started toward her, but Frankie grasped his arm and held him back.

"Whenever you're ready, Miranda." Devon's voice was oddly gentle.

Miranda blocked out the cameras, the techs, her own fear, and focused on Adam, standing at the front of his crew like a pirate captain defending his ship.

"When I first came to Market, I was shocked by the way the cooks here behaved. They were loud and obnoxious, hostile to outsiders. They were like a primitive undiscovered tribe, communicating in a foreign language and distrustful of change. They cursed. A lot."

Some of the crew smiled at this. Frankie mouthed something that looked like "Too fucking right."

Miranda went on. "I soon found that those very qualities that made them such a closed society were the qualities that allowed them to work as a seamless unit in the kitchen, with absolute trust. But that trust had to be earned. My source was someone who never managed to do that.

"Journalists are taught never to give up a source. But I believe there's no moral imperative higher than common sense. My source was Robin Meeks."

A gasp went up from the assembled listeners, along with a rumble of unsurprised grumbling.

Miranda panted lightly, pushing through the moment. No matter what she said, or how convinced she was that it was right, it still went against the grain to reveal Rob's name.

"A week ago," she said, "Rob Meeks held this very kitchen at gunpoint. He'd been fired for poor performance and carried his grudge all the way back here, gun in hand.

One of the cooks was injured as a result of this troubled young man's actions. Clearly, Meeks was an entirely unreliable source and nothing he told me should be considered true or accurate. As a journalist, I should have worked harder to verify the stories he told me about the staff at Market. I should certainly never have implied anything about the honor of Chef Adam Temple, based on his past relationships. In my heart, I knew that particular bit of gossip to be a lie. Adam Temple is a good man, who built this restaurant with his brains, his dedication to the pursuit of perfection, and his uncanny knack for hiring a crew that would follow him to hell if he asked them."

Miranda took a shaky breath and met Adam's eyes across the room. His arms were crossed defensively over his chest, his handsome face set in blank lines she couldn't interpret. But he was listening.

Miranda took the plunge.

"Although I ultimately thought better of the book and intended to remove it from the publisher's hands before it ever saw the light of day, I take full responsibility for the lies that have been spread in public about the people in this room."

That was the bit she and Claire had argued over long into the night. Claire pointed out, quite rightly, that it opened Miranda up to civil suits. Miranda's feeling was that she was liable anyway; she might as well own up to it.

Swallowing hard, Miranda braced herself for the hardest part.

"I wrote the book in the first place," she explained, "because I needed the money. My brother was accepted at NYU, and the tuition was more than I could pay."

She looked up to see Jess shaking his head, and hurried to say, "None of this was my brother's fault, and it certainly wasn't his idea. He was and is willing to work his way through college, applying for scholarships and student loans." She smiled at him. "He's a very independent young man.

"I hoped, though, that by paying for his school, I'd be able to convince him to quit his job here at Market. I wanted to get him away from a man who works here, who I thought was a dangerously bad influence on my impressionable young brother."

Adam shifted his weight. Jess linked his fingers with Frankie defiantly.

Miranda lifted her chin and continued. "I was entirely wrong about Frankie Boyd. The night Rob Meeks brought that gun and threatened everyone here, Frankie proved himself a hero. And he proved how much he truly cares for my brother. Not that I have anything to say about it at all, since Jess is of age and mature enough to make his own decisions, but—" Her voice cracked. Jess grabbed a hand towel and pushed through the crowd of onlookers to put his arms around Miranda.

She hugged him, tears threatening again.

"I know that if Mom and Dad were alive, they'd want you to be happy and to be yourself. I know because they loved you every bit as much as I do, and that's all I want in the world. Since I can't have the other thing I wanted," Miranda said, her eyes going to Adam over Jess's shoulder.

Adam wasn't opaque any longer. He looked shell-shocked.

"That's why I sent the manuscript in," she told him. "I did it the day after Jess was attacked. I'm sorry. It was wrong on so many levels, and two nights later, I decided to pull the manuscript, but it was too late. Rob's escapades thrust this place into the news again, and I guess it was too attractive a prospect to turn down for some poor, under-paid assistant at the publisher's offices. But those excerpts on her blog are all anyone will ever see of the manuscript. I returned the advance money a few days ago and filed an injunction to have the material removed from the Web site. For all the good that'll do. If your business has suffered as a result of all this, I'll do my damnedest to make it up to you somehow."

She meant every word of that vow, even if she had no idea what she could possibly do, short of promising him her firstborn (a child who was looking extremely hypothetical at this point), so she was a little affronted when Adam laughed.

"I'll let you know," was all he said before turning to Devon. "We done here? I need an off-camera word with Miranda."

That's it? she thought in disbelief. That was Adam's big reaction to her arduous soul-baring?

Devon smirked while waving a languid hand in the air, "Oh, I think that's a wrap. We've got plenty of footage." Turning to Miranda, he said, "It was everything you promised, and more, love. I hope you'll think of me for all your self-flagellatory needs."

Under Devon's direction, the camera crew started to disperse. The Market crew, meanwhile, swarmed Miranda and Jess. The first clap to her back made her wince, but once it became clear that everyone was thanking her and smiling, Miranda relaxed.

"Took guts, what you just did," Frankie said. "And spunk. I love a woman with spunk."

"Don't be gross," Jess laughed, smacking him.

Miranda was too dazed to follow the thread of innuendo, but it didn't matter because Adam grabbed her by the wrist and started hauling her away from the group.

"By 'off camera,' I meant 'private,'" Adam said. "Get out of here, you miscreants. It's been a long damn week and you've all earned a night out at Chapel. Tell Christian to put a round on my tab."

A loud cheer went up from the cooks. Miranda looked

over her shoulder to Jess, who gave her two thumbs up and shouted, "Good luck!"

From the iron grip around her wrist and the purposeful haste of Adam's strides, Miranda thought she was probably going to need all the luck she could get.

There was something about Miranda that encouraged Adam to embrace his inner caveman.

Right now, for instance. He was not unaware of his resemblance to a marauding hunter-gatherer dragging his woman off by the hair. But rather than accepting that as a deterrent, Adam let himself enjoy the image.

Because it felt damned good. And Adam had never believed in curbing his impulses.

The pantry was the closest room with a door. He kicked it open and pulled her in after him, slamming it shut with a satisfying bang.

Miranda jumped at the noise, then stuck her chin in the air as if daring him to do his worst. Adam savored the moment. He'd missed her like he'd miss cooking.

"You know what hurt the most?" he asked conversationally. "It was that you didn't fight for us."

"I didn't . . . what?" Miranda was obviously having a hard time switching gears.

Adam elaborated helpfully. "When I left you, that day at the Greenmarket, you just stood there and took it. You didn't fight back. I'd never known you to lie down and give up before. I thought it meant you didn't care enough to fight for what we had."

Miranda closed her eyes, holding herself still. "No. I cared more than I've ever cared about anything—enough to plan out an organized attack rather than simply flailing about uselessly."

Adam nodded, satisfied. That confirmed what he'd read into her little performance piece, too.

"You made up with Jess," Adam said. "That was good."

"Yes, it was a huge relief. I hated not being part of his life."

"I know. But the way you did it, in public like that. In front of the whole world. And that bit at the end, about what you want. That was for me."

Miranda's eyes popped open like he'd slipped her a surprise habanero pepper.

"No, I . . . that was to make up for the bad publicity."

"There's no such thing as bad publicity, it turns out. We've been turning away customers all week."

"I'm glad," she told him earnestly. "I love this place. It made me sick to think I'd hurt it."

Adam identified with his restaurant as much as the next obsessive chef, but he wasn't about to let her get away with that.

"For someone so good with words, you've got to work on your communication skills. Come on, admit it."

She colored up nicely, her cheeks and ears vying with her sweater in terms of redness. "I know you don't feel the same anymore," she said haltingly, "but I love you. I never stopped."

Burning satisfaction swept through him. He wanted to howl for joy and get those cameras back in here so he could tell everyone; he wanted to do a victory lap around the kitchen and invent a whole new menu.

He settled for pulling Miranda's startled body close and kissing her.

She stiffened with shock for only a second. Then, with a soft mewl of pleasure, she sank into the kiss, opening wide for him and sucking on his tongue.

With difficulty, Adam pulled back. Miranda looked dazed, the bright blue of her eyes clouded with bewildered lust.

"You made your big confession in public," he said

hoarsely, "to prove that you could open up. You always held back before, but tonight, you gave it all up, like a gift."

That spark he loved chased some of the haze from her vision. "It was the only way I could be sure you'd listen," she said tartly. "I know how stubborn you are."

Adam grinned. "Stubborn enough to keep loving you, no matter how many mistakes you make."

"Really?" she breathed, face glowing.

Adam kissed her again for an answer. She took it in the spirit it was intended, twining around him lusciously and making those noises he loved.

When they came up for air a few minutes later, Adam said, "You said something before about making it up to me."

Miranda blinked, then frowned. "Adam, if you are about to use my heartfelt regret and desire to make restitution as an excuse to cajole me into having sex in this pantry—"

"Not what I meant!" Adam laughed, then pretended to go thoughtful. "Although . . ."

A muffled thud sounded through the pantry door, followed by several giggles. Adam turned the knob and essentially the entire Market crew fell into the pantry with them.

"Shag her blind," yelled Frankie from the floor.

"That's my sister," cried Jess, in tones that suggested he expected Miranda to go to her grave a virgin.

"The pantry's not the best place for sex," Violet said critically. "You'd think fifty-pound bags of flour would be soft, but they're not."

Milo leered. "Tell us more, Vi!"

"Shut up," Adam bellowed. "I'm trying to offer Miranda a job."

That effectively silenced everyone, including Miranda, which wasn't the reaction he'd been hoping for.

"Come on," he wheedled. "It'll be fun. You can do all the menus!"

Miranda took his hand. "You're amazing, you know that?"

Adam shifted his weight uneasily. Maybe she hadn't enjoyed writing the menus as much as he thought. But no, she was smiling widely, her eyes as light as a summer sky.

"Somewhere along the way," Adam said, "I stopped cooking for anyone other than you. When you were gone, it was like all the flavor had drained out of the world. Without you, nothing tastes as sweet."

Her eyes filled with tears for the second time that night, but this time Adam was pretty sure they were happy ones.

Throwing her arms around his neck, Miranda said, "I guess I'd better accept. You're at Market all the time; if I don't work here, too, I'll never see you!"

He swallowed her smile with a kiss, which prompted a round of catcalls and wolf whistles from his incredibly immature crew, reminding Adam that they were all still there, watching with rapt attention like he and Miranda were their own private soap opera.

Gazing into Miranda's flushed, lovely face, he said, "If you all aren't out of here in ten seconds, I'm revoking that round of drinks at Chapel."

Within eight seconds, Adam and Miranda were alone in the blissful silence of the pantry.

Adam smiled.

"So. I've got this great idea for a book."

"Oh? Tell me more."

"It's about this chef who falls madly in love . . ."

THE "MIRANDA" COCKTAIL

1 ounce rose-petal-infused vodka

3 whole raspberries

Your favorite champagne or sparkling wine

For infused vodka:

2 cups of vodka

2 large red roses

Remove petals from flowers and wash well. Add petals to the vodka and stir around. Let sit, covered, overnight to allow flavors to steep.

Put the berries in the bottom of a champagne flute or saucer, pour in the vodka shot, and top up with your favorite bubbly! For a drier cocktail, choose brut or rosé; if you want it sweeter, the next level would be a crémant, followed by the sugariest of all, a spumante. Makes one cocktail.

GINGER LEMONADE

2 ounces gin

1½ ounces ginger syrup (see recipe below)

1 ounce fresh-squeezed lemon juice

Club soda

Mix first three ingredients in a glass with ice, then top up with club soda. For a "mocktail," increase the amounts of ginger syrup and lemon juice to 2 ounces each—very refreshing! Makes one cocktail.

Ginger Syrup

1 cup sugar

1 cup water

1 cup peeled fresh ginger, thinly sliced

Bring all ingredients to a boil in a small saucepan, stirring to dissolve sugar. Simmer until reduced by half. Strain out the ginger slices and bring the syrup to room temperature.

PORK BELLY WITH CANDIED WALNUTS AND APPLES

1 pound of pork belly (fresh uncured, unsliced bacon), cut into 4 rectangles
Apple cider
1 teaspoon cinnamon
1 teaspoon nutmeg
6 whole cloves
2 Granny Smith apples, cut into matchsticks
2 cups candied walnuts (see recipe below)

Place the pork belly, fatty side up, in a lidded sauté pan and pour in enough cider to come halfway up the sides of the meat. Add the spices and bring the pan to a boil, then turn the heat to medium low and simmer, covered, for twenty minutes, until meat is cooked through. Remove the meat from the braising liquid and blot dry on paper towels. Season with salt and pepper, then sear on all sides in a hot, dry pan, starting with the layer of fat on top. Each side will take 1–3 minutes, long enough to give it good color and caramelization.

Divide the apple sticks between four small plates. Rest a portion of pork belly on each mound of apples, then top with the candied walnuts. Serves four as an appetizer.

Candied Walnuts

2 cups halved walnuts
3 tablespoons unsalted butter, melted
2 tablespoons ginger syrup (see recipe p. 346)
¼ cup dark brown sugar
¼ teaspoon cayenne pepper
1 teaspoon salt

Preheat oven to 350 degrees. Toss the walnuts with the other ingredients, then spread in a single layer on a rimmed baking sheet lined with wax paper. Toast in the oven for 10 minutes, tossing when they come out. Don't worry if they seem sticky or mushy when they first come out! Toss them around on the pan and let them come to room temperature— they'll crisp up and darken a bit as they cool.

Read on for a preview of the next book
in Louisa Edwards' Recipe for Love series

ON THE STEAMY SIDE

Available soon from St. Martin's Paperbacks!

When Devon walked into Market, he didn't necessarily expect to be greeted with a red carpet and a phalanx of trumpeting heralds.

Sure, he'd become used to a certain level of fawning admiration during his meteoric rise to fame and fortune as the darling of the gourmet food world and the Cooking Channel's biggest star. That, plus his undeniably perfect face, was usually enough to get him the best seats/floor tickets/ungettable reservation. Special attention to his needs and desires was a fact of life.

Well, most of his life. There were still a few places left in Manhattan he could go to remind himself of what the real world felt like. A certain dive bar on the Lower East Side, for example. And here. At Market, the all-organic hit restaurant owned and run by his former executive chef, Adam Temple.

Devon deliberately, with the ease of practice, blanked his mind of the spot in New Jersey that could pull him out of the heavens and back down to earth with a single visit.

Adam Temple was a friend. Or as close to a friend as Devon got these days. And he'd never admit it, but part of why he valued Adam was for exactly that lack of interest in

Devon Sparks: Star! When Adam talked to his former boss, Devon felt like . . . Devon Sparks: Talented Chef and Ordinary Guy. Considering he hadn't been either of those things in a long time, and had worked hard to reach that state of affairs, talking to Adam was oddly restful.

Which was why he'd come running when Adam called this morning. Normally, Devon's hectic television shooting schedule wouldn't allow a last-minute detour, but with the current and final season wrapped last night, Devon was a free man.

The final season, he thought with satisfaction. The news that the show was cancelled hadn't hit the public yet, but it was only a matter of time. Until that tabloid explosion, Devon intended to enjoy himself. He could charter a jet to St. Maarten, go out for tapas in San Sebastian, do a London pub crawl, or visit friends in Paris. The world was his fresh, harvested-that-morning-off-the-coast-of-Prince-Edward-Island oyster, with a bonus surprise pearl inside.

So no trumpets at Market. Fine. No red carpet. Check. But was it too much to ask that when he let himself in the front door at ten o'clock Saturday morning, there'd at least be a peon or two polishing glassware and setting tables? Granted, Devon hated waiters of every size and stripe, but they had their occasional uses. For instance, greeting a visiting chef during off-hours and telling him where the hell everybody was.

Instead of the busy, bustling front of house Devon expected, however, he got an abandoned dining room, tumbleweeds all but blowing between the tables.

It was such a different experience, standing in an empty restaurant without the distraction of customers. After designing and opening five fine dining establishments in the last ten years, Devon was a veteran of the decor wars. He could pick out fabrics and choose between leather seat coverings with the best of them.

With a critical eye, he scanned the still, dim Market dining room with its soft moss-green walls and hammered bronze light fixtures with their swirls of vines and leaves. The tables were blond wood, bright and glossy with clean, minimalist lines. Devon liked the banquettes, too, straight-backed and private, in some sort of velvety material that looked very inviting. Striding toward the horseshoe-shaped antique zinc bar that connected the smaller back dining room to the larger front room.

Hoping to find a sous-chef barking orders, a pastry chef kneading dough, a freaking dishwasher, for Chrissakes, Devon pushed through the swinging doors that led into the kitchen.

There were signs of life back there; Devon heard the familiar, comforting clang of a stainless steel pan hitting a cast-iron cooking range, followed by a breathy rasp of sound, almost like a moan.

Devon quirked a brow. The restaurant wasn't as abandoned as it seemed. He paused, suddenly struck by the fear that he was about to come upon his friend, Adam, in a state of nature with the woman Devon had played Cupid to set him up with.

Well, sort of. Invading his friend's kitchen with an uninvited camera crew and filming the very private confessions of Adam's lady love, Miranda Wake, might not go down in history as the all-time most romantic matchmaking scheme. In fact, Adam had been beyond ticked about it, as Devon recalled. Still, Devon stood by the results. Adam and Miranda were disgustingly happy together; every time Devon saw them, he expected to hear the faint twittering of cartoon lovebirds swirling overhead.

Familiar with the aphrodisiacal effects of an empty restaurant on a newlywed, or even just newly-in-lust couple, Devon cracked open the kitchen door with a measure of caution. He could stand to go his whole life without viewing

Adam's unmentionables doing the naked mambo with Miranda's.

Not that he'd be opposed to seeing Miranda's unmentionables—he'd be willing to bet she stripped down pretty well, for an obnoxious, snarky, red-headed firecracker.

But the sight that greeted Devon sent images of Miranda's potential hotness flying out of his head.

A woman stood on the gleaming work counter running down the center of the kitchen, balanced precariously on the tips of her black leather clogs to reach the top shelf of stacked pots and pans. She was taller than Miranda, he registered instantly, and sported a halo of untamed dark curls obscuring her profile from view. The breathy moan he'd heard before sounded again. It rose and fell in a gentle, swelling rhythm that suddenly resolved itself into a tune, a snatch of song that tickled Devon's memory.

He had a mere five seconds to admire the delectable roundness of the backside presented very conveniently near eye level before the woman's ankle wobbled dangerously, causing a lightning-fast chain reaction of shriek, flail, slip, and hey, presto! Devon's arms were full of warm, wriggling womanhood.

"Well, hello," Devon said, amused.

The woman stopped squirming and peeked out from behind her mass of sable curls. Devon got a brief glimpse of bright green eyes and round, pink cheeks before she swept the curls back and revealed a fresh-scrubbed, pink-cheeked face, more interesting than strictly beautiful. Her chin was too pointed, her dark brows a touch too heavy for her face, and her skin was too pale, making her brilliant green eyes appear almost startling. This woman spent zero time at the spa getting buffed, plucked, and tanned. She looked nothing like the perfect, sophisticated women he usually dated, models and socialites and actresses, but there was something compelling about her, some mysterious allure in her sweet, wide-eyed gaze that kept Devon's attention.

Even when he knew, instinctively and immediately, that she was way too nice for him.

"Hey there," she said, the molasses-slow greeting drawled out low and husky, making him think of tobacco and bourbon. Devon blinked. It was a surprisingly sexy voice coming from a woman who clearly bathed in eau de innocence every morning.

She had the face of a nun and the voice of a phone sex operator.

"Not from around here, are you?" Devon asked. Of all the many and varied accents heard around New York City, one of the rarest was a real Southern drawl. Grant Holloway, Market's incomparable manager and maitre d', was the only Southerner Devon could think of among his acquaintances.

"What was your first clue, sugar?" she countered with a toss of that messy head. "And not that I don't appreciate the White Knight routine, but do you think you might be willing to let a lady stand on her own two feet?"

"I don't know," Devon said, curiously unwilling to surrender his burden. That drawl was killing him. "You didn't seem to be doing such a good job of that up on the bar."

She shrugged cheerfully, not a hint of blush or embarrassment darkening her cheeks. "I'm better on good ol' Terra Firma. Well, not tons better, I'm still pretty much Queen of the Klutzes, but at least there's not as far to fall and therefore less chance of a broken ankle." She twisted in his arms, eyeing the distance from her perch to the ground. "Speaking of broken ankles—be careful when you put me down. I just got this job; I can't afford to be limping around the restaurant."

"Adam hired you?" He'd never seen her before, he was

certain, although that didn't necessarily mean anything. He was a frequent flyer at Market, but hardly a regular. And while he didn't like to venture far from the kitchen—too much chance of being recognized and mobbed if he hit the front of house rooms—he didn't pay much attention to the lower level line cooks. Although women were a rare enough feature of professional kitchens that Devon was surprised he'd never noticed her.

He'd never seen her at Chapel, either, the after-hours dive bar Devon and his chef friends, including Adam, frequented on nights when they needed to blow off steam after a difficult dinner service.

He looked at the woman more closely. He couldn't quite picture her against the grimy, punk-rock backdrop of Chapel. And she had yet to betray any evidence of knowing who Devon was. Somehow, he doubted she was playing it cool.

It was weird. Devon couldn't remember the last time he had any interaction that didn't somehow involve or reference his celebrity status. His chef friends ribbed him mercilessly for selling out and becoming successful, all the while wishing they could find some sucker to sell *their* shtick to. Women mostly tended to fawn and gush, all with an eye toward getting into his Ferrari, bed, and wallet. Not necessarily in that order.

"Yup," she said, answering his disbelief about her job status. Then she temporized with: "Sort of. It's complicated." She was starting to squirm again, which felt outrageously good, so Devon put her down before he got distracted and dropped her, thereby fulfilling her broken-ankle fear.

"Hmm. Seems like a yes or no situation to me," Devon said.

Curly Sue wobbled slightly when her feet hit the gleaming hardwood, but she righted herself quickly and ran a careless hand over her shirt. It was pink with embroidered blue flowers on the collar, and it hung on her, as if she'd bought the wrong size. The cut of her baggy brown pants did very little to showcase the assets he'd noticed when he first caught sight of her swaying on the bar like a drunken co-ed. If he'd seen her across a crowded gallery opening, or at an opera gala, he might not have given her a second glance.

She turned back to the counter for a moment, swiping her palm across the shiny metal surface as if checking for incriminating evidence. Devon eyed the way the curve of her waist flowed into her hips.

Maybe he would have given her that second glance, regardless.

"You'd think so, wouldn't you? Unfortunately, my life doesn't really seem to work like that. I exist in a constant state of maybe, almost, and who knows. Hey, you're not a customer, are you? Because we're closed. I think. You'd have to ask someone who's been working here longer than five minutes, and they're all downstairs, havin' a meeting about something top secret."

Apparently satisfied with the state of the bar top, she turned back and looked at Devon expectantly. He followed the slightly meandering thread of conversation backwards in search of her question.

"No, I'm not a customer."

"Huh. Then you must work here. Sorry, I'm so new the tags are still on me; haven't met everyone yet." Grabbing a large spoon from the counter, she bustled around him to check a large pot of something, bubbling away on the stove. For the first time, Devon noticed the hot, slightly bitter scent of hot oil—was she frying something? Ugh. He wrinkled his nose and tried not to cough. Maybe it was shallow, but Devon hadn't been able to bring himself to enjoy anything resembling fast food in weeks.

To distract himself, he studied the woman before him. There was a smudge of floor along one high, pretty cheekbone. She didn't move like any line cook Devon had ever worked with. There was no economy of motion to her, no swift moves at all. She was all elbows and leaning, taking her sweet time, as casual about whatever she was cooking as Devon was about choosing a tie. It was disconcerting; nothing about cooking had ever been casual for Devon.

"No," he replied absently, most of his attention now centered on the pot. "What the hell are you doing with all that oil?"

She looked down as if surprised to see her hand circling the slotted spoon through the frothing, spitting oil. "Cooking lunch," she replied, a touch uncertainly. "What's it look like?"

"It looks like you're performing some sort of science experiment," Devon told her bluntly. "What are you frying? It smells . . . odd."

"I found some chicken livers way at the back of that fridge over there. Didn't look like anyone was gonna use 'em for any fancy dish anytime soon, so I appropriated them."

"Good God," Devon said, revolted, as she began lifting golden brown nuggets of fried liver from the oil and setting them on folded paper towels to drain. "You're not actually planning to serve that to anyone."

"Hey, now," she bristled. "This is my Aunt Gertrude's recipe. It won first prize at the county fair four years running."

"I don't care if it won an Emmy, it looks sickening and it smells worse." Devon had nothing against organ meats, in general; they'd been en vogue among New York chefs for years now. But these humble balls of artery-clogging noxiousness were a far cry from sautéed sweetbreads with butter and sage, or seared foie gras with quince jelly. There was something so . . . peasant about chicken liver. It seemed trashy, in the sense of being destined for the garbage bin. Or possibly a dog biscuit.

"Well, you don't have to eat it," the girl said crossly. "Grant asked me to fix up a quick lunch while he talked to his boss, so that's what I'm doing. It wasn't easy to find anything to make in that larder, either, let me tell you."

"I find that supremely difficult to believe." Market had one of the most varied, interesting menus in the city— Adam stocked his pantry and walk-in with the freshest, most beautiful produce the local farmers' markets had to offer.

"Are you s'posed to be in that meeting?" the girl asked, switching gears abruptly. "I swear, you look familiar. Did Grant introduce us when he brought me by Market yesterday? I know we didn't spend a lot of time here, and everyone was working in the kitchen and out front, getting ready for dinner and all. Dang, that's embarrassing. I'm bad with names. Not faces, usually; I can almost always place people. You're stumping me, though, I hafta say. Wanna give me a hint?"

Devon tucked his tongue in his cheek and tried not to smirk. She didn't recognize him. She obviously hadn't been in the game very long; it was no exaggeration that every young line cook and chef wannabe in Manhattan knew Devon's name.

Not this girl, though. In spite of her egregious assault on Adam's hapless kitchen, Devon found himself more intrigued by this odd conversation than he had been by anything in a long while. A pleasantly reckless feeling overtook him, and it made him stupid. That was the only way he could account for the words that flew out of his mouth.

"We did meet yesterday. I'm devastated you don't remember—does this mean you also don't remember agreeing to have a drink with me tonight?"

Had he lost his mind? This babbling, too-nice woman

with no makeup and no cooking skills was completely and entirely not his type. Far from it. But it had been a while for Devon, what with shooting and the restaurant openings and getting that bad review of Sparks Vegas—he hadn't really been in the mood lately. That had to be it.

Meanwhile, Shirley Temple, over there, looked about as taken aback by Devon's smooth lie as he felt.

"R-really?" For the first time since she tumbled off the counter and into his arms, she looked flustered. "Wow, now I'm real embarrassed. And a little afraid I might have a brain tumor or something, because I have no memory of any spectacularly good-looking, unfortunately rude guys randomly asking me out yesterday. And you'd think after the dry spell I've had, that would be something I'd recall."

Devon spread his hands innocently and made an attempt at a winsome smile, but it must've fallen flat because those pretty green eyes narrowed slightly.

"What did you say your name was again?" she asked.

Before he could decide whether to give a fake name in hopes of continuing this ridiculous charade, or tell her the truth and accept that she might put two and two together and come up with Famous TV Star, Adam's loud voice rang out through the empty restaurant like a clarion bell.

"Devon Sparks!"

Devon winced and shot Little Miss Muffet a swift sidelong glance, but her eyes were wide with something that looked a lot closer to panic than recognition.

Clutching his elbow, she only had time for a quick whispered, "Please don't tell them I was standing on the counter!" before Adam was upon them, his entire crew clomping up the stairs like a herd of rhinos behind him.

"Temple," he said, acknowledging the chef/proprietor of this successful, trendy restaurant, who was currently doing a great impression of an overgrown puppy.

Adam bounced over, flush with happiness, excitement

radiating from every pore. Normal, mundane day-to-day life tended to get Adam flying like a kite; the guy had the gift of passion, for sure. Still, this was something extra.

"Thanks for stopping by, man. See, Frankie, what'd I tell you?"

"Told me the man would be here. Didn't venture to say much about whether he'd be amenable to your little proposition. Hello again, Lolly."

The laconic cockney voice drifted over from the kitchen doors where Frankie Boyd was leaning, fingers of one skinny hand rummaging in the pocket of his painted-on black jeans. Presumably for smokes. Frankie was famously addicted to silk-filtered Dunhills; he'd once told Devon he plunked down his hard-earned for the outrageously expensive British imports because he took his vices seriously.

Devon sneered a little, more out of habit than real animosity. He and Frankie had butted heads when Frankie was one of his line cooks back at Sparks NY, but that was years ago. Frankie was Adam's sous-chef now, and by all accounts, an integral part of the kitchen.

"Wait a second." Devon turned to the woman at his side with an incredulous eyebrow lift. "Your name is 'Lolly'? Like, short for lollipop?"

She stiffened visibly, her thick, straight brows drawing down thunderously. "Lilah Jane Tunkle," she said. "Which you'd know if we'd actually met yesterday."

Busted.